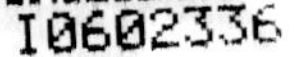

Could Forrest Fenn Be D.B. Cooper?

SOLVED

Stephanie Thirtyacre
Mindy Faucey

ISBN 978-1-7362363-8-3

Table of Contents

Chapter 1: The Thrill of the Chase

I am a city girl, I repeated to myself, poking around the dirt with my shovel. *What the hell am I doing out here in New Mexico? I mean, the scenery is breathtaking, but really, Stephanie!*

Idaho was a bust - a wasted plane ticket on a fruitless venture. Too late did I realize Fenn had knocked Idaho out of the running - but that only came to light after forking out airfare and motel money. I'd lost two weeks of precious time.

New Mexico was just as amazing as Idaho. But now, in the height of summer, it was warmer, at least. The creek water was less frigid, too, even with a little nip in the air. Winter exits gradually but returns quickly in the mountains. *Nearly froze my toes in Idaho! As well as my tushie.* That state certainly has its own definition of "spring."

This wasn't my first trip, and definitely not my last. That is, unless I got lucky and discovered the treasure.

I've driven up the sides of enough mountains that I no longer fear falling off the winding roads and pitching into the canyons below. And I've flown enough times where I'm now comfortable to nap on my flight from Texas. Of course, the pickaxe and metal detector in my checked baggage probably raise some TSA eyebrows, but they allow me to keep the huge flashlight in my carry-on. Plenty of people use backpacks these days – though most don't contain an extra backpack rolled up inside. *I mean, when you go treasure hunting, you have to carry something to bring the loot back in, right?*

In the last few action-packed months, I've learned more than I ever anticipated. I'm getting to be quite the veteran of the search for Forrest Fenn's "secreted" treasure. If you didn't already know, Forrest Fenn is the eccentric retired fighter pilot and art dealer who hid a treasure worth about two million dollars in the mountains north of Santa Fe in

2010. In his memoir, *The Thrill of the Chase*, a vague and cryptic poem contains nine clues that supposedly lead to the famed hoard of gold and precious artifacts.

I know just what and how to pack, whether traveling by air or by car: GPS, flashlights, radio, metal detector, shovels - one medium size, with an adjustable handle and one small garden trowel – a compass, waders, a few pairs of jeans, T-shirts and over-shirts, a light-weight jacket, a hiking stick - though sometimes I prefer to find one when I get to where I'm going - and a medium-sized cooler to hold lunch and water. This time, I even packed a wetsuit and mask, and brought rubber water shoes for walking over sharp rocks.

Although I sometimes fly to my search areas, it's easier to drive. It only took me a few days to get to the location I'm currently searching. My on and off boyfriend, Jay, has come out with me before – first to Cimarron, New Mexico, then to Idaho, before wandering off again. However, he never took the search seriously, as I did.

Lately, my friend, Emma, has accompanied me on my searches. She's been very patient and understanding, tolerant of my ambition and she's good company on the road to boot. I think she got over what happened in Wyoming. It has been hard, for both of us. If Fenn's treasure was ever out there to be found . . . But Emma and I enjoy our time together, and our searches make nice road trips. My new 4-wheel drive makes it a lot easier to navigate the rough country and explore the less trodden paths. Isn't that the point, anyway? To get out into nature? To see what we would otherwise overlook? To try things we would normally avoid without a specific reason or strong motivation? You must focus on more than the gold. It'll drive you crazy otherwise.

Not that I've particularly bragged about these searches to those who have no clue about the treasure I'm searching for- Forrest Fenn's near legendary treasure.

Most people who have never heard of the treasure think I'm crazy. But there is an entire world of people who are still searching. Most of them are nice people, and we've formed a sort of community. There are lots of chat rooms, forums, and websites where avid treasure hunters share their tips and experiences exploring in the wild. And while there has not been a shortage of experiences, some we need to treasure, while others we fight to forget.

Some people have made the hunt their sole purpose in life while others just search to stay occupied and explore the countryside on vacations. Still others make it a family project, while the true dreamers entertain visions of wealth. I have a very different reason for searching. It's not the value of Fenn's hidden treasure that lures or motivates me. I know that something bigger than even the riches is out there, waiting to be discovered.

I rose, stretched, my gaze drinking in the expanse of brilliant shades of oranges, reds, and browns surrounding me. This trip brought me to the Sangre de Cristo Mountains, sandwiched between Santa Fe and the border of Colorado – and, despite the moans and groans elicited by endless climbing and hiking, I relished the experience. The Rocky Mountains are truly spectacular with their sharp crags edging skyward, distant peaks crested with snow, and waterfalls that cascade powerfully, thunderously, into tumbling rivers winding through meadows and valleys to calm pools. Valleys are peppered with streams, dark sloughs, steaming eddies, and boiling geysers that erupt without notice. Rivers and streams creep across the valley floor to form placid lakes filled with several varieties of trout and other fish, all surrounded by towering pines. The various ranges along this chain are sometimes alive with seismic activity, shaking periodically with normally modest tremors reminiscent of an exhausted steed shaking off its loosened halter and saddle after a long ride. I imagine pioneers crossing the rough terrain, driving clumsy wagons pulled by tired horses up the steep sides of mountains, the wagon occupants fueled only by meager rations and hope of a better life at trail's end. I stand in awe of their achievement.

When I started this accursed hunt over six months ago, and a little further south than I am today, I was surrounded by the pastel mesas of New Mexico-- formations striated with varied colors layering the rock and soil deposited over time. They lent enchantment to the landscape when the setting sun threw its golden glow onto the mesas and gilded the tops of subtly colored mountains, lighting them up like a Georgia O'Keefe painting. She lived around there - Santa Fe, that is - and painted the landscape that bewitched her to her dying day. Painted flowers, too - lots of them - in a way that made them appear almost sexual, Forrest once said. I couldn't see it. But he was the art dealer-- made a lot of money at it, too, so I guess he knew what he was talking about.

Blowing a wisp of long blond hair out of my eyes, I stood straight in the hot sun, then wrapped my gloved hands around my waist, stretching my 5'9" frame to get the kinks out.

Damn! Digging for treasure is hard on the back. And I'm not even that old!

Well, not yet, at least. Getting there, though. And what do I have to show for it? A hard-earned business degree, an unearned divorce, the modest condo I call home, and an equally modest income that is less than I'd hoped for. Oh – and my "new" used Jeep.

People always used to tell me I should be a model. I'm tall for a girl. Real pretty - or so I've been told all my life. But did I pursue that? No. That would have been too frivolous for my family to accept. I never would have heard the last of it. Mom especially was super religious before Alzheimer's took hold and erased what was left of the woman who had run away from a rigid and abusive home as a teenager, defying her family for her true love, my father. People are odd. The older she got, the more my mother reverted to the things she had run from as a girl, and the more she tried to push others into her way of thinking. It never worked on my Dad. Or Buster. Or me. But my older sister, Sue, took to it like a fish to water.

Well, most of the family is "Upstairs" now, hanging around with the angels. Dad is gone, at last. And I miss him. Really, really miss him. My older brother, Buster, died when I was sixteen. Mom sort of melted away mentally over time, and then one day, she was physically gone too.

Not everyone's gone, however. My sister, Sue lives with her husband and kids in Austin. Sue's not like me at all. I have deep personal faith, but you will never find me on my knees or in a church. I maintain a running dialogue with The Big Guy, something along the lines of "Let's Make a Deal."

As for men, I love'em and leave'em. Or vice-versa.

It's vice-versa right now with Jay. He and I have been on the outs longer than usual. I have no idea how long it's going to last this time. But he'll be back eventually. We're both commitment-phobes, and who else would put up with his behavior and take him back?

So no close family ties any longer, and no man. Not even a cat to meow a "welcome" when I come home from work. I have no one to share my adventures and my travels with except for a used, four-wheel drive Jeep I call "Betsy," and Emma, my belated stepmother. I originally hired her to take care of Dad when I was unable to, but their relationship quickly progressed into romance.

Dad is gone, but Emma's become a dear friend.

I have many close acquaintances, a handful of close friends, my associates at work, and the construction firm's clients. We get some interesting ones, and great projects - but they come and go.

And then there's *The Search*. My Dad and I shared a passion for *The Search*, and that has kept me sane through all of this. Now, it has morphed into something even bigger, something that could change my life. And that is my current struggle.

At almost 39 years old, I don't have much to show for the time I've spent on this earth. Maybe that's why I got drawn into this - hunting for a hidden treasure. As I've said,

I'm not in it for the money, although a cool two million could go a long way toward fixing what is wrong in my life.

Maybe it doesn't exist at all-- the treasure, I mean. The possibility of it all being a hoax has crossed my mind several times. It would be just like Forrest - sitting back in that big leather chair in his study in Santa Fe, admiring some new discovery from a pueblo dig and chuckling to himself that out on a mountainside, or beside a babbling brook, some fool is working up a sweat and perhaps risking his life to search for an empty treasure box - if even the box itself exists - with dreams of buried gold infecting his imagination and stoking his desire.

"And so, my legend grows, . . ." he'd think as he typed a response to one of the thousands of emails he receives from rabid fans.

He's big on legends, Forrest is. On history. On people. On remembering. On people remembering *him*. On *his* legacy – *his* legend.

What an ego! Prankster, too - loves a good joke. Good Lord, I don't know how his lovely wife has put up with him all these years! He did give credit for her amazing tolerance in one of his books, consenting that Peggy deserved praise for having patience with him. I met her once-- pretty lady, nice and all. He's a decent guy, I suppose. Forrest has performed countless exciting ventures in his eccentric life. Heroic feats. Daring acts. Amazing achievements. Plus, he's funny… a charmer, actually. And boy, can he spin a tale!

He always holds something back, though, then springs it on you just when you think the story is moving in another direction. He's admittedly walked a tightrope with the law on occasion, and survived FBI investigations unscathed. He's attracted media attention galore – sometimes unintended, but most intentional and for a specific purpose. Simply Google his given name and watch how many web pages pop up. He certainly has a dedicated following! There are times, however, when I curse him and his damned treasure box! And the bronze bells he's buried, Lord knows where.

The chat room folks – I've read their posts. They all say the same thing: they're addicted. Sometimes even entire families catch the obsession. The pursuit of his famous treasure is all a person thinks about after a while; all they dream about, save for, and plan for, as they remain convinced that the next trip is surely the one that will turn up the gold. Or the trip after that! And when they've gotten too old, sick, or just had enough, they pass on their notes and theories, like a preemptive inheritance, to friends or family.

Old Fenn should be required by law to put a warning label on his memoir, where he threw out the challenge about finding his "secreted" treasure. He's since elaborated on, expanded - or narrowed - the scope of the nine clues hidden in his poem over the years. But he doles out just enough to hook new souls, or keep the jaded ones going – usually in a new direction.

I think he does that to keep the attention on himself and on the hunt – and likely in part for fun too. He's certainly taught me the meaning of "Gold Fever."

Personally, I've made six trips since April, and its only October. Emma's joined me before, and . . . well, so have others. Betsy's been with me on every single trip since Wyoming.

But Emma wasn't with me today She pulled a muscle yesterday, so she's resting back at the motel.

It's insane really, the number of people who are still hooked on the hunt for the treasure, considering the money and time spent searching! A few foolish people have even lost their lives in the hunt, unfortunately. I thought – well I don't know what I thought. It's crazy however you think about it.

But that book of his and his vexing poem are not what got me started, not at all.

But I'm getting ahead of myself in the story I want to tell. My story goes beyond the treasure, and my contribution to *The Search* may be even more legendary than the box of gold itself.

Chapter 2: The Heart of the Storm

Everything I'm going to tell you is the truth. Some of the information I'm going to include in this book is already common knowledge found in the FBI archive or newspapers that covered D.B. Cooper's hijacking. The additional information I have acquired over the years mesh perfectly with the known facts and will demonstrate connections most researchers haven't made.

It was an especially cold and dark night when a man who'd purchased a one-way ticket from Portland to Seattle under the name of Dan Cooper strapped on a modified Navy parachute and twenty-one pounds of cold, hard cash, then stepped into oblivion from the lowered rear stairs of a Northwest Orient Boeing 727 on its way to Mexico - by way of Reno - after having politely commandeered the jet. Dan Cooper demanded and received $200,000 from Northwest Orient, along with four parachutes to aid in his escape. The hijacked airliner was flying low and slow through a wicked storm when he jumped from those steps then vanished into history and straight into American folklore.

This was the first event of its kind in U.S. aeronautical history. The 150 or so skyjackings that took place between 1967 and 1972 had all been political in nature. But D.B. Cooper did it for the money - and the newspapers covered every detail of his crime for months following the daring heist on Thanksgiving Eve, November 24, 1971.

Years afterward, articles, documentaries, and new information still occasionally pop up to renew interest in the mystery.

The dozens of both genuine and hoax leads reported in the days following the event kept the FBI busy for months. False leads took investigators down long, winding trails to dead ends. Several investigating agents spent years on the case before retiring to write books about their experiences.

Younger, fresher agents picked up the thread where they left off, spinning their wheels for years before reluctantly passing the torch to the next generation.

The occasional article on D.B. Cooper published today is either a nostalgic feature story, summarizing the case to fill copy space, or – much more rarely-- bona fide news articles revealing new details discovered through modern forensic technology on the remaining little evidence the notorious skyjacker left behind. On Thanksgiving Day, 1971, however, front page headlines across the nation blared the scant details to inform the populace of the astonishing act of air piracy and ask their help in finding the perpetrator. The major television networks reported on the drama that unfolded the night before. Their reports rocked the nation.

Described as being in his mid-40s, between 5'10" and 6' tall, 170 to 180 pounds, well-built and physically fit, with close-set dark brown eyes and a left-side part in his dark brown hair, the skyjacker was issued a boarding pass with the name "Dan Cooper written in all caps with a bright red, felt tip pen. "Dan" took the boarding pass from the airline agent and quietly took a seat in the terminal.

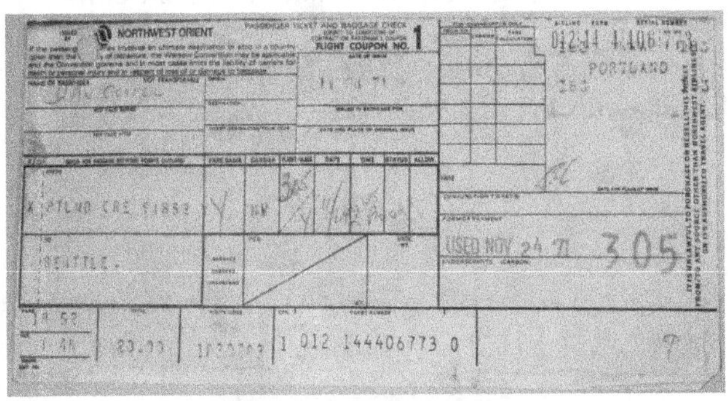

Figure 1 Dan Cooper's boarding pass.

He wore a dark business suit under a dark overcoat and leather shoes some reporters described as loafers. He stepped onto the plane carrying only a brown paper bag and a black attaché case. Nothing about the man gave any indication of what he was about to do.

He waited an hour in the Portland airport before the flight. Neither his appearance nor his actions attracted attention. However, individuals who remembered Dan Cooper would later give the FBI nearly identical descriptions of the man.

Northwest Orient Flight 305 was only about a third full- - 37 passengers including Dan Cooper and six crew members. Upon boarding that afternoon, the lone traveler took a seat in the 18th row at the rear of the plane, with several empty seats ahead of him.

He beckoned to a stewardess, then asked her to sit next to him before takeoff. She complied. Once airborne, Cooper passed her a note. The attractive 23-year-old woman told reporters she thought the hijacker was merely making a pass at her, so she tucked the note in her pocket as the plane rose through the clouds. Cooper, with a calm, composed whisper told her she had best read the message. Florence Schaffner then proceeded to unfold and read the note, which she described as neatly printed in block letters with a black felt tip pen. It informed her the plane was being hijacked. That was bad enough, but what she read next chilled her to the bones. In the nondescript briefcase resting on Cooper's lap was a bomb, and the note boldly declared he was ready to detonate it if his demands weren't met.

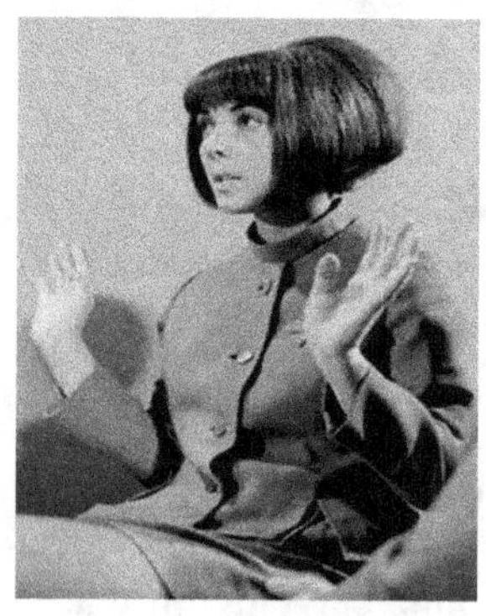

Figure 2 Florence Shaffner

At Miss Schaffner's request, "Dan Cooper" quickly opened his briefcase to reveal what appeared to the stewardess to indeed be a bomb: Eight red cylinders of dynamite ("four on four" as she described them) had detonators connected to red-coated wires attached to a large cylindrical battery. In those days, carry-on bags were not scanned with x-rays as they are today. According to Florence Schaffner, the sinister-looking device filled the briefcase.

The man then gave her his demands:

He wanted $200,000 in "negotiable American currency" and four parachutes - two primary chutes, and two reserve. Cooper also wanted a fuel truck standing by on the tarmac when the 727 arrived in Seattle, and the full cooperation of the crew. While "no funny stuff" was the phrase the FBI said he used as reported by nerve-wracked crew members, the exact words exchanged are unknown, nor the exact wording used in the note. He retrieved it and took it with him when he escaped the plane mid-flight.

When a very shaky Florence Schaffner carried the note forward to the cockpit, another stewardess, 22-year-old Tina Mucklow, promptly took Miss Schaffner's place beside the man "to ensure passenger safety."

Figure 3 Co-Pilot Bill Rataczak and Tina Mucklow

After reading the note, the jetliner's commanding officer, Captain William Scott, immediately radioed Northwest Orient headquarters and relayed Dan Cooper's demands. In those days, the position of the airlines was to first cooperate with hijackers, then sort things out later. Donald Nyrop, President of Northwest Orient at the time, authorized the ransom payment and instructed the pilot to cooperate with the hijacker. Nyrop informed Captain Scott the money and parachutes would be delivered to the plane immediately after touching down at the Seattle-Tacoma Airport.

The plane went into a holding pattern on its arrival, circling Sea-Tac International Airport and Puget Sound for about an hour and 40 minutes while law enforcement and the FBI mobilized emergency personnel and scrambled to gather the requested amount from several Seattle banks. Each unmarked bill was microfilmed to record serial numbers as the packs were prepared. Parachutes were requested from nearby McChord Air Force base and delivered to Northwest's Seattle office.

By 5:24 p.m. the cash and parachutes had been collected, and a call from the FBI to the control tower indicated the plane could now land.

Fifteen minutes later, the plane taxied to an isolated but brightly lit section of the tarmac. While the jet was being refueled, Northwest Orient's Seattle Operations Manager, Al Lee, acting as courier, delivered the approximately 21 pounds of cash. The $200,000 was comprised of 10,000 unmarked $20 bills neatly wrapped in rubber-banded packets of 100 bills each in a fabric knapsack. The delivery took place via the aft stairs in the plane's tail. None of the passengers were aware of the life and death drama unfolding around them.

Cooper refused the military-issue chutes offered by McChord, and instead asked for civilian parachutes with manually operated ripcords. The local Issaquah skydive center offered chutes they'd recently purchased from Earl Cossey.

In the end, one of the parachutes Cossey provided, and the one Cooper ended up using for his jump, was military issue after all: an older nylon NB6 with a broad conical canopy. The Navy used such chutes in emergency situations. Until his unrelated murder in 2013, Earl Cossey complained the FBI frequently harassed him to identify every single of the many shreds of parachute material found in subsequent years within the vast search area, but not a single one bore any resemblance to the parachute used in Dan Cooper's Thanksgiving jump.

Once delivery was complete, the hijacker allowed the other 36 passengers to disembark - all still blissfully unaware of what was happening - along with two stewardesses, one of whom was Miss Schaffner.

But Tina Mucklow remained seated next Cooper, who had donned his dark sunglasses while he continued to relay demands to the cockpit via the plane's intercom. The pilot, co-pilot and navigator stayed in the cockpit the entire time, and never laid eyes on Dan Cooper. While the jet refueled, Cooper detailed his flight plan to the crew—a southeast course to Mexico City.

Law enforcement were concerned the odd request for four parachutes opened the possibility that Cooper wasn't acting alone, or that he planned to take hostages. Neither of these possibilities turned out to be the case.

Since his plan was to jump from the plane's rear, the hijacker instructed the pilots to keep the landing gear down and angle the flaps, lowering them by 15-degrees. Speed was not to exceed minimum airspeed, 100 knots, or 120 mph, just enough to keep the plane aloft without stalling. The cabin was to be kept unpressurized and the maximum altitude maintained at 10,000 feet. This made the plane considerably less aerodynamic and less able to shift speed or alter its direction without warning. However, it also caused the plane to fly inefficiently by using more fuel.

William Rataczak, First Officer and copilot, told Cooper the specified configuration limited the flight range of the aircraft to only 1,000 miles before a refueling was necessary. Therefore, they would have to stop en-route to refuel. After unsuccessfully discussing alternate options, Cooper reluctantly agreed to refuel in Reno.

When Cooper asked for the aft stairway be left deployed and open on takeoff, Northwest Orient's personnel objected, citing safety issues. Cooper allegedly countered that it could be done safely, but ultimately relented. He would lower it manually, himself, once the craft was in the air.

While refueling at Sea-Tac, a vapor lock developed in the pumping mechanism of the tanker. The skyjacker grew suspicious as a replacement truck ran dry before refueling was complete and yet a third fuel tanker had to be employed to complete the job. He was visibly irritated by the delay. An FAA official's repeated attempts to board the plane and talk with Cooper were rebuffed.

Through all of this, Miss Mucklow and the crew reported the man was polite, well-spoken, and considerate, offering to demand meals be delivered for the crew since events were unfolding so slowly. He ordered and paid for a bourbon on the flight from Portland, then ordered and paid for another while the plane was on the tarmac. He even offered Miss Mucklow a tip.

At 7:44 p.m., the plane carrying Cooper and the four essential crew members finally departed Seattle-Tacoma airport and headed to Reno, Nevada. Soon after departure, Cooper asked Tina Mucklow, the one remaining stewardess, for directions on lowering the rear staircase, or "airstair" - a feature exclusive to the design of the 727. No other airplane had an aft staircase in the tail that could be manually lowered, and it appears "Dan Cooper" selected the 727 precisely for that reason.

Figure 4 The crew of Northwest Orient Flight 305.

Cooper then told Mucklow to join the others in the cockpit for the remainder of the flight, instructing her to close the first-class curtain, then shut the cabin door behind her. As she pulled the curtains together, Miss Mucklow reported catching one final glimpse of the skyjacker as he tied something around his waist - perhaps a tether attached to the 21-pound sack of $20 bills that comprised the $200,000. The FBI reasoned that if the money were tethered to a length of parachute cord, its landing would warn the parachutist in the pitch dark that the ground was close and thereby prepare him for landing.

Tina Mucklow's final image of Dan Cooper as she closed the curtain was the last anyone ever saw of the hijacker. The stewardess had spent the most time face-to-face with the man. She later gave the FBI a complete description, telling agents Cooper was polite and calm throughout their time together, but repeated that he became somewhat impatient at times during the wait in Seattle.

When she vanished from public view shortly after Cooper's disappearance, there was little doubt it was due to the young woman's natural desire to escape the unbearable amount of publicity that followed.

Around 8:00 p.m., the navigator, Rataczak, and Captain Scott noticed the flicker of a red warning light indicating the aft "airstair" had been activated. Based on Tina Mucklow's report of what transpired, in addition to a sudden change in air pressure, they deduced the hijacker successfully deployed the stairs in the tail of the 727 at that time. At a normal cruising altitude of 35,000 feet, an opened door would prove fatal to all aboard. At the 10,000 feet maximum and with the unpressurized cabin, the crew was alive to notice the warning light.

Alarmed, Scott reportedly asked over the intercom, "Is everything okay back there? Is there anything we can do for you?"

Cooper shouted back, "No!" That was the last word ever heard from Dan Cooper.

It was thought that perhaps he was looking for a place he had predetermined to jump, since it was not until 8:11 p.m., and again at 8:13, that the crew first felt pressure bumps and then a sudden, sustained upward movement of the tail section so significant it required the pilot's effort to bring the aircraft back to level flight. Only later did they realize those disturbances probably signaled Cooper moving about on the stairs, the moment when he pushed off from the steps and threw himself into the storm.

Another theory argued the pressure bumps may have resulted from the steps snapping shut briefly before springing open once again. However, some speculated Cooper could have intentionally caused that effect in order to throw off the investigating agents as to the exact location of his jump.

If, indeed, he did not leave the plane at 8:11 p.m. when the bumps were initially felt, or at 8:13 when the tail moved so significantly, and given the unknown distance the 727 might have flown before he did choose to parachute, investigators had to ultimately acknowledge they easily could have been searching the wrong locations for the man or his remains for nearly 40 years.

A pair of F-106 jets were deployed in pursuit, flying out of McChord AFB. One flew below the 727 and one above, and both remained well out of Cooper's sight. Although they were never more than five miles away from the 727, they saw no indication of Cooper's jump. The helicopter bearing the lead FBI agent, Ralph Himmelsbach, was never able to catch up at all.

The plane arrived in Reno at 10:15 p.m. At that time, Captain Scott could not be certain Cooper had jumped and assumed he was still on the plane.

Upon landing, the aft "airstair" was still fully extended, although shredded. The airplane was immediately surrounded by law enforcement officers and FBI agents. State troopers, Reno police, and local sheriff's deputies also arrived at the scene. Armed FBI agents thoroughly searched the airliner and determined Cooper was gone, then set about collecting evidence left behind.

Figure 5 The hijacked 727.

A total of 66 latent fingerprints were lifted from the area where Cooper sat beside the two flight attendants. The skyjacker abandoned his black clip-on tie with its mother-of-pearl clip on his seat along with two of the four parachutes. One of the parachutes had been opened, with two of the shroud lines cut from the canopy.

No other trace remained. Cooper's crime was committed prior to DNA testing technology, so the glasses from which he drank his bourbon, rich with undetected DNA, would have probably provided enough clues to close the case had the crime been committed in more recent times.

Whenever he chose to leap, Dan Cooper parachuted from a plane traveling between 120-196 miles per hour at 10,000 feet straight into the blackness of a driving rain. The mean ground temperature was seven degrees below zero, although the wind chill factor pushed the temperature to minus 70 degrees Fahrenheit. If the jumper's shoes were loafers as reported, they would have blown off his feet as soon as he jumped.

Attached to his body by tether or in a backpack bound to his waist and chest, the money added only 21 pounds or so to Cooper's lean and fit form. And although that night's temperatures were severe, searchers initially anticipated he conceivably could have survived the fall - barring the failure of one or both parachutes to open, or being impaled by a tree. More likely, his death would result from an inability to locate adequate shelter or being unable to find a way out of the forest in bare feet and clothing unsuitable for the weather conditions. It seemed Dan Cooper had not prepared adequately for his survival.

To the world's amazement, Dan Cooper was simply gone, vanished without a trace into the black of night, and has remained so for 45 years.

Chapter 3: When I Was a Kid

Okay, I know you're asking, how do I know this much about something that happened seven years before I was even born?

This is where it gets interesting. My dad was ex-military. He and my mom married right out of high school. Instead of going to college, he found a job to support them, as many of his friends had done.

Dad worked in a machine shop to support the two of them after they'd graduated. They tied the knot just two weeks later. Well, going to work like he did, straight out of high school, and with no children and none on the way, there was no draft deferment for him. He was registered 1A and - whammo! – don't you know, his number came up that January, just six months later.

That was back when they drafted you by lottery. Kennedy had been shot and Johnson was in office and the buildup of forces had started in Vietnam. Dad was immediately deployed: "Do not pass Go; Do not collect $200." It was that fast.

He was always smart and clever and somehow ended up working with field computers, which was usually kind of out of the line of fire, because - above all - the Army needed to protect its computer equipment. Computers were new, important, and expensive. It was the first time they had ever been used in war and no one really knew how to work the things. The Army trained Dad, who had an aptitude for electronics and math.

Like all geeks back then, he was considered a god. Even the Generals listened to him. The hazard pay was good, and there was the promise of college on the GI Bill. So Dad did three tours of duty, and soon he had a career. Every time he had the chance to leave the Army, another one of us kids came along. He couldn't risk losing that steady income, even for a short while.

By then, Dad had completed three tours in Vietnam, and he, Mom, Buster and my sister, Sue, moved a few times to posts in Georgia, Tennessee, and South Carolina. Mom could never get used to the South, though. Military housing and the bugs that came with high humidity never agreed with her. When Dad finally received orders to Germany, she was thrilled. I was born right after we got there, at the U.S. military hospital in Heidelberg. That was in 1978.

Dad was stationed a few miles away in Mannheim, and we lived "on the economy" in German housing. Mom drank in the culture and even learned a little German.

Hold on - have patience! This really is going somewhere.

After the three-year stint in Germany, Dad was transferred to Fort Polk, Louisiana, where I started first grade in '84. We lived there a few years before receiving orders to his last post in Fort Hood, Texas. Mom hated Louisiana, and when Mom hated something, we were all miserable. Germany's beautiful scenery and cool climate spoiled Mom. She wanted to live in a special, fairytale location, with trees and water for picnics and fishing - when Dad finally retired. We found Temple, which is a real pretty little town within driving distance of Fort Hood. It looked like a good place for Dad to find a job, or set up his own computer repair business, so when he became eligible for retirement, we settled there.

We bought a rambling old frame house with a wide porch on North Main Street. It was just big enough. Buster was older, and a boy, so he got his own room. I had to share a room with Sue, who was at an age where she seriously resented my presence in her microcosmic world. Consequently, I spent most of my time staying out of her hair and escaping chores by hiding away from everyone.

I was about nine or ten at the time and read constantly – anything and everything I could get my hands on – even cereal boxes at the breakfast table if there wasn't anything else to read. Shortly after we moved into the house, I discovered a closet in the huge second bath at the back of the house.

Anyway, shortly after we'd moved into the house in Temple, I learned to shimmy up the door frame of that bathroom closet and climb onto the top shelf, which was a huge, deep, thick square of solid wood, recessed just enough from the top door frame for me to clamber onto its broad boards. Above the top shelf, the capacious open space only had to be shared with a large box of my father's stuff, filled with military papers and whatnot. Once up there, I could pull the door almost closed and I could read, undisturbed.

This was my refuge, my hideout, my secret place. I would climb the door frame to my hideout with a light book, small flashlight and a snack or a soda stuffed in a paper bag I held tightly between my teeth as I clambered up the door frame. Tucked away out of sight, I would read for hours, avoiding sibling arguments and the chores Dad freely assigned to whomever was within his line of sight.

A day came when I was left with no books to read. It was summer and a promised trip to the library fell through at the last minute, so I was desperate to find something to read for an hour or so in my hideaway. Once in my hidden space, flashlight in hand, I tackled the box-- Dad's box. It was mildly interesting to dig through all my father's old orders to exotic places in Vietnam with names that defied pronunciation, and peruse the shipping receipts for household goods, and orders to the various other bases we'd lived. There was paperwork detailing his promotions, congratulation letters, and a news clip about a medal he'd earned. I quickly flipped through about a thousand TDY orders. Then there were joking and affectionate "Goodbye" cards from coworkers or fellow soldiers he collected whenever he transferred.

The cards talked about how smart he was, how funny he was—his jokes apparently made everyone laugh. He was the "go-to" guy whenever there was a technical question or a problem no one else could fix. This was my Dad? I wished I knew him in that same way. He always seemed so serious around us.

And then I found the motherlode. Newspaper clippings – seemingly hundreds of them. All were from the 1970s and early to mid-1980s, from various publications. Long articles, short articles, and a number of dog-eared magazines with turned-down corners marking the articles for which they had been saved. All of them dealt with just one thing: the mystifying and unsolved disappearance of a hijacker known to the world as D.B. Cooper.

It was the first I had ever heard of him. I was not quite ten years old. But why did my dad save all these clippings? It was a mystery I was determined to unfold.

Chapter 4: The Search Begins

A severe thunderstorm and a lack of ready manpower stalled the massive manhunt for Dan Cooper along the 727's flight path for nearly 36 hours.

On Thanksgiving Day, 1971, the events that transpired on Northwest Flight 305 saturated the airwaves. Every television set in America was tuned in to the news. The public watched, riveted to their seats as the drama unfolded.

Multiple reports detailed the audacious hijacking of Northwest Orient Flight 305, and the mid-air escape of the parachuting perpetrator who had given his name as "Dan Cooper." It was speculated Cooper had leapt to certain death from the tail of the jet airliner somewhere between Seattle, Washington and Reno, Nevada.

The weather in the search area - which had been below freezing when he jumped - was still very cold when approximately 1,000 military troops began to comb the wilderness area around the Lewis River where the foothills of the Cascades ascended rapidly into the thickly forested mountains. The rocky terrain grew more treacherous with every mile. Roads were few and shelters non-existent. It was in this dangerous general area authorities had calculated Cooper would have landed after his jump if he survived the perilous descent. The hunt for the fugitive would be difficult on foot, and even the helicopters would still have a rough time navigating the mountains.

Figure 6 The search for D.B. Cooper.

Local law enforcement joined federal agents in the search for the man, his corpse, or for any evidence of his survival. Composite sketches were drawn up based on descriptions by the flight attendants and the Portland ticket agent, along with the Northwest Orient manager of the airline's Seattle office, who had delivered the items the hijacker had demanded, and anyone else who might have encountered the criminal face-to-face. FBI investigators worked around the clock and conducted extended interviews with everyone who had the remotest link to any male named Cooper, particularly those whose first name began with a "D." Every interview with a person of interest - no matter how fleeting the interest - was written up in the newspapers and led the evening news in those first few months.

A minor criminal in Oregon named D.B. Cooper was briefly picked up by Portland police on the unlikely chance the hijacker had used his real name. An inexperienced reporter from one of the wire services, writing on deadline, confused the name of that poor suspect - who had an alibi and was immediately eliminated as a possibility - with the alias used by the actual hijacker, and the misnomer stuck. Other media outlets and newspapers picked up the mistake, which was repeated over and over, nationwide. The unintended error is now seared into the collective memory of the nation, from whence spring our legends, our American mythology.

Inclement weather delayed the manhunt by a day and a half, and the delay prompted officials to debate the precise location of the landing zone, which was nearly impossible to ascertain. When you consider the speed of the aircraft when Cooper jumped, even as relatively slow as it was, just a few minutes' delay could mean a difference of dozens of miles in any direction. The landing point could have been affected by variables in the terrain and environmental factors along the 727's flight path, including the intensity and direction of the wind and driving rain at the time of the jump. A particularly significant variable was the amount of time Cooper continued to free fall after pushing off the airstair before he located and pulled his ripcord. That detail was crucial to narrowing down the search zone, but impossible to know. All searchers had to go on was their "best guess," and oftentimes, that isn't enough. The pilots of the Air Force jets following the commandeered 727 reported they saw no one jump from the aircraft, either visually or on radar. But, admittedly, there was limited visibility that night and Cooper jumped wearing dark clothing. Cloud cover at 5,000 feet also obscured any view of what lay beneath. Rain and wind would have pummeled the parachute canopy, hampering the hijacker's ability to open it fully in the driving elements.

Simulations were run under several possible scenarios in an attempt to pinpoint the moment of exit. The same Boeing 727 Cooper had hijacked was flown in the identical configuration insisted upon by Cooper, and the airstairs were lowered while weights were tossed from the stairs in an effort to learn at what specific point the tail rise could be replicated. That would prove Cooper had indeed jumped at the precise moment when the tail movement occurred. After several tries, a 200-pound weight, pushed from the plane on a sled, was successful in reproducing an identical upward movement of the tail section. Investigators definitively determined 8:13 p.m. as the moment when Cooper jumped from the aft stairs of the 727.

Flight data retrieved following the hijacking indicated at that moment, the jetliner, which was flying slowly and inefficiently through the heavy rainstorm, was passing over the Lewis River in southwestern Washington,

Calculations and educated estimations initially put Cooper's landing zone within a few miles of Ariel, Washington, near Lake Merwin, and near the southernmost outreach of Mount St. Helen's. Clark and Cowlitz Counties were the focus of the search efforts. FBI agents and Sheriff's deputies from the two counties scoured the forests in the mountainous area, on foot and by helicopter, immediately north and south of the Lewis River. Surrounding farmlands were also searched and included door-to-door canvassing of area homes. Nothing, however, was found.

When the weather cleared, a top-secret spy plane, the SR-71, flew over and photographed the entire flight path of the 727, but failed to uncover any trace of evidence. "Victor 23" - aviation language for the flight path from Seattle to Reno - was searched after the spring thaw, using fixed-wing airplanes. The 200-foot depths of Lake Merwin were even probed by submarine.

Bodies *were* found. While searching, two local women came upon an abandoned building in Clark County that housed a skeleton later identified as the remains of an abducted teenaged girl who disappeared weeks earlier. Another body was also unearthed elsewhere during the search, but bore no resemblance to the missing skyjacker, Dan Cooper.

Eventually, closer study of the variables shifted the focus of the hunt. Captain Scott piloted the 727 manually that Thanksgiving Eve due to Cooper's specific and detailed demands for the restrictive flight configuration. At some point after the event, the captain realized his flight path had been a great deal further east than initially calculated. Tom Bohan, a pilot for Continental Airlines, had been flying only four minutes behind the Northwest Orient jet piloted by Scott. Bohan's flight data indicated the wind direction originally factored into the calculations to determine the drop zone for Cooper's jump was off by as much as 80 degrees. Other data, gathered subsequent to the initial investigation, indicated the probable drop zone would have likely been south-southeast of the original estimations, and was likely to have been over the drainage area of the Washougal River, which winds through a valley bearing that same name.

With no body for evidence or person to testify to Cooper's fate, or his whereabouts, interest in the case faded over ensuing years, although the FBI still devoted limited resources to the continuation of what had become perhaps the most extensive and expensive manhunt in the history of the United States. FBI agent Ralph Himmelsbach, whose involvement in the search had taken him from the night of the air heist into his retirement and beyond, wrote a book in 1986 detailing his efforts and his deep frustration at his inability to solve the crime of the century. The book was his swan song as he handed off the torch to the next lead FBI agent, Larry Carr, to continue the ongoing search for the enigmatic character - and budding folk hero - now popularly known in song, book, and movie as "D.B. Cooper."

Chapter 5: Closeness Is as Closeness Does

The newspaper clippings fascinated me. How long had it taken Dad to accumulate all these? The deeper I dug into the box, the more I found. A lot of the articles were repetitive, especially in the beginning months when little was known. The meager facts and pertinent details were written in a dozen different ways, each article adopting a slightly different slant on the case, depending on the date, the author, and the format or medium in which it appeared. Some accounts were sensationalized while others were dryly factual. One can only imagine how, if a 24-hour news cycle had existed at the time, the airwaves would have been inundated, day after day, with the same details, images and interviews repeated ad nauseum.

My birthday rolled around, so, by the ripe old age of eleven, my goal in life had been set. Organizing, then reading the articles to get the whole picture became my most immediate objective. I was drawn further into the story with each hour spent reading the many clippings in my chest of treasures.

I brought fewer books up into my hidey-hole to read and, instead, devoted myself to the articles and the growing sense of mystery. I had received a thick spiral-bound book of light pink, lined notepaper for my birthday. I was thrilled when I unwrapped the gift and began noting all the different bits of information I gleaned from the articles I devoured. Repetitious as it was, I gleaned a little gem of expanded understanding in each new piece I read and captured in my notebook. I studiously added to my growing collection of factoids on the page I had penned the elaborately flourished title: "The Legend of Dan Cooper, aka D.B. Cooper."

I memorized the composite images distributed by the FBI just in case I ran across Dan Cooper on the way to or from school. I could immediately recognize him and report his whereabouts to the FBI. The two images publicized widely after the hijacking were so indelibly fixed in my mind that I saw them in my sleep, where magical dreams of my solving the mystery resided.

Curious as to why so much of Dad's focus had, for so many years, centered on this one person and his unsolved disappearance, I asked Mom obliquely one rare day when she was in a particularly good mood if Dad had any hobbies or ever collected anything. I certainly had no intention of informing her of my hideaway. I was afraid if I admitted to rummaging through Dad's box, she'd prohibit me from returning to that special closet space. I couldn't bear that.

To my great surprise, my usually dismissive Mom took the question under consideration as she smoothly, silently slid back and forth in her glider chair. "Well, not really," she replied.

My heart sank.

"But," she added, leaning back, and crossing her arms, "your father did have this fixation for a long while about a man who hijacked a plane. The fool jumped from the plane and no one ever saw him again--probably died as soon as he jumped."

"Why was Dad obsessed with him?"

"*Everybody* was real interested in the story for a while. Every time you turned on the news or picked up a newspaper, the story was staring you in the face."

"But Dad doesn't seem like the kind of guy to obsess about a crime."

"He isn't. But this Cooper fellow…well, your father apparently had a suspicion the hijacker was a fellow military man he'd known in Vietnam."

Just like that. I stood there, dumbfounded. Could it be true? Could my dad really have known the *real* Dan Cooper?

Mom paused in her gliding and cocked an eyebrow. "Why did you ask, anyway?"

"Just wondering," I replied, spinning on my heels then tearing off down the hall to my bedroom.

That Saturday, when Mom was teaching a church class, Buster was at a game, and Sue was in our bedroom with her door closed talking on the phone with her boyfriend, I managed to corner Dad. I told him what I had been up to, and showed him my carefully printed notes, with all the new facts I had found. His eyes lit up.

I expected a scolding for going through his stuff, but instead, he asked me to read my notes to him. All of them. He listened intently, silently, as he casually smoked a cigarette.

Then we talked. For the first time in my life, I had my dad's complete attention. I was thrilled.

My dad and I had never shared much common ground, and so never had much to say to one another. Well, the silence between us ended that day. We shared a secret now. A real hobby.

And a passion to get to the bottom of the D.B. Cooper mystery.

Chapter 6: Follow the Money

By the end of 1971, the FBI was chasing its tail in the hunt for D.B. Cooper. Without any other clues to go on, the authorities entertained the idea that Cooper had most likely perished in the jump. A hunter or woodsman could have stumbled across the remains, found the cash, and neglected to report the find to keep the money. If so, the bills would possibly be in circulation.

The decision was made to follow the money instead of the man. Lists of the microfilmed bill's serial numbers were distributed to banks and retail outlets. Even Northwest Orient stepped in, offering 15% of the ransom money, up to $25,000, as a reward to anyone who recovered any amount of the purloined cash.

The FBI was confident that sometime, somewhere, those bills would show up and they would have the lead they desperately needed.

John Mitchell, the U.S. Attorney General at the time, released the list of serial numbers to the general public in early 1972. This widespread information, however, did not have the intended effect. Rather, in an infamous, widely publicized swindle, two men, Donald Sylvester Murphy - who had represented himself as "D.B. Cooper" - and his accomplice, William John Lewis - used those published serial numbers to create several counterfeit $20 bills purported to be a portion of Cooper's loot. The counterfeit bills were employed in a clever scheme to defraud $30,000 from Karl Fleming, an unsuspecting and over-eager reporter for the nationally distributed *Newsweek Magazine*. Fleming was duped into believing he'd the real skyjacker. He interviewed the fraudulent "D.B." and printed the full "interview," in which Murphy, in the guise of Cooper, provided Fleming with very basic, previously published information accompanied by heavily fantasized and imaginatively fanciful elaborations on the details of the heist.

Lewis initiated contact with Fleming and successfully convinced the eager reporter he knew the real identity of the Northwest Orient skyjacker and could put Fleming in contact with him and arrange an exclusive interview - for a healthy fee, of course. Lewis demanded $45,000 for the interview. The offer enticed Fleming to fly from Los Angeles to Seattle, where Lewis had made a reservation at the Swept Wing Inn, where the interview was to take place. Murphy displayed the counterfeit $20 bills with serial numbers identical to those listed in John Mitchell's report. Karl Fleming, perhaps blinded by the potential fame he would likely achieve with the interview, was hooked. The resultant article was published in the May 5, 1972 edition of the *Seattle Flag* newspaper.

Subsequent background investigation by Fleming, however, and extensive FBI contacts revealed Murphy to be a fraud. He and Lewis were eventually prosecuted for swindling $30,000 from *Newsweek* for the fraudulent interview.

Meanwhile, a rash of copycat crimes were attempted on aircraft around the world. Airlines reacted defensively, tightening their regulations by restricting and examining carryon baggage. Various "wanna-bes" surfaced from time to time as well as bona fide suspects, but on interrogation and follow up, none proved to be Cooper.

With the ransom money from the real crime still unaccounted for, *The Oregon Journal* reissued the list of serial numbers and offered $1,000 to the first individual who turned in even a single ransom bill to the newspaper, or any FBI field office. *The Seattle Post* made a similar offer, upping the reward for recovery of a single bill from the stolen cache to $5,000. Many hopefuls submitted similarly numbered bills, but none matched the numbers on record, and the newspapers' offers were retracted after a year.

Fast forward to 1976. With the crime growing ever colder and the statute of limitations looming, a Portland,

Oregon, grand jury was convened and returned a criminal indictment, *in absentia*, against "John Doe, aka Dan Cooper, for air piracy and violation of the Hobbs Act, a 1951 legislation that prohibited actual or attempted robbery or extortion affecting interstate of foreign commerce."

An immediate result of the Oregon indictment was the initiation of a formal prosecution that remained in suspense but could be reactivate at any point D.B. Cooper be apprehended in the future.

In February 1980, nine years after the skyjacking, eight-year-old Brian Ingram was vacationing with his family on the Columbia River, southwest of the original search area, approximately nine miles downstream from Vancouver. While digging in the sand near a fire pit, Brian's small hands tugged out three eroded packets of $20 bills, held together with aged but intact rubber bands. While the stacked bills were significantly worn around the edges from being tossed in the rushing water and rubbing against vines and rocks, the serial numbers were still visible on all of them, and they matched the numbers on file with the FBI.

The bills were still in the order in which they had been stacked and banded before being handed over to the hijacker waiting in the commandeered aircraft on the Seattle tarmac. Two packets contained 100 bills each, which was expected. However, the third presented a mysterious complication—it contained only ninety bills. Ten of the bills were missing. How or why those ten bills happened to escape the elastic binding remains a mystery. A total $5,800 of the ransom money was recovered by Ingram.

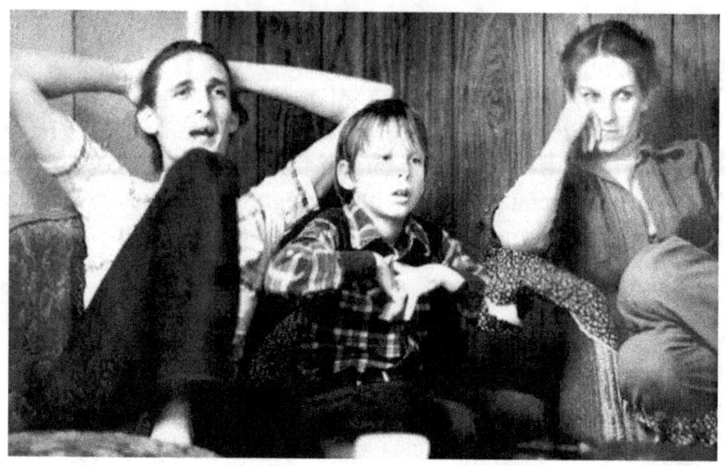

Figure 7 Brian Ingram with his parents.

Brian Ingram eventually split his find with Global Indemnity Company in 1986 after protracted negotiations. The FBI retained fourteen of the $20 bills as evidence and granted Brian the rest of the bills, netting a reward of $2,760 from his find. He sold fifteen of his 138 bills at auction in 2008 for $37,000. The balance of the settlement was paid to Northwest Orient.

None of the other bills have since been found.

Brian's surprise discovery fanned the flames of renewed interest in the mystery of D.B. Cooper, propelling the story into legend.

Chapter 7: Discoveries

"Oh my gosh, Dad!" was my astonished exclamation as soon as I finished reading the clippings from the November 1976 *Oregonian* aloud.

"If they caught Cooper today, he could still go to jail - did you know that, Dad? I mean, that's what this article is saying, isn't it?"

My father nodded grimly as he affixed another clipping to the scrapbook page with a swipe of rubber cement. Our scrapbook was growing. Soon, it would be time to start Volume III of what Dad and I had now dubbed "The Search." He'd presented me with the scrapbook as a gift on a Sunday morning six months prior, while my siblings were still in bed and Mom was at church praying for us all. I squealed with joy as I took the scrapbook from his hands and cradled it against my chest. Within three months, we'd filled that scrapbook and Dad purchased Volume II, which was already one third full.

With everyone asleep or busy, we had the coffee table in Dad's office to ourselves. The Scrapbook lay open with clippings orderly placed in every available space around it. Dad used rubber cement adhere the news clippings to the scrapbook pages with minimal damage to the delicate newspaper clipping. I was in charge of handing the articles to my father in chronological order, then alphabetized by newspaper name, whenever several articles appeared on the same date – which was often. Dad sat cross-legged on the floor on one side of the low coffee table while I sat in the middle of the couch, directly across from him. Stacked envelopes with still more clippings waited on the floor for sorting. We were building a data base, Dad explained, one we could easily use for reference in the future as *The Search* progressed. If new suspects emerged or new evidence came to light, we would be ready.

The Search scrapbooks held more than news clippings. Dustcovers from paperback books we'd read carefully also were preserved in its pages. A cassette of a mildly popular song about the skyjacking filled a plastic sleeve stapled to a page. Newspaper ads pitching a new fictionalized movie about the notorious air pirate were also destined for the ever-growing volumes of information.

The Columbia River find of 1980 resulted in a tsunami wave of new articles, photographs, and maps, shifting the direction of the evolving investigation.

Every day Dad and I explored new articles, added to our scrapbook, and speculated on what had really happened, or read a book together by one of the FBI agents who had worked the case, or an author whose pages fancifully elaborated the scanty facts and paltry evidence, was fun for both of us. *The Search* had given our lives new purpose and built a unified camaraderie between us.

For four hours every week, while Mom was tending to her soul, and Buster and Sue were pursuing the latest romance, doing homework, or just hanging out with friends, Dad and I would huddle over the scrapbook, adding to its contents and sipping hot chocolate or iced tea while we speculated about D.B Cooper.

Not only was I spending time with him, but I was also learning things - like civics, geography, the court system, how planes, airports and the FBI operated, how banks worked and the significance of serial numbers on our money. Dad would answer my questions but usually made me look things up in our encyclopedia set or the dictionary. After researching each question, Dad would look at me expectantly—my cue to discuss what I'd learned. He would elaborate on my simple explanations, speaking to me not as a child, but as a peer. Those times with him made me feel very grown up.

Dad never told me whom he suspected among his past acquaintances, and I knew better than to introduce my conversation with Mom into the mix. I figured he would tell me in his own good time. And Mom's mild hostility to his past efforts made her opinion off limits for discussion. I didn't want to mess up what had become a great way to pass time and build a terrific new relationship with my father.

Dad occasionally told a story about his days in the service, but talked about those times only briefly, just touching on the easy-breezy stuff. I was still only eleven - but with a birthday coming up in a few months - and I somehow knew he would reveal more to me as I grew older. I knew a few kids from school who had relatives that had died or been maimed in skirmishes with the Viet Cong. And I had seen the movie, *Apocalypse Now,* with a school friend at whose home I had stayed over for a night. A lot of what happened in the movie was all very strange to me, although I watched the news and had a general sense of the war and the terrible things that happened in battle. But there was an undercurrent of secrecy in the movie too, and I hoped one day Dad would make it all clear to me.

All in good time, I thought, *all in good time.* I am a firm believer in that old saying, "Good things come to those who wait." Unfortunately, while waiting for those good things, terrible things would also squeeze into the timeline of life.

Chapter 8: Free Floating Conjecture

Brian Ingram's 1980 discovery on the shores of the Columbia River brought home the realization that the focal point of the largest and most expensive search in the country's history had most likely been off by many, many miles, a significant difference that not only changed the nature of the renewed search activity, but also the likelihood of Cooper's survival. What if the area into which he had parachuted that night had been far more hospitable than the mountainous wilderness area that had consumed so many man-hours and air reconnaissance resources?

Theoretically, it was possible that D.B. Cooper was still alive!

New rounds of speculation, however, left many questions unanswered. Following the find by Brian Ingram, initial statements by local law enforcement, FBI investigators, and scientific consultants assumed the still-bundled bills had washed into the Columbia from one of the river's many tributaries. The bundles of eroded, matted together twenties were disintegrated in a "rounded" fashion, an Army Corps of Engineers hydrologist observed. In his estimation, this signified the money had been deposited on the shore of the Columbia by the natural action of the river, rather than deliberately buried.

Figure 8 One of the bills found on Tena Bar

In that event, Cooper could not have landed in or near Lake Merwin, nor on any part of the Lewis River, which feeds into the Columbia River at a point downstream from the site of the young boy's discovery on Tena Bar - a location also known as Tina Bar - along the shores of the Columbia River. Rather, this new theory supported a later conjecture targeting Cooper's drop zone near the Washougal River, which joins the Columbia River upstream from where the money was found. The money could have washed down from there.

The prevalent hypothesis at the time, which assumed the cash found its way to its discovery site by freely floating there without any human intervention, failed to account for several anomalies, such as the ten missing bills from a single pack with its rubber bands intact, and how the three separate packets of cash managed to float together down the river then inter themselves in the sand at the exact same location, despite the rivers' variable currents and changes in weather conditions. Furthermore, how did these three packets become separated from the rest of the money? And the greatest mystery of all—who removed the ten twenties from the securely banded packet? And why?

The bulk of the cash had to be out there, somewhere. If only it could be located, who knew where it might lead? The Portland FBI agent heading the investigation at the time, Ralph Himmelsbach, was adamant the physical evidence was not compatible with the geologic evidence. Scientific reasoning demonstrated the improbability of the thick rubber bands withstanding the deterioration expected while floating for a long period of time. He reasoned the bills had to have washed ashore within two years at most of the skyjacking. Himmelsbach's theory was confirmed, many years later through several advanced technological experiments conducted by a newly established civilian investigative group dedicated to the D.B. Cooper case in 2009. The group became known as the "Cooper Research Team" and maintains a website, even today, that cites their conclusions in the case.

In 1980, geologic evidence suggested the bills settled upon the sand of the Tena Bar shore area of the Columbia River well after 1974, the year the Army Corps of Engineers dredged that particular stretch of the Columbia. Leonard Palmer, a Portland State University geologist, identified two distinct sand and sediment layers between the clay, He deduced the clay had been deposited by the 1974 dredging operation in the top layer of sand in which the bills were found buried, indicating the three packets of the ransomed bills arrived onshore long *after* the river dredging.

When Palmer's conclusions were challenged by the findings of the Cooper Research Team 18 years later, they cited the clay layers Palmer believed were evidence of the dredging done in 1974 were, in fact, natural deposits. With this later discovery correcting the record, the estimated arrival time of the bundles reaching the shore of the riverbank would have been just under a year after the skyjacking of Flight 305. But how did they get there? And where did their journey downstream originate?

While multiple alternative scenarios were offered, one more fanciful than the next, the most interesting one - at least to my Dad and me - was proposed by the Sheriff of Cowlitz County, who theorized Cooper had accidentally dropped a few of the cash bundles onto the airstair then blew off the steps after he'd jumped and dropped into the Columbia river as the plane passed over.

The FBI has yet to close the case on Dan Cooper and his mysterious escape. No single hypothesis has fully explained the meager initial evidence. One additional find-- a Northwest Orient placard-- was discovered by a deer hunter in 1978. It contained instructions on how to lower the aft airstair of the Boeing 727. The placard was found near a logging road located around 14 miles east of Castle Rock, Washington, and considerably north of Lake Merwin. However, the find was within the proposed flight path of Northwest Orient Airlines Flight 305.

Chapter 9: The Pursuit of D.B. Cooper

I remember the day when Dad awkwardly maneuvered a large box through the front door. I knew immediately what it was. I had watched *Apocalypse Now* on one of those machines. Sue nearly tripped over her own feet as she launched herself toward Dad, screaming, "A VCR! I love you, Daddy!" She flung her arms around him, nearly knocking the box from his grip. I distinctly remember the harsh intake of my breath as I imagined the precious cargo shattering onto the floor. Dad carried the device to the dining table and set it down as though it were a Faberge Egg. "Gift for the family," he muttered gruffly. Buster placed two plastic bags next to the box. One bag held cables. The other held six videotapes. It was March 1991; the year Blockbuster came to our town and into our home. It was my birthday, and I was thirteen.

One by one, I removed the videos, holding them so carefully you'd think I was a priest handling the Sacrament at Mass. My heart leapt and a delighted shriek escaped my lips when I pulled the last tape from the bag and held it in both hands, like a huge pearl. My gaze rose from the title to meet Dad's eyes, and his enormous grin mirrored my own. I held a genuine copy of *The Pursuit of D.B. Cooper*. "The other five videos are just rented, Pumpkin," Dad said, "but I bought that one for you. Happy Birthday, Stephanie!"

Figure 9 The Pursuit of D.B. Cooper movie poster

A magazine photo of the red, white, and blue film poster of a man, in a suit and goggles, falling from a plane in a "thumbs up" posture with a parachute strapped to his waist and a grin as wide as mine was at that moment was displayed in all its glory on a page in Volume III of our treasured scrapbook series that now rested proudly on the shelves in Dad's office. We'd had nothing more to put into that last volume, and the last few pages were unused. That hadn't stopped us from reviewing the information from time to time, arguing the finer points of Cooper's disappearance and discussing the various theories surrounding the case. Hundreds of imposters' tall tales, thousands of leads and countless numbers of suggested suspects had been investigated and set aside upon closer examination. But the FBI doggedly continued pursued their man. And, in our own way, so did Dad and I.

Buster and Sue were now in on the secret, but they were completely uninterested, Mom was her usual distracted self, oblivious to much that happened around her and seemingly completely unaware of our interest in D.B. Cooper.

Only, she was more distracted and increasingly forgetful these days. I pointed it out to Dad one day, and he sadly nodded in agreement. Mom was losing her memory - little by little, and I was helpless as I watched her grow ever more distant.

My mother had an unhappy childhood. My brother and sister and I were kept in the dark regarding her background. While none of us knew much about her childhood, I always suspected she was struck in the head by a flying fist more than once.

Mom meandered through life only partially present. Her mind was often wandering, visiting a malignant past whose essence dominated her mind and yanked her back, time and again. Whenever I saw sci-fi movies about space travel and alternate worlds, I thought of Mom, and wondered what kept her from enjoying present reality and her children. At first, I was convinced it was me - that I wasn't good enough to hold her interest and attention. As I matured, I realized she behaved the same way to all three of us. Only Dad could raise her from her malaise and indifference, channeling the mental meandering that stole her from us.

On that day, my thirteenth birthday, it was evident her condition was worsening. She wandered into our celebration as Sue and I supervised Dad and Buster setting up the VCR in the entertainment center, its black case disappearing against the dark wood. The silver control knobs were a stark contrast against the dark grain and glistened in the afternoon light. Mom stood off to the side for a while watching Dad, glancing vaguely at our bright faces as we crowded around to observe the installation process. She appeared vaguely mystified but didn't venture to ask a question or say anything at all. Eventually, she turned around, then wandered back to her glider and her Bible. Dad paused for a few seconds to watch her retreat. Our eyes met, and we silently shared our worry.

But, being thirteen and flighty, my attention was quickly drawn back to the red and blue VCR case in my hands, and - because it was my birthday - it was the first film we watched together that night, as a family. Even Mom sat with us, although she gave no indication she knew who D.B. Cooper was. She fidgeted throughout the entire movie.

The Pursuit of D.B. Cooper was a 1981 movie starring Treat Williams as D.B. Cooper, with Robert Duvall - then still a relative unknown - in the fictitious role of a fellow named Gruen, the airline insurance company's lead investigator, and the only one able to track Cooper through the wilds of Washington State. Kathryn Harrold was Hannah - another fictitious character playing the role of the wife of the character portrayed by Jim Meade, another actor of modest note whose totally invented role was that of an Army ranger instructor of Cooper's. Have I confused you yet?

Figure 10 Scene from The Pursuit of D.B. Cooper.

With so few clues and so little information to go on, the movie was solely the creation of imaginative minds and bore little resemblance to the actual known facts of the mystery.

When we next met for one of our D.B. Cooper sessions, which were growing farther apart as my own interests developed and my social life and after-school activities expanded, Dad and I literally rolled on the floor with laughter as we mocked the movie and imitated its characters and their unbelievable lines.

The many books written about Cooper were far better. They stuck closer to factual fragments of information, the real-life speculation of those involved, and the investigative channels pursued. The books detailed the many twists and turns and false leads in the case, as well as the personal biases, histories and individual characteristics of the FBI agents involved.

Figure 11 Ralph Himmelsbach with his book, Norjak.

Mom's deteriorating condition became the family's primary focus over the next two years as her mind and memory took a sharp dive. Dad had to work to keep a roof over our heads and food in our bellies. His concern for her took a toll on his concentration and his vitality. Stubbles of gray crept into his five o'clock shadow, and the spark grew ever dimmer in his deep blue eyes. He looked so tired, all the time.

The VCR helped. With a good Bible movie playing and a glass of iced tea at her side, Mom was likely to stay put until the credits rolled. After Dad had rented every Biblical movie Blockbusters had to offer, he special-ordered a few more from their other outlets, then found a TV series with multiple seasons of recorded episodes. The series kept her enthralled. Dad and Buster rearranged the living room, moving her glider from the back of the house to a position in front of the television. A small table next to the glider held her tea, some tissues, and her Bible. The office furniture and his workshop tables were then arranged so that Dad had a clear line of sight to Mom's chair from both the garage workbench and his office desk. He waited until I came home from school before making his deliveries and pickups.

With Mom's deteriorating mental abilities, D.B. Cooper's unsolved disappearance receded from our mutual attention and individual imaginations.

In 1993, Buster graduated and left home. He scored a football scholarship to an out-of-state university in Baton Rouge, Louisiana.

Dad lumbered on, though his exhaustion was evident in the increasing lines on his forehead. His work hours suffered as Mom required increasing attention to keep her both safe and occupied. Sue, too, had a part-time job after school to pay for her extras. She was a junior at Temple High, and a cheerleader, so we rarely saw her. On the rare times she was home, she was in the room she had commandeered when Buster's left for college.

That left me and Dad to look after Mom, who had started to wander the house. Dad slept with one eye open and kept the doors locked both day and night.

The word, "Alzheimer's" was still relatively unknown in the American lexicon, but Dad had spoken to her doctor and he and I were sure Mom had it.

Our scrapbooks and long talks about Cooper became a thing of the past.

I was fifteen. And scared.

Chapter 10: The Internet Opens a New Door

Preoccupied with Mom, my father seemed to have lost all interest in *The Search*, but I kept plugging away, researching the character known as D.B. Cooper whenever I could capture a moment or two alone after homework and chores. With Buster gone and Sue fully invested in her senior year and dating a "college man" who attended university in Austin, it seemed a lot of heavy responsibility had suddenly fallen on my young shoulders.

At sixteen and a half, approaching the end of my sophomore year, I was missing out on a great deal of the fun high school is supposed to be remembered for. After-school activities were now an impossibility. Dad needed me at home right after last bell. One by one, my friends peeled away and found other, more available friends to hang around with. I found myself more isolated than ever.

Every day through the fall and winter saw me trudging home beneath a load of books, head down, moving as quickly as my legs could carry me. Even with spring in the air and buds on the trees, I marched home relentlessly after school, offering only a curt nod or smile to those I once had sleepovers with. Those days seemed lost and long gone, but I didn't even have time to regret it. I dearly loved my Dad, and I wouldn't and couldn't disappoint him. Innately and instinctively, I sensed his need for my help, and I made a choice to do whatever I could to lighten his load.

Sometimes, when he wasn't aware of my presence, I would watch him tend to my mom. He spoke to her softly, tenderly, taking her hand and leading her to her chair as though he was handling fragile porcelain. Sometimes, his breath would catch in his throat when, for a moment, her vacant gaze focused, and she looked into his eyes as if searching for a memory. Tears of my own would then obscure my view, but I'm sure my dad shed many of his own during those trying times as well.

Charles Ward had met and married Elizabeth Taylor Sanford and given her his name long before she became the thin, frail, willful creature with the distant, faraway gaze. Sometimes she acknowledged my presence, but she called me Sue, and spoke as if I had never existed. She seemed to recognize Dad, though. A weak smile fluttered across her lips whenever he entered the room. But he knew that recognition would end someday soon. And it broke his heart.

The Internet - a "network of networks," as Dad described it - had come into being some years earlier and, between both his work and the military contacts he still had at Fort Hood, Dad had been introduced to it early on, He had a modem and full access far sooner than most of the general population. Heavily used by academics and several government agencies, as well as the military, civilian companies were just getting wind of its existence, and its potential spread with lightning speed across the entire world. Dad showed me how to use it, cautioning me that it was still for "official use only," but to me, those words meant, "Stephanie, bar the door!" If I had a spare moment in my day, you'd find me glued to the computer screen, exploring every nook and cranny the early Internet had to offer. My favorite discovery was the FBI's website.

The most current information on the continuing hunt for the hijacker, D.B. Cooper - the OFFICIAL information - was now at my fingertips. Much of the material the online FBI file contained reiterated what Dad and I already knew. Our collection, I realized, was quite extensive. But some of it was still new to me, such as agent reports and, particularly, the memorandums discussing a massive amount of conjecture surrounding the case. It seemed that everyone who had worked on, was interviewed during, or was otherwise close to the investigation had a pet theory or opinion. I read them all. I also grew almost intimately familiar with the plethora of suspects that had come under

FBI scrutiny over the years. I relished being so close to the actual FBI investigation. I could now follow it, step-by-step.

Cooper's physical description had remained the same over the years, but I reread it again and again until it was seared into my mind. And I memorized the images once more, although they were the same composites a police artist had sketched in the earliest days. The more I looked at the online images, however, the more it occurred to me the sketch of the man, without his sunglasses, depicted a decent looking, normal-appearing man.

Exceedingly normal appearing.

Yet Florence Schaffner, Tina Mucklow and others who were interviewed and gave descriptions to the FBI - every one of them - had described the man as having close-set, piercing brown eyes. Every one!

I had read a book for a school paper about how your memory can play tricks on you, and how police and trial lawyers have to piece together the consistent bits of witnesses wildly varying recall to get the most accurate description of the event. So the hijacker's eyes must be significantly close-set, I thought, remarkably close-set, for every witness to describe them with the same degree of certitude.

But no matter how many times I looked at the published sketch, the spacing of the suspect's eyes appeared perfectly normal to me. I knew people with "close-set eyes" and boy, they looked nothing like the artist's rendering of Dan Cooper. Holding an enlarged copy of the sketch next to my face in front of a mirror confirmed my suspicions. The spacing of Dan Cooper's eyes was no different than my own, or the majority of the population.

Figure 12 Police sketch of Dan Cooper.

How could D.B. Cooper be found if the police sketch wasn't even accurate?

I suddenly had a brilliant idea. I took my already-enlarged copy and printed out the biggest, clearest version of the FBI image that I could. Setting the photocopier in Dad's office to magnify the image by 200%, I pressed the "Copy" button and ended up with a decently enlarged picture for my little experiment. Very carefully, I proceeded to fold the copied image in a manner that considerably thinned the nose and lips, but also brought the eyes together. Using similar care, I redrew the outline of the lips and nose. The bridge of the nose was still a little bit narrow, but it would have to do. I taped the folds so they would not open and photocopied the revised picture I'd created from the artist's composite sketch. The difference in the face that emerged from the photocopier was remarkable. This seemed right, and somehow, I knew this image was more accurate than the widely distributed police sketch.

I showed it to Dad later that day. But I was not expecting his reaction.

Dad was seated at the dinner table, trying to get Mom to eat something, and feeding her with a fork, which he almost dropped when he saw the picture I'd created. To my surprise, he looked visibly startled when I held the image up for his inspection. He muttered something beneath his breath that I couldn't catch and didn't dare ask him to repeat. Was that a name he had muttered?

As Dad stared, the food plopped back onto the plate and Mom - with mouth open wide to receive the bite of pancakes she expected - grunted unhappily." I'll take a closer look later, Pumpkin," he said, then turned back to Mom, stabbing forcefully to retrieve the dropped bit of pancake.

Back in my room, I taped the new image of Dan Cooper to the mirror over my dresser, then stepped back to admire my handiwork.

Something had shaken Dad. Did my revised image remind him of the person from his past he'd suspected was D.B. Cooper?

I opened my butterfly notebook to a fresh page and carefully wrote *Dan Cooper -Thoughts, Theories, Conjecture and Evidence.* I wrote everything that had just happened-- how I had altered the FBI sketch, and Dad's reaction when he saw it. When done, I closed the notebook and took it with me as I tiptoed past the dining room, where Dad was still trying to coax Mom to "eat just this bite, just one bite more." I sank into Dad's desk chair and booted up the computer. A few moments later, the FBI homepage appeared on the screen.

With the unsolved mystery receding in public memory, the FBI jogged it once in a while by opening their files and making some of its working hypotheses public, as well as venturing tentative speculations as to what might have happened. The hope was that at some point, someone might recall a detail previously forgotten that would progress the investigation out of its current stalemate. I devoured every morsel the website had to offer, returning as often as I could for another bite of information, which I dutifully jotted into my notebook. I felt like a real detective.

Well, except for the butterflies on the cover on the cover of my notebook and the pale pink paper inside. Perhaps such frivolity was acceptable for a really sharp lady detective, I rationalized. A really smart girl detective, like. .

.

Like Detective Stephanie Storm! I would call myself Detective Stephanie Storm. It sounded so much better than Stephanie Ward. Delighted with my new name, I printed, "This notebook belongs to Detective Stephanie Storm," on the inside of the cover in block letters with a red felt pen ink--a reminder of Dan Cooper's boarding pass. Then I sat back and looked at the inscription. I sighed. Detective Storm was onto something - something new and related to the unsolved hijacking case. That "something" involved Dad. The question was, where do I go from here?

Further investigation was absolutely necessary. But a good detective had to have a plan. The new plan could lead her into dangerous territory, and she would need a plan that accommodated every contingency.

Detective Stephanie Storm leaned back in her desk chair, then tapped the cap of the red felt pen against her lip as she pondered the new evidence she had cleverly uncovered.

I just knew I was on the brink of a major discovery.

Chapter 11: Adjustment

The FBI file was a godsend.

When I returned home from school each afternoon, a pall descended and hovered over me until I left again the next morning. I didn't know if Mom's deteriorating condition and Dad's almost tangible exhaustion affected Sue in the same way. We didn't talk much. She was absorbed in her own life, and Dad and I in ours. Buster was quickly rising as the star quarterback of the LSU Tigers, so we didn't hear from him much at all. His team's yellow and purple banner hung on my bedroom wall, although its bright colors failed to lighten the persistent, invading shadows that darkened the home's atmosphere.

As Mom continued to slip away from us, Sue's presence around the house was scarce. If she wasn't busy with her friends, after school activities and her part time job as a hostess, she was locked in her room, doing homework, or lying in bed flipping through teen magazines while listening to the radio. I would grumble to myself a hundred times a week: *She'll do anything to escape responsibility!* I begrudged Sue the freedom she seemed to selfishly hoard for herself. Secretly, however, I wished I could just walk away, too.

Mom was Mom - what else could I say? We couldn't desert her! We just had to adjust, each in our own way. The FBI online website was my escape. It kept me sane. Dad and I had grown so close, and we were so happy when we were wrapped up in our search for information about Dan Cooper. It had been so much fun! But those happy days seemed long past as worry took its toll on Dad. I tried to focus on those good memories. One of my favorite's was when we concocted our own conspiracy theories about D.B. Cooper, and Dad had acted out a scenario where aliens had plucked Cooper right out of the air as he parachuted down.

He could barely make it through the scene without laughing, which would make me laugh too.

Yup. Those days were gone.

As I turned the key to the bright red front door (Mom insisted that Dad paint red, in order to add color to our drab, gray frame house), and pushed it open to step inside, I felt the hollowness of dreams fading.

Adjustment can be very hard.

The clinking of tools and metal components told me Dad was working on computers in the garage workshop. The open garage door into the kitchen allowed his direct view of Mom sliding to and fro in the glider in front of the TV set that had become her babysitter, humming absently as she watched some inane cartoon I had long outgrown and clapping her hands wildly whenever her favorite character came onto the screen.

As computers grew more user-friendly and issues could be fixed through troubleshooting or a quick telephone call, Dad's repair business suffered.

Dad's sadness permeated the house like a living, breathing cloud of darkness seeping into every corner. It was so palpable I started calling it by name—The Fog— after a movie I'd once watched.

Sighing, I called out to him. "I'm home!" I set my books down, then went to Mom and gave her a peck on the cheek. I imagined she responded with a slight smile, but it may have just been wishful thinking on my part.

From that point, a well-established routine kicked in: check in with Dad, ask how Mom had been that day and what she needed; go to my room to change into jeans, then tend to Mom, making sure she drank her tea or water. Check her clothing for any accidents and change, dry and powder her if needed. Then I was free to eat a quick snack. Then - weather permitting - I would take Mom for a walk around the neighborhood, greeting the neighbors as they tried to connect with Mom and convey their good wishes for her to "get well soon." Sometimes she remembered them. Sometimes she didn't.

Sometimes I just wanted to crawl into a hole and die. Not because of Mom's condition - people in the neighborhood understood what was happening. Dad had explained her deteriorating condition with many of them. They responded with casseroles.

Don't laugh! How else would you respond? There are few ways to truly convey regret and sympathy, other than bursting into tears and mourning alongside someone. That's why funerals overflow with food.

No, I was embarrassed because Mom had developed an awkward kind of "Tourette's Truth Syndrome."

As we walked the neighborhood, she would mutter or loudly remark on those people whom she did recall, and every unflattering thought Mom had ever had about them would audibly spill from her memory. Most of the time, she belted out those memories at the top of her lungs.

Certain people started crossing the street when they saw us coming, nodding at me tersely with a grim expression, and quickly averting their eyes so as not to catch hers. Kids sniggered at her outbursts - until she blessed them out, in less than kid-appropriate language. Adults nearby chuckled as they masked their response with a garden-gloved hand, but ducked their heads as she approached, fearing her merciless recall. Our walks started getting lonelier, albeit louder.

After one particularly brash incident that ended with my mother flat on her bottom in a neighbor's sprinkler-soaked yard, I'd had enough.

"Never again!" I shouted to Dad as the screen slammed shut behind us and Mom stood dripping on the carpet. "Never again!" Our late afternoon walks were over. I was done.

I was true to my word. But now, more than ever, I was housebound after school. Mom was calm and manageable as long as she had some tea by her side, a regular snack, was tended to and made comfortable every few hours, and a continuous string of tapes playing in the VCR

I would cook enough on Sundays to last a week, so Dad was available to keep Mom from a hot stove while I tended whatever was baking on two racks in the oven and stirred the four pots bubbling away on the stovetop. On Saturdays, I gave Dad a well needed break and took over the responsibility of watching Mom like a hawk.

I would steal some time while VHS tapes captured Mom's attention, and it was then I could shift into my alter ego, Detective Stephanie Storm, a legend in my own mind, hot on the trail of D.B. Cooper.

The Internet opened a whole new world of investigation for me. I could peruse the full list of FBI suspects at any time, and there were a lot of them. Some were legitimate suspects; others were wannabes, either pathologically hungry for some form of notoriety, or using the unsolved crime as a springboard for fraud. Every delicious detail was now mine to examine. I wanted to learn the characteristics that made these men suspects. I wanted to profile the profiled and unravel the details that caused Dad to think he knew the real identity of Dan Cooper.

I read and researched voraciously, booted up the computer at every opportunity and made copious notes in the butterfly notebook that belonged to that great female detective, Stephanie Storm, aka me.

Chapter 12: The Theories

FBI agents first assigned to the case surmised that Cooper was either from Seattle, or familiar with the Seattle area. The hijacker had recognized Tacoma from the air when the jet flew over the city, and when the 727 circled Puget Sound while awaiting the go-ahead to land, the air pirate had remarked that McChord Air Force Base was just about 20 minutes' drive from the Seattle-Tacoma Airport. That observation led investigators to surmise D.B. Cooper was an Air Force veteran. Who else would know something like that? Then there was the parachuting itself. Who else but someone familiar with planes and parachuting would attempt such a risky, if not downright foolish method of stealing a large amount of cash?

Interestingly, around the time authorities entertained an Air Force connection, a comic book attracted the FBI's attention for a time. The comic's hero was, perhaps not so coincidentally, named Dan Cooper.

Les Aventures de Dan Cooper, was a Franco-Belgian comics series in French, and had a primarily Franco-Belgian and French-Canadian audience. It never aspired to wide distribution and was never translated into English.

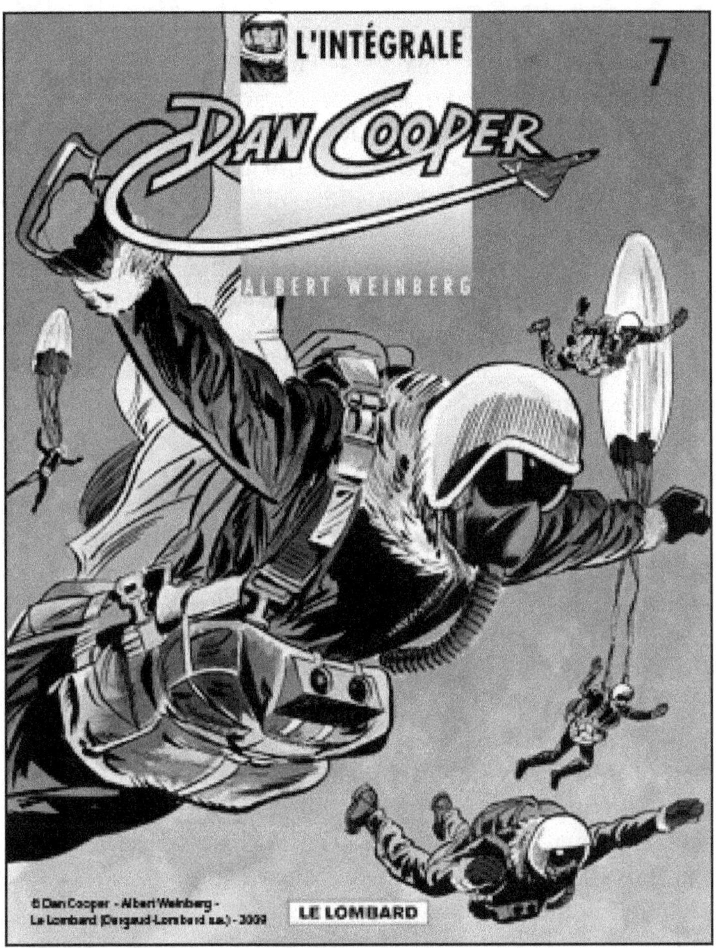

Figure 13 The Adventures of Dan Cooper comic.

The comic introduced its hero as a futuristic military flying ace and rocket ship pilot named Dan Cooper, whose adventures took him to planets in outer space. Later, the storylines evolved, becoming more realistic, occurring in a present-day setting, and tied to current events of the time. Dan Cooper was, by the late 1960-early 1970s, a daring Royal Canadian Air Force test pilot, often depicted in the cartoon images as parachuting and skydiving from high altitudes. When the FBI first uncovered the connections between the comic and the skyjacking – they surmised that Cooper was either Canadian - where the French-language comics were sold around Montreal, or he'd become aware of this publication while on a tour of duty in Germany.

This supported an FBI profile of the hijacker having a close affiliation with the Air Force or Army Special Forces. Either way, agents believed the comic Dan Cooper had served as inspiration for the name the hijacker used when purchasing the ticket for Flight 305 out of Portland, if not actually for the deed itself. Some of the comic's storylines had Cooper illustrated as he jumped from a plane wearing a parachute; another story had a ransom being delivered in a knapsack. Both aspects matched details of the air heist perpetrated on Thanksgiving Eve, 1971.

The hijacker's request for "negotiable American currency" was a strange phrase the FBI assumed no American would use. But when Cooper spoke to the two stewardesses, and to the Northwest Orient ticket agent, none of them detected an accent. That didn't rule out the theory the hijacker was Canadian, however, as the Canadian accent is similar to speech patterns of the American Northwest. Larry Carr was a lead agent who spent years trying to crack the D.B. Cooper mystery. The Seattle-based FBI agent worked with The Cooper Research Team, led by Tom Kaye. The two men were convinced the hijacker chose his alias, and possibly elements of his criminal exploit, based on the fictional Franco-Belgian comic hero.

Figure 14 Special Agent Larry Carr. Source: fbi.gov

The Air Force angle reinforced by Cooper's knowledge of flying. Additionally, authorities saw him - at least, initially - as a shrewd and careful planner, one who was very well informed when he calculated his escape from the plane. When Cooper asked for four parachutes, law enforcement feared he planned to take hostages with him when and if he jumped. Afterward, they arrived at the conclusion the request for extra parachutes was his way to prevent anyone from sabotaging the equipment they provided to him.

Smart.

Then he apparently chose the 727-100 airjet because it was the only aircraft with a rear door that could be opened mid-flight, and a stairway he could descend to jump from. The plane's engines were positioned so they would present no threat to the safety of a jumper, and more specifically, no threat of being fried by the jet's exhaust. This specialized information was never disclosed to the flight crews since it was unnecessary for normal operation of the plane. So how the heck did Cooper know all that? FBI agents were mystified.

The plane had a "single-point fueling capacity," according to the FBI website, which would make refueling quick and easy. That particular airplane also had the capability of flying at a low altitude for an extended period without stalling - something the hijacker obviously knew when he ordered the pilot to fly "low and slow." And Cooper knew other things no common criminal would ever have been aware of--such as instructing the pilots to maintain the 15-degree setting of the flaps, the exact cruising speed to be maintained, and how long it would take to fuel a plane.

Dad didn't even know stuff like that, and he had been Army Air Force and said he knew quite a few guys who were pilots.

My fascination deepened as I read that the aft staircase, the "airstairs" on the plane was operated by a single switch in the rear of the plane that not even the pilots could override from the cockpit! Had Cooper known that?

And then, as I read on, I thought, *Wow! Just wow*. In Vietnam, the CIA used this particular model of 727 to drop supplies and agents behind enemy lines! Cooper *had* to be Air Force, or maybe Army Air. Probably why Dad thought he knew who the hijacker might be!

Every paragraph led me further into the Air Force rabbit hole. Why hadn't Dad told me about his suspicions? I grimaced. *Probably thinks I'm still just a kid. And not only a kid, but a girl as well.* Maybe he thought I'd blab his suspicions to someone. I blinked back a tear at the realization he might not trust me. But how could he not trust me after we had kept our D.B. Cooper research a secret from Mom for so long?

I read on, determined to ferret out clues that might help me discover who Dad suspected. He'd often mentioned people he'd met to Mom. I racked my memory for any mention of some super-pilot he'd known, but came up with nothing.

The FBI agents surmised Cooper had calculated his heist to the last detail, from his choosing a busy pre-holiday afternoon, when everyone was distracted by thoughts of Thanksgiving and family obligations over the extended weekend.

Funny how the FBI search had not turned up anyone who was unaccounted for on that big family day!

Agents agreed that the business suit Cooper wore was likely a ruse - who knew what the guy actually did for a living? But dressing that way made the hijacker look respectable. And he would have to look respectable if he had to hitch a ride after making his way through the woods to a road.

When I scrolled to the next page, the same FBI agents undermined their initial theory about how experienced and clever the hijacker appeared to be. They speculated Cooper couldn't have had the parachute training and experience they initially believed, or he never would have jumped from a plane moving at close to 200 miles per hour into a driving rain on a freezing pitch-dark night over mountainous and forested terrain in an area where he couldn't pinpoint his landing zone with certainty, since he couldn't even see the ground, due to thick cloud cover at 5,000 feet. Speaking of ill-equipped! The hijacker was inadequately dressed in his suit, trench coat and loafers to withstand a sustained wind chill temperature of *negative* 70° Fahrenheit,

Loafers! Loafers would have blown away on his way down, or more likely, as soon as he jumped. If Cooper really knew what he was doing, agents concluded, he would have chosen more appropriate shoes!

As the years progressed, the FBI had given up hope that Cooper was still alive. They'd abandoned the early idea that the hijacker knew what he was doing. No experienced paratrooper could have missed the fact the reserve chute Cooper selected to use for the jump was for training purposes only. It had been provided accidentally in the rush to comply with the hijacker's demands after Cooper had refused the military parachutes first proffered by McChord AFB. The panels of the training chute were sewn shut-- it would never open properly. A trained paratrooper would surely have checked that important detail before trusting it with his life. The "dummy" chute that Cooper taken with him had an inoperable ripcord and was designed for classroom use only. The chute was also clearly marked to as such, and any experienced paratrooper or skydiver would have immediately noticed. Cooper took the functional reserve chute apart, using its shrouds to secure the money bag, possibly tying it around his waist. Of the two primary chutes he had been provided, Cooper chose the older parachute, which was technically inferior to the newer one he left behind.

Figure 15 D.B. Cooper's Parachute.
Source: Washington State Historical Society

I got goosebumps as I read more about the weather conditions Cooper experienced during his jump. *Brrrrrrrrr* - even the thought of a temperature that cold chilled me on that warm spring afternoon.

The FBI concluded that although Cooper may have been in the Air Force at one time, he could not have been a seasoned parachutist, but perhaps a cargo loader. Because loaders often throw cargo from an aircraft while it is in flight, they wear parachutes while they work, but they have minimal jump training– and that would mean Cooper had only a rudimentary working knowledge of parachutes and of jumping. If he was indeed a cargo loader, it solidified the probability that Cooper couldn't have survived the jump, and if he by some miracle did make it to the ground alive, he was injured and incapacitated and most likely succumbed to exposure and dehydration.

The investigation still left many unanswered questions. Why hadn't a hunter or hiker found any evidence of remains in the twenty years since the jump? And if by chance, someone had found the remains and kept the cash, why hadn't any turned up in circulation? And what about those three bills mysteriously missing from the banded packet? *Arrggggghh!* I could understand why Special Agent Himmelsbach was ready to tear out his hair by the end of his career.

The only way Cooper could have survived was if he'd had an accomplice and, by the spring of 1994, absolutely no evidence of an accomplice had turned up, despite intensive efforts by the FBI. By this time, FBI agents had questioned thousands of persons and publicized their search widely. Others had posted substantial rewards for evidence or information, but not one legitimate claimant had come forward in response.

The authorities were stumped. And although I hated to admit it, I was too.

Chapter 13: Suspects and Copycats

The first man to come under suspicion of law enforcement after the hijacking was an unfortunate soul named D. B. Cooper in Portland, Oregon. He had a minor criminal record, so Portland police knew his whereabouts and promptly brought him in for questioning on the remote chance that the hijacker had used his real name when buying the airline ticket. While this suspect was quickly eliminated from consideration, a junior wire service reporter confused this individual with the hijacker of the 727, who had purchased his ticket with cash, under the name Dan Cooper. The mix up was never corrected in subsequent reporting, and it stuck.

So, D.B. Cooper it was. And when I noticed that even the FBI website, blazoned with the official seal, referred to the hijacker as D.B. Cooper, I shrugged and accepted it, at last. Who was I to question the FBI? It was time to stop being such a purist and forget about "Dan" Cooper.

I traced the outlines of Cooper's face with a fingertip as I peered at it closely for the thousandth time. The bland, ordinary face depicted by the police artist stared back at me. It was prominently displayed on the FBI website, but its very blandness resulted in thousands of suspects being interviewed by the agency, with no results. He could be anyone. I was sure the improvised image taped to the mirror in my bedroom with its truly close-set eyes and thinned bridge of the nose was a much better likeness-- particularly since it drew such a dramatic reaction from my father. But how could I get this image in front of someone who would give my opinion any weight?

Cooper's hijacking tactics were certainly unique, and his assumed success, early on, only served to spawn a rash of imitators, all heartened by Cooper's lucrative exploit and by the FBI's evident inability to capture him. Through mid-

1972, a total of 15 copycat crimes were committed against U.S. airlines.

But had Cooper been inspired by a Canadian hijacking that occurred just two weeks before his own Thanksgiving Eve heist?

FBI records stated that a Canadian citizen named Paul Joseph Cini had hijacked an Air Canada DC-8 flying over the U.S. and demanded money at gunpoint. The money was provided, but while the aircraft was flying over Montana, the fellow put down his shotgun in order to strap on the parachute he'd brought on board with him. As soon as the hijacker self-disarmed and struggled to don the parachute, crew members overpowered him. Cini was arrested upon landing and prosecuted in Canada.

Examining Cooper's modus operandi, it seemed to FBI agents that lessons learned from the botched Canadian hijacking were incorporated in Cooper's planning. For example, Cooper maintained a low-key presence, carried his "weapon" in a briefcase, and released everyone but essential members of the flight crew, forcing them all into the cockpit before preparing for his jump in complete privacy. Personally, I saw little connection to Cini's fiasco, and a great deal of creativity in D.B. Cooper's plan. But then, I admit to a slight prejudice.

Gary Brock Trapnell began 1972 by boarding a TWA flight from LA to New York, with the intent to hijack it. He demanded $306,800 in cash (an oddly specific figure, I noted, and a full third greater than Cooper's modest request for $200,000), plus release of the jailed political activist, Angela Davis. I recalled Mom and Dad talking about her with Buster on one occasion, so I sort of knew who she was. I jotted a note to myself to read up on her. Trapnell also wanted a face-to-face meeting with Richard Nixon. He got none of that. Trapnell's luck ran out when the plane landed at Kennedy Airport in New York. FBI agents waited for the plane to land, then shot and wounded the man before arresting him.

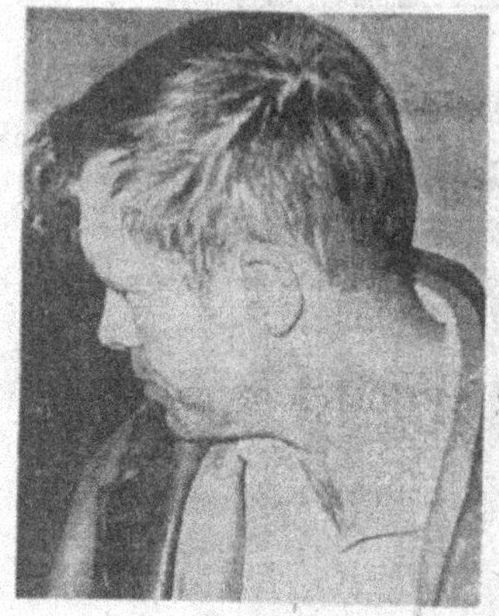

Figure 16 Garrett "Gary" Trapnell in the news.

Then, on January 20 of that same year, an Army veteran named Richard Charles LaPoint brandished what he said was a bomb in his attempt to hijack a Hughes Airwest flight leaving Las Vegas - while the aircraft was still on the taxiway! LaPoint demanded a modest ransom of just $50,000 (he was obviously a man of small ambition. I chuckled when I read the amount - but then, he did self-identify as a New England "beach bum"). LaPoint also requested a helmet and two parachutes. He released the passengers and two stewardesses before ordering the pilot to fly toward Denver, and bailed onto a treeless plain in northeastern Colorado, where law enforcement was able to track his locator-equipped parachute and, following his tracks in the snow and mud of a spring thaw, nailed him only a few hours after his landing.

In April of 1972. a former Army Green Beret, Richard McCoy, Jr. diverted a United Airlines 727 to San Francisco, following its take-off from Denver, and successfully parachuted from the airplane over Utah with a cash ransom of $500,000 (nearly double Cooper's haul - I was rapidly losing respect for old Dan as a criminal). McCoy almost got away with it but was arrested after spending just two days as a man of some wealth.

Then there was Frederick Hahneman, who - apparently homesick - used a handgun to demand a ransom of $303,000 (where do they get these odd numbers from, anyway?) and ordered the Eastern Airlines 727 to fly from Allentown. Pennsylvania to the land of his birth, Honduras. He successfully parachuted with the cash onto his native soil, but freedom was not in the cards for him. With the Feds in hot pursuit and a bounty of $25,000 on his head - which I imagined was a lot of money in the early 1970s, and especially in Central America - Hahneman walked into the American Embassy in Tegucigalpa and surrendered to American authorities. His life on the lam lasted just short of a month.

June of 1972 recorded the dramatic, and almost funny, hijacking episode of another ex-military air pirate. This time, a paratrooper and Vietnam veteran named Robin Dolin Heady reportedly "stormed" a United Airlines 727 departing Reno, demanded $200.000 and two parachutes, which were duly provided, then launched himself into the Nevada night near Washoe Lake, just 25 miles south of the Reno airport. Unfortunately for Heady, police located his car - which ironically, and proudly, displayed a bumper sticker of the United States Parachute Association - parked near Washoe Lake, and so were able to arrest him when he showed up to retrieve it less than 24 hours later.

Another June hijacking that drew attention was undertaken by an unemployed gas station attendant who used a submachine gun to force his will on the flight crew of an American Airlines 727 flying from St. Louis, Missouri to Tulsa, Oklahoma. The hijacker, Martin McNally, diverted the plane's course eastward toward Indiana and parachuted from the plane carrying the $500,000 in cash he had extorted from the airline. Dogged by misfortune,

McNally lost the cash when wind carried it away as he jumped from the aircraft. He safely drifted to earth near Peru, Indiana. He was tracked to Detroit, where law enforcement officials took him into custody only a few days after his disappointing attempt.

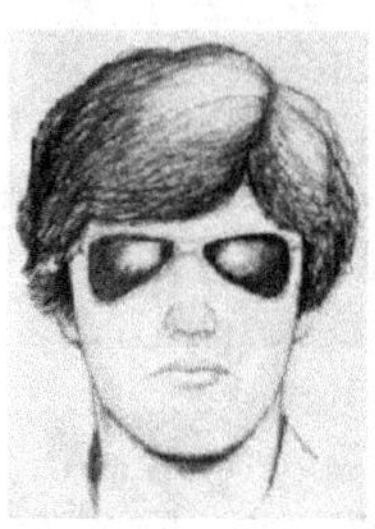

Figure 17 Martin McNally, 28 years old.

When airlines began checking carry-on bags in 1973, the incidents of air piracy stopped. The last such hijacking attempt for monetary gain took place, according to FBI records, in July of 1980, when a man by the name of Glenn K. Tripp commandeered another Northwest flight at the Seattle-Tacoma Airport. The aircraft was still on the ground when he demanded either $600,000 or $100,000 in cash - accounts varied, according to the FBI report - plus the now-customary set of two parachutes. But what was truly extraordinary in this attempt was that Tripp also demanded the assassination of his boss - not a run-of-the-mill request from a hijacker. He was arrested and subsequently prosecuted on multiple charges.

But some people never learn. Tripp was still on probation from his first extortion attempt involving an aircraft when he hijacked the very same Northwest flight - Flight 608 - three years later in January of 1983. However, this time Tripp waited to hijack the plane in mid-flight before demanding flight to Afghanistan. FBI agents showed no mercy when the aircraft touched down on the tarmac in Portland. Glenn Tripp was shot and killed.

It was 1994, twenty-three years after the stormy pre-Thanksgiving night in 1971 that marked D.B. Cooper's entry into the annals of airline history and his inclusion in the panoply of dubious American criminal heroes, joining the infamous ranks of Willie Sutton, Butch Cassidy and the Sundance Kid, Ma Barker and the Barker gang, and Bonnie and Clyde. The FBI had seen a series of agents assigned to the hijacking case, and several devoted the last decades of their careers to the search for the man or his remains. In the interim, thousands had been considered but rejected as viable suspects after interviews and alibis discounted the possibility of their involvement. To confuse the issue, pretenders hoping to claim the spotlight abounded, but only a few merited significant attention.

One of the strangest imposters was Barb Dayton. Yes, a woman. A librarian at the University of Washington and a recreational pilot, Barbara Dayton confessed to a number of friends in 1978 that she had not always been a woman. She been born and lived as Bobby Dayton until late in life, undergoing Washington State's first gender reassignment surgery in 1969. Stretching credulity, she informed her friends she was also the notorious D.B. Cooper. Photos showed that Bobby Dayton owned and flew a Cessna 140, which Barb Dayton continued to fly following her transition. Her close friends, Ron and Pat Forman, waited until Barb died of pulmonary disease in 2002 before researching Barb's claims, detailed in the book they subsequently published: *The Legend of DB Cooper - Death by Natural Causes*. The case was never investigated by the FBI during Barb's lifetime and while there was much commentary on Dayton's claim, only a very brief history verified that Barbara Dayton had, indeed, been born Robert Dayton and served in both the Merchant Marine in 1926, and then the Army during WWII. On discharge from the military, Dayton found work in the construction industry handling explosives. Frustrated by several unsuccessful attempts to obtain a commercial pilot's license, Dayton's shattered dreams of a career as a commercial aircraft pilot supposedly fueled the revenge motivation behind the Cooper hijacking, which took place two years after the sex-change operation. However, upon learning the Cooper case was still open and the potential of conviction for the crime still existed, Dayton recanted her story.

The Formans included photos of Bobby Dayton in their book, placing them side by side with the composite the FBI used. The resemblance was strong. But then, looking at similar side-by-side facial comparisons of the other significant suspects, I was struck by how many of them strongly resembled the FBI composite. They all bore less resemblance, however, to the modified image I had created on a whim.

Richard Floyd McCoy, Jr., I noticed, was the same copycat hijacker whose air piracy attempt had been briefly documented elsewhere. These entries in the file, however, were more detailed. He had done two tours of duty in Vietnam, first as a demolition expert and then as a Green Beret. McCoy returned to the war as a helicopter pilot. On retiring from service, he remained in the Utah National Guard as a warrant officer. Richard McCoy had ambitions of becoming a Utah State Trooper and he was an avid skydiver. McCoy's copycat attempt was widely publicized. What he had declared was a bomb as he brandished it about to create fear turned out to be nothing more than a paper weight, designed to appear like a hand grenade. The gun he waved around as he made his demands wasn't even loaded. McCoy had the plane fly to San Francisco International Airport, where the $500,000 he had demanded was delivered to the aircraft, along with the four parachutes he requested. Ordering to plane to fly east, the former Green Beret leapt from the lowered aft stairs over Provo, Utah, leaving behind his handwritten instructions and a magazine covered with his fingerprints.

Figure 18 Richard Floyd McCoy Jr.

McCoy was arrested two days later, still in possession of his ill-gotten gains, and received a 45-year prison sentence upon conviction. Incarcerated in the Lewisburg Federal Penitentiary, he and several acquaintances plotted an escape two years later. They succeeded, crashing a garbage truck through the prison gate. McCoy headed for Virginia Beach, where he was tracked by FBI agents and died in a shootout with them after three months of freedom.

McCoy's parole officer, Bernie Rhodes, joined with retired FBI agent Russel Calame to co-author *D.B. Cooper: The Real McCoy*, a book that was published in 1991. The pair claimed McCoy was D.B. Cooper, highlighting similarities in the hijackings. They interviewed McCoy's family members, who claimed the black clip-on tie with the mother-of-pearl tie clip that Dan Cooper had left behind belonged to McCoy. The authors further cited McCoy's refusal to admit whether he was, in fact, D.B. Cooper. The agent who had shot McCoy in the Virginia Beach shootout was more than happy to claim a few minutes of fame, based solely on his opinion at the time that, in shooting McCoy he had also killed D.B. Cooper.

The FBI didn't put much stock in the flimsy evidence presented in the book and never considered McCoy a serious suspect for many reasons - most convincingly, the documented fact that McCoy was in Las Vegas the day of

Cooper's Oregon hijacking, and sat down with family members in Utah for Thanksgiving dinner the day after Cooper was thought to have parachuted into the thickly forested wilds of Washington State's rough and mountainous terrain.

William Pratt Gossett was a career soldier, veteran of the Marine Corps, Army and Army Air Force, and had been trained in wilderness survival and as a paratrooper. Gossett retired in 1973 after seeing action in both Korea and Vietnam. A talented individual, he kept busy after retirement teaching military law at Utah's Weber State University, where he was also an ROTC instructor. But Gossett's interest in the paranormal - he hosted a radio talk show in Salt Lake City that discussed paranormal experiences and activity - and his obsession with the D.B. Cooper mystery set him apart. It was another 'oh, my gosh' moment when I read that Gossett had amassed a collection of articles on the hijacking similar to Dad's and mine! At an advanced age, Gossett reportedly told a Salt Lake City friend, a retired judge in Utah, and three of his sons that he had committed the hijacking attributed to Cooper, and his file photos from 1971 bear a strong resemblance to Cooper's FBI composite drawing.

However. Special Agent Larry Carr, who spent many years following up on leads in the Cooper case, went on record saying, "There is not one link to the D.B. Cooper case, other than statements made to someone. The FBI had no direct evidence even placing Gossett in the Pacific Northwest at the time of Cooper's hijacking and disappearance." And that settled that.

John List was briefly considered as a possible suspect. Fifteen days before the Thanksgiving Eve hijacking in 1971, John Emil List - an accountant who had served in both WWII and Korea - murdered his wife, three teenaged children and his 85-year-old mother in Westfield, New Jersey, where he lived, and withdrew $200,000 from his mother's account before vanishing. These factors somehow attracted FBI attention with regard to the Cooper case. They considered List's timing of the murders, a physical description that closely matched Cooper's, and the fugitive's desperation. List was not captured for another 18 years. When taken into custody in 1989, the man admitted to the murders of his family, but absolutely denied the hijacking. No real evidence turned up to implicate List, so the FBI eliminated him as a suspect.

Jack Coffelt was another dead end in the investigation. He was a real piece of work, though. The man was described in the FBI file as an ex-convict, and a con man who had supposedly been a government informant. His assertions were far-fetched and unprovable. Coffelt claimed he was the chauffeur and confidante of the last undisputed descendant of Abraham Lincoln - a great grandson of the 16th President, named Robert Todd Lincoln Beckwith. And, in 1972, Coffelt began insisting he was D.B. Cooper. Of course, it was a scam. He engaged a former cellmate by the name of James Brown - no, not *that* James Brown! - to sell his tall tale about being D.B. Cooper to a Hollywood production company. Working as an intermediary for Coffelt, Brown attempted every angle to solicit the tall tale.

The story was, supposedly, that Jack Coffelt, under the alias of Cooper, conducted the hijacking and then parachuted over Mt. Hood, landing about 50 miles southeast of the town of Ariel. Coffelt allegedly lost the extorted cash as he descended and injured himself in a rough landing.

Interestingly, Coffelt *was* in Portland on the day the Northwest Orient 727 was hijacked. Furthermore, it appeared Coffelt had sustained injuries to his leg consistent with injuries from a skydiving accident. Photos of Coffelt bore some resemblance to the composite Dan Cooper (didn't every one of the suspects?). But the FBI dismissed Coffelt's account when they found significant discrepancies in his story and the facts and timeline of the case. Brown persisted in peddling the fiction long after Coffelt died in 1975, and the FBI report said *60 Minutes* considered airing the story before they, too, dismissed the idea as improbable.

Chapter 14: Not All Surprises Are Good

I had been working on my notes from the FBI file, jotting my comments and pithy observations in my butterfly notebook, when I looked up to check on Mom. I gasped as I saw my father's lanky frame swaying the doorway. He clutched the door frame on either side, his large, white-knuckled, bony hands gripping the wood to steady himself. But it wasn't working. His face was pale, sweating and although his mouth was working, jaws moving, no sound came out. I was terrified.

Oh no, a stroke! Dad was having a stroke! What had Katie Dougan said about what they did to help her father until the ambulance came? My mind raced. *What do I do?*

Dad had been running errands, making deliveries. When did he get back? What was happening to him? It was as if he had forgotten how to speak. Fear paralyzed me. I couldn't say anything or do anything but blink and stare.

Then he croaked, "Buster," and slid down the door frame. I was up like a shot. I wasn't strong enough to support him, but at least I could break his fall. When he crumpled, Dad brought me down with him. He sobbed. Then howled. All he had said that was remotely understandable was my brother's name, and now our big, strong father was blubbering like a baby, his head on my shoulder, clutching me so hard I could hardly breathe. This no longer seemed like a stroke. A cold stone of dread crushed my chest as my throat tightened and my heart sank. There was only one way Buster's name could be associated with this scene, and I started crying, too. Time was suddenly wildly distorted, moving both agonizingly slowly and racing madly. In the distance, Mom glanced at us with a curious expression before losing interest and turning back to her cartoons. The glider's slight creak as it rocked back and forth was amplified in that moment. I still hear it in my dreams. It was surreal.

When Sue got home from cheerleading practice, Dad stood up as she mumbled a greeting and dashed for her room to change for work. He followed her into her room. Silence, then Sue's banshee-like howl - a keening wail I can still hear today when I think about it. She sobbed for what seemed like hours and wouldn't leave her room to eat that night. Dad called the restaurant to report the news and make Sue's excuses for not showing up. He made a couple of other calls, too, but I was on the living room sofa, hugging myself hard and rocking with grief as tears streamed down my face, so I didn't hear much of his muted conversations. After he hung up, Dad went to comfort Sue. He spent a little time talking to her before he came into the hall, shut her door behind him, and joined me on the sofa to fill me in on the details. I was numb but needed to hear every word.

The news was grim. The Baton Rouge police chief had called the Sheriff's Office in Temple to deliver the news personally to Sheriff Johnson.

Sheriff Johnson, too, had been crushed. He had known Dad and Buster for years. Temple was still small enough that people mattered. He met Dad in the driveway just as Dad arrived home. The Sheriff had wanted to wait to tell Dad the news inside, but strangers in the house upset Mom, so Dad insisted on hearing the news outside. It was the right decision. We both looked at Mom holding her big sippy cup filled with tea as she laughed at her cartoons and glided to and fro. We imagined her throwing her cup at the Sheriff and screaming for him to "get out, get out, get out, get out!" at the very moment that Dad was trying to absorb Sheriff Johnson's tragic message.

In a calm monotone, Dad recited what the Sheriff had told him. It was a single fatality crash. The accident occurred on LA 410 at Gurney Road in East Baton Rouge. Buster had been driving too fast for road conditions. It had been raining - pouring, actually. Visibility was poor. An oak branch had fallen into his lane and Buster apparently swerved to avoid it and lost control of the car on a left-hand curve. He ran off the left side of the roadway and . . .

I struggled to digest the news. New tears blurred my sight as I gulped down a sob. Buster had flown off the road, only to crash head-long into the trunk of the giant oak the branch had fallen from. I was already becoming a terrible cynic at the ripe old age of 16-going-on-17.

Buster didn't have his seat belt on. *He didn't have his seat belt on.* Buster, who *always* wore his seat belt and *always* made sure Sue and I were buckled in before he would even start the car! How could that have happened? All it took was one moment of negligence. One branch in the road . . . a rainstorm. A wonderful life destroyed, along with the lives of everyone who loved him.

"Alcohol was not involved. It was the middle of the afternoon and apparently, Buster was just running late for practice."

Late for football practice? I couldn't believe my ears. What a stupid reason to die!

The calls Dad had just made were to Baton Rouge. A funeral home was going to ship Buster's body back to us, unless we wanted him buried there. Dad told the man we had a family plot in Temple's biggest and oldest cemetery: Hillcrest. Buster would be coming home to rest.

Sue was never the same after that. She suddenly became nicer, like she realized it was not worth fighting over little stuff—like our time on this planet was far too short. Her grief caused her to skip Senior Prom, and her date that night (her future husband), drove down from Austin and came over to our house that night to play Scrabble with Sue, Dad and me after Mom went to bed early. Dad roasted hot dogs on the grill and made popcorn and hot chocolate, and we played until one in the morning.

I don't know if Mom understood what happened. I don't know if Dad ever talked to her about it, or explained Buster was gone. At the funeral, dressed in black, with strands of big white beads around her neck and a black hat we had to beg her to keep on her head for "just a little while," Mom kept asking where we were, why we had to stand in the sun for so long; and - this is really funny - why had we dressed her like a penguin? I don't think she ever realized her firstborn was gone.

83

Chapter 15: All in Good Time

But perhaps Mom had gleaned something about Buster's death, after all, despite our attempts to shield her from the disturbing news. Her condition spiraled rapidly downward after the funeral. And she became very, very good at escaping the house.

No longer placated by endless cartoons and comedies, she would wander from her chair, then fidget endlessly when we led her back to it, her eyes darting everywhere, but never meeting ours. The cursing was incredible. We didn't think Mom even knew the meanings of the words she now used freely whenever we tried to dress her or change her Depends. Tending to her personal needs now took two people: One had to hold her arms to keep her from swinging wildly at whoever approached first to care for her, while the other bathed and changed her as one would a child. That's all she was, really. I compared her to an overgrown two-year-old. She had degenerated to an infantile stage since Buster died. Sometimes I would even catch her sucking her thumb or twisting her hair.

When a frantic sunrise search found her splashing contentedly in the neighbor child's inflatable pool wearing just her nightgown and an adult diaper, Dad had to face harsh reality. We could no longer care for her. Sooner or later, her wandering would put her in real danger and threaten others. We could only imagine the repercussions if she wandered onto a major road and was struck by a car.

There were long discussions with state social services, and examinations and tests that her doctor had to provide to establish she could no longer be cared for at home and was a danger to herself and others. Mom was taking multiple medications for a number of conditions but had a bad habit of spitting them out and stuffing them in a pocket or shoving them beneath the cushion of her glider. She'd grown more hostile when her will was thwarted. She refused to eat, so her physical condition was also deteriorating.

Standing and walking were increasingly difficult for her, but that development somehow only fed her need to escape. Eventually, after all the red tape had been cleared, Mom was accepted into a long-term facility that specialized in caring for those with advanced Alzheimer's disease.

I was 17, approaching graduation, and facing huge life choices.

Sue was engaged to the college kid from Austin - Matt Jordan - shortly after Buster's death, and he and his family persuaded her to attend college in Austin.

Dad didn't object. Matt was studying engineering and was a nice, genuine guy. Dad and I liked him a lot. And he motivated Sue to improve herself in ways Dad had never been able to inspire her to do. So, Dad gave Sue and Matt his blessing. Austin was close, 65 miles and only an hour and fifteen minutes' drive from Temple, but for Dad, her move away from home was just one more loss to deal with.

I felt closer to Dad than ever, but at the same time, I had to confess I kind of resented the fact I was the only family he had left to cling to.

Then it struck me. Maybe, at last, Dad could be coaxed to tell me just who he thought D.B. Cooper was. Was my modified composite police sketch a match to the man Dad knew?

Who are you, D.B Cooper? And where did you go? The answer to those two questions, I knew, would be my true life's work.

Chapter 16: Wedding Bells

Sue and Matt were married just before Thanksgiving, 1995.

I was 17, just a little over two months into my senior year of high school and starved for friendships and activities after two years bound to the house by a duty I could not shirk. I think Dad appreciated my being there for him during that difficult time. I was certain that was why he gave me no grief when I joined every club I could and returned home late after school activities every afternoon.

At Sue's wedding, Dad seemed to regain his vitality. He looked so much better than he had for the past year. Best of all, Dad had recovered his marvelous sense of humor. This heartened Sue and me--we had both been concerned Dad might bring the cloud of doom dogging his footsteps and darkening his horizon into this happy setting. I worried his continued grief might make him appear unappreciative of the warm hospitality and generosity exhibited by Matt and his family.

I was delighted to see Dad laugh again. Even diminished in number, it felt like we were a real family for the first time in ages.

At the wedding, I met *him*. Danced with him. Flirted with him. Michael James Giordano. He had to be much older than I was-- I couldn't even begin to guess by how much. But he was so good looking-- movie star looks. And while I'd had more champagne than I probably should have, I was just barely tipsy and in full possession of my faculties. He was a charmer, and I didn't take him seriously when he told me he was entranced, enchanted, under my spell, and would have to see me again. I hesitated for a moment when he asked, but - against my better judgment - I gave him my telephone number at the end of the evening. Why not? I was certain I would never lay eyes on him again.

If only I had known at the time where it would lead . . .

Chapter 17: If Only . . .

Since returning home from the wedding, I'd received two phone calls from Michael Giordano, but had not been home when Dad took his name and number. He'd handed each message to me without question or comment, and I'm sure he thought the calls were from some boy at school. The subject of my age had never come up when we were dancing at the reception, but surely, when my father answered the phone the two times he called, Michael must have figured out I still lived at home--there's no way he could have thought I was married! So, why had he called back? I was sure he'd seen me with Dad at the wedding and had to know I was far too young for him. Maybe Sue's husband, Matt, would be able to give me a little more information about the persistent yet charming Michael Giordano.

When I found a moment, I asked Matt about Giordano.

I hesitated to utter his first name. It almost felt too intimate to call him Michael - Michael James Giordano - and say his name aloud. When I did let the name flow from my lips, I could see his thick-lashed dark eyes, feel his lips gently press against the soft skin on the back of my hand, feel his breath on my neck as we danced. I hadn't thought much about him since returning home, but in that instant, as I relived the memory, I got goose bumps.

After I asked Matt about him, he repeated the name, almost in disbelief: "Michael? Michael Giordano?" Matt looked down at the pot he was scrubbing and cleared his throat before answering. "Yeah, I guess you could call him a friend-- business associate, actually. We're not all that close. I met him through the firm. He belongs to a professional organization I belong to, so we see each other occasionally." Matt turned to look at me directly, quickly wiped his hands on the apron he had donned to protect his suit pants, then grabbed my shoulders and held me at arms' length, staring intently into my eyes, "Honey, believe me when I say, you don't want to get involved with him. No way, no how. Besides, he's thirty-two. You're seventeen. And he . . . well, I'll just have to have a word with Mr. Giordano."

I don't think Matt could have known how alluring his words made the prospect of an older man being interested in little old me. Where I had been annoyed and grudgingly determined to return Giordano's calls simply to inform him I was much too young, and not at all interested, Matt's mysterious behavior had given birth to a sudden fascination and opened Pandora's Box. What was it about that handsome and charming man that made Matt so insistent I stay away from him? Why would he speak that way about a business acquaintance? Was Giordano married? I saw no ring, and he was unaccompanied.

Forbidden fruit beckoned and the potential of romantic danger Giordano offered was an aphrodisiac. In my innocence, I scarcely knew what the word meant - just that it was potent, and exciting, like the thought of those darkly seductive eyes set into his very handsome face. I recalled his compliments and the words of enchantment he spoke to me that night. So he was 32? I knew a few girls at school who professed in hushed voices they were being romanced by older men. Those girls were pretty. Sophisticated. Knowledgeable. Everything I longed to be. As I dried the plates and Matt scrubbed pots, I daydreamed. The late-blooming tomboy in me was growing into womanhood.

Chapter 18: So, I Finally Asked . . .

When report cards arrived on a Friday in January, Dad was not pleased. He was upset to see how my grades had slid so sharply from my usual As and Bs to abysmal Cs, and even one D.

We argued - something unheard of between Dad and me. I had for so long been the obedient daughter, where Sue had been the rebel, talking back, flouncing off and slamming doors behind her to show displeasure at being disciplined or called on the carpet for something she had done - or neglected to do.

Now I was the one displaying "attitude." The quarrel ended badly, with both Dad and I feeling miserable, so we talked it out. I promised to cut back on a few "non-essential" clubs and after-school activities, and to spend more time hitting the books. He told me what a huge help I had been with Mom's care, and how much he appreciated my sacrifices. We cried, hugged, and celebrated our promises to do better over an ice cream soda in a sweet shop by the Food Court at Temple Mall.

"You know," Dad said as I delicately bit into the frosting-filled wafer that accompanied my strawberry shake, "there's a new suspect in the D.B. Cooper mystery."

I stopped chewing then gulped down the wafer. "Oh?" How long had it been since anything new had turned up in the newspapers? How long had it been since Dad and I had even thought about the unsolved case the FBI still pursued with a weary, but dogged determination?

Like a computer program, the FBI was running continuously in the background, quietly pursuing dozens of investigations the public had long forgotten about.

It had been many months since the Cooper case had even crossed my mind. The modified composite drawing of Cooper I had created was still taped to my mirror, but the edges were curled and yellowing, the tape lifting, and I was ready to take it down a month or two earlier. But removing it seemed like a sacrilege. Plus, I realized I would have to clean the mirror with Windex to get the sticky stuff off the glass. So, it stayed in place.

"What did you read, Dad? What did they find out?"

Dad drew the last of his chocolate shake up the straw, swallowed, then leaned back on the hard bench of the booth. He looked like he was settling in to tell me a long story. We were good again, so I sipped my water and listened as Dad brought me up to date on the latest information about our favorite topic. Nothing new had occurred in the investigation since 1988, when part of a parachute had been located - retrieved from the bottom of the Columbia River near where the money had been found in early 1980, close to Tena Bar.

I wondered what Dad had learned.

He ceremoniously cleared his throat, carefully wiped the table before him with a paper napkin, then reached into his back pocket to pull out his wallet and remove several neatly folded newspaper clippings. With the utmost care, Dad unfolded each of three articles and spread them open on the tabletop.

"These two articles came from the Houston Chronicle - Wednesday, Thursday editions. And this is from the Dallas paper."

I leaned forward, eager to see for myself what he had.

I could see a prominent name in the headlines, Duane L. Weber. I leaned back and sipped my shake. This was Dad's story, and I could tell he was going to enjoy the telling of it.

"Almost all these Cooper suspects have been ex-military, and some of them had criminal histories. Well, this guy, Duane L. Weber, fought in WWII, and was an Army vet. But he was also a career criminal and served time from 1945 to 1968 in about six different prisons, mostly for forgery and burglary. He died this year from kidney disease. Now, listen to this. Three days before he passed, he supposedly confessed to his wife that *he* was Dan Cooper. Not D.B. Cooper like everyone has been calling the hijacker for the last two decades, but the original name on his boarding pass. Well, the man's widow didn't know much about the case so basically dismissed his confession until she read up on the D.B. Cooper story after a friend she'd told pointed out the significance of the name her husband uttered on his deathbed.

Duane Weber and Sketch of D B Cooper

"Anyway, Josephine Weber checked the story out at her local library, and while she was doing her research, she came across a book in her late husband's possessions about the hijacking by a man named Max Gunther. I don't think I've ever heard of it. But, anyway, right there, in the margins of that book, the widow found quite a few notations she said were written in her husband's handwriting! How strange is that? And then she remembered a bad nightmare he'd had one night, when she said her husband talked in his sleep about jumping out of a plane and was worried that he had left fingerprints on the 'aft stairs.' And when she'd asked him once about a knee injury, he'd told her he was hurt jumping from a plane!

"None of this made any sense to her at the time -- not until she started her research after he'd died. The man was a chain smoker, like Cooper. And Duane Weber drank bourbon. We know Cooper had ordered two bourbons. Weber's widow kept remembering things, so she eventually contacted the FBI. Apparently, Duane Weber had also taken her along with him on a trip to the Seattle area in 1979. She accompanied him to the Columbia River, where he left her on the riverbank while he went for a walk, alone, in the Tena Bar area - where the money was found the following year by that kid."

I nodded, digesting the new and fascinating information.

"Actually," Dad mused, "the article said their trip took place just four months before the kid found the bundles of twenties from the ransom money. Some coincidence, huh, Pumpkin? The FBI, of course, is checking the story out."

Then Dad dropped his voice conspiratorially. "I've read that the FBI is still sitting on details of the hijacking that have never been publicly released. Those unreleased details are what tripped up most of the imposters over the years. And they still won't release those details because that's how they cross-check answers, using them as a gauge of truth - the only gauge, really, that they have to recognize whether someone is really who they say they are. But the FBI is *really* interested in closing this case. Not only is it a black eye for the agency, but all the songs and books and TV shows and movies have made a folk hero out of a criminal. And that just rubs the Feds face in the fact that the case is still unsolved after 23 years - 24 years, this Thanksgiving."

I pored over the clippings, but they held no more information than Dad had just related.

"There's more, though" Dad said, after a brief silence. "The FBI always thought Cooper had a criminal mind - just the audacity of the hijacking and his escape, parachuting into the storm like led them to believe he was a desperate man. FBI agents believe the real Dan Cooper may have been familiar with prison. And Weber's series of incarcerations fits that profile perfectly. Plus, Jo Weber had given the FBI an old Northwest Orient airline ticket she had found in the couple's tax papers. She's completely convinced her husband was exactly who he said he was: THE Dan Cooper.

"And here's another interesting detail we've never run across before that turned up in one of the newspapers from the Northwest: There was a passenger the FBI never mentioned publicly. His name was Robert Gregory. See there? I noted his name on that clipping you're looking at, so I wouldn't forget to mention it to you. Anyway, Robert Gregory was able to give a very detailed description of Dan Cooper. He was the owner of a paint store in Seattle at the time and sat directly across the aisle from Cooper during the flight from Portland to the Seattle-Tacoma Airport.

"His was actually the best and most detailed description of Cooper, but for some reason I'm not clear about, he was never interviewed by the sketch artist! Go figure that!"

"Maybe that was one of the elements, Dad, which the FBI was holding back, to see if anyone else offered those same details, like their "truth" screen."

"Could be," Dad replied. "But he gave a lot of details others missed. Gregory was the only one to point out the sunglasses Cooper wore were actually 'horn-rimmed,' and that his suit jacket had 'wide lapels' and that the color wasn't brown or black like the other witnesses described, but 'russet' - kind of a reddish-brown. Of course," Dad said with a short laugh, "the man owned a paint store, so he knew his colors! And Gregory had told one of the first FBI investigators on the case that Cooper's hair was 'marcelled.'"

Marcelled? I'd never heard the term. My dad must've seen my confused look, so he said, "What's that, Stephanie? You don't know what that is?" A mischievous glint appeared in his eyes.

"No, maybe vaguely, but don't remember what it means."

"Well, honey, you know how everyone described Cooper's hair as 'wavy"? Well, a 'Marcelle wave' is something far beyond normally wavy hair. Nobody marcels their hair anymore. It's a type of tight, artificial, undulating wave - not a curl - but it's kind of fancy. It requires use of a curling iron to create." Dad chuckled, and drew a series of tight, measured waves on a paper napkin, which he held up to me. "A Marcelle wave looks like that," he explained. "It was very popular during the Roaring Twenties. A lot of the silent movie stars wore their hair that way."

I loved old movies in black-and-white, and the silent films, and immediately recognized what "marcelled" meant: Mary Pickford and Charlie Chaplin and the early Groucho Marx immediately sprang to mind.

"Apparently, since this Gregory character's description slipped through the cracks, the marcelled hair never made it into the composite drawing and was never released publicly. But the information remained in their files. And according to his wife, Duane Weber's hair appeared marcelled. That's the extent of the new information that's recently turned up. Now you know everything I've learned about the guy. We have to follow up on this as they check it out."

I laughed, then said, "So the FBI started out looking in the wrong area for the hijacker's landing zone, and they ignored a more precise description and publicized a composite image of the hijacker that not only did not depict the close-set eyes everyone described, but missed a lot of detail in Gregory's description - no wonder they haven't found him! He had every opportunity to disappear when law enforcement focused all their resources in the wrong place, and they didn't even have an accurate description of the guy - I mean, in 1970, the marcelled hair would really make him stand out! And then they assumed he had a criminal record! What if the hijacker was squeaky-clean and had no criminal record at all?"

At that point, I saw the opening I'd been waiting years for, and I took it. "I need to ask you something, Dad. It's important."

He leaned forward, listening, one brow cocked inquisitively.

"Well," I started, hesitantly, then paused - how should I put this to him? *Just grab the bull by the horns!* The next words tumbled out rapidly.

"I know you had a conversation with Mom a few years ago where you mentioned you were sure you knew who Dan Cooper was. Remember that? There was a suspect you mentioned to Mom. You told her you thought you knew who Cooper was. And when I showed you the composite that I had folded to bring the eyes closer together - remember, the one I taped to my mirror? You were so startled when you looked at it that you spilled the forkful of food you were ready to feed Mom, and almost dropped the fork. Did I make the drawing look like the guy you thought might be Dan Cooper? Is that why you reacted that way?

Dad studied me with a calculating gaze, then looked up at a dove that had flown into the mall and was confused, trapped, and frantically flapping around thirty feet above our heads. He glanced back at me again almost nervously, then looked back up at the dove.

"Who is it, Dad? Who is it that so closely resembles the modified FBI composite I showed you? You must know someone who looks just like the image I created, don't you? Who is it? You said you knew someone. Tell me, who?" I had leaned forward, intent on getting my father to meet my eyes and spill the beans.

The barrage of questions caught him off guard. Again, Dad's reaction spoke volumes. He was grasping for the appropriate answer to a question that had come out of left field. All he could manage to say was, "She told you?"

He appeared incredulous. Had he sworn Mom to secrecy?

"No one else knew about that conversation. No one. I'm just surprised your mother brought that up."

"Did you make Mom promise never to tell? Is that why you don't know how to answer? Don't you trust me with the information?'

He paused for a moment before answering.

"Of course I do. I was just surprised. I - it was so long ago that she and I talked about it. And with her mind slipping away -- who would have ever thought she'd recall something like that? I do trust you. It's just that it brought back a lot of memories.

"The man I have reason to suspect is named - at least, he was named, Fenn. Major Forrest Fenn. I met him in Vietnam. I was new to the country and he was on his way out after one year and 368 missions, or thereabouts. Had his jet shot out from under him twice and walked away without injury or capture. Lucky guy if I ever met one. Who knows if he's even still alive? He was a good twenty years older than I was at the time we met. I don't even know if he was alive when the hijacking happened. I have no idea if he ever went back to Nam, or where he went after he left. All I know is that he had a reputation for an ability to get out of a tight spot, and a slew of medals to prove it: Purple Heart, Silver Star, and a lot of flying medals. He loved a challenge and got himself into some scraps. But he was a legend - he always walked away. If anyone made it out of Nam, he did. He was one lucky bastard. Some name, huh? Forrest Fenn. Like the kind of name movie stars with last names like Humperdink change their real names to for their careers.

"Everyone either knew Fenn or had heard of him. You don't forget a name like that. Not ever. And when I started collecting the clippings, it was because the whole Thanksgiving Eve hijacking thing reminded me of his similar adventure.

"Fenn was a real character. Great storyteller. One situation - it was one of his favorite stories in those last days he was there - was how he'd had a pretty hairy escape when his plane was downed over Laos, just a week before he was due to go home. Right before I met him. The conditions he'd faced were much like the conditions on the night of Cooper's hijacking . . .

"Only Fenn could tell it right, but the situation he described, it sounded just like what Cooper faced. Problems with the equipment, trouble bailing from the jet, not knowing what he was flying over, cold, and rainy weather and then, the Pathet Cong searching for him right after he parachuted into the jungle. He'd had survival training and talked about how he'd really given thought to trying to walk out of the jungle, rather than wait to be rescued. Somehow, I was left with the feeling that he regretted never doing that, never testing his survival skills. From what people said about him, Fenn was always pushing himself that way - testing himself to find out what he was capable of. But he had a family he was going home to, and that, he said, was what made him take the safer route out of there."

I had a million questions, but in that moment, not a one came to mind. A thousand thoughts tumbled about in my head, but none came together to form a cogent sentence, or ask a question.

"Well!" Dad slapped the tabletop to end the tale. "You ready to get on home?"

Dad carefully put the clippings back in his wallet, stood and stretched, then waited for me to gather my things.

I had a lot of new information to digest, especially the story of Forrest Fenn, the man Dad thought could be Dan Cooper. I needed to find out more about this character. I grabbed my purse and sweater, then followed Dad to the car.

All those years of waiting to ask - waiting for him to reveal the big secret, and the discussion of the mystery man he suspected was wrapped up in less than five minutes! Dad never even acknowledged my comment about his reaction to the composite picture I'd folded to more closely resemble the description. Was it a close match to Fenn? I'd have to pursue that line of questioning another time.

Now that I knew the hijacker's hair had appeared to be marcelled, I could add that to my composite. I thought about how Dad was distracted by the bird flapping, rather than answer immediately. His response to what I'd said about Mom seemed rather strange. Uncharacteristic. Yet grief is funny, I told myself. I still was growing up, yet I had already suffered a double loss of those I loved. I was learning life was definitely *not* a "bowl of cherries," like that old song claimed. Death and disease happened to good people, and grief never left, but lingered like a specter, appearing at the times we were most vulnerable. All it took was a smell, an image, a song, a memory, to trigger a great tsunami of emotion and memories to rise up without warning, carrying with them the power to level even a full-grown man.

At least now, I consoled myself, now I had a name to investigate, and new details to research. A good pilot with exploits like Fenn's and had a number of medals to his name had to have a few write-ups in the military newspaper of record, *The Stars and Stripes*. So I had a point from which to start investigating. And maybe - just maybe, when I had a few additional details, I could get Dad to open up a little more.

Chapter 19: The Plot Thickens

The telephone rang. I glanced out the window. Dad was mowing the yard. I picked up the receiver and moved to a quieter spot. "Hello?"

"Hi. This is Michael. Michael Giordano. Remember me? From Matt's wedding?"

For a moment I was breathless, but I summoned all the dignity and sophistication I could muster. "Of course, I do, Michael. Who could forget all the baloney you were feeding me while we danced?"

"Baloney?" He laughed. "I don't do baloney - not when the truth is so much easier, and the subject of my admiration is so very unforgettable. I'm glad I finally reached you. I take it that was your father who answered before?"

"It was, Mr. Giordano. I still live at home, and I am still in high school. It's my senior year. The subject never came up when we were dancing, but I feel obliged to tell you I am still only 17. I turn 18 in May. I'm a Gemini." I cringed. Why did I just blab out my sign? He would probably laugh and think I was a silly little girl, hooked on horoscopes.

"Well, I'm a Scorpio, Stephanie."

Giordano laughed a deep, fluid laugh that complimented his amazing radio-voice, and the liquid brown eyes with thick black lashes which had latched on to mine the moment he led me out onto the dance floor and never left my face until his cheek brushed mine as he pulled me closer for a Latin number and guided my steps. He led beautifully on the dance floor. The way his body moved against mine helped me anticipate our next move, and we danced well together. I recalled thinking that, with a few lessons and more practice, we could be phenomenal dancers.

Before I could say anything, he continued. "Matt called me today. I figured he might be the one discouraging you from returning my calls. Him, or your dad. But when he warned me to stay away from you, I knew it was him, and I had to find out what you had been told."

"Nothing, really. He just said I shouldn't get involved with you. His exact words were, 'No way, no how.' Why would he say something like that? And Matt also told me you're 32 years old. That's 15 years older than I am - even though I'll be 18 in May, and you just turned 32 in what, October? November?"

"November. November 21."

"Okay. And my birthday is May 22. So the difference is 14 years, six months. It's still a huge gap. I'm sure that's a big part of why Matt feels the way he does."

"It's a huge gap, my dear, only if you are very immature, and if I'm a fuddy-duddy at my ripe old age of 32. Are you? Immature? If so, I might as well hang up - though you seemed like you had it pretty together that night."

Suddenly nervous, I stuttered, "Yes. No. I mean, yes, I'm mature. I graduate in June. Things have been rough for the whole family the past few years. But I can handle myself. And I don't think you're a fuddy-duddy. I just need you to know how young . . . "

"Good," he interrupted. "Then you'll have no problem meeting so I can explain why Matt runs hot and cold where I am concerned."

"Tell me now," I insisted. "I need to know."

"Okay. I'll tell you. I'm a building contractor. I own my own company, which is very successful, I might add. I hired his firm to do the engineering on a large project. Matt and I got into it in front of his boss one day. He was insisting that something could not be done the way I wanted it done. But I had worked with the same situation -- identical parameters -- on another project, and I knew what I proposed would work. Apparently, Matt's the Golden Boy around the firm - he was kind of full of himself - and he insisted I was wrong, and he was right. So I called my foreman - the guy who'd worked on the other job. I put Scott on the phone and did a conference call with Golden Boy and his firm's CEO, who was sitting in on our meeting.

"Scott convinced them I was right, and Matt ended up with egg on his face as a result. In front of his boss. Yeah, I was invited to the wedding - but so were a lot of other clients. I'm in and out of their office a lot lately. But I can't say Matt has regarded me warmly since that day."

"Is that all?" I asked. "No other reason? He acted like there was something else, but he wouldn't say."

"Nope. That's it. Meet me for a coffee - you do drink coffee, don't you? There's a place around the corner from my office on West Avenue G. It's called The Town Pump. They have coffee and sandwiches. Let's say, Monday after you get out of class?"

"I cheer," I mumbled. "I'm a cheerleader. I have practice until 5:00 on Mondays. I go to Temple High on 31st Street. I'll need a ride."

"Then I'll pick you up in front of the school at 5:05. I just want to show you I don't bite - I'm a nice guy."

"Monday, in front of the school then," I repeated. "Five after five. I have to go now."

"Until then, Stephanie. Have a good weekend."

"Bye, Michael."

I could've swooned right there. How could I have known what would happen later on? I was just a kid and still believed in happily-ever-afters.

Chapter 20: Secrets and Sentiments

I had dithered about what I wanted to do after graduation, in part because of my own lack of direction, and because of my involvement with Michael, an involvement I kept from Dad. Michael had become my secret love. We met as often as possible.

My terrible grades that year damaged a very acceptable grade point average. To say I was a distracted student was an understatement. It was senior year, I had friends and was popular and could finally get involved in all the activities denied me the two prior years. The additional after-school responsibilities during those years had hurt my grades a bit, too, but I'd still managed to maintain a B- average until that final year. I was having way too much fun. And I was seeing my secret love.

Unbeknownst to Dad, I'd resigned from all extra-curricular activities but cheering, and was using that free time to meet Michael after school, instead. He always dropped me off at least a block away from our street, at a different location each time, and I would walk home from there. Our meetings were discreet, public, and more friendly than romantic for many months.

Only a few friends knew Michael picked me up three afternoons a week in his glamourous, navy blue 1996 Jaguar XJ6. Its well-appointed interior with mahogany trim smelled of fine leather and Michael's intoxicating cologne.

Michael felt friendship was the basis of all successful relationships, and he said he wanted our relationship to be solid before we moved to the next stage. He was serious when he said he wanted our relationship to be successful, gazing deep into my eyes. The memory of that moment still sometimes gives me goose bumps.

My age surely was a factor in Michael's delay in moving the relationship forward. But I was now 18, my graduation was just a few months away, and I was confident things between us would continue to grow more serious after my birthday. At 18, I would be a woman in the eyes of the law. A woman in every way but one. Well, two… The drinking age in Texas was still 21, except if drinking at home in the presence of one's parents. I hoped to remedy the other, however, once I was sure Michael saw me as an adult. Our relationship wasn't entirely platonic, though. We kissed, we cuddled, and the passion grew, but Michael had tremendous self-control, even when mine wavered.

Dad still dodged and avoided the subject of Vietnam, despite my guarded queries, and he rarely answered direct questions about Forrest Fenn, often changing the subject when I pumped him for more information.

He seemed to have lost interest in the D. B. Cooper case following our afternoon at the mall. In fact, once major press inquiries about the new suspect in the FBI case died when Weber's wife could no longer find a reporter who would give her the time of day, nothing further was written. True to form, the FBI continued researching Weber's alleged "confession" in their thorough, plodding way, but they were reluctant to make any comment until they were as certain as Weber's widow her deceased spouse was, in fact, D.B. Cooper.

I couldn't really fault Dad for his lack of interest. His attention turned to his business, and as he landed several new accounts, his time for hobbies was scant.

I had started trying to learn what I could about Dad's Vietnam acquaintance, Forrest Fenn. There was something there, I just felt it. Whenever possible, I surfed the internet to discover what I could. Nothing had popped up yet on the guy. But I was undeterred.

With Michael on my mind, I spent less time on the phone chattering with the other girls about guys my age, who now seemed so immature compared to Michael. I read *Time* magazine and *The Wall Street Journal* so I would have something to talk with Michael about on our long walks by the lake or through the city's parks, or while sharing a sandwich or sipping coffee or iced tea from the thermos he always brought along. We talked about books, movies, his golf and tennis games, my cheerleading and school. And my future.

While I had toyed with the idea of studying nursing, I was still not sure what I wanted to do with my life. As we discussed my ambivalence, Michael came up with a brilliant solution. He wanted to hire me that summer after graduation. I would have a great job with the added benefit of seeing Michael more often,

Michael also encouraged me to enroll at Temple College while I considered my options and explored my interests. Temple College offered a two-year degree that would give me an opportunity to register for several different courses, improve my grades, and therefore make it easier for me to be accepted into a four-year university. The college had strong programs in business administration, nursing, and the growing field of information technology. My work at his firm would give me an introduction to business and construction, and Michael offered me an additional stipend to help with my education, which I refused until he mentioned the tuition assistance firms awarded as scholarships to their best and brightest, implying that I was in that category. Matt was the beneficiary of just such a deal.

I went home after that conversation floating on a cloud of self-esteem and good fortune. Michael was turning out to be all I ever could have dreamed of in a boyfriend.

Dad was delighted when I announced I had found a job as the assistant to the owner of a local construction company, and that my junior college education would be paid by my employer. He accepted that my hiring was an arms-length transaction and never questioned it, nor the late hours I "worked," in addition to attending classes. It was a brilliant solution, and before long, I learned a great deal about the construction business.

I was smitten, and Michael appeared to be in love with me, as well. I still didn't understand what he saw in me and pinched myself regularly to assure myself I wasn't dreaming. He was a good boss--tough but fair, and he cut me no slack. After five o'clock, however, once the office emptied, he turned into the sweet romantic guy who first enchanted me.

Life was good, but experience had taught me a harsh lesson. Everything could change in the blink of an eye.

Chapter 21: Sometimes You Can't see the Forrest for the Trees

Still living at home, and with Dad now enthusiastically absorbed in building his small business, I found myself with more free time than I knew what to do with. I saw Michael Monday through Friday, at and after work, but not on weekends. I needed that time to focus on my studies.

I was not yet twenty, and Michael had just turned thirty-five. We had still not been physically intimate, although we came close. I was still as virginal as the day I was born.

My situation was what I think they used to call "between the devil and the deep blue sea." I could not get any forward progression out of Michael, although I strongly hinted I was ready to take things to the next level. I wanted to introduce him to Dad so we could officially be recognized as boyfriend and girlfriend, and - hopefully - his fiancée, before too much longer.

Michael's attentiveness could not be mistaken for a brotherly interest. He exhibited an undefined sexual attraction, evident but not fully acted upon, despite my eager willingness. I was now on "the Pill" in eager anticipation of that day when we would slip over the line to fulfillment. Perhaps I should have wondered about the peculiarity of a grown man so in control of his emotions and libido when alone with a more than willing partner of legal age. But I didn't.

Our relationship "limbo" afforded me a perfect opportunity to develop a dossier on Forrest Fenn on weekends throughout the spring and summer, between homework assignments and term papers. I intended to enroll in more courses at Temple College that fall and anticipated losing my free hours on weekends to more studying.

For the longest time, my search for any online mention of Forrest Fenn went nowhere. Then I found him. At least,

I was pretty sure it was the man my father had spoken of so sparingly but suspected of the unsolved skyjacking.

Fenn had written two very expensive books, both limited editions, possibly self-published or printed and bound by a small publishing house, as there were no publication dates given. The books, however, boasted beautiful color plates and photographs, which boosted the prices into the stratosphere. They were art books, essentially, with fascinating text that combined the artist's biographical information with the Southwestern influences and history that had influenced their work. The volumes were offered in hardcover, and even in leather bound editions. I read the synopses and the reviews. Evidently, Fenn had owned a gallery in Santa Fe, New Mexico, and was a respected amateur archaeologist who specialized in the history and archeology of the Southwest. The Southwestern Indian tribes and the early Spanish presence in the Southwest fascinated him, and he had a vast collection of artifacts Spanish settlers and soldiers had left behind. Fenn was also quite knowledgeable about art and artists who had worked in that region. He promoted their works in his gallery.

He sold the art business - Fenn Galleries - in 1988 and, by that time, written several books about Indian artifacts and the customs of the Southwest tribes, particularly as depicted in the art of Joseph Henry Sharp, who I'd never heard of. Another artist who painted African animals, William R. Leigh, was the topic of a similar collection of art plates and sketches, with commentary and biographical information Fenn co-authored. Both books looked interesting.

Fenn sells his gallery to art dealer

By PETER EICHSTAEDT
The New Mexican Staff

Forrest Fenn, one of Santa Fe's leading art gallery owners, has sold his gallery, property and art inventory to local art gallery owner Nedra Matteucci for an undisclosed amount of money.

Fenn and Matteucci said the sale was concluded at 5:30 p.m. Tuesday, but that very little will change because of it. The name "Fenn Galleries" will remain, as will the gallery's current employees.

Fenn said the terms of the sale call for him to continue to manage the gallery as a consultant. Fenn also will continue to live in the residence above the well-known gallery at 1075 Paseo de Peralta.

"We've (he and his wife, Peggy) been thinking about selling for a long time," Fenn said Wednesday. "We've done what we wanted to do. We love the art business.

"The only difference is that I have a boss now. I have all the fun part. Nedra has all the work part."

Fenn said he opened his gallery on Thanksgiving weekend in 1972, and after 15 years, he wanted a change. He said he does not plan to leave Santa Fe, but probably would take some long, "well-earned" vacations.

"Santa Fe is our home," Fenn said. "We intend to live here. I intend to work an eight-hour day just like I always have."

Fenn said that the sale will benefit art-buyers seeking art other than the 19th and 20th century Western and regional art he specialized in.

Matteucci said that her gallery, Matteucci Fine Arts, offers contemporary modern art. The two galleries under one ownership will offer a wider selection of art, she said.

Matteucci said she and Fenn have had a working relationship and friendship that began

See Fenn on Page A-2

Nedra Matteucci and Forrest Fenn in front of the Fenn Galleries.

Figure 19 Newspaper clipping announcing the sale of
Fenn Galleries, LTD.

From the brief biographical sketch and some additional information, I was able to gather that Forrest Fenn had served in the Air Force, like Dad said, and became an art dealer shortly after leaving the service in September 1970, receiving his discharge while living in Lubbock, Texas.

Hmmmm…interesting. Particularly in view of the notorious hijacking, just over a year later - if, of course, he had indeed been the Dan Cooper of legend.

Fenn had collected arrowheads and artifacts since he was a young boy growing up in Texas. Texas! Another interesting bit of information. And Fenn was still very much alive.

My question was simple: Was Dad right about him?

With a whoosh of exhaled breath, I plunged. I wrote out a substantial check for my order with slightly trembling hands. With ready funds and few expenses to claim my paychecks, I went wild and ordered the leather-bound copy of *The Beat of the Drum and the Whoop of the Dance* that Fenn wrote and published in 1983. It was even available in a signed edition. *Why not?* I ordered the autographed copy.

With only the most rudimentary knowledge of handwriting analysis, I was aware a lot could be learned about a person from his signature. I figured I could learn more about Fenn if I could find information on how to discern character from a person's cursive hand - or at least give it a good try.

I added a leather-bound, autographed copy of *The African Animals of William R. Leigh* to the order sheet I'd printed out to accompany my check for the purchase. Fenn appeared to sign many of his books. I anticipated Fenn would write more books in the future.

Santa Fe was a well-known art colony, and Fenn's was the premier gallery. The bio mentioned even Jacquelyn Kennedy Onassis had visited once. Fenn had time on his hands and the resources that enabled him to write and excavate his pet project - the huge San Lazaro Pueblo - for artifacts. The latter also fueled his writing, as I was to find out.

An order containing two large and no doubt heavy art books would certainly get Dad's attention if delivered to the house, so I had the books delivered to the office.

How better to learn about Forrest Fenn, than in his own words? For some reason I could not express, I wanted to do my research on Forrest Fenn without involving Dad. He had enough to keep himself busy these days, anyway, and I wanted to know all I could about Fenn before I broached the subject again to my father. He had acted so peculiarly, both with me and with Mom, and I wanted to see if I could identify for myself whatever it was that made Dad suspect his old acquaintance might have successfully pulled off such an astonishing act of criminal bravado. And then become an art dealer, of all things! Retiring from the Air Force in 1970 after 20 years, Fenn had traded jets for art - an unlikely and odd exchange.

Michael was curious when the heavy box bearing my name arrived. I laughed his questions off, saying I wanted to fill the empty shelves in my office space with something other than construction manuals and engineering books to add a more personal touch. He laughed.

I unboxed the Southwest art and archeology book and the earlier publication on African animals. Michael joined me in glancing through the books, He seemed impressed by the quality. I lined them along the shelf and had Michael stop on our way back from a quick lunch at a shop that carried Native American wares. I bought an attractive woven basket and a painted clay jar. They were inexpensive but attractive and would complement the books and help fill the shelves.

I set my native clay jar beside the Joseph Sharp book on the lower shelf. I stood back and admired the way it complimented the Indian painting on the leather cover of my new art book. I positioned the colorful woven basket on the shelf above, next to the large leather-bound book of art depicting African beasts, then stepped back again to observe my handiwork. The arrangement balanced the two shelves, with the books and native items exhibited on opposite ends. The simple decoration filled me with a satisfied warmth and a sense of belonging.

From my online reading, I discovered Forrest Fenn had a wide range of interests. A more than competent pilot, he had evidently flown just about every plane the Air Force had during the years he was in the service. But art became his forte and his path to a comfortable retirement.

I couldn't wait to begin looking through the books whenever I had a few minutes to do so, and I kept searching online whenever possible. *Forrest B. Fenn,* I thought, *I am going to keep digging, and I intend to get to know you very, very well.*

That evening, Michael and I got a bite to eat at his favorite restaurant, and I had him drop me off at the bus stop close to my house much earlier than he would have liked. Now that I had the name and address of the gallery

Fenn had owned, I also had a direction for my search for information on Fenn. I was anxious to start surfing online to see what else I could turn up, and so claimed a headache and asked Michael to take me home early.

Once in my bedroom, I changed into my nightclothes then booted up my computer, a Christmas present from Dad, now several months old. The computer desk crowded the small room, but I'd occupied this space for far too long to make a change now.

Drumming my fingers on the desk as the screen crawled through its start-up sequence, something suddenly clicked in my mind, triggering a memory. I pushed back my chair, then headed for my dad's office.

The three thick scrapbooks still waited on the shelves, gathering dust. Something I'd read persistently nagged at me to reexamine the trove of articles and find the photo of the letter I suddenly needed to look at once again.

I removed them from the shelf then carried them to my room, one by one, grimacing and trying not to breathe in the dust. The scrapbooks hadn't been opened in years, and the office hadn't been dusted since before Mom . . . went away. I quickly wiped the covers with a t-shirt from my bathroom laundry hamper and blew the dust from the edges of the scrapbook pages.

Then I settled on the bed to find the news clippings that described the letters purportedly sent by Cooper after the hijacking.

In the weeks following the stunning act of sky piracy, three letters were received by city newspapers in several locations, allegedly composed and sent by the perpetrator, but postmarked from different cities in Canada and California. Those newspapers printed the first few letters alongside articles describing where they had originated and the contents. There may have been more, but Dad and I could only find three. The letters were composed in different styles, with some of the envelopes displaying the newspaper address printed in block lettering - all caps - and some in angular letters, also all capitalized. I recalled that one of the letters was completely hand-printed in blocky capitals, although the others used the magazine cut-and-paste style often adopted by kidnappers to make their demands. The messages were brief and cryptic, made little sense, and only complicated the search.

Now, where are they? Aha! Found them.

The first letter was received on November 29, 1971, just five days after the air heist. The letter was postmarked in Oakdale, California just two days earlier, and was sent to the *Reno Evening Gazette* in Nevada. As you know, the 727 had landed to refuel in Reno after Cooper jumped from the tail into the raging storm, and onto mountainous, thickly forested terrain.

FBI records described that first letter as a cut-and-paste message along the lines of a typical ransom note. The letters used by the sender were cut from the evening edition of the Friday, November 26 *Sacramento Bee* newspaper. The message sent to the Reno paper was comprised of just three lines and a "signature" of cut-out letters.

"Attention! Thanks for the hospitality. Was in a rut. D.B. Cooper"

Figure 20 The Reno Gazette article describing the hijacker's letter.

Oakdale was a small town just northeast of Modesto, California. *The Reno Gazette* had published a photo of the letter and its envelope, but the writing on that particular envelope was sharply angular, with the first letter of each word trailing far below the general line the printed words in the address had followed, and a peculiarly small "o" on the end Reno was followed by a period rather than a comma. The postal abbreviation of Nevada contained a strange, floating letter E rising above and between the capital letters, N and V.

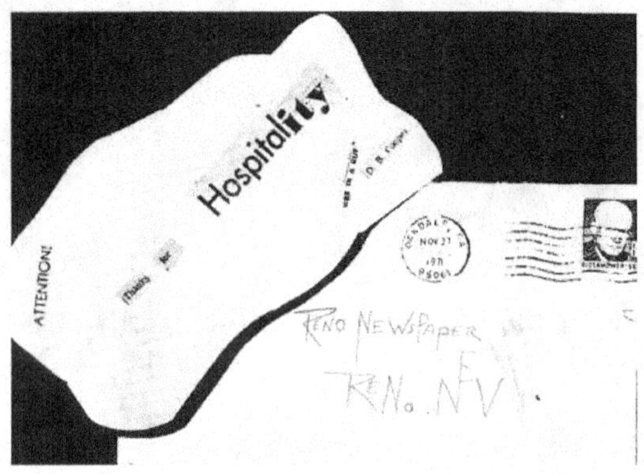

Figure 21 Detail on the envelope.

How very odd! Had the letter E been floated like that as a belated insertion to correct the postal code, or as an affectation to somehow mock and mislead authorities?

The second letter, sent to the *Vancouver Province* newspaper between the 30th of November and the 2nd of December was mailed from that same city, Vancouver, British Columbia. It was printed in pencil and was in all capital letters, but they were not what I would call "blocky" and bore no resemblance to the printing on the first envelope. What made it unusual was the sender's message was that it verified my own thinking. The sender stated the published FBI composite of D.B. Cooper was *not* accurate and "did not represent the truth," according to the letter's signatory: D.B. Cooper.

Figure 22 The hijacker's letter sent to The Vancouver Province newspaper.

I'd had been right. No wonder the FBI had never caught Cooper! If the police composite was totally wrong, it was only natural no legitimate suspect was ever located, and none of the potential suspects who were referred to the FBI or picked up for questioning had panned out!

The hand-printed letter said further: "I enjoyed the Grey Cup game. Am leaving Vancouver. Thanks for your hospitality." The "signature," of course, was "D.B. Cooper," printed in all caps. The accompanying news clip from the Vancouver paper explained that the Grey Cup was the championship game played by Canada's top professional football teams on November 28 of that year, in Vancouver, British Columbia.

The third post-hijacking letter published was a second mailing to the *Reno Gazette*, postmarked December 1, but sent from the area around Sacramento, California. The letter itself was never published - at the FBI's request - although the *Gazette* did mention the existence of the letter in a contemporaneous article they *did* publish, describing it as being pasted together from cut-out letters, with this message: "Plan ahead for retirement income. DB Cooper"

Aha! My memory proved excellent!

I applauded myself. I had recollected that important phrase, and it made even more sense now with my new information about Forrest Fenn's post-Air Force career. This was the information I'd been looking for!

Was the act of air piracy simply a means to fund an otherwise unfunded or underfunded retirement?

I had never thought about the heist from that angle before, even when I had mused about what it might cost to establish an art gallery handling the caliber of art Fenn's gallery did.

Internationally acclaimed artist's works graced its walls, most of it very costly. Even in 1970, the expense of setting up a gallery in a city the size of New Mexico's state capital, Santa Fe - was more than a retired Air Force officer with a wife and two young daughters could have accumulated in savings. I figured Fenn could have saved, say, maybe $20,000? Dad had retired as an Army Aviation Major, and for three tours of duty he had been attached to the 1st Cavalry unit in Vietnam, working with aviation computer equipment used in logistic and battlefield support - primarily to support transport and helicopter operations. Most likely, he had met Fenn while assigned there. But as a Major, retiring quite a few years later than Fenn, he still didn't pull in much more than a Major retiring as a pilot in 1970, even with consideration of his pay raise awarded for valor in combat.

From what I understood of galleries, not all artists can afford to wait for a painting to sell through consignment. Many made their livings, at least early in their careers, by reselling paintings sold to the gallery, usually on the basis of size, priced per square inch. Gallery owners essentially "pick horses," often gambling on the potential of a particular artist, encouraging certain artists' personal and artistic development, and assisting in cultivating a following within a geographic area or a specific clientele.

Was it possible, I mused, that an adventurous and fearless man with aviation and parachuting experience, possessing no criminal record, but with a penchant for antiquities and a few years of rich exposure to the art and cultural wealth of the European and Asian continents could have dreamed up a risky scheme to fund a new business - say, a gallery - with ill-gotten gains acquired in an audacious manner?

Lying on the bed, waiting for the computer to boot up, my mind whirled with "what- ifs." What if the ransom money was laundered, then used to purchase notable paintings in Europe from a dealer who was unaware the cash was stolen?

What better way to launder traceable money than in a foreign country that accepted dollars for cash transactions? Because of the international appeal of United States currency, and the pervasive American military and tourist presence, monetary exchanges frequently utilized dollars. There was a chance purloined U.S. currency, exchanged for paintings in a foreign land, or even overseas, might never make it back to the States, and could continue to circulate in foreign exchanges. Twenty-dollar bills are common and if, in the years long after the fact, a few isolated bills made their way back into this country, who'd be looking for the serial numbers by then?

The hijacker had not specified a currency. If the airline and the FBI had really thought it through, they could have furnished the extorted cash in $50 or $100 dollar bills, which are far less common and therefore scrutinized far more frequently and more thoroughly than twenties. It would have been much more difficult to exchange those larger denominations in another country. And that was where the hijacker was headed - another country. Remember, Cooper demanded to be taken Mexico, which accepts dollars along the border and in major tourist destinations throughout the country, and where money changers have few scruples.

As for the three packets of twenties found by Brian Ingram along the Columbia River in 1980, it had occurred to me years earlier that a really smart hijacker would have intentionally dropped a small amount of the ransom money over a different spot than where he actually intended to jump, in order to mislead investigators and keep them off his trail.

D.B. Cooper didn't seem stupid. I pondered that with my eyes closed, and by the time my computer was up and running, I wasn't. I'd made myself much too comfortable while continuing the line of speculation Cooper's letter had prompted. After less than a few minutes' contemplation, I fell asleep.

Chapter 22: True Love?

It happened. It finally happened!!

Shortly after my 20th birthday, Dad had to spend several days in Austin on business. The house was empty, except for me.

That Monday, I invited Michael in for a drink before he went home. Although our liquor cabinet was sad, a bottle of bourbon, a bottle of vodka, two bottles of red wine and just enough Scotch to make one hefty drink remained on the shelves. Michael opted for the double Scotch. I made a mental note to buy more.

We sat on the sofa and kissed and cuddled. It slowly progressed into some heavy petting before Michael, breathless, stood, arranged his clothing, kissed me goodbye, and left. So close…

Tuesday brought a repeat, except a new bottle of excellent Scotch whiskey was stocked in the liquor cabinet. Michael had two drinks. It was now or never. I took matters into my own hands. And the magic happened.

Touchdown! Score!

It was a home run, all four bases, and we ended up in my bed, at last. Michael stayed the night, then made an early morning escape to go home to shave and change clothes. He returned to pick me up at 8:45. We were only a few minutes late for work, but our faces must have given our secret away to the inquisitive staff.

Michael stayed over every night that week. The whispers grew stronger as the week progressed and reached fever pitch by that Friday. That morning, my good friend Evelyn, head of the secretarial pool, came into the office and shut the door behind her.

"Is it true?"

I asked, "Is what true?"

"What everyone is saying."

"And what is that?"

"That you and Michael are sleeping together. Don't think people haven't noticed what's going on between you two! So, 'fess up and tell me. Spill it," A mischievous half grin boasted a dimple in her right cheek.

I didn't have to answer. The flush creeping from my chin to my forehead gave her the answer she desired.

Evelyn threw her arms around me, "You did it! You did! Well, congratulations. Are you two going to make it official now?"

"What do you mean?"

"Oh, I don't know - maybe stop pretending nothing is going on?"

At lunch with Michael, I mentioned Evelyn's impromptu visit earlier in the day.

"Well, maybe she's right," Michael responded. "Maybe it is time we acknowledged the relationship officially and put an end to the whispers around the water cooler. We have, after all, been working up to this for a while now." He grew serious. "You're my right hand, Stephanie. You know that. I'm not blind. Or deaf. There's been a lot of talk, and I think it's time to put an end to it. Put an end to all this silliness."

"How do you mean?" I held my breath. Where was this going?

"You're twenty now, and our relationship is no longer the scandal it would have been if a 32-year-old man had seduced a 17-year-old."

I blushed again as I reminded him, "But that's precisely what you did."

"And don't think I didn't know it, silly girl. But I think it's time."

"Time for what, Michael?"

"Time to announce our engagement and let the staff know we're seriously involved, not just fooling around. And we'll let your Dad in on our deep, dark secret as well."

Stunned does not even begin to describe my reaction. I'd wanted to hear him say these words for so very long, but Michael's declaration came without prelude or warning. I didn't know how to react, so I simply sat there for a moment, stunned, with a blank stare on my face.

"That's not quite the response I expected," Michael said. His tone conveyed alarm and a nervous edge. "This *is* what you wanted, isn't it, Stephanie? For us to marry? Or was I reading your hints all wrong?"

I leaned across the café table to kiss him then, nearly knocking over my iced tea, which he fortunately caught before it spilled, and planted a huge kiss on his waiting lips. It was a light workday, so Michael excused himself to pay the bill and call the office to say we would be in before the end of the day. We spent the rest of the afternoon shopping for a diamond.

When Michael called the office out of my earshot to inform them we'd be late, he also broke the news to Evelyn and asked her to dip into petty cash to buy a cake and a few bottles of Korbel for a brief celebration at the end of the workday.

We found the perfect ring at the third jewelry store we visited, located in the lobby of the poshest hotel in Temple. The stunning emerald cut, two-carat yellow diamond, flanked by two white diamonds in a trillion cut was simply gorgeous and it fit as though made for me. Michael slipped it on my finger before we left the store.

As we pulled into the office parking lot, a glance up at the office windows revealed several faces staring down at us as Michael parked the car. I poked him and pointed. "Look at them! See how they've been snooping on us all this time? And we never once looked up to catch them in the act!"

Michael just chuckled.

My eyes widened in awe and delight as I walked in the door. A mass of red and white helium balloons hovered on both sides of a table displaying a large similarly decorated sheet cake that read, "Congratulations!" I felt like one of those balloons in that moment, but instead of helium, I was filled with happiness.

I wanted to surprise Dad, who was due home the following evening after five. Michael and I were waiting for him in the living room when he unlocked the front door. And boy, was he surprised! Dad dropped a plastic bag of groceries and stood there, speechless, as an apple escaped the bag and rolled across the floor.

Michael took the lead, explaining how we had met at the wedding, saw each other on the sly until he hired me, and waited until I was old enough before he made his move to claim me for himself. Dad listened silently, nodding, looking from Michael to me as Michael poured his heart out, insisting we had no intention of deceiving him, but simply held back out of respect for Dad and his many struggles over the years. As Michael spoke so earnestly, I watched this strange smile creep across Dad's face until he was grinning from ear to ear. The moment Michael asked for his approval, Dad turned to him and said, Maybe I'll get a grandchild yet who's a little closer than Austin."

Dad hugged me tight, then slapped his future son-in-law on the back as he wished us both well.

Chapter 23: News Travels Fast

News travels fast.

After wishing and hoping and waiting for the day Michael would make a move to bed me for the first time in my life, it had finally happened and now I was publicly engaged to marry him! It seemed too fast; we moved too rapidly. Was I ready? Was this really what I wanted?

If marriage was forever, as my parents and my religion taught me, was this really the "forever" I wanted?

Matt's congratulations when I called to tell Sue had been less than hearty, most likely the result of my ignoring his warning about getting involved with Michael.

I had seen nothing in Michael's behavior toward me that was less than respectful, appreciative, and loving. He hadn't hesitated to make me his assistant, even in the face of office jealousies, and his advice and guidance had matured me into a true professional, despite what some considered my insufficient education - which would be remedied once I got my associate degree from Temple College in a year, and then pursue a four-year degree in business at Texas University. Better yet, I had learned the ins and outs of the construction business and had every right to hold my head high. I'd earned the respect of an office full of men, who followed my instructions without question--quite an achievement.

But Matt's warning still bothered me, so I asked him, "Why did you tell me not to get involved with Michael Giordano - 'no way, no how'? Just what were you warning me against, Matt?"

"I can't recall now, Stephanie. It was . . . it was probably something personal. It's been a while since I've had any dealings with him or his firm. I didn't even know you were working with him."

I found that amusing and couldn't resist confessing I had answered his call for Michael on two occasions, but never let on who I was. He was surprised to hear that.

"So there is no dire warning this time?" I asked.

"If you're happy, then I'm happy. I know Sue is over the moon about the wedding. You had better watch out, though - she'll take over the whole show."

Marriage was a big step, and cold feet in the face of a lifelong commitment was expected. I had my parents as an example of love and loyalty. Although their situation was a sad one, I reminded myself no one knows what life will bring, And, anyway, "tis better to have loved, and lost, than never to have loved at all."

On the heels of what seemed like endless wedding showers and celebratory luncheons and dinners, and a whirlwind of shopping and planning and shopping some more, our wedding went off without a hitch, and we honeymooned in Hawaii for two glorious weeks.

The news traveled just as fast when the marriage ended, one miscarriage and two infidelities later.

Chapter 24: All Good Things Must Come to an End

Michael continued his weekend activities after we wed - whatever they might be - without stop. He ran errands, he bowled with his old team, went to sports events, and played pool with the same group of guys as he had for years. Never church-goers, I slept in while Michael golfed on Sundays with a few beers afterward with the guys at the 19th Hole Grill. While I pushed myself in school those first years, my husband's weekend absences were almost a blessing. He continued to be my best friend, always was supportive of my ambitions, and tender and considerate whenever we did finally get around to making love.

I, in turn, was focused, ambitious, and determined to make him proud of me. After graduation from Temple College with an Associate's in business, I'd applied to Texas University at Austin, and was accepted. Fridays were our "date nights," complete with once-a-week sex. But whenever I asked Michael to accompany me somewhere on the weekend, or just take a break from his routine absences, he would get bristly.

"Look, babe, I was a bachelor for a long time before I fell for you. You see me all day, every day, five days a week. We sleep together every night. Weekends are my 'guy time.' Besides, with your course load, you certainly don't need me in your hair and underfoot."

I could never hold my tongue and usually responded along the lines of, "Well, does that mean you'll include me on weekends with the 'fellows' once I graduate?" –to which Michael would throw up his hands, roll his eyes, and walk out of the room.

That ended the discussion, every time.

As graduation from UT approached, we started trying for a baby. At least, I did. After four years of marriage, I was ready to be a mother. But try as we might, it wasn't happening. We followed up with a physician, who ordered tests. Results revealed Michael had a low sperm count. There were natural things we could try to improve our chances, but we had to face the cold fact I might never be able to get pregnant naturally. Our fertility specialist informed us there were more involved measures available to achieve conception . . . for a price.

However, as Michael and I left the doctor's office, we agreed it was not yet time to take those extreme measures. Months passed before the miracle happened. I was pregnant!

Things seemed to be going well. I was used to being alone much of the weekend. Michael now carried a cellular phone with him everywhere and was available the moment I called. I kept busy. I painted in watercolor, did needlepoint, and read what seemed like a hundred books on motherhood, having a successful pregnancy, and childrearing. I went to lunch and shopped with friends. Weekends found Michael on the golf course, in the bowling alley, the billiards hall, playing handball, or shooting the breeze with his buddies at the 19th Hole after a game of golf. No further away than a phone call.

When the pains started, I was at lunch with friends on a sunny winter afternoon. We had just been seated for a late lunch, with shopping bags piled at our feet. My girlfriends and I were laughing and chattering when a sharp pain cramped my swelling belly. I placed my hand on my just barely showing "baby bump," and winced.

Allison, my friend sitting beside me, noticed the flinch and grasped my hand. "You okay?" she asked in a concerned whisper. The pain only lasted a few moments. I nodded before blowing out a long, calming breath.

We ordered our food, but I had no appetite, and secretly worried about the brief sharp pain I'd experienced. I had an appointment with my obstetrician Monday afternoon. If the pain recurred, I would mention it then. I'd read a side effect of pregnancy was increased gas, so I dismissed the pain as a result of an empty stomach and too much bean dip the night before.

My friends drove me home after we dawdled late into the afternoon. When we pulled into my driveway, I noticed the front tire on the passenger side of my SUV looked low. I made a mental note to have Michael check it the next morning before his golf game. He and some friends had cooked up an impromptu fishing trip to Belmont Lake with the guys, so I didn't expect him back until around 8:00 or 9:00 p.m., at the earliest. He'd promised to call if they decided to camp overnight.

Waving goodbye to my friends, I unlocked the door and walked in, then pushed the door shut behind me with my behind. As I did, an excruciating pain ripped through my belly, followed immediately with a rush of warmth between my thighs. I dropped my packages onto the floor and gripped my stomach. The pain was so bad --I could scarcely breathe.

Michael. I need Michael! My purse had fallen nearby. I sank to the floor, then fumbled through it for my phone. With trembling hands, I pushed the number which autodialed his phone.

It rang and rang. I hung up and called again. No answer. I hung up and called again, hoping by this third call he would realize it was urgent and answer. Tears streamed down my face as the phone rang to voicemail. I left several gasping, tearful messages as waves of agonizing pain slashed through my stomach.

My head swam. I put my hand on the tile floor to steady myself. The floor was wet and at that moment, the unmistakable metallic smell of blood bathed me in a bitter, agonizing dread. My baby was dying, and maybe I was too. So much blood…

I fought the encroaching darkness but lost the battle to remain conscious.

When I came into a fuzzy awareness of another presence, my eyes opened slowly. The man bending over me smelled of liquor and a strong after-shave I did not recognize. It was dark. When the hall light glared on, I was temporarily blinded by its brightness. I heard a slurred, "Oh, my God!" I blacked out again.

Matt and Sue were at my bedside when the bright daylight pouring into the flower-filled hospital room woke me.

Michael, was there, too, slumped in a chair in a corner, looking shamefaced and exhausted. I learned, through the fog I had to swim through to arrive at full awareness, that they had been there all night. Michael had finally come home very late. His friend had dropped him off because Michael was too drunk to drive. His vehicle had been left wherever he had been. When he found me out cold on the entry tile in a pool of blood and shortly afterward discovered the flat tire on my vehicle, he'd panicked and called Matt and Sue, who left their pajama-clad little ones with Matt's parents and raced to Temple. At some point an ambulance had been called, and Michael rode with me to the hospital, leaving just before Sue and Matt arrived at our residence.

I was in pain and felt so… empty. The realization hit me like a cannon ball to the gut-- I was no longer pregnant. An almost tangible tension overshadowed the bright hospital room. Matt glared at Michael, who, had he been able to crawl into the woodwork, would have done just that. Their concern was obvious, but I didn't understand the fierce tension between the three of them.

I remembered calling Michael over and over as our baby was dying inside me. Was my husband the man I vaguely recalled, whose strange scent and alcohol breath had worsened my nausea? Where had he been all that time? And why hadn't he answered when I called?

When Matt and Sue went to the hospital cafeteria for breakfast and coffee, Michael sighed, then came to sit beside me.

My husband cleared his throat. Somehow, I knew he was preparing for a confession.

Tears ran down his face as his words spilled out in a rapid, almost unintelligible babbling. His fingertips stroked my brow, but after his first touch, I turned my head away. I squeezed my eyes shut in an effort to prevent the tears from escaping as he rattled on. He liked women. He liked men. He was confused. He was sorry. He loved me, really. But Kent had shown up one afternoon this past week at the office while I was at a dental appointment. . .

I whipped my head around. "Kent? Who is Kent?"

They had history. They had been roommates at Texas A&M where they were studying engineering. Then one night, after a frat party where they drank far too much, they became lovers, and maintained the relationship long after they sobered up. After starting the firm where I now worked, they'd had a falling out, and Kent left the business, and the relationship.

It was an irreconcilable separation, Michael persisted – as if I really wanted or needed to hear this. They hadn't seen each other in more than eight years when Michael met me at Matt and Sue's wedding. He thought he was over all that . . . it was a youthful indiscretion, a friendship that had escaped its boundaries . . . and whatever it was that had prompted their attraction, that physicality - that was not him.

He was happy with me - so happy. He loved me desperately. But when Kent showed up at the office, unannounced, last Thursday at lunchtime when I was in Austin for classes, it all came rushing back - the memories - the friendship - the good times - their struggle to get the company up and running - their first successes - and Michael could not turn Kent away. Behind a closed office door, he explained to Kent he was happily married. Michael further alleged he told Kent he would soon be a father. He had a family, a great business, everything he could ever ask for. There was nothing between them any longer. Kent's visit was pointless.

Michael's words washed over me, taking a minute to register as they flooded my spirit, battering it against the hard rocks of truth from which his copious protests could not shield me. Numb, I found myself shaking my head, denying his confession. I struggled to process the meaning behind his pained and painful words, convinced this was not real, but a cruel dream. Surely, I was living a nightmare. It *had* to be a nightmare.

The scene was surreal. Relentless sunshine poured into the room, floor to ceiling, through the tall window. My sobbing wreck of a husband, leaning over me with tears streaming down his cheeks, the silent fury of my still-absent sister and Matt, the horror of my now-empty belly, and the cobwebs of anesthesia still impeded my comprehension. And now this, whatever it was that Michael was trying to tell me.

There had never been a fishing trip. It was a fiction. A lie. Michael and Kent had agreed that Thursday afternoon after lunch together, to meet again on Saturday for a round of pool at the billiards hall, then drinks and an early dinner at the hotel where Kent was staying.

Michael insisted he had no intention of carrying the "date" further than an afternoon playing pool, a quick dinner and a few drinks for old times' sake.

Michael thought he could handle it. But they had talked too long, gotten too drunk, and had to stagger upstairs so Michael could sleep it off somewhat before attempting to drive home.

Kent had taken advantage of his drunkenness, Michael insisted, acting the innocent. He was scarcely aware of his surroundings, he claimed, and passed out as soon as they got to the room. When his phone woke him, after ringing many, many times, Michael said he was shocked to realize they were in bed together, both naked, and it appeared - it felt . . . he knew some kind of intimacy had occurred, but he had never wanted that - I had to believe him! He was still drunk when he woke. And Kent wasn't exactly sober, either. Accusations flew, they almost let fists fly, but he could barely stand. Kent insisted on driving him back to our house, despite being as intoxicated as he was. Somehow, they made to the house without incident.

Michael lost it when he walked in the door and found me in a pool of blood. He ran back outside and waved Kent down, screaming. Kent called the ambulance. They loaded me into the ambulance and Michael, distraught and terrified, rode along. Kent got into his car to leave but passed out and never made it out of the driveway. That's where Matt and Sue found him when they arrived, no more than ten minutes after the ambulance left for the hospital.

Wakened by Matt shaking his shoulder, Kent mumbled something about being with Michael and driving him home, then bragged he was the one who had enough presence of mind to call an ambulance. That's when it all clicked for Matt, whose firm had been working with Michael and Kent since the partners had started their business. He'd apparently been aware of their previous relationship in the firm's early days.

But I *had* to believe whatever happened between them was not my husband's fault. Michael professed he was in love with me, and we would make another baby, and it would be all right again. He *promised*.

My perfect world was turned upside down, and the emotional and physical pain prevented me from thinking logically. My belly cramped and I crossed my arms across my stomach and gripped my sides, then began rocking to ease the pain. My thoughts maintained that same rhythm as I rocked and silently affirmed: *Matt knew, Matt knew. Matt knew*, and he still let me marry Michael. Matt knew, but he betrayed me, Matt knew, but he kept silent when he should have spoken. I kept repeating the words to myself silently, rhythmically, as I listened to Michael's pathetic recitation drone on. How he'd resisted. How confusing this all was. Why had this happened when he was trying so hard to love me and be a good husband?

I couldn't watch his performance any longer. All I wanted to do was shut out the pathetic noise. Michael now had a red nose and the hiccups but was still going on and on. I turned my head away, closed my eyes, and pulled the covers around my ears.

Eventually, Michael fell silent. I heard the shuffle of his clothing as he stood, then retreated to his chair in the corner.

Why didn't Matt warn me more strongly? Why didn't he tell me about Michael's interest in men?

"It was second-hand information," Matt later protested when we had a moment alone. "At first, I figured you'd find out for yourself in due time, if that was truly Michael's sexual orientation. And Kent had been gone from Temple for so long, I thought it really might have been a college thing. Call it ultra-male-bonding, youthful indiscretion, sowing wild oats - whatever you want. I'm sure it happens more often than people will admit, and between girls, too. At that age, everyone's a little confused.

"And I did call him, as I'd originally promised after we first talked, Stephanie. Warned him away, in no uncertain terms. But he absolutely insisted he was heterosexual - that men were never his primary orientation - although he never denied a close relationship with Kent. He said he was enthralled with you, really wanted to get to know you on a serious level. He wanted to settle down in a traditional marriage. So, cut me a little slack. You guys kept your relationship a deep, dark secret for so long that by the time we found out, you were already engaged. You seemed happy. Michael had caused no waves in the community and had a great business reputation. How could I know Kent would show up again and start things up with Michael? And how was I supposed to know how Michael would respond?"

Sue and Matt left as soon as the doctor cleared me for release the following day. They offered me a place to stay should I need it, and Sue's long embrace before they left made me feel like I still had *someone* who cared about me.

Once we were alone again, Michael reverted to the pathetic, overly apologetic fool he'd been when he confessed his infidelity. He swore he'd get counseling. He'd go to AA. He'd do *anything*. It had been a moment of weakness - he was drunk, confused. Kent had seduced him when he was not fully conscious of what was happening. He wasn't even sure anything *had* occurred between them, but if it had, Kent was the aggressor. Michael had been too drunk to fend him off. They had history, he repeated, as if that alone were grounds for my understanding and absolution.

The whole thing just made me tired. The only truth I believed was that Michael was very, very confused.

Once released from the hospital, I went to Sue and Matt's for a few weeks to cool down and focus on my physical recovery. Did we all talk about Michael? Of course, we did, at great length. I told them what Dad said when we were engaged, and we all had a good laugh. Ironic, indeed, we all agreed. If we'd only known at the time . . .

Whatever my ultimate decision, the consensus was to keep Dad in the dark. There was no need for him to know. At least, not immediately. He'd been a wreck when he learned I'd lost the pregnancy and was hospitalized, and when I told him the child I'd been carrying was a little boy, he was visibly crushed. I think Dad hoped of having a grandchild in Temple, where he could teach him to ride a bike, play ball, see games together. I knew how badly he missed Buster.

Now that he'd lost both a son and a grandson, he did need the extra strain of knowing of Michael's indiscretion. Dad was keeping busy, his business was going well, and there was no reason to have him worrying about another situation over which he had no control.

Michael called every day. He was seeing the best psychiatrist in Temple. If I wanted to go with him to marital counseling, he would be more than willing to go for as long as it took to "set things right" between us. Kent was back in Austin. He would not return. "Please come back," Michael begged, tearfully. "I can't live without you. And everything at the office is falling apart without you. You mean everything to me. I would crawl across broken glass, walk over burning coals for your forgiveness. Please come home."

I thought long and hard about the situation, Society was coming out of the Dark Ages. It was a modern era where sexual mores had changed, psychological understanding had advanced. I spoke to Michael's therapist who convinced me that Michael was not gay, and that under certain conditions, unaccountable attractions and bisexual tendencies could develop between two human beings of the same sex, encouraged by shared interests and goals, and based in deep friendship. But he was convinced Michael's primary orientation was heterosexual.

After so many years together, I didn't doubt my love for Michael. Because of him, I had marketable skills, business experience, a percentage of ownership in the construction firm, and a four-year business degree from a fine university. Michael was an attentive and devoted husband. All marriages had problems of one kind or another; rising above those difficulties with understanding and compromise were essential for long relationships.

Persuaded, I gave Michael another chance. It lasted two years.

Kent resurfaced. They met secretly for nearly a year, but once their secret liaisons were discovered, I pushed Michael to make a decision. Him or me.

He chose Kent. I accepted Michael's decision as gracefully as I could. Kent bought out my shares in the firm and the two of them became business partners, once again, as well as lovers. I was grateful I'd never given in to Michael's repeated entreaties to try for another child.

The divorce was as amicable as we could manage. Michael wanted to keep the house and bought out my half. Dad only knew that we had grown apart, had different interests and ambitions now, and were no longer in love. My divorce would be finalized by the end of January 2004.

I worried about Dad. He wasn't looking as robust these days, and when we all gathered at Matt and Sue's for

Christmas, we all remarked on the weight he'd lost. Dad brushed it off as getting older and working too hard. After some persuading, we were able to convince him to make an appointment with his doctor after the New Year.

Chapter 25: When Happily Ever After Is No More

I rang in 2004 with high hopes. Matt and Sue announced on New Year's Eve they were expecting their third child. We toasted with champagne and looked forward to the year that lay ahead.

Dad sold the family home after Michael and I married. He'd bought a small two-bedroom condominium closer to his work, and I had nowhere to go once I returned from Matt and Sue's. I started looking for a condominium apartment of my own in Temple.

I found a good job with a real estate development company and was hired as Vice President of their construction division, an achievement both Michael and Kent had applauded when they heard about it. There was no room for bitterness in our parting, and they even took me to lunch to celebrate my new position.

Let bygones be bygones, I decided. I had seen too many people live with seething resentment, nurturing an anger that ate them alive. They nursed their misery until it consumed them, rather than learning from a bitter experience and putting it behind them. On the whole, I had to admit that my relationship with and marriage to Michael was exactly what I needed to climb the corporate ladder, and I had to acknowledge we'd shared some very good years. I owed him a lot. And now, I had to let him go and focus on building a new life of my own.

So I sincerely wished both men good luck and great happiness, and they wished the same for me. We hugged and parted ways. Live and let live. Then I went home and mourned, eating nearly a quart of ice cream, and drinking an entire bottle of wine. Then I slept for two days.

Once I awoke, I was over it. I could carry on with my head held high. I was determined to experience the best of every situation and learn from my errors and heartbreaks. I could spout appropriate homilies to make myself feel better 'til the cows came home, but there was no substitute for moving on and refusing to look back. So that's what I did.

Dad followed up with his doctor, who ran him through a series of tests, then wanted still more. He managed to regain a little weight, and his cheeks filled out some. He took a fly-fishing vacation in the Northwest and returned looking the picture of health. His doctor, however, was still working up a diagnosis. Dad was feeling great, but there was something in his bloodwork that concerned his physician, so more tests were ordered. But Dad didn't not seem worried.

I loved my new job and my new condo, but with time on my hands, I once again turned my attention to Forrest Fenn and the D.B. Cooper mystery to while away my hours alone. Fenn had been a prolific writer during the years I'd been married. After selling Fenn Gallery in 1988 he devoted himself to his archeological fieldwork in the San Lazaro pueblo. He'd authored nine books by this time.

According to the FBI website, the Cooper case was still open. Duane Weber had been ruled out entirely as a suspect when his fingerprints, tested in 1998, did not match any of the prints picked up by the FBI from the plane D.B. Cooper pirated 17 years earlier. His persistent widow, Jo Weber, who had been a thorn in the side of the FBI for years, must have been crushed. A few other suspects turned up since I last checked the Cooper files as well, and I perused the list of new names, faces and stories whenever I had a few minutes to spend online.

Kenneth Christiansen was an individual the FBI had briefly considered after his brother, Lyle Christiansen, watched a televised documentary about the unsolved Cooper hijacking and became obsessed with the idea his deceased brother, Kenneth, was the daring air bandit. Christiansen had, like so many young men, enlisted in the Army in 1944 and trained as a paratrooper, although he never served in combat since WWII came to an end in 1945. Following the war's end, he joined the American occupation forces stationed in Japan and continued to make occasional training jumps with other paratroopers.

After leaving the service in 1954, Kenneth Christiansen became an airline mechanic with Northwest Orient and initially worked in the South Pacific. He progressed in his career with the airline to become a flight attendant and later a purser. At the time of the hijacking, Kenneth was a purser based with Northwest Orient in Seattle. Kenneth smoked heavily, as did the hijacker. He also preferred bourbon, like the hijacker, and was also left-handed, like the hijacker was assumed to be, given that his tie clip had been positioned on the left side of the clip-on tie he left behind when he jumped from the 727. Florence Schaffner, the flight attendant who had first been seated next to Cooper, told a reporter after she had seen Kenneth Christianson's photograph, he was the suspect who resembled the hijacker the most.

A picture of Kenny Christiansen from 1970, the year before the hijacking, compared to the Seattle FBI's picture of the tie that was recovered after the hijacked jet landed in Reno, NV.

When the 727 was commandeered, Kenneth Christiansen was 45 years of age, which matched the age description given by eyewitnesses. But the similarities end there. Christiansen was only 5'8" and a good 20 pounds lighter than Cooper, weighing only 150 pounds, with a lighter complexion than eyewitnesses reported. According to his brother's report, Kenneth had bought a house outright, with cash, only a few months after the hijacking, and when he lay dying of cancer in 1994, Kenneth told his brother, "There is something you should know, but I cannot tell you." When Lyle failed to press him on the matter, Kenneth died with his secret, whatever it was.

According to Lyle, Kenneth's survivors found a valuable stamp collection and some gold coins among Kenneth's effects, along with a folder containing newspaper clippings concerning Northwest Orient his brother had collected from the time he was first hired in the 1950s to dates ending just before the famous hijacking. While Kenneth continued working with Northwest on a part-time basis for many years following the hijacking event, he ceased clipping articles about the airline, for some reason. The family also learned of bank deposits in Kenneth's name that totaled more than $200,000. Despite Lyle's attempts to link his brother to the hijacking, the FBI staunchly denied Kenneth Christiansen's connection to D.B. Cooper. They pointed out the many physical discrepancies and the entirely circumstantial nature of the facts presented to support Lyle's contention, and pointed out Kenneth wouldn't have had the level of expertise to jump from a moving plane under the prevailing circumstances on that stormy night. There was just nothing to incriminate him.

I chuckled as I read the FBI file. I found it amusing the spouses and relatives of potential suspects refused to accept the FBI's measured opinion. Instead, they pursued book, movie, and television attention to "prove" the guilt of one of their own, seeking fame purely by association.

Kenneth Christiansen, like several other suspects in the D.B. Cooper case, had died of cancer. It was a peculiar coincidence with no explanation, except for the prevalence of the disease.

Cancer is such an ugly, terrifying word. Dad's doctor was convinced cancer was present in Dad's body, but was unable to locate it for months, while Dad's weight fluctuated inexplicably. Finally, a routine visit to the dentist provided an answer.

Dad's teeth cleaning and checkup went well, but his dentist noticed the weight loss since his last visit. Only then did Dad mention the irritation under his tongue. "Like an ordinary chancre, except it doesn't ever go away completely," is how dad described it. It got better, then worse, and only bothered him when he ate. However, the sore was painful enough that it discouraged his consumption of anything but soups and soft foods for weeks at a time.

But cancer? It never entered Dad's mind and he'd never mentioned it to his internist. The dentist frowned, lifted Dad's tongue, and there it was--an area beneath Dad's tongue revealed exactly what his doctor fruitlessly searched for. A cancerous growth on the underside of his tongue was something my father had never even considered.

Whenever Dad tried to look at it in the mirror, he'd been unable to find the source of his pain. He discounted it as one of the mouth sores he got occasionally, although this one was far more persistent. He self-treated the area the way he handled mouth chancres all his life, with a daily dab of baking soda applied to the sore spot. It seemed to help each time – but only temporarily.

The biopsy was positive for advanced Stage I cancer of the tongue. He had been a heavy smoker in the service. Cigarettes at the Post Exchange were incredibly cheap, and everyone in the service still smoked when I was growing up. When he'd retired, Dad tried to quit, both because of his work and the changing times - cigarette packs carried warnings since the late 1960s and fewer and fewer people smoked as evidence of its harmful effects were scientifically proven. But though he had curtailed the smoking habit down to a cigarette here or there, Dad still enjoyed a drink or two before dinner, and relished a good cigar.

Dad found a great oncologist who practiced near Scott & White Hospital. The week before Thanksgiving Sue, Matt, and I sat together nervously in the waiting room at Scott & White for Dad's primary tumor surgery, which could evolve into a glossectomy - the removal of a portion of Dad's tongue. I spent some time with Dad the night before, and we had discussed the possibility. He was upbeat, however, and said the oncologist was fairly certain that would not be necessary. But he wouldn't know until he could investigate surgically how extensive the cancer had spread.

On surgery day, we profusely showered him with positivity and best wishes, then Sue loudly said a prayer over him. All there was for us to do now was wait. I fetched us a round of coffee from the vending machine and we talked about inconsequential things until Sue announced she and the baby she was carrying were starving. Matt escorted her to the cafeteria. Sue had come armed with her Bible and her favorite rosary. I dreaded what might transpire on her return. Matt had a magazine and a briefcase full of work to keep him busy, and I hoped to be deeply engrossed in my book by Robert Himmelsbach, the chief FBI investigator on the D.B. Cooper case for nearly a decade by the time they returned from breakfast.

Himmelsbach had written a book about his investigative theories and his experiences over the first decade following the hijacking and was published in 1986. I devoured it, hoping to learn something new from the man who was closest to the investigation in those early years.

My absorption in the book worked. When Sue and Matt returned, I glanced up from my reading only to nod a hello, then returned to Himmelsbach's account of his search for clues in the hijacking and his interviews and background checks of the multiple suspects. Matt busied himself with paperwork, and Sue was relegated to a silent repetition of the rosary, moving her lips in well-defined prayer as she counted the beads. When done, she busied herself on Matt's cell phone, calling friends and offering a play-by-play account of our wait, what we were each doing to pass the time, discussing Dad's diagnosis, the plans after surgery, and Dad's potential prognoses in the most excruciating detail. I excused myself to get a bite to eat and returned quickly, so Sue and Matt could go to lunch. Yet I might have just as well taken my time, for Sue was still yapping on the phone when I returned and continued to chat for the next half hour until Matt made her hang up. I could hear his stomach growling across the room.

Time crept agonizingly slowly. We began to fear the worst.

Other than Himmelsbach's conviction that the wind direction factored into the first estimates of where Cooper had jumped was off by as much as 80 degrees, making Cooper's projected drop zone over the Washougal Valley area, I did not learn much. Of course, the drop zone Himmelsbach suggested had been searched repeatedly by groups of private individuals in subsequent years without turning up any evidence, but this detail considerably increased the chances the hijacker survived the drop.

Finally, Dad's surgeon, Dr. Evans, joined us in the waiting room to explain how he had excised a little more of the area around the tumor than he originally planned, just to make sure he got it all. Dad would need a course of radiation therapy but should recover nicely. Speech therapy would be included in his after-care plan.

Dr. Evans sounded very positive, and we all breathed a sigh of relief. Even as he spoke, I began planning a special surprise for Dad once his year of treatment and recovery were behind him.

Chapter 26: "Life is What Happens to Us While We Are Making Other Plans"

– Allen Saunders, January 1957, Publishers Syndicate

"Steve Roper" was one of my dad's favorite comic characters, the creation of a cartoonist on *The Big Chief Wahoo* comic strip in the early 1950s. Roper was initially a minor new arrival to the scene but eventually the adventures of the news photographer took over the strip until the name was changed to *Steve Roper,* and *Big Chief Wahoo* vanished into cartoon history. A series of five issues of a full-sized *Steve Roper* comic book enjoyed a brief debut before Roper was once relegated to newsprint. The adventurous news photographer chased criminals until he aged gracefully and matured in his career, eventually holding down a desk job at the paper while a new comic cohort, Mike Nomad, took over the role of crime fighter.

In 1969, the cartoon strip was renamed *Steve Roper and Mike Nomad* and continued to be published for decades. Steve Roper eventually became a side character, edged out by other characters during the cartoon's final years, but Dad was an avid reader until the end came on December 26, 2004. Dad never let me forget it was *Steve Roper*'s creator, Allen Saunders, who originated the saying John Lennon altered somewhat and used in his paean to his son, Sean, in *Beautiful Boy,* a track from an album Lennon recorded some years after breaking with the Beatles.

After his recovery from the surgery, I took Dad on a three-week whirl of European countries. Before his illness made eating difficult, my father enjoyed fine food whenever possible. Poor man – although he would never admit it, Mom was a terrible cook, and I had not been much better. Now that his tongue was fully healed, I wanted him to sample the finest cuisine Europe had to offer, so we went on a gastronomic tour of the capital cities of France, Germany, Italy, Spain, and Greece, with side trips into the countryside. It was a vacation guaranteed to add pounds and I confess, I denied myself nothing. Both Dad and I tipped the scales with an additional ten pounds on our return, but for Dad, it was just what the doctor ordered.

Subsequent tests showed him to be cancer-free, and life went on. Years passed. Only memories of Christmases and birthdays and Thanksgiving celebrations, and the occasionally remarkable vacation marked the passage of time. That, and Sue's popping out another child every few years. She and Matt now had five-- three boys and two girls. Just four more, Dad would tease, and they'd have a softball team.

I was determined to build a library of Forrest Fenn's books, and had adopted the habit of ordering each new book as it was printed. During the years I had devoted to my education and marriage, Dad's surgery and recovery, Forrest Fenn had started his own publishing company in Santa Fe-- the *One Horse Land & Cattle Company*. Fenn claimed he always wanted to own a land and cattle company, but could never afford one . . . however, in so naming his printing company, he was able to feel he'd successfully achieved that goal.

I ordered a signed First Edition he'd penned about Russian painter Nicholas Fechin, whose bout with tuberculosis drove him to settle in the arid climate of Taos, New Mexico. Taos was another internationally acclaimed Southwestern artist's colony. Fenn included beautiful color prints of Fechin's work, as well as full page black and white prints from a six-month trip to Mexico. The biography of the man was based on a series of interviews with Fechin's widow, Alexandra. Forrest discovered many Southwestern artists like Fechin, Eric Sloane and Joseph Sharp, and promoted their works, firmly establishing their names among the ranks of the best artists of the West.

The Genius of Nicholas Fechin: Recollections by Forrest Fenn became part of my growing collection, followed by *The Secrets of San Lazaro Pueblo*, which was also a signed and numbered limited edition that described his Indian pueblo located 17 miles south of Santa Fe. He had spent days and months excavating over the years and continued to do so. Not only did the site yield an impressive collection of artifacts, but the book provided real insights into the pueblo culture and the impact of the Spaniards in the Southwest. The book was recently published, and a slice of American history I desired to learn more about. It would accompany and complement Fenn's beautifully illustrated book I had purchased years earlier: *The Beat of the Drum and the Whoop of the Dance: A Study of the Life and Work of Joseph Henry Sharp.*

The fleeting memory of that particular book and the day it arrived at our office brought a sad smile to my lips. I was reminded of Michael, and his endearing response to my excitement. I sighed. We'd had some very good years. But that was then, and this was now, so I shrugged and advised myself to "soldier on, Stephanie!" as I focused on the current book order.

Forrest wrote from his extensive knowledge base in authoring *Teepee Smoke: A New Look into the Life and Work of Joseph Henry Sharp, and Historic American Indian Dolls*, writing both within a short span of time. *Seventeen Dollars a Square Inch*, a book about the early years of his gallery and Forrest Fenn's friendship with artist and writer, Eric Sloane, was his next publication. As Forrest had admiringly described Eric Sloane in a magazine interview, his good friend was a man who "wrote about fifty books in fifty years, and could paint a major painting a day, and still have time to lunch with me." I was quick to order the book, since it promised at last to offer a glimpse into the personality and interactions of the man I was seeking to profile, Forrest Fenn.

By this time, Fenn had instituted the Old Santa Fe Trading Company, and authored a blog by the same name. The Old Santa Fe Trading Co., as the name appears on its website, is an actual building where The Fenn Collection of pueblo artifacts is housed and maintained, exhibiting many hundreds of artifacts collected through Forrest's decades of patient and careful excavations at the site of the Tano pueblo of San Lazaro, a huge Indian complex that covered more than 57 acres and held as many as 5,000 rooms in 27-room blocks that housed nearly 1,800 people at the height of its occupation. His collection was enormous. Fenn had carefully explored and documented hundreds of rooms on digs where he was joined by others who shared his interest and respect for the ruins. Once measured and photographed, the excavated spaces were refilled with dirt to preserve the ruins for posterity.

Nothing in Fenn's collection was for sale, but one could wander for hours on the website viewing photographs of the many marvelous artifacts. His book on the *Secrets of San Lazaro Pueblo* became a welcome reference for many of the beautiful objects my eyes often caressed visually as I worked my way through the vast collection,

How wonderful it would be to see the collection in person! *Someday, I will go to Santa Fe and see all of this for myself. Someday, I will meet Forrest Fenn. And then I will know.*

The Old Santa Fe Trading Co. combined the collection gallery with a storefront where Forrest Fenn's books and many other publications dealing with art and the general history of the Southwest could be ordered or purchased. His blogsite was yet another avenue for Fenn to express himself and highlighted his many interests. Forrest had created the center specifically for the public to view his excavated treasures. Archeological excavation was a passion of Fenn's long before his retirement from the gallery. He was fond of recounting the tale when, at the age of 9, he found his first arrowhead. Forrest spent years excavating San Lazaro and was considered an authority on the pueblo.

Fenn wrote characteristically homey, uncomplicated texts, spun from the skeins of a complicated and complex mind. Forrest Fenn was a man who approached life directly, with a simple set of rock-firm values, brought to life by a flexible and compassionate approach to their implementation. His writing style was such that he could squeeze from or inject a world of insight into any topic, founded on his personal experience and unique viewpoint. With the meaning of even his simplest sentences changing and challenging anew with each rereading, every book was an evolving, adventurous foray into his singular mind.

Then, in 2010, Fenn at last opened the floodgates to his life, and his books gained radically new audiences.

In 2010, Forrest Fenn published the first of what was to be a set of autobiographical novels, and I was thrilled at the thought of reading Forrest Fenn's life story. Perhaps at last, this autobiographical memoir would help me understand just what it was that made Dad think this clever, self-educated man was the legendary D.B. Cooper.

The Thrill of the Chase: A Memoir promised to be just that, so I ordered the book and could not wait for it to arrive.

As Forrest's online presence grew, he gave well-publicized interviews to promote his books and discuss his excavations at the San Lazaro pueblo. A growing number of photographs of the man appeared in various media. One day I finally saw a full-face photograph of Fenn that was large enough to discern his features clearly. As I stared at the man's close-set eyes and his long nose with its narrow bridge, I was reminded of the FBI composite drawing I had modified so long ago, and Dad's startled reaction on seeing it. This face I was staring at . . . I had to see it laid side-by-side with my modified composite image once again!

When I had left my father's home to live as Michael's wife, I had taken nothing but clothes and books, including the three D.B. Cooper scrapbooks. I also took the composite taped to my bureau's mirror, then inserted it between the last two pages of Volume III of *The Search*.

The three volumes rested on the top shelf of the closet in the guest bedroom. I lifted them down with due care. Now over 15 years old, their condition was delicate, and I handled them with respect. I found the composite pressed between the final pages of the third volume - the one Dad and I never completed. Holding up the image beside the current photograph of Forrest Fenn, the first thing that struck me were the eyes.

Unknowingly, folding the FBI composite drawing as I had rectified its defects.

The eyes now were truly close-set to the narrow bridge of the lengthened nose and remarkably resembled Fenn's. No wonder Dad reacted as he had! There had to be a younger photograph of Fenn online. After searching for a short time, I found exactly what I was looking for--a younger Forrest Fenn strapped into a pilot's seat. Another photo showed Fenn, perhaps 40 years of age, climbing into his fighter jet, a large Texas sticker affixed to its side. Forrest's dark brown hair was parted on the left, with his intense, close-set eyes and a slight squaring of a chin that had been drawn too narrowly in the original FBI composite. It was him. It had to be him. The likeness was uncanny.

But now what?

Now, Detective Stephanie Storm, you must build your case, I whispered to myself.

The years had served to peel back the cover on still more of the as-yet-unreleased FBI file information in the D.B. Cooper investigation, and I buried myself in the files on the FBI website, intent on refreshing my knowledge of the hijacking and acquainting myself with new research on old clues as I combed through the most significant developments of recent years.

An old suspect had resurfaced in 2006, after FBI Agent Larry Carr had taken over from Robert Himmelsbach as chief investigator on the Cooper case. Ted Mayfield was a familiar name from my reading of Special Agent Himmelsbach's 1986 book. Himmelsbach knew of Mayfield before the 1971 hijacking because of a previous event at a local airport some time earlier, in which Mayfield was involved.

Despite repeated suggestions that Mayfield was a likely suspect, Himmelsbach had discounted the possibility from the very beginning, primarily because Mayfield had telephoned him - presumably from Seattle, Washington, where he lived - less than two hours after the 727 landed in Reno, Nevada. The purpose of the call, ostensibly, was to voluntarily offer Special Agent Himmelsbach information on various skydiving practices and techniques, and to then speculate as to where the drop zone might have been.

Ted Mayfield had the requisite skills--he was a pilot, a skydiving instructor, and competitive skydiver who was also a Special Forces veteran. He also possessed a criminal record involving armed robbery and the transportation of a stolen aircraft. His pilot's license was permanently revoked in 1984, and in early 1995 he faced new criminal charges over the deaths of two skydiving students killed when the parachutes he provided for their jump failed to open. He was convicted of negligent homicide and served time. Just that year, in 2010, Mayfield had been sentenced to three years' probation for piloting a single-engine plane without a license.

Lest you be tempted to interpret it as a minor oversight, Mayfield's permanent pilot's license was revoked 26 years earlier, and nothing had changed.

Figure 23 Ted Mayfield

The two amateur sleuths who had, once again, proposed Mayfield to the FBI as a prime suspect in the Cooper case had concocted a circumstantial proposition which posited that Mayfield had called Agent Himmelsbach for no other reason than to create an alibi for himself, and somehow he'd located a telephone less than four hours after parachuting into a storm over mountain wilderness. A book deal was in the works, of course, but on closer examination, their theory did not hold water. However, they did attract the attention of Portland television station, KOIN, and were even able to interest *Inside Edition* with their purported "proof" that Mayfield was a viable suspect.

For his part, Mayfield denied any involvement in the hijacking, insisting the FBI contacted *him* for information *five times* while the hijacking was taking place, an assertion the FBI denied. When Dvorak died a year later, the book project was abandoned, and Mayfield was definitively ruled out as a suspect.

Science had caught up with the investigation by that time and in 2007, the FBI announced a partial DNA result had been obtained from three organic samples isolated in 2001 - two of which were quite small, and one fairly large. Subsequent to the announcement, however, the FBI was forced to acknowledge the results of the DNA test on the clip-on tie and its mother-of-pearl tie clip could not be tied to the hijacking suspect, because the actual source of the organic material - and thus, the source of the available DNA - was unknown, and the DNA sample could therefore not be conclusively linked to any specific individual.

Also disclosed at the time of the botched 2007 DNA announcement was some minor additional information pertaining to the items the hijacker had left behind. Cooper had selected the older of the two offered primary parachutes rather than choosing the newer and technologically superior sport parachute. Of the two reserve chutes, Cooper selected the "dummy" – a parachute with its canopy sewn shut so that it would not open during classroom demonstration. That was puzzling because the dummy parachute was clearly marked as such, as any skilled skydiver could have readily determined.

Cooper had also removed cords from the single functional reserve chute to use for other purposes--perhaps to tie the money bag to his body, as was possibly witnessed by Miss Mucklow. Fact sheets and previously unreleased composite sketches were also made public at that time, and the general public was asked to provide any information that might result in Cooper's identification.

With radical new investigative techniques that far outstripped the rudimentary tools available to FBI investigators in late 1971, the Bureau announced the formation in early 2009 of a civilian team of citizen sleuths dedicated to using new scientific technology to reassess the meager evidence in the case. The Cooper Research Team, organized by Tom Kaye, a paleontologist from the Burke Museum of Natural History and Culture in Seattle, was comprised of professionals from a wide variety of disciplines, including a metallurgist and a scientific illustrator. The team planned to use GPS and satellite imagery to retrace the flight path of the Boeing 727 the night of the hijacking, determine the origin of the packets of bills that had floated onto Tena Bar on the Columbia River, and utilize an electron microscope to identify the miniscule particles present on the surfaces of the clip-on tie and mother-of-pearl tie clasp.

The only new information uncovered through the application of new technology, however, was produced by the electron microscope, which successfully identified several particles on the tie, including Lycopodium spores, which can be found in pharmaceutical products, along with fragments of bismuth, an element that chemically resembles arsenic and antimony, as well as flecks of aluminum. Additionally, particles of then-rare titanium metal were found on the tie. These findings implied several things to investigators: First, the perpetrator was very likely someone who worked with chemicals or in metallurgy or was employed by a company that recovered scrap metal from these facilities. He could possibly be a chemist, a metallurgist, or perhaps an engineer or manager in such a plant or production facility. All were positions where a tie would have been part of the required dress in the late 1970s.

Kaye's research team also formed some opinions on Cooper himself after reviewing the FBI files and other evidence in the case. In the absence of either a warm body or cold corpse, and after the extended length of time when not even a bone, shred of clothing or a strip of related parachute fabric had ben stumbled upon by a lone woodsman, camper or hunter, the FBI was at a loss.

The general assumption was that, given the circumstances of his jump, the hijacker had not survived. Accordingly, FBI investigators wavered between preliminary considerations that Cooper was a meticulous planner, a theory belied by his lack of warm or waterproof clothing when a storm was in the forecast, or he was either a highly or minimally skilled jumper, with competing theories based on his questionable choice of which parachutes to use in his getaway, along with his failure to heed the weather for a jump, and the skyjacker's imprecise locational directions to the pilot.

By 2006, Larry Carr informed the national press the FBI's stance on the hijacker's level of experience and his expertise shifted dramatically. Carr told reporters, "We originally thought Cooper was an experienced jumper, perhaps even a paratrooper. We concluded after a few years this was simply not true. No experienced parachutist would have jumped in the pitch-black night, in the rain, with a 200-mile-an-hour wind in his face, wearing loafers and a trench coat. It was simply too risky. He also missed that his reserve chute was to be used only for training and the panels had been sewn shut - something a skilled skydiver would have checked.

"Diving into the wilderness without a plan, without the right equipment, in such terrible conditions, he probably never even got his chute open," Carr added. The FBI concluded the jump could never have succeeded without a waiting accomplice. Cooper's survival was virtually impossible, as was the idea of an accomplice meeting him at a predetermined landing zone, which he no doubt would have missed. The perilous jump had lacked the necessary timing and precision to make that possible.

Kaye's Cooper Research Team arrived at yet another conclusion, and posited Cooper may have timed his jump specifically to take place during the four-day holiday in order to ensure he would not be absent from work and missed by an employer. Curiously, the FBI had never been able to establish anyone had disappeared over the weekend in question – and on a special holiday weekend where extended families traditionally unite, are aware of each relative's whereabouts, and expect to visit with all family members for several hours, at least, if not days.

Furthermore, no employees were ever reported as being conspicuously absent without reason in the days immediately following the holiday.

Tom Kaye wrote in his *Research Conclusions: Cooper Research Team*, "If you were planning on going 'back to work on Monday,' then you would need as much time as possible to get out of the woods, find transportation and get home. The very best time for this is in front of a four-day-weekend, which is the timing Dan Cooper chose for his crime." His words suggested the air pirate had simply returned to his usual job following the heist. As to Cooper's inappropriate dress for such a feat, he added, "If he was planning ahead, he knew he had to hitchhike out of the woods, and it is much easier to get picked up in a suit and tie than in old blue jeans."

That pretty much summed up FBI progress over nearly four decades of investigation. The question remained – and remains to this day: Did Dan Cooper, aka D.B. Cooper, manage to pull off the perfect crime?

Excellent question.

I read with renewed diligence. I dared not miss a detail in the investigation. If I were to construct an airtight case to support Dad's and my suspicions of Fenn, I needed to be certain I knew everything about the case.

Just over ten months after my review, a surprising new development surfaced in the case. At least, as far as my personal investigation was concerned.

I was shocked to learn that FBI investigators *withheld* a fourth, undisclosed letter to a newspaper mailed after the 1971 hijacking! What the public had supposed was the third communication from the hijacker - the letter in which "need to plan for retirement" phrase was used--was actually the fourth communication.

The actual missive, FBI Letter # 3, seemingly also from D.B. Cooper, was postmarked December 1, 1971, but was only revealed to the public on August 1, 2011 when the FBI released the letter back to its original owner: *The Oregonian* newspaper.

At the time of the hijacking, *The Oregonian* was the premier Portland newspaper. The paper received the letter the week immediately following the hijacking. However, they never published it, nor did they acknowledge its existence, but instead turned it over to the FBI. On its return to the newspaper in late summer, 2011, *The Oregonian* promptly published the D.B. Cooper Letter #3 on its website, OregonLive.com, which opened it to analysis by aficionados of the Cooper legend.

It was a traditional ransom-type letter composited from several neatly cut (and one torn) magazine letters. It read: "Am alive and doing well in hometown P. O. The system that beat the system." It was "signed" D.B. Cooper in letters also clipped from a magazine. A later analytic article, prompted by two of the cut-out letters from the cryptic message - the A that began the message and the P in the abbreviation for Portland, Oregon - established with certainty they were clipped from the cover of the June 1970 issue of PLAYBOY magazine. The white lettering against a distinctively curving striped background which - when colorized by an analyst - was readily identifiable by both color and print design, matched the lettering and background for that month's magazine. The blue O used in the abbreviation for Oregon was clipped from the July issue of the same year. The cover photo discretely featured a nude model diving under water, and the entire cover was printed in various shades of blue. (Funny, until the analysis of this letter was publicized on August 11, 2011, I had never realized that every single cover of Playboy Magazine - virtually since its inception - is on the Internet! We learn something new every day).

While the Playboy lettering analysis was completed by an anonymous D.B. Cooper fan provided an interesting factoid, it ultimately added nothing to the investigation.

Interestingly, however, what was long believed to be the third post-hijacking letter, purely because it had been published at the time, was a second mailing to the *Reno Gazette* that was also postmarked from California on

December 1, but was mailed from the area around Sacramento. *The Oregonian's* composite letter, received at the same time, also had a December 1 postmark, but from northern Oregon, a considerable distance from Reno.

The simultaneous mailing in two different states on the same day was a physical impossibility, unless a single person was flying a small plane to make the mail drops so far apart or had a prearranged accomplice in the other location to mail the second letter.

The second letter to the *Reno Gazette* was never published, at FBI request, although its existence was mentioned in a contemporaneous story the *Gazette* did publish. Describing this communication as pasted together from cut-out letters, the message read: "Plan ahead for retirement income. DB Cooper."

Had D.B. Cooper had an accomplice - or two - mailing letters for him from different cities in order to cover his trail and confuse the FBI? And had money indeed been stolen for the purpose of subsidizing the infamous hijacker's retirement? Was that the motive?

Unfortunately, the envelope in which the newly released Letter #3 was sent, was hand-addressed, written in pencil, and released to the public.

When my 2010 book order arrived, the shipment included my first, quaint introduction to Forrest B. Fenn, himself: *The Thrill of the Chase: A Memoir by Forrest Fenn.*

Ignoring the other books, I started reading Fenn's autobiographical story, and devoured the entire book, from cover to cover, in less than four and a half hours. I was a quick reader, but the style flowed, and it was what could be termed an "easy read."

The book was also fascinating in another way: Fenn had used it to throw out a brilliant challenge to all who read it, and had laced his personal stories with clues, he said, to guide the astute to a gold-filled bronze box he had "secreted" away in the mountains north of Santa Fe. It contained gold coins and artifacts – 21 Troy ounces of gold, in all.

Hmmmm, I mused. The wheels of my mind turned. Fenn's words and stories had double meanings and conveyed cryptic messages couched in rich symbolism. While he seemingly recounted a simple personal history and the mundane thoughts of an adolescent, framed with his characteristic *joie de vivre*, Fenn's "under-story" told a different and far darker tale when read between the lines. In this instance, the $200,000 extorted from Northwest Orient by "D.B. Cooper" was comprised of 10,000 individual bills, rubber-banded together in bundles of one hundred $20s - a "treasure" that weighed in at 21 pounds!

Another item of interest the treasure chest contained what Forrest described as his "real" autobiography, written in tiny script on miniscule sheets of paper rolled tight, and protected from moisture in an olive jar with a screw-on cap.

Launching an addictive search for his hidden treasure with a cryptic poem in which nine clues were embedded was a clever way to get people involved in something outside of themselves and their modest lives, promote outdoor activity, and inspire travel though the American West and its majestic beauty.

Forrest's challenge proved a strong draw for the curious and the avaricious. Chat rooms sprang up, parsing suspected clues, examining, and comparing maps and notes and organizing trips to search for the hidden gold and the secret life story hidden within an antique bronze box.

Notoriety wasted no time in seeking out Forrest Fenn. Googling *The Thrill of the Chase* brought up Forrest's many interviews on radio and television, news articles and magazine spreads, dozens of blogs and chatrooms, glowing commentaries from a coterie of Forrest Fenn fans, hundreds of theories on the location of his "secreted" golden treasure, tales of treasure hunts, and maps, maps, and more maps.

Bemused, I flipped through Fenn's illustrated book once again. It deserved another read. And another. It wasn't long before it became my Bible, my treasure map, and the challenge that kept me sane when Dad learned his cancer had returned - metastasized, after lying dormant beyond the vaunted five-year implicit promise of good health that normally ensured a cancer was gone for good.

The book was a charming rendition that both amused and informed, and I was tickled to learn Forrest Fenn was born and raised in Temple. Forrest's father had been a renowned and beloved school principal and pillar of the community, and had a park named in his honor. Just as the shoemaker's children are reputed to have no shoes, the educator's sons had no tolerance for formal education. Although Forrest and his older brother never had more than a high school education, both were clever and resourceful, with a good deal of common sense, street smarts, useful aptitudes in mechanics, electronics and aviation, and an unlimited curiosity about the world around them. They also had an exceeding quantity of courage. Risks were taken by both with great enthusiasm.

Growing up, Forrest and his older brother, Skippy, and their sister, June, had lived on North Main Street, close to the cemetery where their parents are now buried.

One story in the fanciful book featured traveling gypsies. Gypsies? I had never heard of gypsies visiting Temple, Texas, let alone camping in the field next to the cemetery, which was spread over a broad swale between rising hillocks on either side. Nor had Dad. However, we lived farther up Main from the cemetery and open land. And although I'd had a friend who lived on the crest above the cemetery and visited her often, she and I never spoke of anything but boys and clothes and makeup and teachers. Googling "Gypsies in Texas," on a bet I had with Dad, we found there was an established Romani Gypsy population in Texas of at least 20,000 – and so learned there could have been a gypsy encampment in Temple, just as Forrest had described in his book.

Toward the end of that year, I read *The Thrill of the Chase* to Dad as we sat waiting for blood draws and test results and scheduled chemo sessions. It was during those readings I finally pried out of my father the circumstances under which he had met Forrest.

Their contact was brief, and hardly one-on-one, except for a parting handshake. It was in December 1968, just before Christmas, when a group of airmen gathered around the famed pilot in a hangar where they had been working, and a newly made friend pulled Dad toward the gathering, insisting the man at the center of everyone's attention was an amazing storyteller and a much-decorated combat pilot who'd flown 368 missions during the year he'd served in Vietnam. He had been shot down twice - once in South Vietnam and once in Laos - and the last incident had happened just a few days earlier. Both times, Major Fenn had survived with barely a scratch, avoided capture, and lived to talk about his adventures.

Fenn had undergone survival training in the Philippines that no doubt helped him survive, the friend breathlessly added, but Major Fenn was "one tough mother-f" and was going home with a Silver Star, a Bronze Star, a Purple Heart, a bunch of Air Medals, and three Distinguished Flying Crosses.

When Dad laughed and told his new acquaintance he sounded like a rock star groupie, the man responded in hushed tones, "We all are. Groupies, that is. We admire the really good ones. Fenn is one of them. He models himself after a famous WWII pilot and West Point man, Robin Olds. Ever hear of him? He flew in Nam at the beginning of this mess. Big WWII hero. Major Fenn talks about him a lot, you know? I mean, Fenn's not a particularly modest man. Don't get me wrong – he's not *exactly* full of himself, but he doesn't hide his accomplishments. Come on - you gotta hear this guy!"

Crossing the hangar, Dad witnessed that Fenn obviously earned the respect of his fellow airmen. He was an all-around good guy and could apparently tell one hell of a terrific story. Dad told me he had never, since that day in the hangar, seen so many men so enthusiastic about another man since he attended a Jim Morrison concert on a trip to San Francisco before his first rotation in Vietnam.

Dad was new to Nam. As Army Aviation, he was assigned to the 1st Aviation Brigade as their resident computer expert and was moved about between combat aviation groups as the need arose. Dad's particular talent was his ability to enable computer systems to "talk" to one another, and he was often on loan to other branches of the service operating in country. This was back when computers were a mystery and programmers were minor deities.

Just as Dad was acclimating to his first tour of duty and a new role in support of combat efforts through the management of the prevailing computer systems, Major Forrest Fenn was on his way home to the States within just a few days, and so he was making the rounds, saying his goodbyes and extending sincere appreciation to the many who supported his air exploits and pulled him out of a bad situation, in danger of enemy fire, capture and imprisonment on the two harrowing occasions when his downed planes left him stranded in a rice paddy or a jungle of southeastern Asia.

It was a memorable encounter, Dad said, that burned Major Fenn's features into his memory for all time as he listened rapt to the pilot's accounts of his aeronautic adventures and misadventures. Over his year in Vietnam and multiple valiant flights for a variety of dangerous purposes, many of which involved Air Force and Army Aviation attempts to disrupt of the flow of the enemy's weapons, manpower and supplies along the Ho Chi Minh Trail, the network of roads built from North to South Vietnam, and through the neighboring countries of Laos and Cambodia, and which comprised the primary logistical system of the Vietcong, Pathet Lao and the North Vietnamese armies. Its disruption was a necessary component of U.S. efforts to defeat and deflect the repeated North Vietnamese incursions into the democratic South.

Fenn had engaged in firefights, dropped bombs, and flown reconnaissance on an enormous scale and his tales kept his audience mesmerized. Before Fenn walked away, however, Dad grabbed his hand to thank him for his service and express his admiration and enjoyment of Fenn's stories. As he gazed into Forrest's intense, closely spaced hazel eyes that appeared dusty blue in sunlight and almost a light brown in the dimmer hangar. Dad told me the intensity of Fenn's gaze was softened somewhat by crinkles at their edges that bespoke Fenn's amusing perspective on life. The Major smiled and wished him well. Fenn had a gift, Dad said, a way of making you feel you had known him forever, even when you'd only just met.

Dad said he grew effusive at that point, almost gushing expressions of praise and admiration as he walked with Major Fenn out onto the sunlit tarmac. Dad laughed, then said, "Hero worship was evidently contagious – and, being young and impressionable, newly stationed in a war zone, I'd caught a bad case." Fenn listened with amusement to Dad's glowing praise, then laughed and told him, "It didn't seem like such an amazing feat at the time. Everything that could go wrong in exiting that jet certainly did go wrong. But good training keeps you calm and focused on the steps you need to take to survive. But the fun of telling a story is in embellishing the truth. And I'm good at embellishing, as you might have noticed. I survived because I have always believed I was invincible, when the truth of the matter is, I was just lucky. Stay safe, my friend."

That was the last time Dad had laid eyes on Forrest Fenn.

But when the headlines trumpeted the news of the audacious Dan Cooper hijacking, Forrest Fenn's face immediately sprang into Dad's mind. The audacity, the skill exhibited in parachuting under those circumstances, so similar to the conditions under which Fenn had to eject from his fuel and armament-laden jet into unfamiliar North Laotian terrain on a cold and wet night, with a lack of visibility and surrounded by hostile forces seeking him out. Add to that his knowledge of the use of the aft stair on the 727 to jump from, the survival training in the Philippines, and his characteristic desire to test his skills to the limit, all triggered Dad's suspicion. Then the composite drawing of their suspect was released by the FBI, which caused Dad to doubt his instinctive hunch. But my simple modification had mirrored Fenn's face. He had finally admitted that. And now we had Fenn's homey memoir to support our suspicions.

That, and an intriguing new challenge. When we weren't reading from Fenn's book, we passed the time speculating on the treasure hunt which Fenn had challenged his readers to pursue. I'd had the wisdom to photocopy the pages of his book. The original was pristine, but the photocopied pages were highlighted, starred, bracketed, underlined, and dog-eared, read, and reread. Each reading revealed a word or a phrase that had been overlooked in the prior reading. Many lines could be read as having two meanings. It was a game to a man skilled in hiding in plain sight. And our working copy of his personal history was a mess.

Was there a treasure or not? It would be just like Fenn, Dad maintained, to set the world off on a wild goose chase, then sit back and chuckle at the predictability of human nature. His book was evidence that while he cherished life, he didn't take it - or himself - too seriously, and a colossal joke like that would not be beyond him. But that was just Dad's opinion.

I begged to differ. The man seemed to have an overwhelming need to be remembered. Setting the world off on an unsolvable chase for hidden treasure was the perfect way to be remembered far into the future. The treasure was valuable enough that, until found, it would remain the focus of many searchers, and he would be talked and written about well into the future, until his secreted treasure chest – and the "real" autobiography it contained – was either found or forgotten. Fenn was ill with cancer, wasn't he? He had admitted that in his late 50s, he'd been stricken with cancer, but was fortunate enough to undergo a full remission following surgery. It was during those trying years when Forrest Fenn was battling the disease, supported by his wife and daughters, that he both sold his gallery and conceived the idea of hiding his treasure, to send the world off on a mad hunt for the end of his rainbow. For some persistent, intrepid, and intuitive fortunate hunter, the payoff would be massive. But even more intriguing to me was the certainty that his true autobiography would reveal him to be what Dad and I suspected more strongly than ever: that Forrest Fenn was *the* D.B. Cooper!

The chase after a fabled treasure ensured his remembrance for as long as it remained undiscovered. And if there was no treasure, I reasoned, if it were simply a ruse, Forrest Fenn would live *forever* as a legend - just as Blackbeard's pirate treasure is still hunted, three hundred years later, and the hidden caches of the gold and coins hidden by ancient men are discovered or uncovered from time to time, and grab the headlines and inspire research for weeks, months and years. It was a form of immortality.

My career was quite lucrative but becoming a bit of a bore. The job was steady, the projects were still fairly interesting, and all in all, I liked what I did for a living. But it had become only minimally challenging. I had an excellent staff that responded dependably and consistently to support my efforts, and I liked both the clients and my coworkers.

I had recently hired a decorator to update and refurnish my condominium. I had spent far too much, although I loved how it turned out. The unit I had purchased after my divorce from Michael was spacious, convenient to work, and close to a park. An older Temple neighborhood, my block boasted a dozen pecan trees that shed enough nuts in season for every resident to gather an ample winter supply of luscious nuts for baking and snacking. On the whole, I lived modestly. What I didn't spend, I saved, and I now possessed a healthy IRA, contributed regularly to my account in the construction firm's 401k, possessed a respectable investment portfolio with the local branch of a major brokerage, and a had fat savings account in the bank. But, while I enjoyed financial comfort and security, I was coming up short in the dream department. Forrest Fenn, I suspected, would never have approved.

My life had become safe, secure, and predictable - until the recurrence of Dad's cancer came out of left field. He had sailed through the magic five-year span during which a cancer generally recurs, if it is to recur at all. But a little over seven cancer-free years after Dad's successful glossectomy and six months of radiation treatment, nature had reneged on its tenuous promise. The doctors and I disagreed on the origin of the new cancer. They maintained the cancer in Dad's lungs was unrelated to the cancerous growth under his tongue, while I felt strongly the cancer had simply lain dormant for a bit, and then rapidly metastasized.

A few articles I'd read at the time speculated on whether operations to remove cancerous growths could actually spread diseased cells into other areas of the body, suggesting that perhaps the better course was to administer chemotherapy or radiation to destroy as many cancerous cells as possible prior to performing invasive surgery, but I had assured myself that was unproven speculation, and his doctors knew best.

I read voraciously about the phenomenon of cancer while Dad underwent radiation treatment years ago but was ill-equipped to argue with his oncologist at the time, who intimidated me and never quite answered my questions. But I was different now - more mature, better informed, and much more confident. I checked out current medical journals from the library and perused oncology websites to bring myself up to date on new developments in cancer treatment. I brought photocopies and notes with me when we went to see the doctor, having pre-planned my questions and observations. I brought Dad up to speed before each appointment, so we could all discuss Dad's treatment options intelligently.

Matt's father pulled some strings to get Dad seen by the top oncologist at M.D. Anderson Cancer Center in Houston. We drove there twice a week for his appointments. My seniority at the firm was an asset and worked in our favor. The company president was understanding of my need to take two days off per week and knew my well-trained staff could efficiently handle everything in my absence. Besides, I was just a phone call away and would have my laptop with me.

Dr. Benjamin Grissom was Dad's oncologist. He was about my age-- studious, earnest, single, and very handsome. Dad tried - jokingly, I hoped - to set us up on a date. I dated from time to time, but had yet to find someone who could keep my interest, or who didn't resent my earning more than he did, or who was not a "retread" - divorced and bitter (or divorced or widowed, and still grieving). Or emotionally unavailable. Or just a jerk.

At a certain age, I realized, all the good men were taken, gay, or divorced with baggage. Lots of baggage.

Steamer trunks full of unfinished business, needy exes, hostile offspring, and the overhang of debt. The single men who were "still looking," and those who proudly proclaimed themselves avowed bachelors soon demonstrated, and rather quickly, precisely why and how they maintained their unenviable status.

Oy, vey! Where do I begin? Their attitudes and egos, annoying mannerisms, habits, appearance, personal hygiene (or total lack thereof), excessive narcissism, tics, insecurities, aversion to commitment, stinginess, or inability to converse or connect on an intimate level, consistently operated to seal their fate. I found, through a few brief but disastrous attempts to relate to passably attractive single men of a certain age, that they were frequently as difficult to remove from one's life as barnacles from the bottom of a boat, hardened in their habits and unable to adapt, desperately attaching to whatever fragments of affection they could cling to. And, while they were loath to let go, once they "felt a connection" with a woman, they were all too often unable to reciprocate affection in any satisfactory way.

It is next to impossible to express these thoughts and experiences to another male, whether father or brother (in my case, brother-in-law), or a male friend. The comradeship felt among men serves to generate a negative reaction that cannot be reasoned with. There is no simple way for them to understand how undesirable certain men are.

So I no longer bother to explain, and - ever more often, of late - I simply make excuses to well-meaning friends attempting to set me up on blind dates and avoid intent stares from single men my age I encountered in bars or libraries, or even at the homes of friends, thereby avoiding that dreaded lead-in that inevitably results in some lame line to get me to go out with them. I find my "radar" is becoming more finely tuned as I age.

So, whenever Dad joked, as he often did, and Dr. Grissom responded by giving me an appraising look, I would cringe, and suddenly remember a phone call I needed to make at that precise moment, or excuse myself to go to the Ladies Room down the hall or, on occasion, simply retire to the waiting area.

Dad was depressed, although he denied it. I did everything I could to get him involved in anything that took his mind off the dreadful chemo treatments and the possible pneumonectomy once the chemotherapy reduced the size of the cancer - or failed to reduce the tumor at all. Dad tired easily now, His partner, Art, who had finally married a rather mousey but very bright, sweet young woman he'd met at a Star Trek convention, took over a lot of Dad's responsibilities and brought in his wife to assist him in covering both jobs. Tabitha was on top of things in no time.

As always, I turned to the FBI website and my notebook to interest Dad in the latest developments surrounding the D.B. Cooper mystery. I lent Dad all the books I owned written and published by Forrest Fenn. I also bought my father a new laptop for his birthday and bookmarked all the Forrest Fenn and D.B. Cooper websites, along with the Mac Daddy - the FBI website itself. Dad was delighted. Before long, Fenn's books and that dependable topic - the unsolved hijacking - afforded us hours of conversation.

Dad's mood perceptibly improved when he, too, began keeping a notebook and jotting down his observations and any new "evidence," or points of speculation supporting the possible guilt of Forrest Fenn.

One afternoon while we were surfing the web, we paid a visit to the FBI site. It'd been a few weeks since we last visited it. Maybe a new document had become unclassified and added to the archive.

Bingo! We struck pay dirt, and seated side by side, shoulder to shoulder, we leaned forward to view the small screen simultaneously.

The month of July 2011 brought another suspect to the attention of the FBI: Lynn Doyle Cooper.

This new suspect was known as L.D. Cooper and was proposed as a suspect in the November 24, 1971 hijacking by his niece, Maria Cooper, twelve years after his death in

1999. L.D. was a leather worker and a Korean War veteran and was also an avid fan of the Canadian comic book hero, Dan Cooper. Maria Cooper recalled he had thumbtacked one of the Dan Cooper comic books to a wall.

Figure 24 Lynn Doyle Cooper

Lynne Doyle Cooper was neither a skydiver nor a paratrooper, but Maria Cooper recalled a time when she was around eight years old where she witnessed L.D. and another uncle behaving secretively, planning something she described as "very mischievous" at her grandmother's house in Sisters, Oregon. Sisters is about 150 miles south of Portland. Whatever they planned involved a set of "expensive walkie-talkies." The following day, when the brothers were supposedly out hunting a turkey for Thanksgiving dinner, Northwest Orient Flight 305 was skyjacked. When the brothers returned home, L.D.'s shirt was bloodied, the niece recalled. L.D. blamed the smeared stains on an auto accident. Eventually, Maria Cooper's parents came to believe L.D. was the hijacker. Unable to immediately dispute the claim, the IRS referred his survivors to several estate attorneys and began an investigation.

Then in August of 2011, Robert Gregory's more detailed and accurate FBI sketch surfaced, based on his eyewitness account as he was seated across the aisle from Cooper. Among other changes to the original composite sketch, the artist updated the original hairstyle, incorporating the "marcelled" style with tight, crimped waves.

Coincidentally, L.D. Cooper – like suspect Duane Weber - wore his hair in an artificially waved, or marcelled, style. The niece also provided L.D. Cooper's leather guitar strap in hopes that DNA found on the strap might match the partial DNA profile gained from the hijacker's tie and tie clasp. A few weeks after L.D. rose to the level of suspect, the FBI crime lab returned a "not guilty" verdict on Lynn Dale Cooper based on the DNA evidence. The FBI was also forced to acknowledge they were unsure of the source of the DNA material found on the tie and the clasp. There was no way to know if the DNA found on the tie clasp was Cooper's.

A book by a New York private investigator, Skipp Porteous, was published in 2010, and in early 2011 was summarized in an episode of the History Channel's series, *Brian Meltzer's Decoded*. Porteous had been hired by Lyle Christiansen, the brother of Kenneth Christiansen, a 2003 suspect in the hijacking to uncover evidence supporting Lyle's suspicion that Kenneth had been D.B. Cooper.

November 2011 heralded Tom Kaye's announcement that the Cooper Research Team had isolated particles of pure, unalloyed titanium on the tie left on the skyjacked 727 by the daring criminal. This finding of titanium - which was rarer and had fewer uses in 1970 than in 2011 - was only found in metal fabrication or production facilities, or in companies that recovered scrap metal from those sources.

When Dad and I read Kaye's report in the Ongoing Investigation section of the FBI website, we both stared at each other, jaws agape, and almost lost the laptop, which threatened to slide off Dad's lap. I grabbed my shoulder satchel from the side of the chair and rummaged through it for the annotated photocopy of Forrest Fenn's *Thrill of the Chase.*

Once I found it, I thumbed frantically through the pages just as Dad was called for his chemo session. He slowly stood up, then hesitated.

"Go on in, Dad, let them get you started," I urged. "I'll take care of the laptop and be in as soon as I find the paragraph, I promise." The nurse smiled at my frantic appearance before leading my dad into the chemo room.

I closed the laptop, then read through the photocopied book as quickly as possible, flipping the pages and tracing the words with a freshly manicured index finger. Titanium was used in metallurgy - had it been used in a chemical operation, Kaye had written, the titanium would have been combined with aluminum, but the particles on Cooper's tie were unalloyed titanium . . .

There! There it was!

My finger between the pages to hold the paragraph, I scooped up Dad's laptop and tucked it beneath my left arm, strapped the purse and satchel over my shoulder and walked awkwardly toward the door of the chemo room. An orderly held the door open for me.

"I have it, Dad!" I exclaimed. "Here. Let me get situated." Dad's eyes lit with a welcome spark of excitement.

"Here it is, right above Forrest's *ODE TO PEGGY JEAN* - see?"

Dad leaned forward slightly. The nurse glared at us both. "No movement!" she whispered, shaking her head.

"Relax, Dad - Let me read it to you." I cleared my throat. "This is where Forrest talks about making the bronze bell… ready? I'll read it all - the whole page."

Dad grinned. He gave me the slightest of nods. I began reading:

"On many occasions at night, while my wife was watching *Dancing with the Stars* I was making wax bells and writing words on them in elevated letters. The later bronze castings of the bells are exactly like the wax originals I took to the foundry. Bronze is a nonferrous metal, meaning it won't rust or deteriorate in any way. One must pound it with a sledgehammer, or melt it down in order to change its shape. All of my bells were cast in that material so I could bury them. Each one is signed and dated or there would be no point to the madness. Some of the bells have clankers that I made from large copper nails taken from 17th century Spanish galleons. Skippy's son, Crayton Fenn, is a professional deep sea diver. He gave the nails to me.

"I buried those bells about three feet deep so a metal detector can't find them. Some may be on land owned by the American people but tended by the Bureau of Land Management. Other bells have words that say:
GOD WILL FORGIVE ME, THAT'S WHAT HE DOES.
IMAGINATION IS MORE IMPORTANT THAN KNOWLEGE.
IT DOESN'T MATTER WHO YOU ARE, IT ONLY MATTERS WHO THEY
THINK YOU ARE.

"There are others but these illustrate my point if not my logic. Hopefully no one will happen upon a bell for many years. Around 1,000 would be perfect. The Rosetta Stone was . . ."

I stopped reading mid-sentence when Dad had raised his hand. His lips moved, almost silently, and I quickly went to his side and leaned forward to hear his soft words. "He's looking for God's forgiveness. He wants God to forgive his crime. And the D rings were missing from the parachute. Isn't the 'd' missing from that word, knowledge? And remember? He was praying for 'Ds' in school? Who does that?" Dad paused, then continued with a startling statement, "The D rings were missing from his parachute. I think this whole book is full of clues, about more than just his treasure. I think the clues are about his sky-coup--the hijacking. I think these are all clues about the hijacking. That last sentence, and the writing on the bell: *It doesn't matter who you are, just who they think you are*? And the bit about God forgiving, because that's what he does?"

Dad started coughing from his prolonged whispering. The nurse shot over, glared at me, then offered Dad a sip of water. She crisply informed me, "I'm going to have to ask you to wait outside, if . . . "

"I know, I know. I won't disturb him again. He just had to say something to me. I'll be good. But he enjoys being read to while he's having this done. We can talk about this in the car on the drive back, Dad. We have to follow orders." I smiled at the nurse and mouthed, "Sorry."

Dad was on an acute central line. I think that's what they call it. It's designed for short term treatments. Since the line went through a vein in Dad's neck, the slightest cough sent the attending nurse flying over. The chemo drugs were highly toxic, obviously, and I was only in the room thanks to Dr. Grissom's good graces. I knew better than to push the envelope and lose the privilege of keeping Dad company through his ordeal, so I meekly retreated to my chair across the room, mulling over Dad's remarks.

Sick as he was, he was still sharp as a tack, and his memory was superb, recalling every detail of both the D.B. Cooper investigation and Forrest's breezy autobiography. He remembered the man who furnished the four parachutes to the 727 waiting on the Seattle-Tacoma Airport tarmac after Dan Cooper turned down the four military parachutes originally obtained from McChord Air Force Base. When Cooper refused the military parachutes because they would have all been equipped with location devices to enable rapid rescue, the aircraft was forced to circle Puget Sound as they waited for delivery of chutes from a local skydiving school. The parachute packer was Earl Cossey. When the press discovered his identity, he was interviewed multiple times by reporters anxious to learn details of the parachutes the hijacker had selected.

Cossey told reporters the hijacker had left behind the modern sport parachute used for recreational skydiving, the one he would have chosen for himself. It could be steered directionally and had an easily located ripcord, as well as modern safety elements and padded straps. Instead, the hijacker selected an N-8, a Navy emergency pilot rig, worn for the express purpose of ejecting and escaping a downed jet aircraft.

Since its use was exclusive to pilots operating in a very tight space, there was no room to wear a reserve chute. That's why, Cossey explained in an article I'd found, the primary chute Cooper donned for the jump had no attachment rings, known as D-rings, to connect a reserve parachute.

No D-rings. Damn, Dad had a good memory!

Cossey was convinced Cooper used the container of the accidentally provided "dummy," parachute to carry the money. In the absence of D-rings, Cooper had to cut two lines from the usable reserve parachute in order to tie the moneybag to his chest. That's probably what Miss Mucklow saw just before she pulled the curtain shut and entered the flight cabin. Cooper's jumping without a reserve probably did not influence the outcome. The Navy parachute had a round canopy, according to Cossey, with little chance of malfunction. Cossey didn't know if all the money fit into the reserve container, or whether any had been stuffed into the briefcase Cooper took with him. There was no indication of what was in the paper bag the hijacker had carried aboard. Nothing but the three packets of money had ever been found. Were they dropped intentionally, perhaps a few months after the crime? I had always questioned the missing twenty-dollar bills – why that specific amount, just $200? And I'd always wondered what happened to the rest. Did it survive the jump? Not a single other bill was ever found, despite dredging the Columbia and other waterways.

I found it fascinating that Dad viewed Fenn's book as a confession and interpreted the author's words as they related to his act of air piracy. I tried to think of the book from Dad's point of view, and remembered the mention of the Rosetta Stone . . .

The Rosetta Stone! It *was* all right there, plain as day. Dad was right! We just had to use one language to translate the other, the way Champollion had discovered the key to unlocking ancient hieroglyphs by using the other two languages inscribed on the famed stone -- ancient Greek and a later old Egyptian script known as Demotic, or popular, everyday writing – linking their translations to understand and catalogue the meanings of the hieroglyphic symbols that evaded interpretation and had mystified linguists for so long!

The details of one mystery – words and phrases and stories in Forrest's autobiographical book he employed to launch a national hunt for his 'secreted' treasure - were necessary to unlock the secrets of another mystery – utilizing Fenn's oblique confessional statements and actions proffered through the text that hinted at the truth behind a nearly forgotten and still unsolved crime of air piracy, of which the putative perpetrator was actually quite proud.

Wow Just wow!

I would need to reread the entire book again from Dad's perspective. But right now, Dad waited for me to continue reading Fenn's words aloud while the healing poison dripped slowly into his veins.

Settled back in my uncomfortable armchair, I prepared to continue, but not before grimacing in Dad's direction, rolling my eyes, and nodding toward the vigilant nurse now tending another patient. Dad smiled.

"The Rosetta Stone was undiscovered for 2,000 years and don't you just know the guy who carved it was proud?" Fenn's words – not mine. I continued reading aloud to Dad:

"I'm also burying bronze jars for the same reason, about eight in all. My friend, Tommy Hicks, who owns the Shidoni Foundry didn't know how to cast jars with screw lids, so I had to teach him. It's a secret technique I discovered when I ran my own foundry many years ago."

There it was. The link to the unalloyed titanium particles on the hijacker's clip-on tie! I looked at Dad, who grinned. He winked at me before I read on, repeating Fenn's sentence:

". . . It's a secret technique I discovered when I ran my own foundry many years ago. The same autobiography that's in the treasure chest also is in the jars, which are decorated mostly with dragonfly or frog designs."

I paused and thought of those small creatures and their characteristics, viewing Forrest Fenn's written statements through Dad's lens to interpret his words. Dragonflies are fast, agile flyers, found around water. They migrated across oceans and are predators. They symbolize courage, strength, and happiness in Japan, yet are sinister in European folklore. Dragonflies are ancient and have been found as fossils with huge wingspans. What a great deal of symbolism in a single insect! Forrest Fenn was an agile flyer, had crossed oceans, loved fishing and history, flying and archaeology, and could often be found around water - and what behavior could possibly be more predatory than commandeering an aircraft for profit and escaping with the cash?

And frogs - frogs are known for adapting. Frogs can see clearly in all directions and are also said to have an amazing sense of hearing. They can adjust their body temperature to their surroundings, and often burrow underground to hibernate. And, of course, they are renowned jumpers. Recalling a fascinating survival show I had seen recently, I recalled one survival technique recommended on the program was to burrow into the ground, forest cover, or even snow to retain body heat.

Was that how Forrest Fenn had survived that cold and rainy night in sub-zero weather if the radio Skippy made for him didn't summon his brother quickly enough? Or if Fenn had overshot his drop zone due to complications with the aft stairs?

In describing the contents of his treasure chest, Fenn mentioned a gold frog - a jumper. Was it symbolizing his harrowing experience of parachuting from a damaged jet (under similar conditions to the Washington State jump) in northern Laos in Southeast Asia? Fenn said his treasure chest also contained a Columbian necklace – gold. Could that symbolize the cash found along the Columbia River! *Oh, my Lord*, I thought. Fenn has put all the clues to the hijacking in his book, and the prize is in finding the treasure, which contains, no doubt, his *real* autobiography, one that will surely reveal all the circumstances surrounding the hijacking and confess to being the perpetrator – to being Dan Cooper!

Interpreting the puzzle in the book will solve the unsolved. Locating the treasure will be its reward. I was ready and eager for the mystery to unfold. It had become my passion.

Of course, with the criminal case on hold, but ready to kick into a full prosecution once the perpetrator was found, Fenn could not hazard the mystery being solved during his lifetime. No wonder the treasure was secreted so carefully, and no wonder 1,000 years would be a good span of time before the bronze jars - which also held Fenn's real bio - are found. Yet I could sense Forrest wanted to reveal he was the one who had pulled off the most daring crime in history without being discovered! Hiding in plain sight. Amazing.

But at this stage of the game – Forrest was 86, and the cancer had returned – it would be virtually impossible to try the man in court and, in the event of a conviction, jail an old man who'd been a contributing member of society.

Forrest Fenn. A truly remarkable man. A Renaissance man. I was convinced he was a moral man, a spiritual man, and a man seeking God's forgiveness, "because that's what He does." His spiritual presence was strong; however, Fenn's ego was totally human, and not that of a small human, either. I felt – still feel - that Forrest Fenn wanted recognition for his coup. He had found "a system to beat the system," as pointed out in the hijacker's fourth and final letter.

His wits – and the fruits of both his efforts and his possible crime - had provided for his family and for his community and had allowed him to build a life beyond his flying years he happily shared with all who were interested. Forrest had been generous to artists, had hosted celebrities without losing his humility and sense of place in the universe, and had built not just a name for himself, but had founded an entire cottage industry that would last long after his demise.

What an amazing character! How fun it would be to reread *The Thrill of the Chase* with fresh eyes! I could not wait to begin reading from my new perspective.

Dad loudly cleared his throat. I'd stopped reading entirely, lost in thought, and had been staring off into space with a ridiculous grin on my face.

I told him I felt like a slot machine with apples and oranges and stars spinning wildly in my mind, hooking up with other random fruits and stars, bells ringing, as facts slipped into the slots of his book. But once the spinning fruits halted, forming a row of gleaming stars, everything fell into place and I startled myself, slipping back into reality and the chilly chemo room.

With a quick apology, I picked up where I left off:

". . . the jars are decorated mostly with dragonfly or frog designs. Frogs are kind of my specialty because I like to fabricate long legs and buggy eyes in the soft wax.

"So now I have to wonder about myself doing all those things that others must think are so foolish. Is there any wisdom in trying to cause momentary excitement in some future millennium? I'm not even sure I can define history in those terms. And what if no one ever

discovers my art? Will my time be wasted? I guess the rewards have been in doing it, and the joy of wondering what might happen someday. No matter. It was more fun to run the risk of being foolish than to watch *Dancing with the Stars*."

I sat back. "That's incredible, Dad-- what a novel perspective you've shown me! I can see all sorts of admissions and confirmations in his words. Very interesting. Thank you, Daddy." I blew him a kiss. It was almost time for Nurse Negative Nancy to remove the tube from Dad's neck, bandage the site, and send us on our way home.

If Dad was up to it, we would have an amazing discussion on the long drive, and I could tell him what it felt like in that moment when I had been so entranced and feeling like a human slot machine on the verge of a huge payout!

Chapter 29: Once More Unto The Breach, Dear Friends, Once More

– William Shakespeare, King Henry V

My father was an amazing man. Truthfully - I'm not just saying that because I'm his daughter. He opened my eyes that afternoon and the ride home was phenomenal. We couldn't stop talking. The first hour was filled with laughter and speculation. Then Dad was sick to his stomach. We pulled into a rest stop so he could sit outside for some fresh air, and I purchased some bottled water for him to sip on the road. When we got back in the car, Dad stretched out on the back seat and fell asleep.

I was proud to be his daughter, yet so sad to bear witness to his suffering. But Forrest had been diagnosed with cancer, too, and his father had cancer as well, taking his own life rather than face an end filled with unbearable pain.

I hate cancer. I hate the word. I hate what it does to families, I hate what those afflicted with it have to go through. For doctor and patient, it's always a crapshoot. While all the treatments are toxic or invasive and as potentially lethal as the disease itself, the world is full of people who suffered and lost their hair, their appetites, their pride, and years from their lives sitting, as my father had that very day, with poison slowly dripping into their veins, surrounded by all the precautions associated with a toxic dump site. But a fairly large percentage have successfully emerged from that agony to live long and productive lives, or at least extend their lives to enjoy all this precious life has to offer. I was hoping, with all my heart, that Dad would be one of those miracles of modern medicine.

And so days, weeks, and months passed, each filled with mind-numbing regularity and routine, with time moving inexorably forward in its inimitable way, ticking off the minutes we have left on this planet, one by one. In what spare time I had, I read and reread *The Thrill of The Chase* through the widened lens Dad had provided, making copious additions to my collected information as I reread the clippings and my notes on the D.B. Cooper case, refreshing myself on the few known details, cataloging new information, and searching the FBI files for whatever we might have missed or forgotten. Before I knew it, it was 2013.

Dad had miraculously recovered his strength and developed a more positive attitude as his tumor shrank and his condition stabilized. His medications were so numerous that dosage schedules regulated his day.

My work grew more intense since the firm started construction on a new wing of the Scott & White hospital and a new classroom building at the Texas A&M Health Science Center.

I hired Dad a nursing attendant, Emma Morgan, a petite widow who lived alone in Temple. She was credentialed, had great references and, best of all, she liked Dad. He described Emma as "a challenging chess partner" who kept him thinking whenever they played, but worked on crosswords, crocheted, or watched the news whenever Dad needed a little 'space.' She tracked his medications and his appointments, drove him everywhere and kept his complicated schedule straight. In addition, she cooked – and very well, according to Dad – and ate with him every evening, both keeping him company at the evening meal and making sure he ate well. Plus, Emma did laundry and light cleaning, took care of grocery-buying, and kept the car running. I loved her to death--she was my lifesaver. And D.B. Cooper was, too.

I continuously had to remind myself when wondering why anyone in their right mind would have undertaken the terrible risks the mystery skyjacker had for a mere $200,000, that $200,000, in 1971 was the current equivalent of $1,052,000 in 2012 dollars.

What a testament to the ravages of inflation!

I paged through the FBI files, which weren't any better than the information we compiled in our scrapbooks - except their files contained news clippings Dad and I had no access to. It was getting late, but I was resolute. Each rereading of *The Thrill of the Chase* continued to offer still more clues that made no sense until removed from their *Thrill* context and compared directly with our documented details of The Search in our scrapbooks. Fenn was a storyteller, all right! And a man who loved puzzles.

Determined, I perused the FBI website that afternoon, pushing myself forward, page by page, reviewing the seemingly hundreds of thousands of articles and reports that flooded the FBI and news outlets in the days immediately following the Thanksgiving Eve, 1971 skyjacking of Northwest Orient Flight 305.

I was starting to nod off from boredom, but kept pushing to absorb one more page, one more page.

Then I found some new information. Well, new to me, at least. The article had been printed in the *Los Angeles Times* a few days following the incident. I read the article and made copious notes. This was surely something Dad would be interested in.

The incident reported by the L.A. *Times* occurred at a "crude airstrip" located about ten miles from Woodland, Washington, just after 8:00 p.m. on November 24, 1971, the evening of the hijacking. A mysterious light plane had "swept in out of the stormy night," according to eyewitnesses, circled the field, then landed amid the wind and rain on the small, obscure landing strip located near a wooded ravine and reported in the news item as being a "bumpy and unlighted hilltop airstrip."

Despite the time and the weather - or perhaps because of it - nearby residents took note of the activity that took place around the same time the Northwest Orient hijacker leapt from the 727.

Due to the extreme weather and "uncertainty as to where to look until flight information was put through computers, the search for the hijacker was not begun on a full scale until 36 hours after the hijacking," the article read. I had forgotten the weather had been so terrible and holiday staffing had been so light authorities were delayed over a day and a half in beginning their search efforts.

Evidently, deer hunters used the remote landing field during hunting season, and other light planes frequently landed on the crude strip fringed by foot-high weeds, but they seldom used the field at night, and never during a driving storm. Nobody in their right mind was flying a light aircraft that night!

Mr. and Mrs. Neiger lived down the road from airfield and its owners, the McClellan family. They noticed a light plane circled the airstrip for much of the afternoon on the 24th. The couple went out and returned around 8:00 p.m., when they suddenly saw the plane fly low over the field with its landing lights on. Just when they thought it was going to land, the plane nosed up and gained altitude once again, leaving them puzzled.

The initial search area indicated by the flight plan and the immediately available flight data from the Northwest Orient 727 covered approximately 150 square miles north and south of the Lewis River. Computer data pinpointed the jump point and anticipated the hijacker's descent would take him about two miles south of the river, around two miles north of the McClellan landing strip. The Clarke County Sherriff commented the area north of the river could only be scanned by air, due to its densely forested and unpredictable terrain. He remarked, "If he landed there, he's in trouble."

A teenager hunting in that thickly wooded area with his father on the 13th of November had become separated from his dad while hunting and had not yet been found by the time the Northwest hijacking occurred on the 24th.

South of the Lewis River, where the McClellan's landing strip was, the terrain found its level at a more hospitable elevation, with fewer forested areas. Land was cleared for several small farms by 1971, and small towns established nearby were growing slowly as people began to settle the rural area.

Those individuals who observed the light plane's unusual appearance and its landing attempt were questioned at length by the FBI, who refused comment on the interviews or on the conclusions reached. Could the sky pirate have had accomplices who were to pick him up by car or truck, and then fly him out of the area? Such theories were supported by a second suspicious report that "someone in a car apparently rendezvoused with a pilot at another nearby air strip the night before the hijacking and went for what could have been a pre-hijack scouting flight, purposely undertaken in equally bad weather (as was forecast for the night of the 24th)."

Mr. and Mrs. Robert M. McClellan, Jr. lived at the south end of the strip. They had owned a private plane at one time, but it was sold long before the hijacking. Robert McClellan's parents resided in an older home on the family property, but it was situated some distance from the airfield itself.

A second article reported that a 100-man posse was raised from the local populace, aided by ten patrol cars and six helicopters, and fanned out the previous day to hunt along a five-mile span that extended through the mountain foothills for any trace of parachute canopies or any other objects or evidence that might be related to the hijacking. After eight hours of searching in misty rains under low clouds, the posse's efforts yielded no results. On December 1st, temporary headquarters of the search was closed-- the end of six fruitless days of scouring the fifteen-mile area around Woodland. Despite strong evidence of collusion with more than one accomplice, interest in this essentially important pairing of events was nothing but a dead lead according to the FBI. Just another bit of forgotten information.

Really? It seemed obvious to me these reported events were practice runs performed by the accomplices of the hijacking. Why did they fail to pursue the matter?

Well, I thought, with over sixty volumes of such exciting "tidbits" and fruitless leads in the case, the FBI agents who dedicated nearly a decade of their careers chasing after D.B. Cooper could certainly not be faulted for leaving a few loose ends flapping in the wind.

"Collusion: A noun denoting secret or illegal cooperation or conspiracy, especially in order to cheat or deceive others."

I would have to pinpoint the exact phrases Fenn used in *The Thrill of the Chase* that made me certain that Forrest's long-time sidekicks, Donnie and Fenn's older brother, Skippy, had been involved in aiding with the heist at some level. Growing up, the boys had been "The Three Musketeers," vowing "One for all and all for one." I was certain the two of them had facilitated Forrest's escape and helped engineer his disappearance following the Thanksgiving Eve hijacking, and the posting of subsequent letters taunting the investigators, posting letters from separate locations which, coincidentally, were from places related to the three of them.

Yup, I smelled a whole lot of colluding between those three.

In 2013, Forrest Fenn published yet another autobiography, *Too Far to Walk*, which I ordered on first publishing and promptly devoured in an afternoon. It was written in the same breezy, enchanting style, centered on the same cast of characters, with a few additions from later years when Forrest Fenn lived in Santa Fe.

His new book built on the themes and stories of *The Thrill of the Chase* but was a little more philosophical and introduced Forrest's impressions of the many celebrities and interesting characters who had peopled his life. Where Forrest had been suffering from what he thought was a death sentence when he wrote *The Thrill of the Chase*, this new book started by recounting his miraculous recovery from cancer, and the impetus for hiding his treasure. But he also related other stories that reinforced my certitude he was a man with a confession to make.

Forrest packed tremendous amounts of information within the shadows of his words. His hesitations and the spaces between the lines spoke to me as well as Forrest recounted his story in personalized hieroglyphics spun of images and imagination. His "catch-me-if-you-can" analogies and cryptic parables mixed and matched "facts" and tall tales, while maintaining that "nonfiction writers have to be right only 85% of the time." That left 15% of falsehoods to be ferreted out.

In his flippant approach to a life well lived, filled with derring-do and many valiant accomplishments, small satisfactions and huge triumphs, Forrest Fenn has, indeed, created "a system to beat the system." His breeziness of delivery often masks the unfathomable truths by which he has lived, and the secrets he has held close for decades. But those secrets had him bursting at the seams with an urge for the world to really know, and long remember, Forrest Fenn.

Forrest's regrets at growing old are minimized by this impressive man's fear of being forgotten.

In the three years since writing *The Thrill of the Chase*, Fenn had rested solidly in the happy knowledge that he beat cancer. He no longer had any trace of the disease, which heartened me in the face of Dad's apparent improvement and, possibly, his complete recovery from the cancer. However, even Fenn was forced to admit a fear of its stealthy return in this latest book.

By 2013, when *Too Far to Walk* was printed by One Horse Land and Cattle Co., Forrest's first autobiographical book and its poem providing the fabled nine clues to his hidden treasure made him an overnight celebrity, netting him multiple television and radio appearances, book sales, and a dozen fan clubs, a score of chatrooms, and thousands of treasure hunts and expeditions into the mountains north of Santa Fe and in the states of Idaho, Montana, Wyoming and New Mexico by ardent followers afflicted by both gold fever and their own thrill of the chase. Fans and treasure hunters congregated electronically in multiple chat rooms, forging alliances, exchanging tips and hints, and striking up friendships founded on common interests-- the hunt for Fenn's treasure, and the exploits of the man himself, as well as an appreciation of the stunning beauty of the Northwest where Forrest and his family passed so many happy summers.

With every book I owned - and I owned them all now - I noticed he had included an email address on the cover page to reach him, but was unaware how heartily he encouraged contacts and welcomed visits and inquiries. An apparent night owl - or a disturbed sleeper - Forrest often read and answered correspondence late into the night, as I learned from posted comments. More than a few people made pilgrimages to the "Shrine of Fenn" in Santa Fe. Others went there simply to see the sights and satisfy a curiosity or interest about the region, as well as the man. Forrest Fenn had become the star of his own life story. Well, what he *chose* to reveal of his own life story.

As Forrest maintained, "It doesn't matter who you are, it only matters who they think you are." No truer words were ever voiced or printed.

His new book just added more fuel to the fire of my suspicion, however. I had learned to read his words as Dad had taught me, as a puzzle or riddle to be solved. Since, as Forrest maintained, a writer needed to be only 85% factual, I read between the lines, putting disjointed stories together and tying much of what he wrote to my simultaneous investigation into D.B. Cooper. My fat butterfly notebook had doubled in size, with no pages left on which to scribble notes, and I was halfway through a second, flowered notebook, with pertinent pages affixed with small plastic tags for easy reference.

I had become a Fenn-o-holic, and now followed several chatrooms where searchers for his hidden treasure expounded their theories and shared tidbits and details of their contacts with Forrest Fenn. I was building my own "profile" of the man. I discovered him on YouTube and waded knee deep in so much information that weekends found me on the computer - two, actually, a desktop and a laptop - so that I could do comparative research with my trusty notebook and pen at my side.   I ordered food delivered in, rather than cooking.

It was Friday evening. The Chinese Szechuan dinner delivered to my door had been outstanding and I had enough General Tsao's chicken to make another meal when crisped a bit in the toaster-oven the following day.

Where was I? Oh, yes, collusion.

In his first book, Forrest offered several peeks into the workings of the trio: Skippy Fenn, his older brother, their mutual friend from West Yellowstone, Donnie Joe Heath, and Forrest himself. They had known each other during their early youth in the 1940s, when the Fenn family spent long, lazy days fishing for dinner in Montana and Wyoming where Marvin Fenn, Forrest's father (a principal at a middle school in Temple), owned a small cabin. Every summer, Marvin would pack his family into the car and make the long road trip to West Yellowstone, a sport fisherman's paradise.

Donnie Joe's grandmother had been the postmistress of the tiny town, which, in those years, had a population of under 1,200 souls – and even fewer in the winter.

Forrest's book and his blog recounted a few tales that illustrated the strength of the boys' ties and their loyalty to one another. As many of us have experienced, deep friendships made in early adolescence last a lifetime. I would have to locate the incidents stuck in my mind as I read stories in his books that illustrated this intense loyalty, but that would come later. The new book, too, was full of stories and elaborations that deserved my attention, but not just now.

At the moment, I was intrigued by what the news article about the post-heist activity at the two Washington airstrips. To me, the meaning of this dated news story was evident. And, although the FBI had not been able to immediately find any additional clues to follow as a result of their brief witness interviews, the 41-year-old report just reinforced what I was instinctively certain of: Forrest Fenn had not been alone in pulling off his skyjacking caper.

It was unfortunate the FBI didn't doggedly pursue the mysterious sightings and follow up on the secretive encounters that reportedly occurred on those remote airstrips within the projected drop zone immediately prior to and following the hijacker's extortion and aerial escape.

I located a flight map of the area over which the hijacked 727 had flown. The Woodland airstrip was not far from the flight path often referred to in D.B. Cooper articles as "Victor 23." Had the FBI not been so pressed for time, the information might have led to Forrest's two accomplices, and to the perpetrator himself.

I mean, pilots and planes have registrations, and private airports are small enough that activity around hangars is easily observed. Surely, *someone* had seen who was flying in and out over the Thanksgiving holiday. There is almost always someone around who keeps an eye on that sort of thing, if only for security reasons. When documentation is unavailable, interviews can trigger recall. Cars have license plates, too.

I was certain that the FBI was receiving hundreds of "tips" a day during those first few weeks, and simply could not spend time pursuing what they considered non-productive leads. However, it was possible that others, too, had seen the same plane repeatedly circling the two isolated airstrips and wondered why. Aerial activity at an airstrip with such intermittent traffic would surely find someone noting it. With more extensive questioning, some individual might be found who could provide information to identify the small private aircraft.

Admittedly, the weather was a huge factor in both the 36-hour delay in starting a search and pursuing the investigation.

But the flight path of Northwest Orient Flight 305 was so close to those airstrips that they were on the flight maps of the projected path of the 727 that night. And the airstrip, ten miles south of the town, was close to both I-5 and State

Route 503, which can be accessed from Vancouver and runs through to Battle Ground, where it crosses the East Fork of the Lewis River, passes Lewisville Park, then narrows into two lanes. From there, the road winds along a scenic route that twists and turns in a northeasterly direction into a heavily forested region of the Cascade foothills, on its way toward Yale. There, it crosses the historical, 532-foot-long Yale Bridge, and continues until it forks at the spur into Cougar, intersecting with the Lewis River Road. It then runs southwest parallel to the Lewis River, passing through the small communities of Yale and Ariel on its way to the I-5 Woodland interchange at the confluence of the Lewis and Columbia rivers.

At the S.R. 503 spur, a driver or cyclist can opt to follow the west branch, traveling toward Woodland, or continue along to its end, about ten miles east of the small town of Cougar, where it becomes NFD 90 - a National Forest road that leads into Mt. St. Helens National Forest. Stables in Cougar have long served those tourists who wish to explore the forested wilderness on horseback.

The distance from Battle Ground to Woodland on 503 is 54.11 miles through forests and the agricultural communities of rural Clark County.

The branch that turns west to Woodland parallels and runs just north of the Lewis River as it flows downstream toward the juncture of 503 and Interstate 5, which passes through the town on its way north. While SR503 is little traveled past the city of Battle Ground after sunset, during daylight hours it has long been a favorite of motorcyclists and drivers out for a scenic cruise. It is not a fast road; the shoulders are virtually non-existent, and the many sharp curves are semi-banked, with signs recommending a speed of no more than 25 miles per hour. As 503 winds through wooded areas interspersed with farmland that hosts the occasional and distant structure, there are reportedly sudden crests that offer a glimpse of what is left of the famous volcano, Mt. St. Helens.

Travel directives caution drivers to heed the "no gas beyond" signs, or risk being stranded. There is no opportunity to refuel and little chance to purchase food or beverages along the route. Only a few spots beyond Cougar offer respite from the road or a pot to slake a thirst or fill a hungry belly. The road heading west toward Woodland puts the setting sun directly in a driver's eyes, making navigation even more hazardous, as woodland creatures abound and frequently do not make it across the road in time to avoid oncoming traffic. Both legs of 503 are minimally traveled and are pitch dark after the sun sets.

According to a 2011 Washington State Department of Transportation highway survey that measured the daily traffic volume, the busiest portion of the 503 was around Orchards, before Battle Ground, which recorded 34,000 vehicles daily. The least busy section of the 503 was the western terminus, just east of Yale, which saw only 720 vehicles daily, mostly during daytime hours. Dial these stats back to 1971, and this was one deserted paved road, the perfect place to pick up someone evading the law, then whisk them away to the nearest isolated airfield, to then be flown to safety by a second accomplice, who might or might not be licensed, but who was capable of piloting a light private plane.

The tale Forrest tells of his brother, Skippy, in *The Thrill of the Chase* immediately came to mind. Forrest's penchant for hiding stories within stories, only surreptitiously revealing vital information, had me referring once again to the story of Skippy's adventure on Hebgen Lake, which he had called his family to witness.

Skippy - although untrained - had competently piloted a pontoon plane and landed it safely on the lake, despite his lack of a flying license or completion of flight lessons. Forrest's older brother had disappeared into neighboring Idaho for a period of time before appearing out of the blue to show off his pilot skills.

Subtle indications in Fenn's story led one to understand that Skippy had most likely "borrowed" the aircraft from its rightful owner, and, unable to fly it back due to the thin air at that altitude - around 6600 feet above sea level - could not provide the necessary "lift" to get the plane back in the air again, Skippy removed the wings, loaded it all into a truck and drove it back to Idaho.

There was no doubt in my mind Skippy was flying the plane seen circling and then again at an airstrip during a rendezvous with a car driven by another - no doubt Donnie – the two practicing the pickup and transfer to occur the next night-- November 24, 1971. And it was Skippy, I was certain, who buzzed the McClellan airfield the night of the hijacking, taking off once again when the vehicle and its passengers missed the timing for the exchange.

Tom Kaye's CitizenSleuths website was a great resource.

The instructional placard for the previously unopened aft stairway was later found on the ground within the eight-mile width of the Victor 23 airway. The Cooper Research Team (CRT) found no reason to give credence to the several theories of deviation in the flight path, whether created to account, somehow, for the bundles of $20s found on Tena (Tina) Bar, or the supposition of Captain Scott that the wind direction originally factored into landing zone calculations for Cooper were off by as much as 80 degrees, and in an easterly direction.

The CRT's final conclusion relied heavily on flight transcripts, which gave the aircraft's specific, timed locations for Flight 305 recorded on Distance Measuring Equipment (DME) and reliably determined precise data, as measured by radio beams. Further, transcripts gave the 727's altitude as 10,000 feet, with a speed that hovered around approximately 165 knots (195 mph). Flaps were at 15 degrees, as the hijacker had specified.

The DME positions, the CRT reported, "…were north and south of the jump point, allowing speed and distance calculations across the important jump zone." Thus, an elementary calculation utilized the time necessary for the craft to move over the distance between the two DME points to arrive at the airspeed. If the known and calculated airspeeds were a match, another, more sophisticated test was used to further verify that initial result.

The family that found the placard on their hunting ground had supplied the GPS coordinates of their find after turning in the evidence to investigators, and, since they owned the land, the coordinates they provided were deemed reliable. In addition, the civilian research group had interviewed the original air traffic controller responsible for the Northwest Airlines flight as it traveled north from Portland. He was certain Flight 305 had not veered from the Victor 23 flight path for as long as it had appeared on radar in the Portland airspace.

These findings successfully debunked "the Washougal theory," in that, when crosschecked against the airliner's prescribed flight path, all calculations and recorded flight data demonstrated there was neither the necessary speed nor the time for heavy winds to have blown the aircraft to the east of Victor 23 by as much as ten miles, and still allow it to return to the flight path in time to be noted by the DME position at the southernmost point of the Portland airspace. The Victor 23 flight path, as noted by the FBI, took the plane over or near the towns of Ariel, Pigeon Springs, *Toledo* (another possible hint Fenn dropped), Highland, Battle Ground, and Vancouver. Tena Bar and the Washougal River and its river basin were not within or even near the eight-mile span of the V23 flight path. Furthermore, the Victor 23 flight path offered no possibility of overflight of the Tena Bar and Washougal River area.

As to the spot on the family hunting ground where the aft stair placard had been found, according to GPS coordinates, it was located near a place called Toutle, twenty miles north of the presumed jump zone near Ariel, Washington, and directly under the V23 flight path.

The online CRT report explained, "Giving the placard a free fall time of nine minutes and a south west cross wind of 18 knots, then the plane would have to be 2.68 miles from where the placard was recovered and 2.6 miles west of V23. This distance is well within the official 8-mile width for the Victor airway and is 4 miles east of the theoretical Tena Bar flight path. This data places a constraint on the planes (sic) position approximately six minutes before the jump and suggests Flight 305 was on the original FBI flight path."

The Cooper Research Team report concluded that:

"Understanding the flight path is a critical first step in determining the history of the money and how it became buried on the Tena Bar. The various lines of evidence all point to the original FBI flight path as accurate and do not support the Tena bar overflight of Washougal Washdown Theory. This research finds no reason to believe the original FBI flight path or the jump zone was in error. This does, however, create a large obstacle in explaining how the money came to rest on the Tena Bar. The flight plan information along with other evidence presented here, provides no basis for naturally transporting the bundles to Tena Bar via the Columbia River. This leaves only a mechanical or human explanation. The human explanation has historically been ruled out due to the belief that Cooper died in the jump. After 40 years, no body or other evidence has ever been found, suggesting that the idea Cooper died in the jump may be in error. A mechanical explanation has additional obstacles, so the processes that transported the money out of the woods and then twenty miles to the sand bar remain a mystery."

Interestingly, the presence of the money on Tena Bar belied the prevalent FBI conclusion that the hijacker had been killed in the drop. Their conclusion that only human intervention could account for the money being present on Tena Bar supported my personal suspicion the cash was placed there intentionally in order to misdirect investigators from the actual site of the hijacker's parachute landing.

The FBI and public supposition were that no one in their right mind would jump from a plane into the driving rain and high winds of a black and stormy night without visibility of the terrain below and in sub-zero weather, wearing just a business suit, trench coat, loafers, and socks, donning a difficult parachute to maneuver and guaranteed to jolt the fillings from a skydiver's teeth once the canopy deployed to slow his pace of descent. Hence, to a civilian mentality, the result would be certain death.

Civilians, however, have little concept of the rigors of war, and few who return rarely enjoy discussing their most harrowing experiences - or, if they do, the experiences are sanitized for the retelling. Only in the post-Vietnam decades have films dealing with war experiences approached the reality. All wars bring out the very best and the very worst of human nature and behavior, from the greatest valor and self-sacrifice to the cruelest and ugliest imaginable actions, and the greediest and most self-serving of motives.

The Internet was, by that time, an amazing resource with computerized military records open to historians. Someone had likely worked up the stats for ejecting from an airplane under the worst of conditions. A Google search found several statistical data sources. Further, I had Forrest's experience to rely on, bits of which were told in his two autobiographical books, affectionately referred to by Forrest Fenn aficionados as TTotC (*The Thrill of the Chase*) and TFTW (*Too Far to Walk*). But his stories were more anecdotal than detailed. Many specifics were left out, and those were the things I needed to know to continue my profiling of the man.

I found a website where a Fenn groupie who had become a Fenn friend, Dal Neitzel, had filmed three videos interviewing Forrest about his Air Force experiences, and listened several times to Forrest's more detailed and specific explanation of the events that transpired when he was shot down over Laos and had to eject from his heavily armed F-100 fighter jet. Delivered in a sober and matter-of-fact manner, Forrest's verbal descriptions were an eye opener. My admiration of him increased…to a point.

The similarities between what he had experienced and survived when violently jettisoned from his downed F-100 into a cold and wet jungle while facing one equipment failure after another, were *so* similar to the conditions Cooper likely experienced upon parachuting from the 727 after his audacious act of air piracy. It was uncanny.

After surveying his surroundings in the northern Laos jungle, Forrest toyed with the idea of attempting to walk out of his predicament. He'd have to navigate through dense growth crawling with Pathet Lao soldiers and rely solely on his hunting knife and a compass. The feat would test his survival knowledge as a graduate of the Air Force Jungle

Survival School at Clark AFB, Subic Bay, Philippines. Fenn frequently refers to it as "Snake School" in his books.

All Vietnam pilots in the 1960s were required to go through an intensive three-day course of jungle environmental training. Known to be the toughest survival school in the world, instructors at the Cubi Point U.S. Naval Station were Philippine aboriginal natives, Negretos, who carried big bolo knives with them everywhere. The natives resided in the jungle and were said to have been among those who helped the U.S. military in WWII.

The training involved both classroom instruction and daytime and overnight "field trips" into the jungles of Luzon. They learned navigational skills, how to build a shelter, how to make soap from tree bark, and other necessary skills. They were shown where to find edible plants and grubs and shown the poisonous ones as well. Snakes, bugs, worms, monkey meat were on the menu, along with the delicious hearts of palm one can now buy in any grocery store.

Fortunately for his family, Forrest fought the temptation to challenge the jungle, and instead called in his location. He was home for Christmas. Good man. He made the three ladies in his small family very happy that year.

But Forrest, it seemed - as well as his older brother, Skippy, and their West Yellowstone buddy, Donnie Joe - had a penchant for tempting fate. I felt strongly that Fenn's certitude he could repeat the experience and survive it lay at the heart of the greatest caper of his life.

My personal theory was the hijacking operation had been perfectly timed and rehearsed, and the drop zone selected with a precision made possible by the flight speed and distance calculations Fenn was familiar with, and which did not require ground visibility if planned in advance, as it obviously had been.

The exact timing of the jump, however, was thwarted by the three minutes of bounce-back of the aft stairway, when it slammed shut at least once. That movement had been felt by the 727's pilots after the first attempt to lower the aft stair was noted at 8:11 p.m., which was when the jump presumably should have occurred.

The approximate three-minute delay between 8:11, when Cooper should have jumped, and 8:14 p.m., when the Cooper Research Team ultimately determined the hijacker leapt from the stairway into the night were ultimately fortuitous for the hijacker. The jet airliner was flying at 195 mph, or 3.25 miles per minute. The three-minute jump delay moved the landing zone approximately 9.75 miles south of the originally planned drop zone in the wooded foothills of the Cascade Mountains, which began near Woodland--a potentially perilous area for a night jump.

The resultant landing zone in the vicinity of Battle Ground was nearly ten miles south of the FBI's 1971 estimate. Battle Ground was a small town with a population well under 9000 in those days, and in an area of flat farmland, rather than heavy woods or mountain wilderness. Cooper would have been within ten miles of Vancouver, with its bus and train stations--well within walking distance for a healthy and fit man in his mid-40s.

Losing his shoes in the jump - his loafers - was a probability, but only a minor issue. A few witnesses observed Cooper wearing long johns - long underwear - beneath his suit. Silk "long johns" were both compact and warm when insulation was required, yet light enough to be relatively inconspicuous beneath clothing. Maybe one of the accomplices stashed a pair of sturdy boots near the predicted landing zone. If that was the case, the loafers may have been part of his "disguise."

But best of all for the legendary criminal, the delayed jump took him far south of the area the FBI presumed he landed. How lucky could one man get?

Some are triply blessed, I thought. As more connections clicked between Fenn and Cooper, I could have turned cartwheels, had I still been of the age and physical agility I possessed when I cheered at Temple High.

The Citizen Sleuths concluded the hijacker had survived the jump. And that confirmed the real suspect in the

Thanksgiving Eve hijacking remained undetected and was very likely still alive.

Citizen Sleuths had also published their final conclusions regarding their analysis of the clip-on tie, which I found quite interesting in light of Fenn's admission at the end of *The Thrill of the Chase* that he had run his own art foundry immediately preceding and for a short while after he retired from the Air Force on September 6, 1970.

I got the feeling Forrest was looking for a post-service occupation to supplement his rather meager retirement pay. Forrest had revealed he not only owned the metal foundry, but he also experimented with the composition of the metals and with the processes to achieve certain results.

Carefully perusing the CitizenSleuth.com website, I copied their facts and conclusions in my trusty notebook:

<u>Fact</u>: Microscopic metallic titanium pieces were found on Cooper's tie.

<u>Fact</u>: In 1971, titanium was a strategic metal primarily used in military aircraft, some civilian aircraft and highly corrosive industrial plants. Metallic titanium was not found in consumer products at the time.

<u>Fact</u>: All titanium used in aircraft is alloyed and the Cooper material was pure titanium.

Interpretation: Due to the lack of alloyed titanium, Cooper did not work in the aircraft industry.

<u>Fact</u>: Spiral chips of aluminum and other exotic metals like bismuth and stainless steel were found on the tie.

<u>Fact</u>: Spiral aluminum chips of the type found on the tie are made in metal fabrication plants that use lathes and drill presses.

Interpretation: Cooper worked in or had access to, an exotic metal fabrication facility that contained titanium, aluminum, and other specialty metals.

<u>Fact</u>: In 1971, only engineers and managers in fabrication plants wore ties to work. Interpretation: Cooper was either a manager or an engineer. Furthermore, interpretation of Cooper's knowledge of the workings of the airplane, the use of the parachute,

and his construction of a "bomb" all suggest that he may have been an engineer.

My notes of the CRT online report continued, "The process of making titanium must be understood in order to place the finding of pure titanium into context. First a beach sand, rich in titanium like Rutile, is processed in a vacuum furnace to separate it from the contaminants. Next, either sodium or magnesium is added to bind with the chlorine, leaving behind the pure titanium metal which is then called 'titanium sponge.' The titanium sponge plant is the first step in manufacturing this metal. From there the sponge is sent to a second plant that melts the titanium down again, adds alloying material as required, then forms the titanium into useful shapes like sheets and bars. From there it is sent to a third plant for metal fabrication to be machined, cut, and welded into parts for aircraft, etc."

The titanium on the tie was unalloyed.

The government contract for the first American supersonic transport (SST) project was awarded to Boeing, and development took place at the Seattle, Washington Boeing facilities. However, the lack of a distinct market for the 250-300 passenger aircraft with cruising speeds approaching Mach 3, making it faster and larger than the Concorde, plus rising costs and the consistently negative press articles that focused on sonic booms and potential effects to the ozone layer, caused the program to be scrapped in 1971. The two prototypes were never completed.

According to the Cooper Research Team, the SST was to be constructed of titanium, and the end of the project in 1971 literally "threw the titanium industry into a turmoil. There were large numbers of layoffs due to the cancellation, so it is still conceivable Cooper may have in some way been affected by the shut down."

I suddenly recalled a seemingly pertinent bit of information from a Fenn treasure chatroom that concerned Skippy but didn't seem important at the time. Flipping through my notebook pages, I found it. Someone in one of the chat rooms - Lord, I wish I had written it down! - Someone had mentioned Skippy might have worked at Boeing. Apparently, a Montana telephone book had a listing for him, and it was believed he was possibly an engineer at Boeing in Seattle. I would have to add this detail to my "follow up" list. I hated that I had neglected to write down the source! Darn!

Sodium and chlorine were prevalent on the tie, according to the CRT report, but not magnesium, a necessary component of the upstream production process utilized by titanium sponge plants to create their product. This fueled an extensive examination by the Citizen Sleuths of the companies producing titanium sponges and the specific processes they employed. The CRT managed to acquire original samples of most titanium sponge produced in the 1970s for the study, but no identifiable titanium sponge particles were found on the tie. Furthermore, the tie bore no trace of the sands from which titanium is extracted for processing, and the absence of magnesium continued to be problematic.

The CRT found an abundance of match residue in the second sampling of the tie particles, and it was established that titanium, sodium, and chlorine signatures were present in the flammable heads of everyday matches. Witnesses reported Cooper had been a chain smoker and left the butts of at least eight Raleigh cigarettes in the seat ash trays.

Match residue! Match residue? Really!

I nearly stopped reading at that point, considering the matter closed with the very disappointing discovery of the vital components' presence in everyday match heads, a finding bolstered by firsthand evidence that Cooper was a heavy smoker,

Then, however, the CRT report took a sudden twist that had me glued to the remaining paragraphs of the page. "The titanium and stainless particle is quite informative. This particle requires several factors to be in place for its production. The first requirement is that there is pure titanium available. Second, a 400 series stainless steel has to be in intimate association with the titanium, third, there has to be some kind of device or machinery involved, capable of producing high-compressive forces that would abrade and smear the two metals together as shown [There was an online illustration here of the titanium piece with embedded stainless steel particle at top (Length = .43 mm)]. The most likely place these factors would come together and produce this type of particle, would be in a fabrication facility using titanium.

Figure 25 Photo courtesy of CitizenSleuths

"Two spiral aluminum chips were extracted from the tie (Fig. 6). These spirals were very small at about 1/16" in length and were perfectly formed by a rotational cutting process like a lathe or drill bit. EDS analysis determined that the predominant ally was magnesium, showing the closest match to either the 500 series cast, or 5000 series wrought aluminum. This series is not found in either of the labs used to analyze these particles. 5000 series is known for its high corrosion resistance and good weldability. This type of particle is again typically found in a metal fabrication shop, consistent with other findings."

In addition, on the sticky stubs and vacuum filters used to collect the various particles, many particles of brass were also found. These particles were not included in the analysis because brass screw plugs were used to seal sample filters. All in all, the evidence indicated to the CRT that the best occupational fit for the hijacker was someone who came from or regularly visited a machine shop or metal fabrication facility.

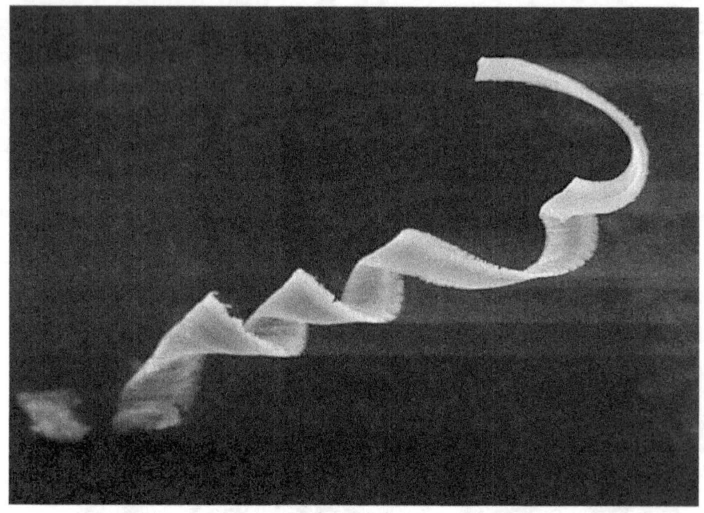

Figure 26 Spiral titanium. Courtesy of CitizenSleuths.

At Christmas time, 2014, I came across a thesis by Martin Andrade, Jr., MBA, entitled "Survival Probability Analysis of the D.B. Cooper Hijacking Using Historical Parachuting Data." *Thank you for the amazing Christmas gift, Mr. Andrade!*

Andrade explained that among skydivers in the United States, there is a single fatality for every 150,000 jumps, primarily due to canopy failures, and that this remarkable safety record was the result of both diligence and regulation. But the Northwest Orient hijacker had faced many more challenges: jumping at night into high winds, sub-zero temperatures, low visibility, driving rain, no functional reserve parachute and 21 pounds of cash contained in a bulky canvas parachute bag affixed with knotted parachute cords to his parachute harness, or - worst case - to his waist.

Despite an unknown degree of training, he'd chosen and donned the heavily modified NB6 Navy-issue pilot parachute which lacked the necessary D-rings to properly affix the canvas bag to the harness of the selected parachute. Its choice, rather than the newer and more comfortable "sport" skydiving parachute, denoted a military background, and the probability of only the most basic parachute training. Sifting through accurate statistical data for RAF pilots, the Cooper Research Team learned that battlefield jumps had a whopping baseline survivability rate of 97.4%, with RAF after-action reports revealing that 90% of ejecting pilots had been able to pull their ripcords. Extrapolation of existing figures for night combat missions and aircraft lost resulted in an approximate range for surviving nighttime combat jumps in WWII of between 73-93%, and a similar success rate for daytime jumps in battle.

The probability of the hijacker surviving a nighttime jump under the conditions Cooper faced were far better than the FBI and sport parachutists surmised.

Concluding my investigation of the FBI files and the CitizenSleuth.com website. I had a few minutes left before my bed called me to sleep. In a fit of a frenzy, and just for fun, I Googled D.B. Cooper on YouTube and found the original CBS report on his Thanksgiving Eve act of sky piracy, as reported by Walter Cronkite. Suddenly, as I watched the 36 passengers disembark at the Seattle Airport, my eyes widened, and my jaw dropped. I kept replaying the video, again and again. *That looks like Skippy!*

The eleventh man to disembark was of average height with dark hair and distinctive eyebrows. He wore a dark cowboy hat pulled low on his forehead. What had caught my notice, however, was the man's perceived effort to avoid looking directly into the camera for a brief moment, as the other passengers had when approaching the KIRO television news camera, each providing a full-face shot before following the walkway as it angled sharply to the right.

The dark-haired man in the cowboy hat seemed to be making a conscious effort to keep his head lowered and turned to the right as though he were searching for something in the distance. His features were distinctly reminiscent of Skippy-- to the position of his ears and the narrow space between his dark eyes and eyebrows.

A month earlier I had studied a photo of William Marvin "Skippy" Fenn, Jr. on a website. The photo featured a mischievous face of a dark-haired young man in a light-colored jacket, a ball cap on his head, and what looked to be a six-inch live fish dangling from his mouth, its tail caught in his teeth. The rippled water behind him implied he was on a dock or in a small boat, and probably fishing. Skippy's photograph was a very casual close-up snapshot that captured his features, which were coarser and thicker than Forrest's. His silly grin lit up his face and drew attention to his dark eyes and distinctive, curved dark brows. Skippy appeared to be goofing around with the photographer. The photograph was attached as part of a memorial note on findagrave.com. Skippy was buried in Hillcrest cemetery, Temple, Texas, just as Forrest had alluded to in *The Thrill of The Chase*. I found another photo of Skippy on the chapter 7 title page of *Too Far to Walk*. Again, I noted the distinctive dark good looks.

I had no doubt he was passenger number eleven disembarking from the hijacked flight on Thanksgiving Eve, 1971. He had accompanied his brother on the fated flight.

My first impression of Skippy was that he was a prankster, restless and unconventional, probably rather immature emotionally, but clever and fun-loving. He appeared about seventeen, maybe eighteen, in the photos.

The information offered as his obituary was taken directly from Fenn's brief comments regarding his brother's death in his book, *The Thrill of The Chase*. Oddly, the memorial notice named Skippy's children as survivors, as well as his and Forrest's sister, June. Skippy's parents were mentioned as being deceased, but the site omitted any reference to Skippy's brother, Forrest Fenn.

Skippy allegedly died at age 50 in what was purported to be a scuba diving accident in Cozumel, Quintana Roo, Mexico. He was found standing upright in 90 feet of water, with his weights on. His father and Forrest had, together, buried Skippy's cremated ashes one night at Hillcrest, in the same grave as his mother, Lillie Gay Simpson Fenn. The ashes were still in the plastic bag provided by the crematorium. The strange obituary falsely claimed his ashes had been scattered in Colorado, however, going directly against Forrest's words in his book.

I ran the ABC news clip at least five or six times, side by side with the photo of Skippy Fenn. Doing so left no question in my mind. I was convinced the young, dark haired man in the cowboy hat was none other than William Marvin Fenn, Jr., a/k/a "Skippy." But what was he doing on the same flight his younger brother had just commandeered?

Was he on Flight 305 to ensure that all went well? Or was the plan to leave essentials under the seat he'd occupied while flying to Seattle for Fenn to retrieve once the plane was empty and the stewardess, Miss Mucklow, had been sent forward to the cockpit to remain with the pilots until landing in Reno? Had Skippy stowed a small duffle bag with a helmet and shoes under the seat in front of his own, or in an overhead compartment, and left it behind on the plane so that Forrest could retrieve it and would have appropriate shoes and a helmet for the jump?

I ran the YouTube video one more time. Yup, no doubt about it, it was Skippy Fenn.

Smiling smugly, I yawned and stretched. It had been an extraordinary day's work and did much to support the theory Dad and I had been nursing for years. Forrest was indeed D.B. Cooper. He had survived…and thrived.

While I still had questions, they would have to wait for another day. I was exhausted, but exhilarated. I slept very, very well.

Chapter 32: Shall We Dance? The Unspoken Invitation

I can't recall what prompted me to email Forrest Fenn. The invitation had been on the flyleaf of his books for years, where Forrest's email address was prominently displayed in a manner that invited contact. His artist's email was similarly displayed, but I'd always discounted that as a marketing ploy.

I had mixed emotions as I typed in his online address, ffenn@earthlink.net. My boldness was undoubtedly inspired by the second glass of wine I'd enjoyed that Friday evening, and by the multiple posts of Forrest Fenn fans in chatrooms who spoke glowingly of communicating directly with the great man.

My boldness was also bolstered by my deep curiosity and a sense it was only fair to confront the subject of even an informal investigation.

Where was I going with this, anyway? I had poured a third glass of wine for courage, nursing it as I mulled over what to write to encourage a response. Forrest did not respond to everyone, but only to those who struck his fancy, or piqued his interest. The wheels of my mind turned, cycling through different approaches.

I could gush about how much I enjoyed his books, which would stoke his ego, but I'm sure he heard that all the time. I needed a fresh approach.

Although no stranger to modesty and humility, Forrest Fenn *seemed* to be a raconteur and prankster with a broad sense of humor and unique perspective on life who seemed not to take himself too seriously. My unschooled analysis arrived at a deeper conclusion and revealed a very complex and conflicted man who sought forgiveness for his misdeeds even as he itched to share his biggest secrets.

He was a man who liked to get right into "the fling" of it, so maybe that was the best approach. I'd just tell Forrest I was writing a book that would reveal him to the world as the real D.B. Cooper. That, I figured, would get a rise out of him, and perhaps, a response.

It must have been that third glass of wine.

Chapter 33: Making Contact - Encounters of the Fifth Kind

So many individuals have reported sightings of Unidentified Flying Objects and of encounters with extraterrestrial beings that such encounters are now categorized as falling into five groups, depending on the intensity of the encounter.

Such close encounters are defined as follows: If a UFO is witnessed within a span of 150 meters, or about 481 feet away, it is considered an encounter of the First kind. When an encounter with a UFO on the ground or in the sky leaves traces behind such as scorch marks or indentations it constitutes an encounter of the Second kind. If a witness observed occupants within a UFO, it is an encounter of the Third kind. At Level Four, an encounter involves the abduction of a human being and the indignity of being subjected to experimentation. Lastly, an encounter of the Fifth kind involves direct communication between an extraterrestrial being and an ordinary human.

If one thinks in spiritual terms - and many of Forrest's recorded thoughts are nothing, if not spiritual - we are all extraterrestrial beings, souls living a human experience. And what human, apart from astronauts, are more "extraterrestrial" than a jet pilot? But, if Forrest were offered the opportunity to fly closer to the stars and observe the earth below in all its astounding beauty, I am absolutely certain he would have done so without hesitation. As a pilot, Fenn had been recognized at least 25 times for his extraordinary actions.

I had seen the man in photographs and on video, read his soul on paper. Now I was ready to communicate with this unique being. I was prepared to experience an encounter of the Fifth kind. If Forrest Fenn decided to answer my email.

So I waited. And waited, checking my email spam folder every time I signed in.

Then waited some more.

Then, five days later, I received a very brief reply:

"Is that so? I would be most interested in hearing your theory. Tell me about it." f

Looking back now, I realize what those few simple words propelled into motion, but at the time, I had no idea what I was getting myself into. I wasn't actually planning on writing a book, but once he began asking questions, a book took shape in my mind. I mean, why not? I had scads of notes and virtually every article ever written on the hijacking. I'd also memorized many parts of Forrest's two autobiographies. And so the dance began.

I say "dance" because our correspondence was a courting of his good humor and a coaxing of information and small facts that drew us closer for a time, electronically, and then, when subjects grew a little personal, forced a temporary retreat. I began to write, and the story developed as our online relationship progressed.

Sometimes, Forrest was chatty and effusive. At other times, he drifted into memory, providing tidbits of information I could weave into the tapestry becoming the story of my investigation. At other times, he seemed guarded and suspicious of my intentions.

Interestingly, Forrest never disputed my initial assertion —that he was the legendary D.B. Cooper. But he never admitted it, either. Rather, he seemed to want me to prove my case. Our online exchanges were sometimes lighthearted, sometimes serious, frequently flirty, and often waxed philosophical. I think we were both entertained by the exercise.

Forrest had become a night owl in his later years, often up late into the early morning hours. I spent my weekends "hanging out" on my computer, busying myself with the book and researching details of Forrest's stories, the FBI investigation, and curious trains of thought that would help me understand Forrest Fenn, the man, from the wealth of information unearthed by the media, his fans, or his own video presence.

Dal Neitzel, a professional videographer, was a big fan. Dal (pronounced "Dale") hosted an interesting blog about Forrest and had shot multiple videos interviews with him. The subjects varied from San Lazaro archeological digs to rambling but fascinating stories about his youth, to his experiences in the Air Force.

Forrest wrote of buffaloes, bears, and the beauty of West Yellowstone, as well as the American West and Southwest. Corresponding with Forrest Fenn provided education on many levels. I benefited from the experience, but I never understood what Forrest got out of our relationship. Of course, we were both teasing out information about the other, and I must admit to being cagey on my end when Forrest probed and asked about my progress on the Cooper case.

Dad's health had taken a turn for the better. He was stronger and seemingly more self-sufficient with each passing day. The cancer was in full remission. His doctor was delighted with his progress. He was considering returning to work again.

An idea had been simmering for a while, and when Dad announced he was officially cancer-free during a Saturday autumn afternoon picnic with Emma in the Temple park now named after Forrest's father, William Marvin Fenn, I decided to propose my plan.

"Look, Dad, before you go back to work, I want to take you and Emma to Santa Fe to meet Forrest Fenn." Dad's excited, incredulous expression amused me.

"Meet Forrest Fenn? How do you propose to accomplish that?"

I flashed a sly smile. "Well, I think he'll invite us."

"You're joking."

I shook my head. "Nope. Dead serious. You see, well…I've been corresponding with him through email for a few months now."

Dad nearly spit out the mouthful of sweet tea he just chugged. "H.. How could you not tell me that?"

I laughed and offered Emma a quick wink.

"When did this start? How?"

I related the events of the past several months. By the time I was done, he was fully engaged. I could almost see the wheels turning in his head as he digested the information.

He grabbed a brownie, then took a bite. "And Forrest didn't deny being DB?"

"Nope. Not in the least. He's just curious how I intend to prove it. And when I started to explain, I realized he actually expected me to be writing a book about him, and, at some point, might ask to read what I had written." I laughed.

"Maybe Major Fenn will publish it himself," Dad shot back, and we laughed uproariously at the thought that Forrest Fenn might actually self-publish a book exposing his perpetration of the crime of the century.

"You know he can still be prosecuted, Steph. Since they filed the court case eliminating the statute of limitations, it's still a pending case that can be kick-started in no time. Have you given that any thought?"

"I know. And I'm sure Forrest is well aware of that. Look - he's how old now? Born in 1930? I've read some articles that mentioned if the hijacker was ever identified, the FBI wouldn't prosecute him for a 41-year-old crime. And if they did, it would be a token sentence - like probation for the rest of his life. There's no way he would go to jail. My gosh, Dad, he's a folk hero! He should be given a medal. He'll never see the inside of a jail. And, besides, he knows too many famous people."

Dad nodded.

"Let's go meet him, Dad - renew your acquaintance, remind him of how you met."

He smiled. "When do you want to go?"

I intended to propose a visit to Santa Fe to Forrest without mentioning Dad specifically. I'd wait until we were face-to-face to let Dad introduce himself and explain who he was and how they had met. It took a few days to connect with him, but to my delight, Forrest responded to the idea of our visit in the affirmative, saying he would be happy to meet us and show us around Santa Fe. He also mentioned he hoped to read a few pages of whatever I had "scratched out" about him.

That sardonic remark propelled me to develop an outline and an introductory preface, as well as my opening. I'd have something to show for my talk.

I worked late into the night. By the first glimmering of sunlight, I'd finished the preface, an introduction, and a very rough first chapter.

I pressed on for the next three weeks and completed several additional chapters in which I introduced and developed Dad's and my theories and observations. I planned to hand Forrest enough to be able to quiz him once he had read all of it.

I was excited – this was really going to happen! Precisely what was going to happen, I was not yet sure. *Should I confront him?* I'd have to chew on that idea for a while – and keep writing.

Chapter 34: Santa Fe

I knew what he would look like. Forrest Fenn, that is - I had scoured the internet for videos of him and his family. That's how I came across the video of Skippy disembarking from the hijacked 727, and newspaper articles with pictures of Skippy's boys, who were granted plumbers' licenses at the ages of 13 and 14 and worked with their Dad.

I mulled over my years of research and Dad's recent observations as our plane labored through cloud-laden sky on its way to Santa Fe from Texas. Looking down from the window, I watched as desert *arroyos* ran strong with the powerful flow resulting from a strong thunderstorm.

The plane hit a pocket of light turbulence. Emma tensed, then twittered, "I...Is this normal? I've never flown before."

"Really?" Dad and I asked in unison, sounding like the Japanese twins in *Godzilla*. Or was that *Mothra?* Anyway, you get the picture.

The idea that a 46-year-old woman had never flown was hard to swallow. I hoped for a smooth flight.

But, of course, it wasn't. When we hit the next round of turbulence, stronger this time, I thought we were going to lose Emma, who turned quite pale and squeezed Dad's hand so tightly   I imagined his bones cracking. He comforted her with a tenderness I hadn't noticed before. Was there a budding romance going on right under my nose? I'd have to ask Dad about it when we were alone.

Our landing at Santa Fe Municipal Airport was uneventful, and by the time we disembarked, Emma carried herself like a seasoned world traveler, although Dad was still solicitous. *Definitely something going on there.*

This trip was well-deserved treat for us all, and I spared no expense. Emma's eyes brightened and Dad grinned as I loaded their bags into the rental car—a Mercedes SUV.

Twenty minutes later, we checked into the historic Rosewood Inn of the Anasazi with its comfortable, charming rooms, authentic Southwestern décor, and architecture. Built in the late 1800s in the heart of Santa Fe, it was just a five-minute walk from the Santa Fe Plaza. Each room had its own kiva fireplace and a flat screen TV with DVD player, an iPhone docking station for music, a work desk and, most important of all, free Wi-Fi. My laptop hummed with excitement.

The Inn had a full bar, and three highly rated restaurants were right on site. That solved the need to pre-arrange dinner plans. And I have to admit, I was ready for a drink…or three.

I was liking this! It was starting to feel like a real vacation – something I had denied myself for far too long. And it would do Dad and Emma a world of good to enjoy a change of scenery. Ten days without a doctor or lab would be a divine relief.

After checking in, and before the drinks I looked forward to, we piled back into the SUV and drove along the narrow streets in historic Santa Fe. Shopping, restaurants, and the town's major art galleries were located less than a mile from our hotel, and Santa Fe Plaza was less than 600 feet away.

I can only speak for myself when I say I was captivated by the charm of Santa Fe – "The City Different," according to its brochures. Dad and Emma had a tour book they studied intently, rather than looking out the window, but I was looking left and right as we passed the city's interesting structures and historic buildings. Santa Fe was an immensely interesting and beautiful little city.

Despite being New Mexico's state capital, Santa Fe was no larger than Temple. I was going to have fun exploring it with Dad and Emma. But I also wanted to venture out on my own, so I could do a little snooping around and ascertain "the lay of the land." I could also ask the natives their opinions of Forrest Fenn.

Back at the hotel, Dad and Emma made their way to their room while I lingered at the front desk. I perused the services offered by the Madeleine Inn's Absolute Nirvana Spa, located in the garden a few steps away. I scheduled a massage and steam treatments for each of us. Dad was squeamish about the idea of a massage, but Emma extolled its virtues and rattled off an impressive list of prominent athletes who routinely got massages. That calmed Dad's machismo angst.

When I arrived back at my room, I slipped off my shoes and stretched out on the plush white duvet. Dad's stamina still wasn't one hundred percent, so he and Emma decided to nap before dinner. A glance at my phone told me I had a couple hours to relax before meeting them for dinner in the lobby at 7.

I reached into my backpacked and pulled out a leatherbound journal in which I'd I had haphazardly jotted notes relating to my correspondence with Forrest.

I settled in and thought of Dad and Emma comfortably ensconced in their own adjoining rooms, but now I wondered if . . . then laughed. They were adults and could rest where they pleased. If in each other's arms, even better!

I focused on my notes. They were a loose conglomeration of undeveloped thoughts and fragments of suspicions, sudden epiphanies, imagined truths, and sometimes, just statements that made me focus on an unusual detail or coincidence. This was going to take a little time.

Sipping from my plastic cup of in-room brewed coffee, I flipped through the pages.

We were both playing games. He had to know it, as obvious as it was. I think Forrest was curious about what I had to substantiate my suspicions. I think he thought I was feigning interest in his treasure hunt to excuse my "hanging around" with him online and to disguise my true intention— to elicit something useful from him to validate my suspicions and theories.

One of the early notes prompted me to reread my second letter to Forrest Fenn, where I softened my approach by making it about the treasure and a mutual interest in art. I intentionally made my choice of words less mature, less intimidating.

I wrote:

Hello again, Mr. Fenn,

I found an article about your treasure hunt that you started with your book, The Thrill of The Chase, and got excited about the number of people you have inspired to look for the gold. Is it really that valuable? I was a bit of a skeptic until I saw the number of people who follow you and have actually gone on several hunts for the box of gold and coins and things you have secreted away somewhere in the mountains.

I actually don't live that far from your area. Or from where you grew up. I live in Temple, Texas, and I was raised on North Main, too, but in a different neighborhood. I know where your house was, though.

I also happen to collect art. Maybe that's part of the treasure hunter in some of us--the love for beautiful things.

I don't know if you can tell me this or not, but since I'm not from your area.... I was wondering if I ever did visit to do some investigating, or look for your treasure, if it's legal to dig in federal lands or state lands etc. Is it? I just don't want to get in trouble.

Also, do they make scorpion spray? LOL.

I already have some exciting ideas about where you might have hidden it as I have read your book, The Thrill of the Chase, about a dozen times already. I love a good puzzle too... and especially, thinking outside the box.

I'm trying to use Google Earth to get familiar with the areas around you. And there are so many maps online – on all the chat sites where people who are hunting for your treasure exchange information and chat.

Thanks for the fun idea. This must be exciting for you. I hope you find out if someone does find your treasure. I think if I found it, I'd definitely want to tell you.... but no one else.

At least, that's what I say now :-)
Stephanie
A few days passed before he replied:
Dear Stephanie,
Thanks for the email and it is fun to know you may join in the search. Luckily, you won't need scorpion spray because I've lived in NM since 1972 and have yet to see my first such critter. But watch the red ants if you look for prehistoric Indian beads on their colonies.

I don't know what the state and federal laws say related to digging. I suppose it depends on what you are digging for. Best to check with those people before you start scratching around. Let me know if you are coming this way, I would like to meet you. F

I waited a few days, then wrote him back:
Hi, Forrest,
**Phew* about not needing the scorpion spray, but I am a little bummed about the fact I probably shouldn't go prehistoric Indian bead hunting on ant hills. It actually sounded like a fun adventure as well.*

I can't wait for your next book to come out. I'm already scouring the Internet for information about you and looking for your updated clues.

I've had some fun ideas I'd love to talk to you about (I know you can't say anything, but I suppose if there is a real chance I might try - though I probably shouldn't. You never know if there are computer savvy people trying to get information in case we discuss something you haven't told anyone else.)

I would absolutely love to meet you if we come out.

Maybe if you've ever been in the springs there, you can show us how to get to them and take a dip. ~Stephanie

Three days later, he replied:
You can look in the ant hills if you want to, just don't let them crawl up your pant leg to a soft spot. I'm the world's leading authority on how much that hurts. Who's coming with you? f

I was determined to somehow encourage Forrest to give me longer answers, and to make him respond at greater length. I needed to draw him into a conversation. So I wrote back:

Hi Forrest,

I work, and help take care of my father, who is fighting cancer. I understand you fought it and beat it? Wonderful! Not many places to look for treasure, and certainly not much time. If – no, WHEN - I start looking, I will take my mission to find the treasure very seriously.

I don't know about New Mexico ants, but I was on a construction site for my job, helping a worker move something when we came across some sort of ants that must have had teeth larger than their bodies, and they sure hurt.

If I came to New Mexico it would be with my sometimes boyfriend, Jay. He's the type who goes along with any of my crazy fun plans, just because. He's not the love of my life-- we run hot and cold. Right now, it's lukewarm.

I just sent you a friend request on Facebook. Now you can see me. Stephanie Ward. I was married but went back to my maiden name because . . . well, for a lot of reasons. I think you've got such a neat name. A movie star or major author kind of name.

Hope my emails aren't boring you. I'm sure you're super busy with people wanting to talk to you in hopes for clues.

~Stephanie

Well, Forrest was evidently not bored with my emails, which he answered promptly. We got into a rhythm of sorts, where one email would engage him by questioning a detail or passage from his books in order to get him to elucidate his past and relate adventures with Donnie and Skippy. The next email would inquire about one of his favorite topics, like art, or Indians, or the Spanish in the Southwest, or the Pueblo digs and his huge collection of artifacts or mention an article I had read on the subject and ask for his comments. I would keep bouncing from topic to topic, then change the subject back to personal information once again.

I slipped in seemingly innocuous questions from time to time and made a point of getting at least one piece of factual, usable information from each email. In this manner, I eked out detail after detail, even - occasionally - luring Forrest to reminisce about his flying years.

One afternoon, when I had some time on my hands, I emailed:

Did you pay much attention to the DB story when it happened? ~ Stephanie (actual email)

Apparently, he also had nothing better to do, because a few minutes later, he replied:

Sure I did, like everyone else. F (actual email)

Feeling emboldened, I made a comment about the titanium found on DB's tie. Forrest replied with this peculiar email:

The eyelids of the F-100 are made of silver plated titanium. It is a very hard metal. When I had to land an F-100 in France without landing gear pieces of the titanium were on the runway burning like wood. Later, I picked up a piece of it and it broke in my hand it was so brittle. f (actual email)

Curiously, he immediately sent another email adding the following:

I'm sorry, I should have told you what eyelids were. They are part of the tailpipe and they move in and out depending on power setting. When they close a little you go faster but the temperature goes up. The pilot doesn't control them, the engine does. When you go into the afterburner range the eyelids go crazy for about 3 seconds, then they settle on a setting and temperature that gives you max thrust. I'm sure that doesn't help you much. F (actual email)

After receiving that response, I grew more daring, and replied:

You more than most must have some thoughts and ideas on how he could have pulled it off and where he landed and if he made it. ~Stephanie (actual email)

Just a short time later, he replied:

My guess is that he made it because his body was never found. When he jumped out, I promise you that he had no idea, within 75 miles, where he would like to land. He didn't even know where he was when he jumped. Jumping out of an airplane during daylight is no big deal, at night is foolhardy and crazy. ƒ (actual email)

Oh, wow. Did I dare ask one more question? I bit my lip, pondering. What the heck…

Forrest,

Apparently DB Cooper asked to have the landing gear down the entire flight. That doesn't make sense to me at all. Do you understand why? ~Stephanie (actual email)

I felt like I hit the jackpot when he replied:

It makes perfect sense because the plane can fly slow with the gear down and hold a high power setting. Pilots don't like low power settings in jets. DB wanted to jump out at a slow speed so he wouldn't hit the tail, I guess, but what do I know? ƒ (actual email)

Wow! I had a feeling Forrest Fenn knew a whole lot more than he let on!

When Forrest had lost a kidney to cancer in the late 1980s (he was, in fact, diagnosed with kidney cancer around a year after his father had been diagnosed with pancreatic cancer and took his own life), he'd sold his private plane, a single engine Rockwell Commander. He missed flying. He had been an avid airman from age 23, and, in contrast to Skippy, who experimented with flying in his teens but never became proficient, Forrest made flying his life.

I couldn't wait to see Forrest and my father interact. Dad would be thrilled to see him again. I hesitated to mention the desire to finally pin down the man we both suspected of being D.B. Cooper and confront him directly. I had no idea how my father would react.

I hoped for the possibility to confront Forrest bluntly, rather than continuing our online fencing, our 'dance,' with each of us dropping knowing hints that proved nothing other than Fenn's playing with my suspicions of him, obliquely acknowledging my results while casting doubt on their application to him, and my all-too-slowly teasing details and tiny admissions from him. As in his books, Forrest was fond of dropping hints – the double plays on words or situations--the innuendoes. I was dying to sit face-to-face with the man. Would Fenn's body language be as cool and non-committal as his casually typed responses?

Forrest was maddening. To me, he was obviously holding a huge secret, fighting his desire to tell all, but holding back, cautious in the face of potential prosecution by a gung-ho State's Attorney with political ambitions and the ready-to-prosecute status of the Oregon court case, cleverly engineered to evade the statute of limitations.

Maintaining his secret had to take a toll on Forrest. After, all, if he really wanted to hide his successful coup of the century, why had he buried at least nine copies of his "real" autobiography, one in his infamous "secreted" treasure chest and at least eight more buried in his cast bronze jars – then notified everyone and their cousins of its existence?

But enough speculation--I needed to focus my attention on my notes. Not even recalling the topic or my impressions at the time of their writing, I studied each page, trying to make sense of the flow and create order out of a jumble that read:

<u>MY D.B./FENN NOTES</u>

It describes him as wearing loafers. In TTotC he speaks many times of losing his shoes and says he wanted a job where he could wear hushpuppies…LOAFERS!

Also, the note he gave the flight attendant was in felt pen, Isn't that marker? There's a scrapbook on Dal's site that has an envelope with all caps and in felt marker.

Maybe this is why the little girl says that her father calls him a fraud.

He writes about Skippy flying a plane without a license. (Did Skippy fly the getaway plane?) Did Donnie pick him up and bring him to Skippy? He tells a story in ttotc where he needs to be picked up. Is the substitution of names intentional – or not?

He talked about how he put an IOU in there. . . (This was in one of the videos where he talks about how he would know if someone found it. Maybe he was joking with himself that he was putting an IOU in there for the money he hijacked.). He later talked about how he almost put large bills inside it, too.

He said that two people can keep a secret if one of them was dead. Skippy and Donnie are both dead now.

He talks about having "hairs for DNA" in the olive jar inside the chest he hid, He might have said "three hairs." Is that to prove he was D.B.?

D.B. Cooper, they think, landed around the Lewis River which is in Clark County in Washington State (he talks about looking for Lewis and Clark and he talks about the Washington painting).

He brags about forgeries. His attitude is what's wrong with a forgery if you liked it before you knew it was? Could he be speaking of himself? He wrote in Too Far to Walk that he and former Texas Governor John Conyers bought a lot of forgeries from Elmy de Hory, who could imitate any style - and sold them all. But everything that comes from his mind is like a parable.

He never says anything straight-out, and when he does, you doubt it.

I caught myself thinking aloud, started, then instinctively looked around even though I was alone in the room. The sudden sound of my voice in the stillness was jolting. Looking back at the notes, I marveled I had made these observations and never looked at them again, leaving some without context. They seemed like they were written by a stranger. I read on:

They say that Bismuth was found on the tie. Is that used in foundry work, or something else he would have been involved in? They do say Pepto-Bismol, though, could be indicated, so it could be just from drinking that. Lycopodium spores were found on it and that's from a pharmaceutical. Breathing some things from the foundry could cause his breathing problems, too.

Also, aluminum was found on the tie. That could definitely relate to foundry work.

In November 2011 Kaye announced that particles of pure (unalloyed) titanium had also been found on the tie. Titanium, which was much rarer in the 1970s than it is today, was found at that time only in metal fabrication or production facilities, or at chemical companies using it (combined with aluminum) to store highly corrosive substances. Cooper may have been a chemist or a metallurgist, or possibly an engineer of manager (the only employees who wore ties in such facilities at that time) in a metal or chemical manufacturing plant or at a company that recovered scrap metal from those types of factories.

The best place for him to hide money would be within the art world. Forrest told me he was making 80K a year out of his garage, reproducing sculptures.

And I had scribbled Forrest's direct, and oft-repeated quote: *"Yes, it doesn't matter who you are, it only matters who they think you are."*

Apparently from the FBI file, I had noted the following: *"Agents theorize that he took his alias from a popular Belgian comic book series of the 1970s featuring the fictional hero Dan Cooper, a Royal Canadian Air Force test pilot who took part in numerous heroic adventures, including parachuting."*

And, also from the official file: "FBI Suspect Cooper's height: 5' 10" (1.76m) to 6' 0" (1.83m) tall, 170 to 180 pounds (77 to 82 kg), mid-40s, with close-set piercing brown eyes. Passengers and other eyewitnesses gave very similar descriptions."

"Those are his measurements, too," I murmured. *"He told me he was 180 pounds and was 6 feet tall."*

I'd say that Forrest would, for sure, be described as having close together eyes. I think they are bluish or light green-hazel. But colored contact lenses have been around for quite a while. OR maybe a russet suit would shift the color of his eyes to a darker hue, mistaken for brown. I found notes from an interesting online ophthalmological note reporting that, per DMV records, "many people with hazel eyes mistakenly classify their eyes, and tell the Driver's License Bureau and police, that their eyes are Brown, when in fact they have hazel eyes. Many don't even realize it."

Another article excerpt was even more helpful: *"Hazel eyes are brown and green, usually. It may be accurate to say, "Your eyes look light brown or brown to me," but that is not actually the color of the eye...This is what happens. The inner ring of the eye is generally brown. The outer ring is some variation of green. As the pupil dilates, as the eyes adjust to differing light levels – low light, normal ambient light levels, etc. – it causes the pupil (black) to be prominent, with the brownish inner ring the next to follow.*

"With the darker inner ring and the pupil comprising about 80% of the visible eye, and the eye is going to look brown, or light brown, when it actually is not; 74% of green/hazel eyes have a brown ring around the iris. "Hazel eyes are not one color. It is a name for a variety of colors: golds, greens and browns."

Another article mentioned, "The colors seem to change with hair and clothing color. Some hazel eyes are rimmed in blue and have flecks of gold, medium brown and green in them." The author noted, "When I wear certain colors, my eyes change, kind of like a chameleon."

Another of my own notes read: *"Forrest has a distant relative, Ida Cooper."*

Another note referenced paragraphs from his book: *"Reading, 'and it was very cold and raining when the jump was made.' They also talk about turning off the oxygen in the back of the plane. He talks about oxygen in that one story where he's coming back from the party on the East coast. He talks about it raining when he went to Borders in ttotc.*

The captions in his book are all in black felt pen, in all caps.

In one of the letters, DB Cooper said he was "in a rut." FF talks about ruts a lot.

He talks about the postman/postmistress – Donnie's grandmother – and that in the post office they have 'wanted' posters. Was it in his book that <u>he talks about having pictures up on the wall with the bad guys</u>?

"*His poem talks about nine clues; The name Dan Cooper has nine letters.*"

Another note from Forrest' writings: "*Skippy trampled the grass around some pretty interesting events during his fifty years, and I was a tag-along observer with him for my share.*"

My notes: Did the above comment mean that it was Skippy's plan? Or that Skippy was the jumper?

In TTOTC, Forrest talks about Skippy disappearing while in Idaho. Maybe disappearing to find a place for their getaway.

Also questioned whether when Forrest says that Skippy died with weights on his feet - maybe Skippy had secrets – things he had done. Was the story of Skippy dying in Mexico, in ninety feet of water, with weights on his feet the truth? I was told that Skippy's ashes were buried on top of his mom's in the Hillcrest Cemetery. Was there a cover-up? Forrest said they went at night to bury his ashes.

"*His direct words: 'My father and I dug a hole on top of my mother's grave and buried Skippy's ashes there. They are still in the plastic container, but no marker marks the spot.'*

"*Forrest talks in a scrapbook about jumping from the tallest bridge, with no one around.*" *Was that a nod towards this plane being the tallest jump?*

Surfing for data, I had come across Dal Neitzel, a documentary photographer, who has recorded several videos and tapes about Forrest Fenn. Dal is ex-Marine, so he and Forrest share their military experiences. Dal is more than generous in sharing his info on Forrest. I have watched all his interviews of the man I soon hoped to meet in person. Forrest had hundreds of scrapbooks. He had loads of photos from his gallery days. A lot of famous people had visited his renowned gallery in its heyday, and he had pictures to prove it. He was a master of publicity. And of keeping secrets.

And this note was from *TTOTC*: "Looking back now, after almost sixty-five years, I have fond memories of that road trip. Skippy died in a scuba diving accident in Cozumel, where they found him in ninety feet of water with his weights on. His luck failed him in the end. And it didn't surprise me at all. At age fifty, he was plucked from life at the moment of his greatest blossom, and I knew he wouldn't go in any normal mundane way. I had to bribe two Mexican officials to get him home. Skippy had such potential and there were so many things he would have accomplished. We should have buried him standing up."

I'd noted the date Forrest retired: *"...when I retired from the Air Force on September 6. 1970." And I then noted in pencil: "November 24, 1971, when it happened."* It would have made Skippy 43. He died at age 50, and obviously did not die during a jump from a 727. That shot that theory.

Another note read: *Forrest could have flown somehow to and from the different towns to post the letters supposedly sent by D.B. to the various newspapers. One talked about a football game in Canada, and he referenced football in one of his books. He talks in one of his blogs on his website of writing to a newspaper editor about using so much paper for the Sunday edition. The letters DB wrote WERE sent to editors.*

He says that his Dad is probably burning both ends of a candle. Is that one for Skippy and one for Forrest? Did his dad know about it?

Forrest said in one of the scrapbooks on Dal's blog, "In my rush to get over to the MVD I ran out of gas. It was right in the middle of the busiest street in town because I forgot to plug my idiot phone in I had to just sit there until the honks brought every cop in town to my location. Big deal. You'd thought I robbed a bank, or something." Was that from one of his books, or an email, or a chat conversation?

It sounds like a similar situation to D.B. waiting on the tarmac, surrounded by law enforcement." The man speaks in parables.

Forrest and I had talked about his scrapbooks at some length. Forrest had the heart of a collector. He enjoyed looking at the pictures and reading the comments from time to time. I would have to ask to see them. Dal Neitzel had incorporated Forrest's penchant for scrapbooks in his "groupie" website, starring Forrest Fenn.

I remembered a photo on one of his scrapbook pages-- it had a folded five-dollar bill on it with one corner bent. I instantly recalled the page in the massive online FBI file with a similar posting--a photograph of an identically folded bill that – aside from the denomination – appeared exactly like the photo newspapers had used to illustrate one of the bills. Another strange coincidence?

I truly do believe Forrest Fenn wants the recognition of being D.B.!

He does. Absolutely. I was convinced. But it was a dangerous thought since it only fed my desire to bring this to a head. Why was I so eager to prove this so soon? What personal hunger was I feeding? I wasn't vengeful – Forrest Fenn had done me no harm. The need to conclusively prove my life's – and Dad's – ongoing suspicion had grown strong enough to quell an unwise eagerness to jump to conclusions. Proving this would be its own reward. The idea of turning my research over to the FBI had motivated me since my earliest involvement with the story of D.B. Cooper. And I was closer than ever to learning more. I pressed on in my reading:

Forrest helps Dorothy at Collected Works Bookstore, located in Santa Fe. Was she by chance Skippy's wife? Is that why Forrest helps her? I had found an old marriage certificate where he appeared to be married to a Dorothy, yet he speaks of Skippy marrying a woman named Irene. Dorothy's bookstore is the ONLY physical location where his book can be purchased – all other sales are by the secondary market.

Before Dal Neitzel had ever met Forrest Fenn, he was a friend and work associate with Crayton Fenn—Skippy's son. Crayton was a master SCUBA diver and owner of a maritime service company when Dal met him while filming a freelance science news story for CNN in Uruguay. Crayton constantly kept the dive crew amused with tales of his Uncle Forrest's fascinating exploits. That was Dal's first acquaintance with Forrest Fenn, though they did not meet until years later.

Another note: *D.B. told the flight to go to Mexico. That's where Skippy supposedly died. Any connection? Maybe Forrest flew to Mexico to retrieve Skippy's body and brought it – or his ashes - back on a plane. . . he said he'd carried Olga's (another topic of a story in TTotC) ashes in his plane.*

Could there have been a time discrepancy . . . he talks about how Eric Sloane fibbed about his birth date . . . what if Forrest fibbed about Skippy's death date?" Logic kicked in: Why would he do that? Besides, all the records show Skippy dying in the manner Forrest published in *TTotC*. And good luck trying to get any information from Mexico!

Skippy's Social Security records say he died in November of 1978. D.B. Cooper committed the crime in November 1971. If we're right and Forrest Fenn is D.B. Cooper, were they part of other robberies where Skippy could have been killed? Ok Stephanie, one conspiracy is enough.

Forrest never wanted to wear a tie when he worked at his gallery. He never wore a tie in the Air Force, except with his dress blues. D.B. took off his tie and left it behind.

Forrest asked me if I knew what "pie" meant in Spanish. I told him no, and he said pie, or pies meant "foot" or "steps" in Spanish. D.B. lowered the aft steps, or 'airstairs.'

The hidden gold is supposed to weigh 20 Troy pounds; the $200, 000 in ransom money, bundled in 100 packets consisting of one hundred $20 bills that was extorted from Northwest Orient weighed a total of 21 pounds. Forrest has *actually said the chest and its contents weighed 42 pounds at one time. He said he'd made two trips from his car to haul the chest to its hiding spot. That would be 21...twice.*

Forrest talked about a needle in a haystack once-- Seattle has The Needle.

He mentions the word "reward" several times in TTOTC.

Interesting comment from this article: If he's alive today, he'd be about 85 years old," [FBI Special Agent] Carr said. "Maybe one day I'll be sitting at my desk, and I'll get a call from an old man who says, 'You're not going to believe this story.'"

WOW-- this is big. Just looking at ancestry page and found a travel document for a Mr. William Fenn. Here's the info. Interesting. . . that's the same airport and airlines I believe. Skippy was two years older than Forrest-- as of this date, he would have been about 26. Forrest would have been 24, just one year out of flight school.

Name: Mr. William Fenn;
Race/Nationality: USA;
Port of Departure: Tokyo, Japan;
Arrival Date: 17 Mar 1954;
Port of Arrival: Seattle Tacoma Airport, Washington;
Airline: Northwest Airlines

Maybe all three were involved. Forrest told me Donnie died in California! I believe he was from Hawaii originally. There were D.B. letters from and to California and British Columbia newspapers. Skippy's second wife was from British Columbia. So maybe they all did it, and when Forrest flew them all home, he dropped a letter at each place – maybe left two more to be mailed simultaneously on December 1.

June and Donnie were the same age. They lived in Washington State, too, when they were both 36. I wonder what made them all go to Washington.

The fact the letters were in the hometown areas where Skippy and Donnie lived is neat. If Forrest flew them home after the air heist, then they sent the letters from where they were to confuse authorities. It makes perfect sense that D.B. HAD to be a pilot when you consider the letters being sent from different locations so quickly. Also, he must have had accomplices. If Skippy's wife was from BC. . . it would make sense they went back to her family's possibly for Thanksgiving. . . and Donnie would have to go to California to be with his family.

The D.B. Cooper name was the result of a mistake made by a reporter. Forrest talks about errors in his book TTOTC. There was even a kid he went to school with he called "Edard." His real name was Edward. Forrest said he shortened the name because it saved time.

He speaks in TTOTC of Frosty being a 'Ruler.' a King is a ruler, and this happened in King County, Washington. A clue?

He talks of the bottle of Jackie Kennedy brandy. . . But D.B. ordered a mixed drink.

I just saw a photo Forrest took while flying with his grandson, Shiloh, where he's wearing sunglasses similar to the original D.B. composite sketch in one of the Scrapbooks from Dal's blog.

In his book, TTotC Forrest talks about the radio Skippy built for him: 'With the help of my little radio, we were reunited.' So, maybe he had a little radio to connect him with an accomplice, his get-away person. What a perfect way to locate him in the wilderness after a jump. Maybe the "bomb" was actually a locator device for when he was on the ground.

Forrest was stationed overseas. He once told me that he was in Germany (Bitburg, near the border between Germany and Belgium?) when the devastating Hebgen Lake Earthquake aka the 1959 Yellowstone Earthquake hit in West Yellowstone in 1959. The quake literally moved mountains and blocked the flow of the Madison River and caused the water to rise and form what was later named Quake Lake.

Forrest goes out of his way to mention the gypsies in TTotC. Gypsies are often stereotyped as thieves and frauds. Is he dropping hints?

He chose the art and collectables business so he could fly overseas with the money and bring it back in art. Then he could legally sell the art for a profit, thereby laundering the money. The art markets are unregulated and the price for art is variable and subjective, with values and deals that are hard to pin down precisely. How convenient.

I'm reading about D.B. and the parachutes, and read that there were no D rings on the Navy parachute he selected for his jump. . . 'The rigger (Earl Cossey) supplied back-packs without D-rings-- there was nothing to clip the reserve to. In Cossey's statement to the FBI on 11/26/71, 4th paragraph '...he described the missing backpack parachute (the one Cooper jumped with) as having a sage green nylon container, Model NB6, with sage green nylon harness, which harness has no 'D' rings to mount a chest pack.'

In his book, TTotC, there is an image of a jar with the word "KNOWLEDGE" on it that is missing the letter 'D' and as a kid in school he used to 'pray for Ds.'

Forrest drops clues like breadcrumbs!

I glanced at my phone. Almost time to head down to the lobby, but I hadn't yet heard a peep from my traveling companions, so I pushed on.

Forrest mentions being in the electronics class in the military but talks about how Skippy was much better at electronics than he was. I think Skippy built his radio. He carried a paper bag on board. Was it the radio? Forrest also mentioned carrying a paper bag in TTotC. But again, maybe the "bomb" in the briefcase that connected a set of large science batteries was actually the beacon, or radio system-- that would certainly explain why he jumped carrying the briefcase.

His treasure chest - Fenn claims he has a gold frog (jumping), and Asian carving (the Orient), and a Columbian gold necklace (Columbia River where packets of money from the ransom were found).

In one particular interview Forrest has former CIA agent Valerie Plame attesting to his
character. I found an article from an Ohio newspaper that said Forrest was in the CIA. Wow!

Really? Not even in fiction does that happen! But it must be real. It's in my notes. I think he found it amusing.

D.B. asked a stewardess to 'take this down'-- a note of instructions – military notes I found online have what appear to be letters that Forrest had someone else type for him. So maybe Cooper was used to asking others to write things for him.

Then, I had typed a timeline, with the following heading:

"This is a timeline for Forrest, and for the world:

1929-37	The Great Depression Era
Aug. 1930	FF was Born in Temple, Texas
1930s	The Dust Bowl – Result of drought and destructive farming methods
1939	FF found his first arrowhead at age nine.
1930s-1950s	Forrest, his father and friend, Concy, hunted for arrowheads together.
Early 1940s	Forrest's mother owned a cabin at West Yellowstone where the family spent Summer months.
1939-1945	WWII – FF was 9-15 years of age
1947-49 (??)	Forrest's last fishing trip to Grebe Lake with Concy
June '50-'53	Korean War – FF was 20-23
Sept. 1950	FF joined air Force 3 months after Korean War started, at age 20.
Sept. 1953	FF graduated Air Force Flight School at age 23.
Dec. 1953	FF and Peggy wed. FF was 23.
??	Kelly Fenn was born.
1959	Zoe Fenn was born.
1959-1975	Vietnam War – FF was 29-45 years old.

Early 1960s   FF trained fighter pilots at Luke Air Force Base near Phoenix, Arizona

1968-1970   FF flies in Vietnam 1968-1969, flies 368 missions, parachutes from two downed jets and brings home medals, ribbons, stars, and citations

1969-1972   FF operated a foundry 'from his garage' making bronze reproductions of sculptures; sold some (making approx. $80,000 a year), traded some for Indian artifacts.

Sept. 1970   FF retires from Air Force as Major, after 20 years' service and lives in Lubbock, Texas another two years. Retirement pay is $12,000 a year.

Nov. 1971   DB Cooper highjacking.

1972   FF and family move to Santa Fe with $20,000 and FF becomes partner in an existing art gallery. Within a short period, Fenn builds a house, buys out the partner, and establishes Fenn Galleries, Ltd.; FF was 42 years old.

1986   FF's father took his own life, after suffering with cancer for many years. FF Was 56 at the time.

1988   FF himself is diagnosed with cancer at age 58. A kidney is removed.

1988   FF closed Fenn Galleries and began writing books and excavating at the Pueblo de San Lazaro

Early 1990s??   FF's cancer goes into remission and has not recurred.

1995   The Internet was commercialized. FF was 65.

2006   FBI investigates Forrest Fenn for antiquities theft; no charges were ever filed. FF was 76.

Prior to 2009   FF sells his private plane and stops flying solo.

2009-2011   FF decides to create treasure hunt by hiding an antique chest of treasure including gold coins, exotic gold jewelry and gold antiquities and gems, along with "true" autobiography. Hides his treasure chest.

2010-2011:   Writes and publishes *The Thrill of The Chase*, released in Oct. 2010, and proceeds to publicize the treasure hunt through all available media.

The nine clues are first introduced. FF is 79-81 years of age.

2012-2013   FF writes and publishes second memoir, *Too Far To Walk*, in 2013.

I yawned, stretched, then walked to the balcony for some fresh air. It was past 3:00, but still not a peep from Dad and Emma.

The balcony was too warm, I decided, and would have to wait. Back in my room, I adjusted the A/C and turned to the next page.

Forrest told me his dad always told him to grab every banana and said, "The train doesn't go by the banana tree but one time. You should reach out and grab every banana on the way by." If anyone took advantage of that advice, it was Forrest Fenn. The man had collected a lot of bananas in a very full life. He sensed the train moving more slowly, his physical attributes diminishing, the bananas becoming fewer and harder to reach.

It was readily apparent – and he admitted it – Forrest did not like growing old. No more than he liked the thought of someday being forced to leave the train at its station and pass into the next dimension, joining those who had gone before him, and whose artifacts and evidence of life had fascinated Forrest since he was nine.

I clicked on the TV and found the music channels. I switched it to "Adult Alternative," and went back to deciphering my notes.

"...When Tina Mucklow described the battery in Cooper's briefcase, she was most probably describing a No. 6 Dry Cell... these were some of the first radio batteries. Sometimes called the "Columbia Battery," they were common for science experiments and hobby use in the 1970s. They were 6.0625 inches long, and about 2.5 inches in diameter."

Then I'd noted, *"that poker poem in the front of The Thrill of the Chase. . . D.B.'s plane landed in Reno, NV, where you have to walk through a sea of slot machines to find your way to Baggage Claim.*

He mentions Captain Kidd – a pirate. Because he was an air pirate and this was air piracy?

The beginning line of the poem talks about the bronze chest and he talks about his 'secrets,' as in more than one secret being hidden away. So it is not just the secret of where the chest is hidden away, but his secret about being D.B, which is probably in that tightly written autobiography that is supposed to tell the world everything about him that he has not yet exposed in his books. There might be other secrets in the chest that he talks about, too. Like what really happened to Skippy.

Regarding Forrest, you can never tell where the fiction stops and the truth starts – or the truth stops, and the fiction starts! He is the master of the double entendre. This is one smart man, hiding something really big, but all the while dropping clues – again, like breadcrumbs – challenging anyone out there to follow the trail. So far, no one has made the Cooper connection but Dad and me. And that reference of his about the Rosetta Stone! Like no one could figure out what he meant by that! Use a language to translate or interpret a language.

Forrest Fenn was, indeed, the "Master of Hiding in Plain Sight." Kudos, my friend.

Hmmmm. More notes.

Fenn parts his hair on the left side – like Cooper.

And where did this come from? *"I bet if we are right, there's a D.B. bill in the treasure chest, and the serial numbers will match with what they have on record. He kept talking about how he thinks he put an IOU in there, or that he thought he put money in there – in the chest – but then took it out because he thought it would get wet.*

Fenn has that one scrapbook where he says he has a $10,000 bill, and he makes a point to mention the serial numbers of money, and of cars, and stuff.

He paid $20 to learn how to make horseshoes, he wrote in TTOTC, and he paid $20 for the Northwest ticket that afternoon. The ransom money was given in $20s, and he always manages to have $20,000 saved to invest – like in Skippy's motel idea, the Dude Motel in West Yellowstone, or in buying into a partnership with the gallery after moving to Santa Fe in 1972, and the $200,000 was all paid on $20 bills . . . the number comes up again and again in his stories and his writing.

Everything seems to revolve around that figure: 20!

And this: *Read recently that there were reports that a small airplane landed shortly after 8:00 p.m. near where the hijacker would have landed and immediately took off again. A vehicle drove up to the plane on the small airstrip. Is it possible that someone picked up D.B. in a car and drove him to the airplane so he could get away? We knew that both Skippy and Forrest had flown, if Forrest's stories are true in TTotC about Skippy flying a plane to Hebgen Lake.*

It was a hunting airstrip and Forrest speaks of hunting.

And he has talked about finding a little airstrip in the middle of nowhere and landing at it, like Lander, Wyoming.

Forrest talks about Skippy not having a license. . . then shows his picture I.D. in the pages of his book. . . does that allude to Forrest teaching Skippy to fly the getaway plane?

At some point, I checked with Social Security to learn what they had on Skippy's death:

Name: William Marvin Fenn, Jr. (William Fenn, Jr.)
SSN: 516284955
Gender: Male
Race: White
Father's Name: William M. Fenn
Mother's Name: Lilly G. Simpson
Death Date: Nov 1978
Type of Claim: Original SSN
Signature on SSN Card: Marvin Fenn, Jr.
(Signature Name Differs from NH's Name)
Notes:
Jul. 1944: Name listed as William Marvin Fenn, Jr.
30 Dec. 1987: Name listed as William Fenn

In TTotC, Forrest talks about a little radio Skippy made for himself but gave to Forrest. Then he says it didn't have a speaker, but it wasn't needed. If Skippy made him a radio for the event with no speaker, maybe I really was right...was it a beacon? For sight, not sound? Is that how they planned to locate him?

He mentions a Jill Cooper in Too Far to Walk. Really? I missed that!

He talks a lot about Dr. Pepper. But D.B. ordered 7-Up with his bourbon, but it's still a soda.

I think Forrest DID smoke at one time like D.B. In TFTW, he writes about A Vietnamese prison wanting a cigarette. They traded a pack of cigarettes for his sandals cut from a tire. Since Forrest was the one who ended up with the sandals, that means that would have been HIS pack of cigarettes – Forrest's. BINGO! Great connection.

Forrest said there was an unintended clue in TFTW he had been unaware of until it was printed. . . like it might have been in written by someone else. Was it in the forward by Suzanne Sommers? Could this be the unintended clue: 'I wanted to re-route the trip.'? Was he referring to his demand, on the night of the hijacking, that the Northwest Orient 727 divert from its normal route, and instead fly to Mexico City?

Forrest talks about bribing Mexican officials to bring back Skippy's ashes. Had the Mexican authorities already cremated his body? That seemed strange. Why would it be so hard to bring an American citizen back home from a tourist location? My conspiratorial mind wandered, imagining Forrest and Skippy as part of something bigger then even D.B. Maybe Forrest needed a way to bring Skippy's death to a non-criminal conclusion.

Were authorities notified when Skippy died? Social Security does not have a definite date, which is very unusual.

The antique bronze treasure chest is supposed to have a ladder on the lid. Is that a reference to the aft stairs that gave him a problem?

He talks about comic books in TTotC. Dan Cooper is the name of the French or Belgian comic book they think Cooper used to create his alias. It was sold in Canada and in Europe – Belgium and France. And Germany near the border? That comic was around for a long time. He was in Bitburg, Germany in 1959. That's near Belgium, right?

Agent Carr's Theory: Larry Carr thinks it is highly unlikely that Cooper survived the jump. "But he came from somewhere and from someone. And that is what we want to know." Based on what he has learned so far, here is Carr's profile of Cooper: "He served in the Air Force and at some point was stationed in Europe, where he may have become interested in the Dan Cooper comic books."

One of Forrest's "Scrapbooks" contains this image:

Compare that to the photo from the FBI vault of the money given to DB:

And this vague note: *I read somewhere that Skippy might have worked for Boeing in Seattle. I think Skippy moved to Seattle after the Dude Motel was sold, apparently. Or maybe later.*

Forrest has said he always took trips alone, vacations and such, and mentioned that in his book, he went to see his Dad and go fishing, and he would see other people, and he said in his books that Peggy always put up with him and was very tolerant. I think he has always done whatever he wanted in life. He's done a lot. So he would not have been missing from family and friends. In one of his stories in TFTW, he speaks of taking a three-day trip alone. Was he stuck in that wilderness for a while?

This is a repeat, to kind of summarize: This would be something that could be checked out, as long as he's still alive, I think the fact that he was an amazing pilot, was familiar with ejecting into a wilderness situation, became rich just after that, had access to use the money out of the country so that the serial numbers wouldn't be found out. . . he could easily launder it in the art world, had cause to be in California and British Columbia, and Washington, where the letters came from...the titanium on the tie from working in metals...the 'bomb'...not to mention what could be innuendos in the book, and scrapbooks, like waiting in the middle of the busiest road for gas and what did he do, rob a bank? Oh, and the comment he made about the Twin Towers on 9/11 with the plane hijackings."

One time, I asked Forrest how he had laundered the money. Had he done it through trading Russian art? A few days later, he put out a Scrapbook that told the world exactly how he did it. He said his dog had eaten a bunch of hundred dollar bills, then pooped it out into tiny pieces. He had washed the money several times in the laundry machine, and he said if he put the pieces somewhat back together and sent them to the US Treasury, they would replace them with new bills. And most specifically, the serial number did not need to be visible on the bill! Forrest then offered the piles of "laundered" pieces on eBay! He's telling the world exactly how he laundered the money and why none of the money was ever found! How clever is that?

Figure 27 Fenn's "laundered" money.

There! I was done at last, and what a mess I had waded through! My notes from our online conversation – Forrest's and mine - were often repetitive, highly speculative, and loosely thought out – or, more simply, clear as mud! I could see some connections, some things I had researched or followed up on. But did I learn anything new? Not really.

The bulk of the notes were made during middle-of-the-night email or chat conversations. A lot of notes repeated things I had already learned because much of what I was doing when we "conversed" electronically was to verify my understanding or validate a suspicion. I jotted notes when I thought of things to ask him or recalled things I had read that he'd touched upon in conversation. He had always seemed so open in our conversations, but when I thought about it, much of what we talked about revolved around his repetition of the stories in his book, but he persisted in dropping irritating hints and clues that proved nothing, although they served to strengthen my suspicions he was just playing with me. With me, with the country's premier law enforcement agency, and with his readers.

Life had always been a game to Forrest, and – unlike poor Skippy – he had consistently been on the winning side. Was his luck about to run out? Could I interest the FBI in my case and persuade them to investigate the connections I'd made? What would happen if I confronted Forrest with an air-tight case?

Well, for starters, it would have to be totally airtight. This was the kind of hunt where you only get one shot to halt the lion in mid-leap as it goes for your throat.

I had mentioned the book several times to Forrest and he teasingly asked about my progress from time to time, but we danced around the subject. After wading through ten typed pages of scattered information, I needed to tighten my case, build timelines, and persist in my search. Misfiring would only weaken my case and I would be blown off by the FBI, as so many others, and my discoveries would never gain their serious attention. I would play it by ear, learn as much as I could from this visit, and continue to tighten the noose.

I was looking forward to the next ten days in Santa Fe. The city was charming – everything the brochures promised – and our hotel was comfortably quaint. With dusk approaching, I walked out onto broad balcony, supported by dark beams that stood out against the warm adobe façade. That vantage point overlooked Santa Fe Plaza and the mountains beyond. Suddenly, I understood the words, exalted in the popular anthem, "America, the Beautiful."

I was, indeed, looking out at the "purple mountains' majesty." Standing in the glow of the sunset, with the first stars twinkling above and a cool, dry breeze caressing my body, I watched those purple mountains shade-shift with the setting sun. The view was stunning.

I belong here. For some reason, and for the first time since our arrival in Santa Fe, I had the strongest sensation of being exactly where I was supposed to be, at just the right point in time for. . . for what? The feeling was almost religious in its intensity. I felt blessed, with Dad doing so well – and a possible romance in the brew. I had just met Jay – Mr. Hot & Cold – who was running really hot at the time and doing a good job of trying to sweep me off my feet and change my opinion of single men my own age. Life was good.

And tomorrow, we'd spoil ourselves, then prepare to beard the lion in its den.

The temperature dropped rapidly with the setting sun, and we soon understood why we had been counseled against dining outdoors after 7:30 in the evening without a shawl or jacket, and why every room in the city had its own little fireplace. Upon asking, we learned the lovely scent that flavored the chill night air was burning Piñon or Pinyon Pine. Used as firewood for centuries, this useful tree covers the Southwest and yields edible pine nuts that can be used in cooking. It is also New Mexico's State Tree. The aromatic smoke was intoxicating. It didn't smell like other pine resins, but its thick, curved needles had a smooth, sweet fragrance, redolent of the Southwest. Our waitress informed us that woodsy Piñon aromatic candles were quite popular with tourists and residents alike and were sold everywhere.

We were seated outdoors under the stars, with a fingernail moon glowing bright against a navy sky that appeared as though someone had spilled God's saltshaker. Just amazing. The air smelled like no other, fresh, and clean with just a trace of sweet smoke wafting on the breeze.

I felt so decadent I ordered seared foie gras with a dark chocolate and red chile pepper sauce with juniper berries and a brioche. Dad chose the dry aged sirloin and Emma went for the duck prepared with an interesting combination of ancient grain, artichoke, tamarind, dates, and fresh coriander. We moved to an inside table by a crackling fire, in a vast stone-walled room with large beams supporting the ceiling and characteristic arched Pueblo entryways. Low lighting and plush area rugs softened the austerity of its architecture, and neutral tones brought the earth to mind — the desert.

The food was exquisite and presented so artfully on the plate it was almost a shame to eat it and ruin the design. But eat, we did. And talked.

We were at a corner table in a room that allowed for good conversation, both open and cozy at the same time. The restaurant was a place where it was easy to speak, and where the wait staff were quick and accommodating, but not omnipresent.

Emma had an understated presence about her that made her prettiness a slow discovery. I loved the way Dad looked at her. She was obviously good for him and kept him occupied, and constantly on the move. He would do anything for her. Even exercise.

She appeared totally absorbed by Dad's every word and looked after his well-being with a devotion no salary could buy. They were obviously smitten with one another.

I laughed to myself and that – of course – brought instant inquiry as to what was so funny. I admitted I had figured out their romantic interest in one another. Then I asked, like a bemused parent, how long it had been going on. They blushed like teenagers. Yeah, they were sleeping together. I laughed again at my role reversal and gave them my blessing.

Then the talk turned to Forrest Fenn. We were going to meet him at last.

As we spoke about our upcoming encounter in hushed tones, Emma became inquisitive, and I suddenly realized Dad hadn't told her about Forrest, or our interest in the D.B. Cooper mystery and mutual suspicion that Fenn was the individual who had done the deed, with a little help from family and friends.

Referring to him only as "*f*," Dad and I filled her in on the basic details, and that conversation carried us through to coffee, dessert and an after dinner drink. For some reason, I held back on details I had not yet discussed with Dad – like Skippy being on the plane that night.

Emma was agog.

"It all fits," she declared, "I can grasp it all. You're right. There seems to be a distinct possibility that a person of F's character and experience – and wits – and with his brother and friends - could have carried it off. But what you have said, Stephanie, is all just, so circumstantial. What you have been saying is basically unprovable. Isn't it, Charles?"

Before Dad could answer her, I replied "No, it's not unprovable. There's his DNA. That was so weird – he volunteered, in one of our chats that he'd placed three hairs into the bronze treasure chest with his 'real' autobiography for purposes of identification. Why would he do that? Identify him for what, if it's not to prove he was the one who carried out something like this? That he *is* Cooper?

"There was a lot of DNA on the tie they couldn't match to anyone. The bourbon glasses were either cleaned immediately or left with all the other glasses from that flight to be washed later. If the airline used plastic, the glasses he used were tossed. If they used real glass, they were likely mixed together with others. And the prints they did find were useless because, despite his hijinks and risk-taking, Fenn had a clean record--no fingerprints on file.

"Don't know about anyone else in that crew - Skippy and Donnie, or their wives - but I doubt Forrest's *ever* been stopped by a cop, and if he has been, I'm certain he could talk his way out of a citation. I bet he's squeaky-clean."

Dad added, "But I wonder how nervous he was when he was questioned by the FBI for archeological theft, or some such shenanigans involving antiquities. Was that a close call, or what?"

"But F claims he reacts clearly and calmly under pressure, Dad. He's said so himself, many times - in the Air Force videos Dal did with him, and in his books, and to me as well. He can be one cool character. Guess you'd have to be, as a combat jet pilot. Plus, he's a storyteller, always shaping his words to elicit a specific reaction from his audience. It must be second nature to him. Really, after an extended chat, I no longer knew what part of what he'd told me was truth, and what part was fiction!"

"Just how often do you talk him?" Dad suddenly seemed on edge. His eyes narrowed and brow furrowed as he regarded me intently.

"Well, your Mr. F certainly sounds interesting," Emma chirped, helpfully attempting to change the subject.

"Dad, you need to understand I have never really *talked* to F in person. We've been "chatting" online. You know, emailing and using instant messenger to exchange messages, or have a discussion - usually late at night when neither of us can sleep. We just notice when the other is online, and we say a few words."

He clucked disapprovingly. "You should have told me the extent of your *relationship*."

"It started as a lark," I said, trying to sooth his ruffled feathers. I added a noncommittal shrug, and that seemed to ease the tension.

Emma seemed overwhelmed by the download of data we had inundated her with--her head must have been swimming with all those details about the D.B./Forrest Fenn connections we'd made. I could tell she had a million questions she wanted to ask Dad, so I reminded them we needed to be at breakfast no later than 8:30 the next morning in order to arrive on time at the Absolute Nirvana Spa for our 10:30 massages and pedicures.

Dad grinned and laughed nervously when I told him I would be snapping photos with him soaking his feet, and his pant legs rolled up to his knobby knees. Emma giggled, and we said our goodnights.

The next day, we planned our visit to Fenn over tender slices of grill-striped elk tenderloin at the Anasazi Grill. The very mention of my desire to confront Fenn with our knowledge of his misdeed was uniformly met with cries of horror from Dad and Emma.

"Your case is not solid enough yet," and "You can't simply accuse someone like that!"

So, I shelved the idea for the moment. It was a subject that would come up more than once, however.

Forrest had invited us to stop by his home toward late afternoon as soon as we were settled in at our hotel, so I called, heart in my throat. I have no idea why I was so nervous.

Perhaps it was because, through self-promotion in pursuit of doing the things he loved, Forrest Fenn had become somewhat of a minor literary and archeological celebrity. He was a pillar of the Santa Fe community.

His celebrity status was boosted by the excitement generated by the hunt for his multi-million-dollar treasure secreted away in the mountains north of Santa Fe. He seemed to be leading his followers on a merry chase, but was he also the legendary D.B. Cooper, who had gotten away with the one of the most notorious crimes of the 21st century?

Maybe I was struggling with my eagerness to confront the man, eagerness born of ego and an undefined need to push the narrative forward rapidly and learn the truth before it was too late. After all, Fenn was nearly 86. And no one lives forever.

But the smooth, welcoming voice on the other end of the phone line allayed the jitters that put a frog in my throat. Forrest's voice came across as warm and friendly, and I detected a curiosity in his tone. Was he as excited to meet me as I was him?

At 4:30 that afternoon a tall, lanky, still handsome older man in jeans, a short-sleeved plaid shirt, and a dark brown cowboy hat met us at the front entrance to the single-level adobe structure that was the Old Santa Fe Trading Co. I noticed immediately his eyes were grey-blue, with a circle of deep blue ringing each iris. The color that shifted from dark to light – deep blue from some angles and speckled grey-blue from others, perhaps the result of changing light or enhanced by the colors of his clothing.

I had seen his image often in doing my research, especially on Dal Neitzel's website. The site received several thousand hits a day. Dal had more knowledge about Fenn than anyone. He had been working with Forrest for years, and Forrest regularly contributed to his website. The website really helped give a glimpse into who Forrest was…well, who he wanted you to think he was.

While they are friends, Dal is also an admitted treasure hunter. His closeness with Forrest notwithstanding, he *appears* to have no inside access to extra clues to the treasure's location than any other searcher.

I hadn't searched for the treasure yet. Not as of that first trip to Santa Fe, at least. My job left me little time for frequent or long vacations, and what little time I did have was spent housekeeping or running errands.

Emma was a huge help because she was able to drive Dad to his appointments. Besides, I'd rationalized, with some chagrin, he's probably happier in her company, anyway. I was happy for them, but I have to admit their joy in one another just made me feel more alone.

But now, here was Forrest, and it was not the time to philosophize or mope. We were in the lion's den at last.

I stuck out my hand, and said, "Hello Forrest. I'm Stephanie Ward. And, if you recall, I'm the woman writing the book that'll expose your secret. And this is my father, Charles Ward – you two have met before, believe it or not. And this is his friend and assistant, Emma Morgan." I watched Forrest closely while I made my introductions. Forrest's eyes clouded for a brief second or two when I reminded him about the exposé I was writing. But then he turned to Dad and Emma with his hand extended. His lips relaxed into a sincere smile, and the twinkle returned to his mischievous eyes.

Forrest turned back to me and said, "I remember exactly who you are and what your driving mission is, Miss Ward. And I am most eager to learn of your progress. But only after you've all had a chance to look at my prized Fenn Collection, which I think you'll enjoy. At least, I will enjoy showing it. I always do. These artifacts all came from my excavations at Pueblo San Lazaro. It is one of the best archeological collections in the Southwest, if I may brag a little. Let's walk on through and take a look. Then we can all compare notes over a beer or glass of wine. My treat, to welcome all of you to Santa Fe."

Smooth. He'd turned an awkward beginning around and endeared himself to Emma, who had feared the worst. Dad also seemed mollified.

He was eager to reminisce with Forrest and just as eager to examine The Fenn Collection. We spent the next hour and a half listening as Forrest related the history of the Southwest and its Spanish occupiers and of the tribes of Native Americans of the Southwest. Dad and Emma peppered Forrest with questions.

"I have all of your books, Mr. Fenn. I found *The Secrets of San Lazaro Pueblo* and *High Plains Paleo* especially interesting."

"San Lazaro is a special place," he quipped. His features relaxed into a dreamy expression, his lips curling into a slight smile, as if fond recollections of that place glowed from the dark corners of his memories.

I wandered around the large room slowly, carefully, so that I wouldn't clumsily knock over a priceless relic and break it into worthless pieces. I stopped in front of an intricately woven basket. The intricate red zig-zag pattern woven into the beige fibers captivated me. Certainly, this masterful piece of art couldn't be as old as Forrest claimed.

Forrest's slow Texas drawl snapped me out of my reverie. "Stephanie?"

"I'm sorry, can you repeat the question?"

Forrest laughed softly. "I was just saying you can touch and hold anything you'd like."

After a while, Forrest suggested we return to the hotel bar for refreshments. He turned to Dad. "You all are staying at the Inn of the Anasazi? Great choice. I'm kind of partial to their cooking. And they have a great bar."

I brought up the rear as Forrest locked up and we strolled back toward our hotel and across the Plaza. We found a table outside that offered a spectacular view of New Mexico's spectacular, red-tinged sunset.

As I predicted, Dad and Forrest had no problem finding things to talk about. Put two military men together and there's an instant affinity, a connection. Shared experience creates a bond of brotherhood. Emma listened raptly. Sometimes Dad would lean over and explain terminology so she could follow the conversation. I sat back, sipped my drink, and observed.

Forrest was a listener, rather than a talker. However, when he did talk, he could weave a spell with his carefully chosen words. In his memoir, *The Thrill of the Chase*, he'd hinted at his love for language, and it was clearly evident now. He told us the stories of being shot down twice by enemy guns and aircraft, first over an open rice paddy in South Vietnam, where he walked away with a minor ankle injury, and then his terrifying night and day in Northern Laos, when his plane, carrying a load of jet fuel and missiles, was shot out from under him.. Major Forrest Fenn had huddled on the cold jungle floor overnight, ever watchful for jungle creatures and enemy soldiers. The Pathet Lao were rumored to use ferocious dogs to hunt US soldiers. That night, Forrest realized it wasn't just a rumor. He could hear the dogs barking in the distance. It was a harrowing story.

Even with intense danger surrounding him, he battled an internal tug of war between his desire to test his survival skills and playing it safe by staying put and waiting for rescue. He thought of his wife and two young daughters waiting for and worrying about him back home, and the choice was reluctantly made for him—he would wait for rescue. And rescue did come in the form of a helicopter manned by experienced, brave soldiers. They brought Forrest out of his dire situation, and as a result, Forrest was home for Christmas.

Major Forrest Fenn had accomplished things far beyond the meager achievements of many college graduates I knew. Subliminally, however, I was certain Forrest felt a constant need to reestablish himself to himself, measured against the successes of those more formally educated.

I have always felt the true purpose of education was to create a lifetime love of learning. Unfortunately, that's not always the outcome. But it certainly was in Forrest's case.

Immensely likeable. That was my strongest impression – shared, no doubt, by Dad and Emma, who were totally engaged in Forrest's accounts of some of his 368 flying missions during his year in-country.

We ordered appetizers to share with our drinks, and as the sun set and the snacks dwindled, my stomach started to grumble for more substantial fare.

Forrest and I must have had stomachs that operated on the same timetable, because no sooner did I think of dinner than Forrest recommended La Plazuela at the La Fonda Hotel on the Plaza.

"I love this area," Dad whispered loudly to Emma. "Everything's right here!"

"Santa Fe is a food lover's heaven," Forrest informed us as we followed the hostess into the enclosed restaurant courtyard. A two-story-high glass ceiling covered the atrium filled with big trees, heavy wood beams, and splashes of strong earth-tone colors on the windows. A central fountain bubbled soothingly and low, twinkling lights cast their sparkling glow. The overall effect was magical.

"This place ranks 13th out of 381 restaurants. Wonderful wine list."

"Three hundred and eighty-one restaurants?" Emma echoed.

"Yup," Forrest declared, "three hundred and eighty-one restaurants. In a town where food is responsible for around half the tourist revenues-- if not more-- you've gotta offer the people a choice!"

Delicious odors rose from each plate as we passed by. The hostess seated us at a table on the far side of the courtyard.

Emma and I studied the menu while Dad just followed Forrest's lead, ordering Roasted Corn and Green Chile Chowder, followed by Rellenos de La Fonda. I chose the Mexican Posole Rojo – a kind of pork and hominy corn stew, followed by Enchiladas del Norte. Poached Sea Bass was Emma's choice, preceded by salad.

Dad and Forrest kept up their running dialogue. Now they were talking about being stationed in Germany – Forrest at Bitburg, close to the German border with Belgium, and Dad at Mannheim, near Heidelberg. Emma and I listened with but a few asides to praise the food.

When Dad and Forrest began talking about their favorite comic strips, I began paying attention. And the moment I heard Forrest say, "Dan Cooper comics were popular among the flight crews when I was at Bitburg," my ears perked up. But, instead of jumping on that lead, Dad started talking about *his* favorite comic hero, Steve Roper.

I almost kicked my father under the table. I had hoped to hear from Forrest's own lips, and in front of witnesses, that he, too had enjoyed reading the Dan Cooper comics. No such luck. But at least I knew he was familiar with them. *And* it was because he had been stationed so close to Belgium. I was certain he knew enough about the comic to use the "Dan Cooper" alias when he bought his Northwest Orient ticket.

As Emma had pointed out, the pieces to the puzzle all fit.

I would have talk with Dad, who was evidently star-struck.

After dinner, Forrest said his goodbyes warmly – even to me – then invited us to help him excavate in the Pueblo San Lazaro the next morning – "if we cared to come along and had nothing better planned."

If we cared to come along? Boy, did we!

Forrest said he'd pick us up around 7:30 the next morning. He also promised to "sweet-talk" his wife, Peggy, into packing us a hearty picnic lunch, and told us to bring water – lots of it – and sunscreen, and to dress in cotton layers. Big, broad brimmed hats would do nicely for all of us, and we were told to wear long pants, lace-up shoes, and thick socks. If we didn't have appropriate headwear or sturdy shoes, we would stop somewhere to get the right gear for a desert dig. We would be gone the entire day.

I was too excited to sleep. Accompanying Fenn to his pueblo would be a fabulous opportunity to get to know him a little better. I still had a million questions to ask him, but I needed Dad on the same page, so I called his room.

"Dad, I have to come see you for a few minutes. You dressed for company?"

"Sure. I'm in bed, but I'm just reading a bit to relax. That sure was an unexpected invitation! Does he always devote this much time and attention to casual visitors?"

"But we're not casual visitors, are we, Dad? That's what I need to talk to you about."

Dad was sitting in an armchair donned in a plush white hotel robe when I let myself into his room. He'd brewed me some in-room coffee that sat steaming beside the companion armchair. I bussed his cheek with a brief kiss, then plunked down in the seat.

"I know what you're going to say," I began.

"Well, if you already know, and won't follow my advice, then why do you bother to ask?" My Dad liked to answer a question with a question. He and Fenn shared that proclivity. It was maddening.

"That's not what I was going to say. Tomorrow gives us a great opportunity to get to the bottom of this, especially if we tag-team him on the questions."

"Look, honey. You're my daughter and I love you very much. I admire your tenacity, but now is not the time for that kind of tenacity. Let's just get to know the guy – you'll learn more if he's not shut down from suspicion. Just my opinion, Pumpkin, but I think you should take it easy on him. Let him get to know you a little before he has to defend himself from your relentless *charms*."

"But Forrest already knows what I'm up to," I reminded. "We've been chatting online for a few months now. Remember, the draw of the book was my hook to get him to answer my email and take me seriously."

"Does he? Take you seriously?"

I let myself relax in the chair and sipped my coffee before answering. "I don't know. But it's too late to persuade him that I don't have an agenda."

"From what I've been able to gather, he's a straight shooter. He may exaggerate, but I don't think he lies. He's just very good at evading questions. And as far as the Internet goes, you can't take anything said there as absolute truth."

"I disagree. I think people talk more openly online to a faceless acquaintance. It can get like a confessional out there in digital space."

"Well, has Forrest confessed to you yet, in all these online exchanges you've had with him?"

"Not really. That's what I'm after. But he sure has dropped a lot of hints. And he speaks in parables, so he admits stuff but encapsulates the admission in a story, so that you can never really pin him down."

"Well, that should tell you something. He's not ready to give himself up. Who would be, with an arrest and trial set to kick into action the minute he surfaces and his identity proven?"

"But who would prosecute an eighty-something-year-old man for a 45-year-old crime?"

"A state prosecutor after headlines would drag him into court in a heartbeat. And even if a jury found him innocent, Fenn would still have to spend a huge amount in time and expense to defend himself. And if I understand him at all, he'd rather take his secret to the grave than exit this world a notorious criminal."

"But he *wants* to get his story out, Dad. You've even said so yourself. That's why he hid all those bronze things and that treasure chest with what he calls his real autobiography. And I just *know* it's his confession of the truth. I believe to the soles of my shoes that Fenn pulled off the coup of the century! And, bottom line, I think he wants it known."

"In his own time and his own way, Pumpkin. Not yours."

I tried to think of a quick reply, but came up empty.

He seemed to sense his advantage and changed the subject. "Digging in San Lazaro is going to be an education in itself. I'm really looking forward to it, Stephanie. But you've got to let your old man get some sleep. It's going to be a long day tomorrow."

I kissed Dad goodnight, realizing how much he meant to me. Dad, and Dad alone, was what "family" meant to me. And now there was Emma, whom I had grown to treasure both as a friend and a helpmate for my father. If anyone could keep him well, it was her.

As I shut the door behind me, I realized I had forgotten to tell my father about my belief that Skippy was a passenger on the Northwest Orient 727, and that he lived in Seattle. I cursed under my breath. I almost turned around to knock on the door again, but Dad had looked tired, and when I did get around to telling him this, it was going to be a long conversation. As I walked down the hall to my room, I wondered if Skippy had flown with Forrest – anonymously, of course – to ensure his younger brother didn't run into any trouble during the air heist. Was it also to stash a few things Forrest would need under a seat, or in an overhead compartment – like a pair of shoes or boots that would stay on during a jump, and a helmet?

The next morning started well. We met Forrest in the lobby and piled into his Jeep, armed with hats, shirts, sunscreen and shovels, small garden rakes and brushes, containers to hold our finds, and a marvelous picnic lunch Forrest's wife had prepared. She had enclosed a note that introduced herself and invited us for dinner at the Fenn home before our departure. Obviously, a gracious lady. No wonder Forrest spoke so glowingly of their marriage. I imagined that, as a husband, an independent man such as he was, with so many interests, acquaintances, and notoriety and immense popularity, was a handful for any woman to manage. My hat was off to her.

San Lazaro Pueblo was about 17 miles outside of Santa Fe. The first stone and adobe buildings were built and inhabited around 1150 A.D. Construction of the pueblo extended into the 1300s, and it was the largest of the eight pueblos in the Galisteo Basin area over the centuries. A Tano pueblo, San Lazaro has been estimated to have as many as 5,000 rooms in 27 room blocks that cover more than 57 acres, although recent estimates speak of an estimate closer to 2,000 rooms and 22 room blocks. The enormous site measures 1,438 feet, north to south, and 1,738 feet, east to west. San Lazaro at its height may have been home to 1,800 people or more and was, in fact, a small city. Tewa Indians, too, had occupied the site some 300-plus years ago, after the Tano and before the remaining families moved on to the Hopi reservation in Arizona.

In the 1890s, after New Mexico had become a U.S. Territory, Adolph Bandelier was the first archeologist to visit San Lazaro, publishing only a brief description of the Pueblo.

Once New Mexico became a state in 1912, initial excavations were conducted by Nels. C. Nelson, an archeologist who worked for the American Museum of Natural History in New York City. By the time Nelson began his dig, the pueblo had been abandoned for over 230 years, and he described it as "eroded and treeless" – no more than a depression in the soil. Surrounding landscapes were barren, and forested areas had suffered from centuries of exploitation for fuel and food. Nelson excavated only about 60 rooms.

Forrest purchased the 160 acres of the land containing San Lazaro in the mid to late 1980s, and has continued excavations with friends, student and archeological groups, and various interested visitors. Fenn opened his land to excavation by amateur archeologists, primarily students and young people with the intent of inspiring them to treasure history as he does. Sometime in 2014, Forrest sold the land to a man named William Sathers.

While Forrest no longer owned the land, which includes a ranch, he retained his digging privileges and still brought groups out to dig with him.

San Lazaro was the name of Saint Lazarus, friend of Jesus and brother to Mary Magdalene –the same man who was raised from the dead by Jesus.

We drove through a dry and dusty landscape ringed by purple and green mountains - the Sangre de Cristo and Ortiz ranges – covered primarily with savannah grassland and scrub brush, piñon, and juniper bushes stretching as far as the eye could see. But arroyos and mountain creeks, such as the Galisteo and the La Cienega, that fed into the Santa Fe River and the Rio Grande, brought water to the Basin, and made it habitable.

Forrest told us this was home to deer and antelope, bear and coyote, bobcats and smaller creatures, and the occasional wandering steer. Spring rains were due, he said, and would add patches of greenery and wildflowers to the expansive scenery.

Fenn had made the pueblo the focus of his life after selling the gallery in 1988. He had published his book, *The Secrets of San Lazaro*, in 2004, when I first bought a copy. I had seen two used copies of the book online, on a rare book website, just a few months before our trip. They were listed for $438.56 and $651.35, respectively, but were in only "Good" condition. How much would my perfect copy bring?

We drove past a charming adobe church with its dusty-walled cemetery filled with both simple and elaborate crosses – and the occasional plain headstone – that marked the resting place of about two hundred souls. Stucco, stone, and adobe churches dotted the valley, most with an iconic bell tower (or two). They varied in age from ancient to modern. Small villages sprang up around them in the valley and on the hillsides – some charming, and others less so. Broad, flat outcroppings of rock punctuated the Galisteo

Basin floor, and some were large enough for pooled water to settle in the pitted stone. Its rural population and prevailing architecture spoke of the state's history and forcefully reminded one of New Mexico's heritage.

Traveling with Forrest was like traveling with an audio book encyclopedia. Fenn had no need to regret his lack of formal education beyond high school. He knew more than the majority of my friends with graduate degrees. This was a man with a thirst for knowledge and a capacious brain, capable of retaining an immense number of facts. That, and a love of learning, served one far better than a grudgingly earned degree. I was learning a tremendous amount just looking out the window from the back seat of his rugged Jeep, listening intently as Forrest talked. We were all so entranced by his monologue that no one asked a question for miles.

When Forrest paused, Dad bombarded him with questions. Was it far? What does one do on a dig, anyway? Are there any prohibitions about taking a find or two home? Emma wanted to know if there were "facilities," and fretted when she learned there were none. Noting her discomfit, Forrest assured her that in a desert climate, the urgency was to maintain hydration despite daytime temperatures that dried the body as the fluids escaped through the skin. It usually never became a problem, except on the ride home,

In short order, we pulled up to the area Forrest was currently excavating. He had a particular group of rooms he was interested in. He taught us how to gently dig and sift the soil while looking for any small items that might otherwise escape notice. We were to brush off each potential find to determine its nature, then place it where it was found and take a photo of the location and its relationship to identifiable features.

Dad and Emma took their tools and immediately set off to work in a room some distance away. Forrest and I would work together. Following Dad's advice, I bit my tongue and worked quietly alongside Forrest, listening to him talk and wondering how I could shift the topic to the questions I wanted to ask. We dug and dug in the hot sun. Forrest had worn a trusty, beat-up brown felt 10-gallon cowboy hat and long-sleeved plaid shirt, ironed jeans, and hiking boots. I had loaded up on sunscreen and wore a long-sleeved cotton shirt over a t-shirt, jeans, grey hiking boots, and huge sunglasses beneath a large, floppy straw hat.

Forrest fell silent after ascertaining I had "gotten the hang of how to do it right," and we dug independently, occasionally comparing pottery shards and other small finds. I retrieved a nicely patterned clay spindle whorl with a small chip, some beautifully decorated shards of pottery and what looked to be a wooden spoon by the time we broke for lunch.

I was starving and marveled at the feast Peggy prepared for us: cold fried chicken and home-canned pickles, biscuits, and a type of cabbage slaw made with spiced vinegar and shreds of carrot and raisins. Dessert consisted of extra-large sugar cookies. An iced tea dispenser contained a blend of fresh lemonade and iced tea--a refreshing change from the warm bottled water we'd been drinking all morning to stay hydrated.

After lunch, Emma and Dad eagerly returned to the room they had been working on, but not before discussing their own small finds with Forrest. Forrest pointed out the most productive areas to dig and congratulated them on their finds.

Once we were alone again, I couldn't stand it anymore. I had to speak.

"Forrest," I blurted, "let's cut to the chase – no pun intended. You know I'm dying to ask you dozens of questions."

So much for Dad's advice. I held my breath.

Forrest replied, in his slow drawl, "And you know, young lady, that I am just as eager not to undergo an inquisition. Not until I know what you have up your sleeve. Not until I hear some of this "evidence" you've been gathering. I want to hear this case you think you have made against me."

Cool. The man was so cool. He hadn't even blinked.

"Forrest – I would like nothing better. Can we set aside just a little time, just you and me, so we can sit and rationally discuss this? Maybe tomorrow morning?"

"We could probably do that. If I wanted to. Do I want to? Not really. But I must admit I am pretty curious."

"So, do you want to?

"Why?"

"So you can understand what leads me to believe you've been hiding in plain sight, and sprinkling hints throughout your books like Hansel in the Grimm fairy tale!"

"No, I meant, why do you need to do this? What is it that has driven you to 'investigate' me - to hear you tell it - for the majority of years you've spent on this planet?

That threw me off balance. I hadn't thought about that. It had never entered my mind to even contemplate this line of questioning, within myself, or with another.

I had no answer. D.B. Cooper had always just "been."

He had been part of my daily consciousness since I was ten, for heaven's sake, and my absorption with the mystery of old D.B. had carried me through most of the crises of my young life. It had given Dad spirit when I'd feared all was lost. But I'd never really thought about how and why it had become such an obsession for me.

Honesty appeared to be the best policy when dealing with Forrest, so I cautiously replied, "I really don't know, Forrest. D.B. has just always been there for me. And I just know you're D.B Cooper. Am I right?"

He studied me for a second, then said, "Have you ever caught a fish that tested you so well, tried you so hard, that you hated to throw it back? The one that had fought and fled, time and again, and profited from each battle?"

I looked at him with what I'm sure was pure confusion plastered on my face.

"Well, that kind of fish teaches a humbling lesson. – leaving as legacy the fact that he'd somehow escaped the hook, even though the bait was gone. Such fish become legendary among fishermen. Every fishing hole has a huge, wise old fish that has lived on through time, defeating every hook."

That's a not-so-subtle self-reference, or else I'm blind, deaf, and dumb. But it was not proof.

"Look, Miss Ward, you might as well get used to the idea that I'm not gonna admit to anything coming out of your mouth having a shred of truth to it. In case you've forgotten, my true biography has already been irrevocably committed to writing for some time, and copies are sealed with the treasure, as well as in a few of the bronze jars and bells I've buried. *That* is how I will know when the treasure, or any of the bronzes, have been found. Whether I am dead or alive, the news will not be contained."

"Then I *am* on track, aren't I, Forrest? Aren't I? We really need to talk!"

"I thought we just did," was his reply.

What a tough old nut to crack. Maybe Dad was right. Maybe the nut *couldn't* be cracked. Maybe it had to be chipped or worn away instead. Forrest was a sly old dog and was not going to allow himself to be pinned down. Confrontation was not going to work.

I might not remember how my obsession arose, but I did know it wasn't going away any time soon. Especially not if Forrest kept talking, because he couldn't resist taunting me with ephemeral, insubstantial, and quasi-admissions. Cat and mouse. And I felt like an increasingly uncomfortable little mouse. My "interrogation" was turning out much different than I had imagined.

But he *had* agreed to talk to me the next day, right? That wasn't my imagination. We would meet alone the next day to go over my conclusions. Good thing I'd actually started writing the book and brought those first chapters with me! I knew he would want to see if it was a reality, and not just a ruse, before considering any kind of negotiation.

What spurred me on was an intense belief I'd developed during my investigation--Forrest had a final story he really wanted told. If my hunch was correct, at the end of this life, he wanted the world to marvel that he had actually devised "a system to beat the system" – in a final letter to the media.

A sudden clamor alerted us to Dad and Emma approaching excitedly with an object gently cradled in their hands. "Look at this, Forrest," my father exclaimed. "Look! These little bowls, these were in the room under the angle of a fallen rock ledge that could have been part of a table!" Dad and Emma's excitement reminded me of children on Christmas morning who'd just received the one thing they really, desperately wanted.

Forrest duly examined their finds and praised the perfect state of preservation, the undamaged surfaces, as well as beautiful handiwork and finely painted details. Dad was ecstatic, and Emma proudly clung to his arm. "We took pictures, like you said to do," she announced, grinning in celebration of their magnificent find. For the first time, I noticed she had dimples. Along with my earlier finds, I'd uncovered a rolling pin to crush grains and herbs. My finds did not even come close to being exceptional. But the looks on Dad and Emma's faces more than made up for my failure. Those beaming faces were priceless.

Emma pressed against Dad as he showed Forrest the photos of the items he'd taken *in situ* and the measurements he'd taken. Forrest patted him on the back and conveyed his delight when Dad offered their find to his Collection.

"Since history belongs to us all," Forrest said, "I accept your kind offer on behalf of The Collection, and for the many who will have the opportunity to view it as a result."

With the sun well past its zenith, we packed up and called it a day. Forrest paid special attention to the transport of the precious Tano Indian bowls. Cleaned of their dust, they were exceptionally beautiful, with their classic shapes and their hand-painted decorations intact. My mind's eye conjured up images of the artist carefully drawing his brush over the clay in the sharp -edged designs important to their culture.

Dad and Emma held hands as they gazed at the result of their excavating efforts. They glowed with happiness, and I glowed with the knowledge that I had been able to provide my father with this amazing opportunity for accomplishment – something to tell his friends back home.

We said our goodbyes and thanked Forrest for a grand outing. He and I exchanged knowing glances. We had agreed to meet at 10 a.m. the next morning. Our excellent dinner that night, at yet another exquisite Santa Fe eatery, was a two-fold celebration for Dad and Emma. We drank to their archeological find, and to their engagement.

Yes, engagement. In the euphoria following their mutual discovery, Dad had proposed to Emma, and she accepted. "After all," he joked, "Emma's already doing all the wifely stuff." He kissed his blushing fiancée. "We'll need the morning off from whatever you might have planned, Stephanie. We'll be shopping for rings."

Well, I thought, that took care of my problem of keeping them occupied while I bearded the lion in his den! Or something along those lines. At least, I would get the opportunity to explain my line of thought to Forrest, and in so doing, maybe catch a glimpse of where the truth actually lay.

As the sun set and we continued our meal, fireworks began going off around the city. We called the waiter over to inquire as to the reason for the explosive celebrations. "Tomorrow is Cinco de Mayo – big celebration for our Mexican friends. Some people always have to start celebrating early. Tomorrow is a big day around here. Fun time. Can I get you anything else?"

"How about a wedding ring on a holiday?" Dad asked.

"Oh, it's not that kind of holiday, Sir. The stores don't close – they just close earlier. The whole purpose of the festival is to *make* money. You'll have no problem. May I offer the happy couple a complimentary glass of champagne?"

We sipped the champagne and browsed the dessert menu, then ordered fruit tarts and crème Brule, chocolate truffles coffees with liquor, and a cup of tea for Emma. With our bellies and souls satisfied, we called it a night.

I think Dad and Emma slept in the same bed, because the next morning they exchanged their single rooms for a spacious double, without saying a word to me.

Chapter 37: Face-to-Face

Dad and Emma were as excited as kids the next morning at breakfast. It was sweet to watch them doting on each other, barely noticing my presence. Watching them as I ate my huevos rancheros, I vaguely recalled the excitement I'd felt when Michael and I set out in search for just the right ring following his lunchtime proposal so long ago. I tried to remember any deeper feelings that afternoon but drew a blank. The memory remained as but an historical fact brought forth from the shadows of the past in response to my observation of the happy couple sitting before me. Pain had erased every emotion of that day, leaving only the dry facts.

After breakfast, we went our separate ways. "Be sure to check out the Palace of Governors if you're heading in that direction," I suggested as they turned to leave. "I understand the local Indians display their wares under the portico, and they have some beautiful jewelry and other handiwork for sale." Dad turned to smile at me as Emma took his arm. I waved them off and headed to my room.

I immediately regretted eating a big breakfast. Nerves had my stomach churning. I had less than two hours to dress, take a quick glance at my notes, and have the desk call a cab to take me to the Fenn home. I wondered how long Forrest would suffer my questions, whether I would get the answers I hoped for, and whether – if he didn't throw me out and I was actually invited to stay for lunch - I would meet Peggy. If things did *not* go well, and I became persona non grata in the Fenn household, it might jeopardize the tentative dinner invitation Forrest had extended at the dig. He'd promised to firm up the invitation once he had consulted his wife.

Dad would be crushed, but I couldn't waste any more time speculating. Besides, wasn't he as concerned about getting to the bottom of the D.B. mystery as I was?

Flying in the face of Dad's caution, I had pushed this with Forrest and now I was committed to taking it as far as I could go. I had not mentioned this meeting to Dad. But, come to think of it, there were additional details I had uncovered in recent months that I had not shared with my father. Since Emma had entered his life, we hadn't had much time to talk – not about The Search, anyway. I hadn't even had the chance to mention that I had discovered that Skippy was on the pirate 727 that night! Or the airport sightings, or – my gosh, how long had it been since we had actually shared anything about our suspected D.B.-Fenn connection, besides briefly mentioning our suspicions to Emma *sotto voce* on the plane to bring her up to speed?

I had a good grasp of the essential details supporting my case. But I had no clue how our session would go.

I jumped in the shower, dressed quickly, and had the concierge call a cab for me. I had written the address on a slip of paper and passed it to the driver - a rotund gentleman of obvious Mexican descent who introduced himself as Raul and declared his great honor that I had chosen him and his humble taxi to drive me to . . . he looked down at my printed note and I watched the flash of recognition cross his face. His moustache smiled even before his lips parted and spread into a toothy grin.

"Ahhh," he said, sending me a twinkling glance me through the rearview mirror, "The pretty lady is going to visit Senior Forrrrest Fenn." I almost laughed at the exaggerated way he rolled the Rs in Fenn's name. "He is very famous, no?" He was studying my face in the mirror as he asked this, gripping the key in the ignition, but not yet turning it to engage the engine.

"I guess so," I replied brusquely, and pointedly stared out the window for the remainder of the ride. I owed no details to a curious cab driver. I kept an eye on the meter and had my money in hand when he stopped the taxi in front of a sprawling adobe built by Forrest on the Old Santa Fe Trail in the years after he had conquered cancer and sold his gallery.

As I walked up to the door, it swung open, and Forrest stood there, in jeans and a blue and white short-sleeved shirt, with sheepskin-lined brown leather slippers on his feet. A slow, easy smile came easily to his face.

"My inquisitor arrives," he announced, and waved me inside, shutting the heavy door behind me. Transition from the bright heat to the cool, dim interior of the entry left me momentarily blinded, and the faint soft, sweet smell of piñon smoke assailed my nostrils. I had the impression of dark wood furnishings and accents of stone against pale stucco, and antiquities everywhere. I blinked. My eyes slowly adapted to the low light.

"I would offer to take your coat, but you don't seem to have one," Forrest joshed. His eyes crinkled beneath bushy brows and brightened his face when he smiled, even as his other facial features remained stoically composed. Fenn's intense eyes - sparkling with amusement – were set into stern features which softened with a blend of *bonhomie* and unmistakable dignity as he greeted me. It was like he was laughing on the inside at some brilliant cosmic joke that only he understood. In the bright sunlight of the previous day before, I hadn't noticed the gentleness of his expression, nor the kindness in his eyes. His gaze was direct and appraising.

I hadn't expected a warm greeting, and it caught me off guard. I was wearing dress denims, brown leather ankle boots and an aqua and pale green plaid shirt with silver buttons and pale green Western trim. My large saddle-leather bag slung over my shoulder carried a tape recorder, pens, a notebook, and my notes. No mistake about it, I was here on business.

"Let's go on back to my study."

Forrest turned and walked down the hall. I followed, taking in everything I could as I walked behind him. Despite his age, Fenn carried himself well. His stride was even, his back straight. His military posture and still-broad shoulders made him appear even taller than the 6 feet he owned up to. A slight belly had softened his physique, but at almost 86 years of age, Forrest Fenn was still a fine specimen of a man.

Although modest on the exterior, it was an incredible house, with incredible contents. I'd thought The Fenn Collection was fascinating, but it did not even begin to match the items Forrest had displayed in his home. Shelving and long, thin display drawers appeared custom-built to show and store his vast collections. Visually, I was overwhelmed, and could barely watch where I was placing my feet as I looked left and right, up, and down, from eye level to ceiling height to tabletop, as I tried to keep up while not missing a thing. Walls were covered with amazing Western paintings, and a thousand other items. Something fascinating occupied every square inch of the place.

A grouping of Native American shields made from painted leather stretched on wood frames and adorned with feathers and bead trim were hung together on one wall. Assorted artifacts and personal adornments hung on the other walls, joined by beaded moccasins, fringed bags, mounted goat horns and painted hides, Chieftains' headdresses with trailing feathers, big-horned cattle skulls, and ancient weapons. Grey slate floors were covered with oriental rugs. We walked by the dining area, with its long stretch of a table and the dozen or so upholstered chairs drawn around it. Then we passed beneath the structural timber lintel framing a narrow doorway that opened into a truly astounding room: Forrest's study.

My jaw dropped. I spotted a large Remington bronze worth a small fortune on a tabletop. Two mounted cowboys met, face to face, their patient steeds snorting and stamping hooves, ready to move away when spurred by their riders, whose serious faces evidenced an equally serious topic of conversation.

Wood chests, large ceremonial drums and feathered rattles, an antique table covered with small artifacts and a neat row of trapper boots standing beneath competed to attract the eye. A well-loved, tan sofa sat against the pale wall to the side of Forrest's large mahogany double-pedestal desk; mounted above it was an impressive painted bison hide that spanned the length of the leather couch. The couch appeared very comfortable, and I envisioned Forrest stretched out and napping on it before I made note of the colorful woven throw folded over one of the padded arms. That blanket served to confirm my imagined portrait of him.

A long, narrow window that echoed the height and width of the entry stood directly opposite and balanced the long room. A faded red Persian rug warmed the décor.

The magnitude of the room, and the number of artifacts and curiosities displayed on shelves, tables, wall, and Forrest's crowded desktop was just astounding. The Fenn Collection paled in comparison. The room was eye candy for the connoisseur, and truly overwhelming for someone like me. I didn't even know where to begin looking.

The ceiling had to be about 20 feet high, with adjoining walls of book-filled shelves occupying each corner and rising to the ceiling. The shelving stretched from the slate floor to the two uppermost levels upon which Native American pottery was displayed – huge decorative clay pots, big glazed and unglazed pots, imminently useful bowls and urns, plain clay and painted creations all sat side-by-side, one stunningly large piece after another.

The ceiling itself was comprised of three long vaults of finished logs. fitted together tightly and supported by two immense, squared wood beams that ran parallel for the full length of the room.

Artifacts were everywhere – pipes and dolls, bracelets and beaded turquoise neckpieces. Ceremonial elements sat next to everyday items. Cattle skulls and paintings punctuated every available wall space. A cabinet of small collection drawers drew attention to the space beside the leather couch.

A beautiful, fringed shirt of velvet soft buckskin leather hung over the tall, wood-capped window opposite the entrance to the study. The deer leather from which the shirt was softened through one of a plethora of techniques Native Americans used to soften animal skins used for apparel.

Applying mashed Saguaro cactus seeds to the hide was one such method and braining – applying coatings of mashed animal brain mixed with water to create an oily liquid with extreme softening properties was yet another. The result was an incredibly soft leather that could be sewn and beaded and fringed like fabric. The shirt on display was an excellent example of the efficacy of the technique.

As I looked around, taking it all in, I murmured, "My Lord, I'd hate to dust this place!"

Shocked at the words that had just issued from my mouth, I raised three fingers to my lips as if to shush myself, and glanced at Forrest, who was obviously amused at my reaction.

"No need to worry, Missy," Forrest remarked, "Maria here takes care of everything."

I glanced at the tiny Mexican woman who had silently entered behind us, carrying a large silver tray of Southwestern design and ornamentation. On it were two large silver thermos pitchers, a wooden tea box, a glazed terra-cotta cream and sugar set with a painted pattern of stylized dragonflies, cups and saucers of the same design and a similarly patterned plate with a variety of treats. The tray looked far too large for her to carry, but Maria handled it with ease and set it on the large beige ottoman at the side of a large wing chair next to Forrest's crowded desk.

A formal wood armchair upholstered in striated beige silk sat in front of the desk, a conversational distance away from the chair I presumed was Forrest's. I had seen photos of Forrest seated in that very chair, reading glasses perched on his nose, busily tapping away at his laptop.

Forrest introduced us as he lowered himself into the wingchair, praising Maria and thanking her for the beverages. I nodded to Maria as I stood beside the other chair, then took my seat. She smiled, nodded back at me and quickly retreated as Forrest turned to the tray and asked, "Coffee? Tea? What's your pleasure?"

"That's easy," I replied. "Black coffee."

He poured then passed me a cup before proffering the plate of pig-shaped cookies and little squares of what looked like fried dough, sprinkled with cinnamon and rolled in sugar. "These are 'special order' treats - all the cookie calories were removed at the bakery. Both are from genuine Mexican recipes. I wanted to offer you something authentically Southwestern. The cookies are *Marranitos.* Delicious. You do like the taste of gingerbread?"

I nodded and accepted a cookie, placing it on the saucer alongside my coffee.

"I've also heard these called *cochinos,* or *puerquitos*: Little gingerbread pigs – though the funny thing is, there's no ginger in them at all. No cinnamon, either. The spicy-brown goodness comes from molasses. And these crispy squares here are *Sopapillas* – Maria's specialty. She made them for you just a few minutes ago, so do her the honor and try these first," Forrest said, using small tongs to transfer two little cinnamon and sugar-dusted square to my saucer, where they joined the waiting pig.

I tried one immediately. It wasn't bad at all, although a little foreign to my Texan palate.

Within a bite or two, and between sips of coffee, Forrest answered my many questions about the amazing items scattered about the room. I was curious about everything - absolutely everything. I also wanted to cut the tension – *my* tension, not his – and use the opportunity to enjoy the yummy snacks while I calmed down and marshalled my thoughts.

As at San Lazaro, Forrest was in his element as he spoke about his collections, his finds, and the history of the region. A good 45 minutes later, he settled back into his chair and announced, "Well, I guess it's about time we get started."

I nodded assent.

Clearing my throat, I began at the beginning, when I had first learned about Dad's interest in the hijacking from Mom. I reminded him that Dad had met him in Vietnam.

Forrest furrowed his brow as if trying to recall his farewell visit to his comrades in the hangar.

Noting his attempt at recollection, I paused, but didn't hesitate to accommodate his memory process as I plowed on, discussing how Dad's interest in the hijacking and his blind hunch about Forrest being D.B. and our subsequent investigation of the case had strengthened our relationship. I continued, relating how the unsolved case had fueled a fascination that became a lifetime obsession – one that had propelled me through the many rough patches in my life. I emphasized that, although Forrest had been a suspect since Dad revealed his name to me, I had carefully considered every other suspect introduced into the FBI investigation, and had dispassionately arrived at my own conclusions.

I elaborated as I did because I wanted Forrest to understand that my interest in him was not the result of casual curiosity or a wild theory, but the result of years of intensive personal investigation built upon the FBI findings, expanded by my own extensive research.

My studied reinforcement of Dad's initially casual suspicion, however, had been limited by lack of information – until Forrest himself began filling in the blanks, starting with his first memoir– *The Thrill of The Chase* – which I read and reread until I knew every detail, and then realized the book elucidated relationships and events in the investigation, and – like the Rosetta Stone – was the key to fleshing out the D.B. Cooper story. I gave Dad due credit recognizing that Forrest spoke in parables and was a master of the double entendre.

Forrest listened carefully, offering neither denial nor affirmation as I laid out my findings woven into the fabric of my own life milestones. The Search intertwined with all that had happened to me and to my Dad over the years.

I scrutinized Forrest's face closely as I spoke, alert for any micro expressions, those minute muscular twitches about an individual's eyes and mouth that can signal deception, or a suspicious shift in posture or body language that could inform me that my tale was ringing true.

In most people maintaining a false front, psychophysiological changes can unconsciously betray our conscious mind's nervous attempt to hold on to a fictitious version of reality. Such slips can reveal truth.

The majority of us are bad liars under pressure, although it is said that a true pathological liar can fool anyone, even a polygraph, because at the moment the lie issues from their mouths they've already convinced themselves that their words express the truth.

I held no illusions that I was capable of interpreting Fenn's reactions, but I had watched enough videos of him speaking and had seen enough of him in the past two days that I recognized his normal reactions and manner of speaking with individuals – the typical calm tones, direct eye contact, unwavering voice of Forrest Fenn.

Rather than being clever or postulating my conclusions immediately, I was deliberate in my telling, only occasionally referring to my notes to check a detail or observation. I knew every detail by heart.

As I spoke, my eyes strayed only occasionally to the F-100 model that sat on his desk, and I realized his eyes were following mine. Our eyes generally remained locked, however, as the details spilled from my lips, as though we were trying to peer into one another's souls, each trying to read the other at the deepest level.

Did I read respect in his eyes? I had not missed the occasional blink or twitch of facial muscles that seemed to acknowledge – what? They seemed to occur when I introduced my own discoveries and opinions. His face remained impassive when I reviewed known details.

Something was connecting in that brain of his. In spite of every attempt to remain unreadable, Forrest occasionally exhibited the tiniest of "tells" in response to some of the things I said. I became afraid to blink or check my notes while speaking for fear I would miss one of those "tells." Like when I talked about the money found on Tena Bar, and the missing $200 that I posited had most likely been removed from one of the three packets to pay the travel expenses of whomever had planted the cash not long after the hijacking. The twitch of the small muscles around his mouth was unmistakable, and there was the slightest change in the skin around his eyes before he looked past my face for an instant, as if a recollection called him into the past, before his eyes settled back on mine.

I somehow understood I was right.

I had not yet explained how I tied Forrest's books and the D.B. story together – I was not at that point yet, nor did I mention at that point that I was convinced Skippy had buried the purloined packets of twenties a shallow burial on the shores of the Columbia River to validate the prevalent theories of where Cooper had landed. But the Skippy I knew from Forrest's own stories would have felt entitled to reimbursement for expenses, and perhaps some small "bonus" for carrying our instructions. Ergo – the missing $200.

I'd wager that Forrest, on first hearing about the missing $200 in 1980, when the remnants of cash were found, understood immediately what had happened to make exactly 10 of the $20 bills from a single packet disappear, with no disturbance of the rubber band holding the bills together! Forrest knew his brother well, and – to give Skippy credit – they might well have agreed beforehand that the missing amount would finance the venture without raising the suspicions of Skippy's wife over an off-budget expenditure of that magnitude. After all, if the $200,000 garnered from the heist in 1972 would be worth $1.5 million in today's dollars, the missing $200 was the equivalent of $1,500 in today's dollars – a fairly significant sum for a working man to have to explain to the Mrs.

I brought that up later as I laid out the progression of my discoveries for another hour before revisiting the Tena Bar theory once I had disclosed the connections between the stories in his memoir and the Dan Cooper hijacking. Many of those stories also provided information that filled in the blanks missing in the FBI investigation.

I watched his face even more closely when I summed up my beliefs and told him I had read the August 20, 2012 article that Newsweek reporter Tony Dokoupil had written about him and the treasure hunt.

"I read that article, Forrest, and it made me laugh. It *SO* fit my theories and understanding of the case and confirmed my understanding of *you* – don't get me wrong – I am a huge admirer of you, and of all you have done. Knowing what I know . . .   And I could not help but laugh aloud reading – and here I quote Dokoupil, 'Santa Fe society was flush with tales about the invader Texan with the expensive tastes. And yet, despite the attention, Fenn remained essentially mysterious, He had arrived in 1972 as a nobody, a middle-aged Air Force veteran with a modest retirement, a high-school degree, and not a lick of experience in the art world. Shortly thereafter he was a millionaire. The question was how?'

"You remember that article, don't you Forrest?"

He shrugged, and responded, "I've had so many articles written about me over the years, I can't say that I do." He regarded me with a sudden wariness. And he was blinking – a lot.

"I know, Forrest. I've read quite of few of them. But I especially appreciated this one, because it rings so true in relation to your tenuous relationship with the law, and the pride you take in pulling one over on authority and making your own good fortune – although you have been one lucky devil, in a number of respects that we can discuss later."

He raised his fuzzy-caterpillar eyebrows at that.

I continued reading form Dokoupil's article. "In part, his timing was good. He arrived just as people moved to the Sunbelt and adopted a cowboy-and-Indian decorating motif. And he was clearly bright. One of his final military efficiency reports reads like a movie poster decorated with critical raves: 'high caliber,' 'truly amazing,' 'can do anything.' But people kept looking for something more, 'some secret' which would more than adequately explain his far-reaching success,' as a friend wrote in a 1981 book about the Western art world."

I grinned at Forrest periodically as I read the words. He looked slightly baffled. His eyes blinked, then darted from my eyes to my notes and then back to my eyes again. He had to be wondering where I was going with this. I had seized the upper hand and ran with it. I kept reading.

"Another friend took to calling Fenn the 'Wizard of Oz,' 'a former flim-flam man' who inspired a following." Fenn smiled at this, and the blinking relaxed.

"State and federal officials were curious, too. They wanted to know how, exactly, Fenn had acquired so much powerful inventory, and so quickly. 'His name has come up as a person of interest for decades,' says Phil Young, a retired National Parks Service investigator.

"To some degree, Fenn invited this kind of attention, He was a self-described 'hustler,' spending the first hour of every day –"

"Here, Dokoupil quotes you, Forrest . . . This is a direct quote."

I glanced at Forrest. He was avidly listening now, leaning forward slightly in his chair as I read the article to him. He seemed to be enjoying every word of it.

". . . spending the first hour of every day, 'well, scheming isn't a good word, but just planning,' he told me. 'I wanted to play Monopoly. I wanted to turn one into two and four into nine.' And he did precisely that, buying his paintings low, mouthing off about them for a few years, and selling high. As for how he got himself into the game to begin with, it's not so complicated, really. He dug his way in.

"Fenn has always been unusually good at giving himself advantages. As a boy, . . ."

"And here, Forrest, the writer goes on – and most of it is from *The Thrill of The Chase*, which we can both probably recite from memory, and goes on to talk about 'grabbing every banana,' and you and your dad collecting arrowheads. Then here it mentions, "The chase accelerated when he joined the Air Force in 1950, and was transferred to Bitburg, Germany, later that decade."

I abruptly stopped reading, hoping to catch him off guard. "'Fess up, Forrest. That's when you got hooked on the Dan Cooper comics."

His eyes widened, but then, blinking like a strobe light, feigned ignorance and urged me to continue with a slight wave of his hand. I laughed. Unwittingly, he'd surrendered another point to my side.

"Let's see, he goes on to talk about you taking jets, like the F-100," – I nodded to the model on his desk – "to Pompeii and Libya, and you hunted souvenirs in the Sahara, and then, here, Dokoupil mentions your time at Luke Air Force Base in Arizona in the 1960s, then talks here about potentially illegal digs, your 'slapstick trouble' with rattlesnakes and centipedes and being 'yanked' from a cave that had collapsed on you - or your digging partner, and then the helicopter arrival of Sen. Barry Goldwater, who just wanted to join your dig. And then here he writes about your transfer to Texas in the mid-1960s. Lubbock, wasn't it?"

He nodded.

"Hmmm. This says in Forbes in 1978 you started trading trinkets and artifacts for cash, or for more valuable items while you were stationed in Texas, before your stint in Vietnam where you received survival training and survived that terrible parachute into the Laotian jungle. Those extreme conditions were remarkably like those Dan Cooper faced Thanksgiving Eve, 1971."

Forrest blinked several times. His gaze darted to the notes in my lap.

"Go on," he said, with the slightest hint of impatience in his tone.

"Okay, here we go. Here the Newsweek reporter says about you, 'He also says he took in money by casting bronze statues, using a crucible he 'scrounged' from the Air Force, and the metal from a 'midnight requisition' of four sprinkler heads from a Texas Tech practice football field.' I think I recall you telling me in one of our online chats that you were taking in nearly $80,000 a year from that foundry work in your garage. You do realize that the Cooper group identified the aluminum and titanium particles on the tie you left behind as indicative of someone who worked in a foundry? In your memoir, you mention the foundry close to where you mentioned the Rosetta Stone, and I realized what you meant-- that to solve the mystery of D.B. Cooper, I had to use your book to translate the facts and make them meaningful. My dad advised me to look at your words as parables, never quite totally factual, and always having an alternate meaning."

No reaction from Fenn except the darting, blinking eyes. Who did he think he was fooling? I hoped he never played poker.

"Back to the article. I can see you're getting antsy, Forrest. Here's where you went to Vietnam for a year – though Dokoupil doesn't mention a thing about Nam. He just jumps to 1972, and writes, 'By 1972 he had enough cash and inventory to move to Santa Fe, partnering with a local Indian-artifacts trader. Within a year, the trader wanted to back out, fearing damage to his reputation with the Indians. But Fenn had his footing by then.' This is the part I *love*, Forrest: 'He found an angel investor and began to build Fenn Galleries, buying, selling, and trading his way up the totem pole for the next 17 years.'"

I sat back, gazing steadily into Forrest's eyes – when I could hold his gaze. Had he been this visibly nervous when he defended himself against the FBI agents investigating him as a grave robber and black market dealer of Indian artifacts, they would most certainly have arrested him on the spot.

I moved in for the kill.

"See?" I said. His fidgeting and wandering gaze emboldened me. "I told you that you were lucky. You found that 'angel investor' in Northwest Orient, and cashed in on Thanksgiving Eve, November 24, 1971.

"Not only did your delay in jumping take your landing zone miles from a dangerous drop and out of the search area after the heist – Poor Skippy and Donnie had practiced for naught – but when one or the other of them – was it Skippy? Or Donnie? When you were picked up walking barefoot along the road in the flatlands of Washington State, some eleven miles from the Portland airport, all you needed to disappear into the history books was a pair of shoes and a ticket home. Nobody was going to be looking in Texas for the infamous, Dan Cooper-- D.B. – whatever you want to call him. Am I right? And the two of them were perfectly situated to mail those letters for you to throw off the hounds."

My mention of the rural airport "dry runs" in anticipation of the event - the reported sightings of the car meeting up with a small plane - and the aborted pick up the night of the air heist evoked visible emotion in Forrest – suppressed, but visible, as he blinked and squirmed in his seat, more uncomfortable than ever. He hadn't yet denied it, but he hadn't admitted it either. *Damn it!*

"I don't mean to be rude, Forrest – you're a great host, and Lord knows, I'm an unabashed admirer – I really am – but we both *know* you did it; that *you are* D.B. Cooper. And we both know you are dying to tell the world. Well, that wasn't such a good choice of terms at your age, but you do want the world to know. I mean, it – it was the crime of the century with books and songs and movies made of it. It was over 45 years ago, and you are an old folk hero! I want to tell that story for you."

The implacable Mr. Fenn stared right back at me when I finished my triumphant little declaration. His eyelids were batting faster than those of a señorita being wooed by a handsome caballero, and he was squirming uncomfortably, but - gesturing with his chin in the direction of my photocopied Newsweek article - Forrest simply asked, "Can I make a copy?"

I was floored by his reaction. Getting an acknowledgement was going to be tough.

But I could see that he could barely keep from doing just that – admitting what I had deduced was the truth of the matter. I leaned forward and asked, "Will you let me tell your story?"

His response was just this: "You are a very perceptive young woman, and it does make for a good story. But none of that is proof."

"All circumstantial. I agree, Forrest." Then I reached into my bag of tricks for the ultimate *piece-de-resistance* – the one discovery that could not be dismissed as merely circumstantial evidence or pure supposition. It was the one discovery that was certainly enough to kick the dormant investigation into high gear. *It was evidence.*

"I have found irrefutable visual proof that Skippy was on that plane with you, Forrest, and disembarked with the released passengers after your demands had been met."

That got to him. If I had previously questioned the validity of Forrest's facial cues, or my ability to accurately read them – the multiple "tells" that I had observed – there was absolutely no question now. He asked in a shaky voice, "What is the proof, what kind of evidence, I mean. What do you have? Where is it – *what* is it?"

"I don't physically have possession of it - it is on YouTube, for the entire world to see."

"Well, what is it?" he demanded.

"It is a full copy of the videotaped report by Walter Cronkite, with video of the Flight 305 passengers, filmed at the Seattle Airport by the CBS News crew assigned to the story that night. It reveals William Marvin 'Skippy' Fenn, no doubt flying - like yourself – under an alias, disembarking with the other passengers immediately following the hijacking, and while you were still on board. He was the 11th or 12th passenger off the plane. He was wearing a dark cowboy hat and was the only one trying very hard not to be noticed – which, or course, made him all the more noticeable. He was complicit. And I bet Donnie was in on it, too. They are both gone now, and that leaves just you, *D.B.*"

Forrest's eyes grew wide, and he finally spoke, asking abruptly, "How do you know it was him?"

I smiled slowly at him, relishing the moment, and remained silent. My small smile rivaled the Mona Lisa's for vagueness, although – within – I was grinning like a Cheshire cat.

I explained how I had come across the large close-up photo of Skippy on the Hillcrest memorial post on www.findagrave.com when I Googled his brother's full name.

Forrest just stared at me blankly. I then told him how I'd found the CBS videotape within days of that discovery, just to learn how it had been originally reported. Then I used two computers, operating side-by-side, to show the enlarged memorial photo of Skippy right next to the videotape as I ran and reran the tape a good 20 times, and then isolated each single frame as he passed by the camera, to compare the features.

Skippy's attitude, too, as he made his way toward the camera was a dead giveaway. Relative to the other disembarking passengers, Skippy had not been relaxed as he walked, looking naturally into the lens. Rather, he overtly made every attempt to avoid looking at the camera as it was positioned, to the point that he stood out from the other passengers with his strained neck positions and evasive tactics. Then I looked at the background photos of Skippy in *TTotC*. There was not one shred of doubt in my mind that it was he.

"Not one shred," I told Forrest. His silence spoke volumes.

Suddenly he rose, announced that it was about time for lunch and "of course" I was staying to eat a little something, was I not?

"I'll let Maria know we're ready, Missy. Be right back."

Forrest was gone in a flash, leaving me to stare at his retreating back, with mouth agape. I had noticed activity around the dining table, which was visible behind him. But I never suspected he would offer lunch.

There was still no sign of his wife, Peggy, but Maria had laid out a lovely spread. I could barely think about food at the moment and had no appetite. I wondered how Forrest could eat at all.

He graciously filled a plate for me from the assorted Mexican entrees and passed it to me, then filled one for himself, and poured us each a glass of red wine. A full glass of water stood at each place, and we sat at angles to one another, so we could speak quietly.

"Does Peggy know?" I asked.

He looked at me and said, "You know, I don't know. Of course, I don't know what you are talking about, either."

The food almost fell out of my mouth. I was stunned.

"Why haven't you looked for the treasure?" he asked, switching topics on me. "Any answers you're looking for are in the autobiography I included with the treasure. And in the bronze bells and jars I've buried. The world will know what it needs to know, in due time."

"Forrest!" I was horrified. He was not going to admit to what we both knew to be true, and acknowledge what I'd spent so many years and so much effort to discover, but intended to send me on that same wild goose chase that thousands of others were spinning their wheels – and spending thousands of dollars and insane amounts of time on - to find?

I threw down my fork and just stared at him.

"What did we just go through this morning?" I demanded, icily.

"Look, Missy . . ."

"My name is Stephanie."

"I like Missy better. It suits you. Look, I have no desire to spend my last years and thousands of dollars hiring lawyers to defend my you-know-what. D.B. is a criminal and will be immediately arrested should he come forward – you know that. And whether they can prove I am he, or not, is open to question. But I don't want to deprive my family of what could be hundreds of thousands of dollars. You just know some hotshot Oregon D.A. will jump on this case with both feet, aiming to make himself a name, so he can run for the State Senate, or a federal position. Those damn fools always have politics on their minds."

"Well, I don't want to spend the thousands of dollars chasing my tail to find your treasure. I am not quite as rich as you are, Forrest, but I have a good life just as it is. I don't want to lose what I have, thank you very much."

"Then, Missy," he replied, "you know exactly how I feel."

He was infuriating, because – if he really did not want this to come to light until after he was gone, why in the world had he made such a spectacle of this treasure hunt? What if – through some fantastical piece of luck – one of the thousands of treasure hunters actually *found* the darned thing? If his autobiography said what I think it did, the story would be out, anyway! And I told him so.

"Well," he chuckled, "anyone with a lick of sense would very quietly go their way and spend the contents over time, secure for life and free of the 50% the government would siphon off in taxes."

"Not if their egos are as big as those of some people I know," I retorted, crossing my arms for emphasis – emphasis that was lost the minute I reached to take a sip of my wine. It was delicious. I pushed my food around the plate and then took an angry bite. Whoa – why were we fighting, this was delicious. I took another bite and chewed thoughtfully. Maybe he could be reasoned with.

"Forrest, what if I took this to the FBI?"

"You've got to do what you've got to do, Missy," Forrest replied, in an equally thoughtful tone, "But then I don't think I could call you my friend anymore."

I was ready to tear my hair out, and would have stomped off to get a taxi, but Maria's cooking was simply too good. And I was really getting to like the man. He had an endearing quality about him. Sort of. For a moment I thought I'd actually like to count him as a friend. But I was still dissatisfied with the outcome of the morning, frustrated that my labor of love was going nowhere, since the answer still evaded me.

"I am going to write my book, anyway," I announced, deciding then and there that I would tell the tale without a conclusion – yet.

"I will write it, Forrest, and get it published, and I will go ahead and look for your damned 'secreted' treasure while I do!"

It was my "so there!" moment, and I relished the moment he said, "And I just might publish your damned story, anyway, and we'll both make money off it. But I won't admit to it. I'll never admit to it, so long as there's still a little life in me." Forrest took a bite, chewed thoughtfully, and then said, "Find the treasure, Missy. Join the Chase. You're so pale, you could use a little more sun on your face. And I bet you don't see much of the outdoors. It would do you a lot of good."

Chapter 38: When the Dinner Bell Rings

I don't know how the dinner table conversation got around to talking about Pavlov and his dogs, but it did,

Dad and Emma had returned victorious from their hunt for a ring. Emma proudly displayed the unusual ring set that Dad had splurged to buy her. A striking emerald-cut aquamarine was set in platinum between trillion-cut diamonds, with a matching band that alternated square-cut aquamarines with diamonds of the same shape around the entire band.

The aquamarines were a rich color and did, as Dad pointed out, match Emma's clearly ice-blue eyes precisely. They were like teenagers.

Dinner had started on a light note when Forrest made his announcement. "Missy here came to see me this morning about this kind of interesting theory she has," he began, "and she's writing a book about it."

Dad shot me a look that was part query and part fury. I reached for my wine and tried to think of some way to respond, but couldn't, so I just took a sip and nodded – and promptly took another.

"I think I'm going to help her get it published," Forrest announced.

"What's it about?" Peggy asked, passing me the salad as she did, one eyebrow cocked in inquiry.

Forrest answered in my stead, "She thinks I'm D.B. Cooper. And she just might be right." He winked at me.

"D.B. who?" Peggy asked.

"You know how I love a good story, and I think this will be a hit, Peggy. Make us all a lot of money."

I had said nothing to Dad about my intentions to see Forrest that morning, hence the fury he'd exhibited on learning of it. But when he realized Peggy was clueless about the actual significance of what Forrest had just revealed, Dad panicked – thinking she would require an explanation - and brought up Pavlov, out of the blue, saying he had just read a fascinating book about the scientist. His enthused remarks successfully shifted the topic. That's how we ended up talking about the dogs.

And speaking of sly dogs, I suddenly realized that Forrest was ahead of the pack.

It hit me that he had broached the subject to Peggy so that it could now be dealt with over time. It would take at least several months for me to write enough for anyone to read, and that gave him ample time to massage the story and present it to her in a manner she and their daughters could accept. It seemed to me, however, that the ever-present danger of someone finding the treasure box and publicizing his revealing autobiography without warning should have prompted him to introduce the subject to her long before now – like in 2010, when he'd published *TTotC*? Perhaps it was true, as some had surmised, that there was no treasure at all – or that it was so impossibly hidden that it would *never* be found. In that case, he was wise to have withheld the facts from everyone.

I confess I had to agree with his caution in bringing the facts forward, since businesses and individuals wind up enriching no one but the lawyers when forced to defend themselves from lawsuits, or even significantly delayed prosecution. Situations abounded where elderly criminals, caught at long last after years on the run from the law, and having lived long lives without a further hint of scandal, have been forgiven their crimes by society, and granted only token punishments.

In Forrest's case, his status as a folk hero among his treasure hunting followers – along with D.B.'s regaled folk status as "the one who got away with it" - would surely combine with his advanced age and subsequent contributions to society and result in a light sentence, if any at all, were the case against D.B. Cooper ever to be - as he put it - "kick-started" and pursued by some ambitious District Attorney.

By backing my book, Forrest Fenn would demonstrate no fear of the story getting out. By publishing it himself, he could profit from what was sure to be a runaway best seller due to its topic, if not the quality of its writing, and in so doing he could still maintain what politicians dub "plausible deniability." Further, by maintaining good relationships with me and my family, and retaining control of the book as its publisher, Forrest had it all sewn up. It could be published as fiction, or as a "real crime" speculation, and the money and resultant fame would serve to keep the family lips zipped, in our best interests. There was even the possibility of attracting the attention of Hollywood. After all, Forrest did have contacts.

Forrest Fenn. was one smart cookie, and a master of human nature.

We parted that evening with an agreement of sorts written on the back of a grocery list. Fenn promised to follow it up with a generous contract, and I promised to have something to show him within a month.

Pavlovian, indeed.

Chapter 39: And So It Goes . . .

When I returned to Temple, I spoke to the partners of the construction firm and wrangled a six month leave of absence, provided I retained remote supervision responsibilities for my tight little group of managers - who actually needed little more than a seasoned company official to provide occasional guidance or consultation. I was confident in their abilities, and so accepted the conditions.

I bought a new laptop, cleared my calendar, and set to work.

I felt an unspoken obligation to Forrest to at least take a trip or two into nature and put in a few days looking for the hidden gold and the autobiography he promised would tell all. Jay, the sommelier at my favorite French restaurant in Temple, had flirted with me for as long as I had gone there for dinner. We'd begun our on-off relationship some time ago and found it comfortable and pressure-free. Our casual alliance was perhaps a bit more involved than a "friends with benefits" arrangement – but not by much. There was an emotional component, but we had both been burned so badly in the past that neither of us wanted to invest the necessary emotional energy into a relationship to see if it would work.

Jay, a dedicated camper, bought into the idea of heading out for a week or ten days in the mountains with great enthusiasm. He loved the great outdoors, where I only tolerated being outside, unless it was a spectacular day with superb weather. He assured me I could sleep on an air mattress, and that the tent he owned was tall enough to stand upright and had both a floor and a screen door to keep bugs out while letting light in, plus a top of the line cook stove. Good food and decent coffee were also "musts" for both of us. Jay furnished, packed, and pitched the tent and set up our gear. I cooked, and he washed up. That was our deal.

The deal worked for us, but the relationship did not quite make the grade, and we were ready to strangle one another when we left Idaho after our second trip together.

The reason we disagreed so much was the obligation I felt to actually hunt for Fenn's treasure during much of the day and then spend evenings writing. Jay had volunteered to go on the treasure hunt with me because he liked the idea of introducing me to nature and to the things that he loved to do. He thought Forrest's poem ridiculous and, since the instructions were so vague, decided that hunting for the hidden box was a waste of time that could be better spent fishing, hiking, and making whoopee in the tent whenever he was in the mood. Which was often.

While I was flattered that he was apparently so turned on by me, Jay's passionate expressions interfered with both the search, and my writing – as well as with my sleep.

After our return from Idaho, he had not called or approached me and – to be fair – I had avoided the restaurant at all costs. The hunt, to date, had been spectacularly unsuccessful, and I was on a roll with my writing. I couldn't wait to show Forrest my first draft.

I planned a May visit to sign our contract and to show Forrest the chapters I had written. Dad and Emma wanted to accompany me to Santa Fe so they could be wed where Dad had proposed to her, in a city Emma was fast coming to love. Dad had even begun tossing around the idea of selling his business to Art and making a permanent move to Santa Fe. It was still just talk, but I was reluctant to go along with the idea. I was sure he could get better medical care in Temple and said so. When I mentioned it, Dad politely told me to "butt out," and live my own life. So I did and made sure to give them all the space they needed during the trip.

Peggy was a gem. She and Emma hit it off immediately, which was just as well because I was occupied with contractual matters and working with an editor Forrest insisted I use – an older gentleman whom he trusted, but who could simply not "get with the program" in terms of current language usage. He had difficulty wrapping his head around certain terms, and, well – quite a bit of the manner in which I chose to express myself. We were at loggerheads.

Peggy and Forrest took care of everything regarding the wedding and Dad just wrote them a check for what was a beautiful – and quite reasonable – ceremony. We had a marvelous catered dinner at the Fenn home – Forrest's and Peggy's gift to the happy couple. They had invited a few of their friends who they felt would be compatible, so that we celebrated the nuptials and made new friends at the same time, which was extremely important to the happy bride and groom, who were more intent than ever on pursuing the prospect of Dad finally retiring, and of making Santa Fe their home. By the time we flew back to Temple, they were making plans for the future.

Recognizing that, at long last, I had no further responsibilities for Dad, I grew rather sad. I grew even more morose when I admitted to myself that I missed Jay and the laughs we shared whenever we were together. To combat those feelings, I threw myself into my writing.

I refused to change style for someone whose stilted style of composition was dated and cramped my developing personal style. I finally persuaded Forrest I needed no one to hold my hand and approve every word and convinced him what I was writing was really quite good. I got his blessing to "wing it" and submit my work for final grammatical editing only. In the interim, Forrest told me, he would be the one reviewing my work. I found that to be an ideal situation, and Forrest and I struck up a great system for communicating regarding the pages that I submitted electronically for his perusal and comment. He told me that he was pleased with what he was reading, and that was all that mattered to me.

Time, for me, began passing in pages and chapters, rather than weeks, days, and hours.

Forrest's health and energy were good, but his age was always a consideration. I wanted to make sure this was finished . . .well, in time for him to see and approve the final product, even though he stubbornly resisted admitting that any of what he was reading – and correcting – was true.

Although I was not happy about the lack of confirmation, I calculated that much of what he was doing was a form of validation of my research and conclusions. I was detailing my research and had not yet worked in my way to expound on any of my conclusions, so there was time to figure out how to wrap up the story and create an ending that would satisfy us both, recognizing full well that it might have to be revised at some future date.

I studied Forrest's poem, reading and rereading *The Thrill of The Chase,* and *Too Far to Walk* again and again, until every word, every character and every story were etched into my mind.

There was something I was missing here; I just knew it. But I couldn't put my finger on it.

I'd worked late into the night and was sleeping soundly when my cell phone shrilled at me one morning. I tried to turn off the alarm on my nightstand before realizing it was the telephone. A quick glance at the time told me it was 8:55 a.m. I had been asleep all of 5 hours and was owed another three before rising.

It took a minute to recognize the hysterical individual sobbing at the other end of the line.

"Emma?"

"Yes," a tremulous voice on the other end answered. "Stephanie, it's – Goodbye – No, no, no Stephanie – I didn't mean you. Not you. EMS just left. They took your Dad."

"Took him where? Try to calm down, Emma - I can barely understand you. Took him where?"

"It was terrible, Stephanie," she sobbed, "They took him and there was nothing I could to about it. I was sleeping. He was sleeping – who could have known? I don't think I can ever get over it!

"It was horrible. They called the Coroner. And there were detectives here. Can you imagine? *Detectives!*

Because he died at home they thought *I* did it! How *could* they?

"He was fine when he went to sleep. Maybe a little indigestion . . . But he's had that before – even in Santa Fe. But they took your father away. And I don't know what I am going to do." Her anguished sobs sped through the line and threatened to possess me as well.

"Emma! Emma, stop and take a deep breath, then calm down and tell me what happened. What are you talking about?"

"Your father, Stephanie. He was . . . gone. Gone before I even woke up."

"Gone? Where, Emma?" I was still blinking myself awake, grappling for comprehension.

"Dead. Gone. He passed in his sleep, Stephanie. Heart attack, they think. Or heart failure. There has to be an autopsy. He had cancer, but never heart trouble! They took him *away*, Stephanie. He's gone! Your father's gone!"

"Stay right there, Emma, I'm coming over. Give me a half hour to dress and drive over - and I'll be there. By the way, where are you?

"Home."

Then Emma wailed into the phone, "Do you know what it's like to wake up next to a *dead* person? Someone you *love*?"

"Hush, Emma. Hush. I'll be there as soon as I possibly can."

A cold stone had formed in the pit of my stomach and my mind struggled to wrap itself around Emma's terrible words. *Dead. Gone.*

"Dad," I wailed at the top of my lungs. "How could you do this to us?"

I threw on the clothes I'd worn the day before and raced out of the house with slippers still on my feet.

Chapter 40: Goodbyes are Tough . . .

Emma was alone when I arrived at Dad's place – what had been Dad's place – within the half hour. She was a wreck and threw herself into my arms the moment she opened the door to my knock.

EMS had been gone for a half hour, along with two men from the Coroner's Office called by the EMS team, and a pair of detectives – probably from Homicide, Emma angrily declared, "Because the EMS workers had put Charles on the floor to do CPR and whatever else they could, and I was kneeling beside your father, hysterical, and these two men in suits were standing around with their arms crossed while I was sobbing and stroking Charles's forehead, and as I leaned over and kissed him I heard one of them say to the other, 'Well, she looks pretty broken up about it," and I hadn't known who they were until one of them said that, and then I knew they were looking at me to see if maybe I had done something to . . . Oh, Stephanie, how could they!"

I held and rocked her, but I couldn't bring myself to shed a tear because I, too, was in shock - frozen, unbelieving.

After we had struggled through cancer together, Dad couldn't have died of an unrelated problem! Some cosmic contract had been broken, an unspoken agreement between the universe and I, that said that if I could get Dad through the cancer, and those miserable treatments, and give him hope of the future again, he wouldn't die-- he couldn't die. I was a 38-year-old woman, soon to be 39, and I still needed my father. I had earned the right to keep him around a while longer.

This was not fair. It was not part of the deal! And it was not fair to the dear woman I held in my arms, either - or to my father. It was supposed to be their time together-- their time to be happy. They were going to move to Santa Fe. She told me that Dad had even bought their tickets for a trip back to the city in two weeks. They had contacted a realtor and were looking at houses online. There was even going to be a guest room for me to stay with them while I worked on the book.

Emma was rambling, weeping, and babbling about anything and everything. I simply listened and rocked her as the fact sank in that now Dad would never know for sure if he'd been right about Fenn. He'd never get to read my book or hear that I'd learned about Skippy being on Flight 305. I should have told him. He deserved to know.

Why had I held back? Because, with Emma in his life, he had never had time to sit with me and talk, except the night before I went to see Forrest. Why hadn't I told him then? Why hadn't I turned right around when I thought about it and kept Dad up for a few minutes more to tell him about that amazing discovery?

Regrets. Death always brings regrets.

Now Emma was going on about some dish she had promised she would make for him--something Southwestern we'd eaten at the dinner with Peggy. The women had shared recipes. Emma had promised Dad she would cook for him.

It was very weird. As I comforted Emma, I felt my father's presence – I know, scoff if you wish, but I know it was him. I felt his hand on my shoulder and heard whisper, "Take care of Emma for me."

I made coffee and pulled together a breakfast of sorts-- coffee, tea and toast with butter and jam. Emma called her children, and then called the same funeral home that had helped her bury her first husband.

"I hope you don't mind, Stephanie," Emma told her, "They did such a good job handling everything when Morgan died, and they are not pushy, and everything was just beautiful. And I know them. I feel comfortable with them," Emma had explained, as if she needed my permission to make that decision. I was just glad she knew what to do.

"Did he ever tell you what he wanted?" Emma asked. I stared at her, lost for an answer. Finally, I said, "I think there's a vault for his ashes at Hillcrest. When Mom died, he had her cremated and he bought two vaults. His is next to hers. I don't know if you want to use it. He didn't know you then, Emma, and I don't think he imagined he would ever remarry."

"I know. I didn't think of remarriage, either, when Morgan passed. He was buried. He's at Bellwood Memorial. I'll have to think about it. I have to think of a million things! And the kids are coming. They'll be in this evening."

I was still wondering why tears would not come as I held Emma's hand and asked her to tell me about her children, a girl and two boys, one of whom - a Marine captain - was overseas on assignment and would not be coming, but his wife and son would represent him. Her daughter was an accountant. The other son was ophthalmologist with a thriving practice. Their spouses, too, would be coming for the memorial service, and the grandchildren, of course.

I was glad Emma would be surrounded by family. She needed that. I feared I might be her only emotional support and felt entirely inadequate to the task. I had to talk to Sue. And Matt. And Matt's dad, Jim, who had been close to Dad. And Art. I had to tell Art right away.

Calls and planning took up the rest of the day. I went home to shower and change into something appropriate, then made my calls to Art and Sue.

Then I called in to work. Many of my coworkers had known and liked my father. Dad always made our Christmas parties and the 4th of July beach bash in Galveston, and had always reciprocated, extending invitations for the entire office to attend his firm's celebrations.

The firm! Had Dad done anything about its sale to Art yet? Did he have a chance to revise his will after he married Emma? He had been drawing disability for the last year. His death needed to be reported. Lord, there was so much to think about! So much to take care of. . . and Forrest and Peggy would want to know – needed to know. I had another chapter for Forrest to review and would have to ask for more time before turning in anything more.

Emma decided to have Dad cremated. She would keep his ashes. She was planning to go ahead with plans to move to Santa Fe and asked my permission to take Dad's ashes with her. Sue would kick up a fight, I was certain, but a quick call to a friend who was an estate planner and another who worked for the county established Emma's superior right to determine how to handle Dad's remains, so I gave her my blessing, Sue be damned. I don't think she'd had much contact with Dad over the past year, other than holidays and when he called to tell her of his marriage to Emma, Sue responded with a vague promise "to come meet your bride and bring the kids to meet their new Nanna," but had yet to act on her words.

"I still want to use the tickets," Emma announced out of the blue at the end of the day, before her children arrived. "The two tickets Charles bought for Santa Fe. Will you come with me?" I was nonplussed and told her I needed to check my schedule. I would have to think about it.

Sue had not been home when I called and did not pick up her cell, so I hesitated to call Matt's parents until I had spoken with her. This was not the kind of news one leaves on voicemail.

Michael! Michael and Kent would have to be informed. And Dad had other friends; friends I didn't know, like the guys he bowled with, and those he fished with . . . Emma could help me with that – she had his address book.

I hadn't yet given Emma an answer about flying to Santa Fe with her. I considered her invitation as much a plea for moral support as anything, so I would have to make some plans in order to use the visit well. I was concerned that Forrest was making no changes at all in what I was writing and wondered why not. Maybe we could clear that up, along with a few other questions I had.

I could understand Emma's motivation in moving. Her kids lived out West – one in Nevada and another in Arizona. The one who was in the Marines moved often, but I think his wife was staying with her parents in California until his reassignment came through. Besides, I think Emma had fallen in love with Santa Fe. Easy to do as it was quite different from Temple.

I was exhausted, but sleep would not come. I tossed and turned the entire night and then, just before dawn, I awoke bawling my eyes out. I had dreamed of Dad. It was more like a visit than a dream. I could feel his hands as I held them and see the earnest expression in his eyes. His message? "Take care of Emma for me." They were the same words I thought I had heard when I sensed his presence while comforting her.

I promised him I would, then woke up in tears.

When it rains, it pours. On my way to meet Emma at the funeral home, I rear-ended a car at a stoplight downtown. Cursing, I slammed my hands against the steering wheel and hit the horn by accident. I speed-dialed Emma to tell her what had happened and was explaining why I would be late when I noticed the driver who was getting out of the car I had hit. I began to laugh wildly, Life is just too funny, sometimes.

I was still laughing when the handsome man walked up to my window and stood there grinning at me. Of all people, it was Michael Giordano.

"First you hit me and then you honk afterward? It's supposed to be the other way around – honking is what you do to *avoid* an accident!

"My, my Stephanie Ward, struck in the middle of the road by my lovely ex. You could have just called. What's so funny?"

"You – this. But I did intend to call, I needed to tell you . . ." Tears flowed freely and unexpectedly. "Dad died yesterday, Michael. I was going to call as soon as I could. There's so much to do . . . I . . ."

I was a sight to see, bawling like a baby, snot running down my nose, and nary a tissue in sight, Michael whipped out his trusty folded handkerchief. I always loved that about him. He was the gentleman-on-the-spot on many occasions, always able to provide a spotless fold of initialed white linen to quell any disaster.

"Let's get out of the road," Michael said. "Park this heap of yours and let's talk."

"But I'm late for . . ."

"Anybody else, and you would have to call for police and be here an hour, guaranteed. We can grab a cup of coffee there on the corner and settle this like friends, and you can call whomever and make your excuses, then give me the details. Come on."

Both cars were drivable, so I followed his instructions, and a few minutes later we slid into a booth beneath the neon Dunkin' Donuts sign. Michael ordered a cup of coffee and a cruller for each of us – a snack which I initially refused before realizing I had not eaten in nearly 24 hours. I wolfed it down between sips and rapidly brought Michael up to date on everything-- Dad's and my suspicion of Fenn, our trip to Santa Fe, Dad's marriage to Emma, my morning confrontation with Forrest, his challenging me to find his treasure in order to learn the truth, and the book I was working on that had grown out of years of research with Dad, and that Fenn had committed to publish.

"Forrest is not denying a thing, but he won't come clean – at least, not immediately, so I'll attempt to find his darned treasure, if it makes him happy. I think his real motive is to get me out in the sun, and into nature – it's a big deal with him. But he wants to tell his story- badly. I was brutally direct, but he danced around the subject. I *will* get it out of Forrest Fenn. You know how persistent I can be. But now Dad will never see the book or learn the answer."

I used the napkin as a tissue, but succeeded only in reddening my nose, and Michael fished his handkerchief out again and handed it to me.

"Keep it, my dear. You need it more than I do"

"I will. I'm a snotty mess, and this is not quite as nice as a lady's tears, I'm afraid. Thanks, Michael – I'll launder it and get it back to you. Along with a check for the damage. Text me the amount. But I really need to get going. Emma is waiting for me at the funeral home. I told her I would be late, but. . ."

"I know. I understand. I am so sorry, Stephanie. I know how much your dad meant to you." Michael leaned over and wiped a stray tear making its way down my cheek. I got goosebumps. I had forgotten how good looking he was, and how much I had been in love with him. Michael was a gorgeous man, damn it. Once mine – now Kent's. But, more than that, what I was feeling was the loss of our deep friendship. Michael had once been my confidante, my buddy, my biggest supporter, my cheerleader. None of that had changed. And, right now, I could use someone in my corner.

"You are still together, aren't you? You and Kent?" I had to ask.

"We've had our ups and downs, but yeah. I guess. I've found out that he cheats. And I still like women. Go figure, And I miss you so much. But this is where my choices have brought me. I made the bed – now I've got to lie in it. And sometimes, it's really tough."

"Well, Mr. Giordano. I could really use a friend, about now. You think Kent would have a hissy fit if we met for lunch sometime?

"He'll just have to deal with it - like I have with him, many, many times. Besides, you owe me a check for the bumper. I'll see you at the funeral Stephanie – I'll watch for the notice."

"Memorial. Emma wants to cremate Dad, and that's what I think he wanted. When there's no body, I think they call it a memorial. I can give you a call when we get the date set. I will be in the next week or ten days. Emma still wants to use the tickets for Santa Fe that Dad bought. She still wants to move there. So we'll be headed to Santa Fe in two weeks. It holds an of attraction for her – she loved the place – and it's closer to her kids. She and Dad had started looking at neighborhoods . . . anyway, she asked me to accompany her. I agreed. And I agreed to let her take Dad with her."

"Take your father? Oh, the remains. That is very romantic. Very touching."

My eyes welled up again.

"Well, when you get back, then." He kissed my cheek and we parted company.

Emma felt comfortable enough to make a few decisions regarding the service, but she waited for me to finalize things. I approved of her choices, and she signed the necessary papers. Dad had apparently held a whole life policy and he'd made Emma the beneficiary after they married. There would be money from the sale of Dad's shares in the company, as well, and an income of some kind from investments, in addition to his retirement, so Emma would be far from destitute. I had no idea where I stood in his will and didn't really care. I had made a commitment to take care of Emma, and I meant to honor it.

The week passed in a haze. A death brings floods of support and sympathy from friends and relatives, and a million details that must be attended to, accompanied by the blessed shock that makes it all possible. Emma and I struggled through those eight days from Dad's death through the cremation and memorial service.

It went off without a hitch. Emma and I did what the survivors must do. We greeted the other mourners, spoke of Dad fondly, and listened to eulogies given by Art, Sue, Matt, and Matt's father, Jim, who had been Dad's good friend and benefactor. Sue went on overlong, and got rather preachy, but she spoke of her relationship with Dad in a manner that made me wonder where I had been, growing up, that I had failed to see the depth of their relationship.

But once it was over, the friends and their casseroles disappeared, as if death were contagious and they dared not linger. Emma and I were left to console one another, and I marveled that she'd had the good sense to decide to use the airline tickets and go back to Santa Fe. We both needed to escape the gloom brought about by the many reminders of Dad that seemed to be everywhere. Though I was afraid a trip back to Santa Fe would raise painful memories for Emma, that lovely city was also the beginning of a new life for her, and would be a reason for me to visit often.

Six days after Dad had passed she and I were winging our way to Santa Fe. We had reservations at The Madeleine Inn near the historic Plaza. "Hooked on the spa, huh?" I teased Emma as our plane took to the sky.

"Absolutely," was her reply, as the ground receded beneath us. That massage was the best I've ever had."

We talked about Dad a bit and laughed about his reaction to his first visit to the spa. Then I told Emma about oddity of running into Michael – literally – the day I was late to the funeral home to make arrangements. I filled her in on our strange history and Emma nodded empathetically before mentioning she had been somewhat aware of our history, because of her conversations with Dad.

"He loved you so much, Stephanie. Don't ever forget that."

"Who? Dad or Michael?"

"Both of them, I am sure. But I was speaking of your father."

To avoid the two of us becoming teary-eyed, I changed the subject to Forrest's secreted treasure and his urging that I get out and commune with nature a little more often. I talked about the two search trips that Jay and I had been on, a brief trip to Wyoming, and a ten-day trip to Idaho – after which we were barely speaking. They were fruitless trips, in terms of our finds, but they had offered me exposure to the marvels of this country that I never would have sought out without Forrest's urging me to join the search.

Emma was curious as to what was in the ancient bronze treasure box and marveled at the enormous area searchers had to consider when planning their treasure hunting trips. I spoke of Forrest Fenn's immense, almost cult-like following, and of how dedicated the search groups were, the countless chat rooms where the obsessed discussed opinions, recounted experiences, and shared hints. Then there was the infinite number of articles, the tremendous draw of the hunt, and Forrest's apparent reveling in the fame it created.

"Next time you go on a search, I want to go with you," Emma declared. "I will have nothing but time on my hands, and I need something to occupy my mind. Your father got me hooked on computers. He bought the laptop I have with me as a wedding gift, and I've been using it to look for properties in Santa Fe. That's why we planned this trip."

Cozy and pretty, The Madeleine Inn was a delightful B&B. Built in 1886, the rambling structure was 5 minutes from the Plaza. Wine and cheese were offered for guests each evening, and the garden was lovely and tranquil.

We settled in for a week of pampering and house-hunting, and I worked on my book every afternoon when Emma napped in her room.

Chapter 41: Hope Springs Eternal

I met with Forrest just once on that trip to review my recently written chapters. He and Peggy had sent flowers for Dad's memorial service and he expressed his sympathy at Dad's passing. "We never did get a chance to reminisce much, but he was a good man. Pretty bride."

"Emma is with me. I know she'd love to see Peggy if you can let her know Emma's in town. She and Dad were looking to relocate to Santa Fe. Emma's kids and grandchildren are out West-- Nevada, California, Arizona – so she's looking forward to finding a place here. She even wants to go with me the next time I go looking for your treasure! You know, I'm determined to find it. It may be the only way I'll get an answer to my suspicions. You are the most frustrating man I know, Forrest Fenn! And I have no clue how to end this story, without knowing the truth conclusively."

"You're a clever young lady," he grinned. "You'll find a way."

I asked him straight-out why he was making no additions or corrections to the material or to the conclusions I drew from those facts. Forrest replied. "It's a good story. Good stories need to be told. And I think this one is going to be big."

"Well, I appreciate your opinion, and that makes me feel good, Forrest. But is it going to be "big" because it is a good story, or because you really *are* D.B.?"

It was his turn to adopt the Mona Lisa smile. His non-reply was, "You have a very captivating way of writing, Missy, and you are very perceptive. I think the public will eat it up."

"Forrest, you know that's not an answer!"

"Well, it's all the answer I have for you today. I'll escort you out now, Missy. Peggy has something planned and wants me to tag along. I'll tell her about Emma. Maybe you all can get together for lunch. Take care, young lady. Enjoy the rest of your visit and keep up the good work. We'll stay in touch."

Grrrr! I was ready to scream. Forrest was toying with me and enjoying every minute of it. The only heartening thing about our conversation was that he liked what I was writing, and I was evidently on target. However, he was not about to admit to the truth of it.

Emma had never read Fenn's books, and I had photocopies of both *The Thrill of The Chase* and *Too Far to Walk* with me, so I loaned them to her, expecting they would keep her busy for a while.

The next morning at breakfast, however, she informed me she had been up half the night and knew exactly where we needed to hunt for the treasure.

"You do? Tell me, then, because it's still a mystery to me."

"Well, instead of napping yesterday, I started reading and making a few notes. And I

went online and found a few of those chat rooms you told me about. And boy, is that crowd all over the map! But I remembered you talking about Forrest 'hiding in plain sight' for all these years. And, reading his books, I understood exactly what you and your father said about him talking in parables. I'm not up on the details of the D.B. Cooper case, but – just looking at it the way Forrest might think, he gets a kick about people chasing their tails when the truth is right in front of them."

"Absolutely. So?"

"So I thought on it for a while and then read his second book – you're right, they read really fast, and he leaves you, so you never really know what to believe, because he embellishes a lot, to put it nicely. And he leaves a lot out. But the thing that comes through all his writing is how much he loves West Yellowstone. And he was so disappointed his granddaughter did not find it as charming as he did at her age, when he was trying to get her to enjoy his favorite spot. That's where it is. I'm sure of it. Because that is certainly where he would want his bones, and you mentioned a Newsweek article that said he wanted to bury his bones near beside the bronze chest, where they would find his autobiography so people would know whose bones they had discovered.

"The treasure chest is where he says the real story - in that autobiography. Is that why, all of a sudden, you are so interested in finding that treasure? It's been out there for years. I never figured it was the money that got you hunting for it. You have to know, so you can end that book of yours."

Taking a page from Forrest's list of non-answers, I responded, "You are a very perceptive woman, Emma Ward. Very perceptive, indeed. Since my first two forays, I've decided it has to be in West Yellowstone. We should round up some maps and start planning. Shall we shoot for a trip to Yellowstone in mid-June, early July?"

Chapter 42: Fateful Coincidences

I had promised Michael a meeting upon my return, if for no other reason than to settle accounts for the accident. It was just a fender-tap – I had literally rolled into the rear end of his vehicle at the light. Well, okay. Maybe the impact occurred closer to 30 miles an hour. Damages to my car totaled $450. I anticipated damages to his at closer to $800, or more. Because I was already late, I didn't want to report it to police, and I certainly didn't want a ticket and points on my license. Besides, it had been a long time since I had seen Michael, and I wanted to catch up on things that had transpired since our split.

He insisted on taking me to a late lunch at one of Temple's finest restaurants. Pignetti's was noted for its rainbow trout with a pecan crust, and Michael knew I loved fish. He ordered lasagna and a bottle of Fontemorsi Rosato Toscana 2012, an exceptional rosé wine.

I had my checkbook out, pen at the ready, and was prepared to write him a check for damages, but Michael told me to put it away.

"But," I started to protest . . .

"I'm not hearing of it. If you write one out, Stephanie, I will just tear it up in front of you.

The accident was a blessing. You don't know how much I wanted to see you again, but I knew you probably wouldn't give me the time of day if I called you up and suggested our getting together."

My antenna was up, and I was wary. Was Michael hitting on me? He picked

up immediately on my hesitation. He could always read me like a book, and so Michael moved quickly to allay my doubts, saying, "Look Stephanie, I'm not trying to reopen a closed chapter of our lives. I know I've irreparably. . . I recognize it's over between us, romantically."

"You're right, Michael, I just can't go there again, whatever is going on between you and Kent. I gave it my best shot. More than once. You can't say I didn't try to make it work."

"You did. I know that. But I still miss you. And I miss you as a friend. I never realized, until you were gone, that you have been perhaps the only friend I could trust 100% to give me your frank opinion on things – to have my back. You're the only person I can - could -easily confide everything and anything. I've come to recognize how very difficult everything we went through was for you, but I always felt that you made a real effort to understand what I was going through. And you were so gracious when we decided . . . through the whole divorce, and, and after, Life with Kent has been . . . what can I say? Difficult, at best. That's the only way I can put it.

"And I often feel I lost everything solid for something so illusory, and fleeting. Kent is an excellent business partner, but the partnership breaks down privately. Please understand, I am not asking for a second – no, third - chance. I just wish we could get together now and again, just to talk. You have such a great perspective on things. I miss that. I really do."

"Oh, Michael, Michael. You don't know how much I wish it could have worked between us. I haven't found anyone who affects me the way you did, and you did so much for me. I owe you so much. You're right in that it can never be the way it was. Too much water under the bridge. But I will always be available if you need me. We can do that – get together once in a while for a chat. However, there has to be boundaries.. I can't go through that again."

I thought it prudent to change the subject, so I began talking about Emma and her plans to follow through on her and Dad's plans to move to Santa Fe, about the darling two-bedroom adobe she had written a contract on and how she was now awaiting the inspection results and bank approval, and I spoke of Forrest and his maddening refusal to admit anything, although he was committed to publishing the story precisely as I was writing it.

"Without an admission, I don't know how to end the darn thing. I mean, he knows that my conclusions are based on what I consider pretty diligent research, are correct. He refuses to change a detail, however, and he knows that I know the truth. But he said it's all unprovable, just circumstantial evidence. But the thing that really got to him was one piece of evidence that would get the FBI interested enough to open a new investigation – the one publicly available piece of information I don't think he ever realized was still available-- the YouTube video of the original hijacking report showing released passengers disembarking from the hijacked plane. It's as plain as day. Forrest's brother, Skippy, was flying on the same flight – Northwest Orient Flight 305 – and was present during hijacking. Skippy was trying so hard not to be seen straight-on that he stuck out like a sore thumb, straining his neck, and looking away to avoid the camera. And he was the only passenger with a hat on – a cowboy hat, of all things."

"Where did you find a close-up to compare his features?" Michael asked, curious.

"His online obituary – www.findagrave.com."

"They have sites like that?"

"They do, indeed."

"Why don't you take this straight to the FBI? It's still an open case, right? I bet they are dying to close it."

"Yeah. And some hotshot D.A. is dying to jump on a high-profile prosecution like that to ride it into elective office."

"No one would be able to successfully prosecute a case like that and use it for political purposes – not prosecuting an 80 something-year-old man with an otherwise good record, and not for a 45-year-old crime."

"I know. That's what I told Forrest. But he rightfully pointed out he would still have to spend a ton of money holding the legal hounds at bay. And he doesn't want that. Forrest is eager for the tale to come out – that's why he is going to publish the book I have been writing, telling all I know – but he won't corroborate my conclusion – that he is D.B Cooper, so I don't know how to end it. It's terribly frustrating. And so he's sent me on a hunt for his treasure. for the autobiography – his real autobiography – rather than owning up to the truth."

That elicited a round of questions from Michael about the treasure, and Forrest's "real" autobiography, and the searches I'd already undertaken with Jay.

"Jay?"

"Jay is no one. An occasional friend. Someone just as afraid of getting emotionally involved in a relationship as I am. No one of consequence."

"I did this to you. Hurt you that badly. How can you ever forgive me, Stephanie?"

"I can't. There's nothing to forgive. Just a lesson to be learned. And it has been. Emma is coming with me on my next search."

"Oh? And where will that take you? Where will you search?

"West Yellowstone. I hear it is beautiful. And Emma says she has a strong feeling this is the place Forrest would have hidden it."

"That's insane. Do you know what is going on there? Right now? Haven't you read – of course not, first your Dad, then your trip. It's dangerous out there. Very dangerous right now." Michael's face was earnest as he uttered the warning.

"Says who? What's going on? Yellowstone always has tremors, and geyser activity, silly. The last big earthquake was years ago, in 1959 – the one around Hebgen Lake that dammed the Madison and formed Quake Lake. I researched it. I know they are expecting "The Big One" to hit the San Andreas Fault. They've been saying that every day since after the Oakland quake years ago. 'Any day now' - for the last two decades. We'll be fine."

"Stephanie, you have been out of the loop for quite a while, I guess. The warnings started in March of this year –

yes, this year. Since 2015, actually. You are aware of the "Ring of Fire," right?"

"Of course, Michael. I'm not a total ignoramus."

"I never said you were. So you know about the earthquakes that have been occurring fairly steadily since last year, moving from location to location around the Ring of Fire, all through Asia – Japan to Indonesia, and an uninhabited area of Alaska? That last set of earthquakes were just in Ecuador, on the coast of South America, and in Indonesia. Earlier in the year, Chile was hit with severe earthquakes. The tectonic plates are shifting, and the earth's crust is very unstable right now. There have been volcanic warnings, as well – Mount Io, on an island in Japan had dozens of volcanic tremors, and Iceland is watching several volcanoes as well. Etna in Italy is still active, and the Italians are worried about Vesuvius, too. In this country – in Oregon and Washington, Mounts Hood, Rainier, and St. Helens have all had huge numbers of volcanic tremors, as well. There are over 40 active volcanoes erupting worldwide right now, including at least one in Costa Rica, and another in Mexico. A huge eruption in Indonesia is causing chaos, and volcanoes that have lain 'dormant' for decades – centuries – are showing activity now. Globally, there have been over 3,000 earthquakes of 1.5 magnitude within the past month alone!"

I listened intently and nodded. Michael was telling me nothing I didn't already know. I had heard about most of those events before. Well, maybe not the activity around Hood and Rainier – but St. Helen's has smoked on and off since it blew, years ago. And 3,000 earthquakes sound like a lot until you realize that most of those can barely be felt, except by finely calibrated scientific devices. I wanted to mention that, but I held my tongue.

"In fact, Stephanie, if you're not a geology and tectonic plate buff like I am, chances are you haven't heard about anything other than the worldwide reports of those actual earthquakes and eruptions– and nothing about the numerous signs and indications of what might be coming. The mainstream media in this country isn't reporting a word about it, probably because of the abysmal ignorance and lack of curiosity of most reporters, although one could argue it would be in the government's interest to clamp down on or dismiss any reporting of these things, because it would likely cause panic."

"So now there's a government conspiracy to keep us all in the dark?"

"Look, the first I heard of it were some reports from Yellowstone National Park of unusual activity. They have cameras and monitoring equipment all over the place. Geysers have been erupting in spots that have never had geysers, and there have been huge, lingering flashes of light that have nothing to do with lightening.

"Like you said, Yellowstone has always had tremors, but they seem to be increasing in number. And – get this – the official seismological organization and the University of Utah have cameras that monitor Yellowstone 24/7, and have caught instances where the ground has actually been *glowing*! There are videos on YouTube too. Magma is moving close to the surface, like only 5 to 10 feet underground. That's how close the magma chamber is to the surface – that's what heats most of the geothermal attractions at Yellowstone – just like in Iceland. These videos were taken just this past March and April. *March and April, Stephanie!"*

"All sorts of supposedly true malarkey are online. The major news outlets haven't reported a word of this."

"Stephanie, on April 22 the London Daily Express online - it's a legitimate online site, reported about occurrences at Yellowstone and included a recent video of the Yellowstone Caldera in Wyoming. That volcano's a little over 2 9,400 feet tall, and its last major eruption . . ."

I rolled my eyes. "I know – was about 640,000 years ago. Really, Michael. That's ancient history. Where is this going?"

"For your information, Miss Smarty-Pants, the last lava basaltic magma eruption was 70,000 years ago. Anyway, the video the Daily Express featured – again, available online, so you can take a look at it – it shows the lake that fills the caldera is heating up with rising steam. The volcano sits atop a huge reservoir of magma. And heat signatures throughout the Yellowstone area are through the roof. While all the geyser activity and ground lighting was going on in Yellowstone Park itself in March, a river near the Yellowstone Volcano in Wyoming began *boiling*, and still is. Geologists think a new vent opened up beneath the river. Long-time residents have never seen this level of activity before."

"But I checked the, the - what is the Park monitoring service? The U-something."

"USGS."

"Yeah. That. The Yellowstone Park monitoring service was giving the green light and said everything was normal and even that the weather was great. That's just fear-mongering you're repeating, Michael. You're too smart to trust everything that comes across the Internet."

"I know what the USGS is saying – publicly. They're a government agency. What they report will always be green until the point of evacuation. That service is also neglecting to report the great number of earthquakes happening around the globe. Besides, Mount St. Helen's didn't post warnings or make announcements until just before it blew. Its dome had grown substantially in a very short time, and it was not long before the explosive forces could no longer be contained. Yellowstone National Park is not in the business of scaring off tourists until they are absolutely certain of an impending event."

"There – you said it, Michael. They are obviously *not* absolutely certain – so how can you be? They say animals have a sixth sense about natural phenomena, so when the animals start acting antsy or weird, I'll believe it. Next thing you'll be telling me it's because we're not all driving a Prius and don't have solar panels on our houses and windmills in our back yards."

"I tell you; something is definitely about to happen. I told you I follow this stuff avidly. And if you are going to wait for the animals to react, how about this? On June 7, just weeks from now, FEMA is planning to hold a huge multi-state drill to prepare for a large-scale 9.0 Cascadia Subduction Zone earthquake and tsunami. The code-name for the drill is 'Cascadia Rising,' and it's supposed to simulate the effects of a huge earthquake along a fault no one ever talks about, the Cascadia Subduction Zone. It's a much bigger threat that the San Andreas. This is the fault zone where the Juan de Fuca tectonic plate meets the North American plate. In all, it stretches about 700 miles from Vancouver Island, in Canada, to Northern California."

"Come on – 9.0? There has never been an earthquake of that magnitude, has there?"

"That's where you're wrong. There have been a considerable number of earthquakes that have registered that much, and more, all over the world - in the U.S. as well. Chile had a 9.5 earthquake in 1960, Indonesia experienced a 9.2 in 2004, Japan had one that registered 9.0 on 11-3-11, the 11th of March, 2011 – easy date to remember; Portugal had one in 1983 that registered between 8.5 to 9.0 in 1755, Russia had a 9.0 in 1952, the United States had the 1964 earthquake in Alaska that was a 9.2, and the last time the Cascadia fault caused an earthquake was in 1700, in Canada, that is estimated to have been between 8.7 and 9.2 on the Richter Scale – which of course, didn't exist back then, so they estimated it this past century based primarily on the extent of past ecological damage, given the fact that the area was sparsely inhabited."

"You do know your stuff! I'm impressed."

"I've told you; this is my "thing" – has been since grade school. But I confess that I also have an excellent memory. Plus, I looked it up only a few days ago, because of the news about the FEMA drill. You're right in that a 9.0 and above is pretty rare. Most severe earthquakes register between 7.5 to 8.8.

"What I want to emphasize above all, however, is that the largest earthquake ever to hit continental North America struck right along the Cascadia Subduction Zone."

"And the fault runs along the mountain range by that name? The Cascades?"

"Bingo. The 1700 earthquake unleashed a powerful tsunami that inundated coastal villages as far away as Japan. So this is not a foolish exercise the government is planning at every level across three states. It's not preparation for a Zombie Apocalypse, like some of the local police, fire and medical units have joked about in an attempt to keep it light-hearted while they practice emergency procedures. The Cascadia zone can produce an earthquake as much as 30 times stronger than the San Andreas fault, Stephanie, and generate a tsunami greater than the ones that hit Thailand and Japan in 2011. This is serious stuff.

"The FEMA guy responsible for the affected area told the reporter that if a 9.0 happened and the fault ruptured, FEMA's assumption is that 'everything west of I-5 will be toast.' Do you realize how bad that would be? Everything west of I-5 totals more than 140,000 square miles! It would destroy all of Washington and Oregon and affect over 7 million people.

"A couple of geologists whose posts I follow are convinced that we will soon witness major earth changes, the likes of which we have never seen and could never imagine. The "Ring of Fire" is kicking to life, my dear, and the Cascadia fault lies in the Ring. This one guy I follow, a geologist named Michael Snyder is convinced these are warnings, and it's not long before a crisis strikes.

"And regarding this exercise, FEMA sent out official notification flyers to over 50 counties and major cities, to Indian tribal nations, state and federal agencies, private businesses and other organizations across Oregon, Washington and Idaho. They will all be participating."

"Idaho is right across Hebgen Lake from West Yellowstone."

"That is exactly what I have been trying to tell you, Stephanie. It's not a good idea to head out there."

"Well, Emma and I had been thinking of going much later in the month, and the exercise – drill – will have ended well before that. All of this is just speculation, Michael. Really, there is always one group or another fear-mongering."

"Well, this is something you can't adapt to until long after it has happened. Haiti is still rebuilding from their 7.0 in 2010."

"Haiti's a Third World country."

"Well, this country will be, too, if a disaster of that magnitude occurs."

"Oh, Michael. Absent a direct waning, we *have* to go. Emma's convinced she has figured it out - where the treasure is. And I *need* that autobiography. I have to get to the bottom of this, and find an ending for my book, and Forrest won't give up a damned thing! I'm convinced he's playing me. I think he's going to publish my book as fiction!"

"There's always the option of writing it all down to the point that the facts have all been set out – including the Skippy thing – your only major proof – and then give it all to the FBI and let them wrap it up."

"The Skippy video is not the only proof-- there's Forrest's DNA."

"Of which you don't have a sample."

"Do too. I have a water bottle Forrest drank from when we went to San Lazaro to dig up antiquities. And there was DNA on the tie that he left behind on the plane he hijacked."

"And who has that DNA to match with your water bottle?"

"FBI."

"See, that's the only way - you've got to turn in what you have pulled together and have the new evidence examined by law enforcement. You don't have possession of the tie for your DNA evidence to prove a match, and you have no lab that can match it for you – only the Feds can do that. What's your hesitation, besides the fact you think he's a nice guy?"

"He's a brilliant guy. When I threatened to talk to the FBI, he said I should do what I needed to do. He did. Then I kind of gave him a loose commitment that I wouldn't do that, when he said he would publish my book. . .I figured I could get the information out that way."

"Honey - I'm sorry. Stephanie, I know how you feel about this guy, and the situation, but what you are saying makes no sense. You need an ending to your book. Fine. You need to tell his story, and you think he wants it told. Okay. But both of you are at odds because he won't confess, and you need to know for certain.

"So he has you putting your life in danger to look for a treasure chest that he says holds several million in gold and antiquities, plus this mysterious autobiography he says reveals everything about his life that he hasn't already written in the two books he's already published and profited from, and this treasure is something that thousands of people have been fruitlessly looking for since 2010? You do realize how ridiculous all this sounds?"

I put on my best disappointed pouty-face that had worked for so many years to let me get my way with Michael. I chewed a fingernail as I looked away and willed some tears to the corners of my eyes. Then I said, in a very small voice, "What I'm doing is just as much supposition as what you just spent the last hour explaining to me."

"Stephanie, this is insane."

I looked down at the table, still chewing my nail, still acting as though my world had crashed, and it was all his fault.

Damn, if it didn't still work!

"Okay, okay if you two ladies intend to persist with this cockamamie idea, at least let me tag along and keep you safe. Kent can take a flying leap if he complains. I have the camping gear, and a Land Cruiser with 4-wheel drive and a v8 engine that can haul ass, if need be. And I have the knowledge and good sense to know when to get the hell out of there. I'll map an escape route, just in case."

I could have kissed, him, but I simply squeezed Michael's hand and mouthed a "thank you" instead. I rose and excused myself to use the Ladies Room while he paid the bill, and thought about what he'd said while I relieved myself. Scary stuff. But there is so much scary stuff in the world that the media goes on about, but never happens: The Cold War ended without a bomb being dropped by either Russia or China, cranberries and red lipstick and saccharin never killed anyone bigger than a mouse, the sky has never fallen, and the seas have never risen, and we haven't run out of oil. And yet, things that *are* proven harmful often come from supposedly safe sources. For example, every bit of dietary advice doled out by the Federal Government has been dead wrong - and potentially harmful, and drugs approved by the FDA have actually killed and maimed people! Lethal events with no precedent often come out of the blue, with no warning at all – like the deaths of 2,996 non-combatants who went to work one morning and were dead by noon in one of the greatest disasters to hit this country.

We would be just fine. And Michael had been as chivalrous as always, so we now had a ride, and full camping gear, plus a guardian angel who would know just what to do should his direst predictions come true. All we had to do was find that damned bronze box! I hoped Emma's hunch was right on.

Chapter 43: This is Not a Drill

Emma was delighted when I told her the outcome of my lunch meeting with Michael. We were going to Yellowstone National Park with an experienced camper who had all the necessary equipment and who would drive us around in the perfect 4-wheel drive vehicle. Furthermore, I explained that Michael knew the outdoors, and was a superb diver who had a wetsuit and diving gear. I had learned to dive when we were together and so would bring my diving gear, as well.

Both Emma and I had a sneaking suspicion the treasure was actually stored underwater and was the reason Forrest had such a preoccupation with things like keeping his autobiography and any cash he wanted to include in the chest dry. All else – the treasures, the containers, coins, jewels, and antiquities were impervious to water.

I had previously told Emma a good deal about Michael, our marriage, and the reason for the divorce. She was understanding. She had already heard much from Dad on the subject and was delighted we were still on such good terms that he would assist us so wholeheartedly.

I failed to tell her, however, the real reason he had been concerned enough to volunteer. She was aware of Yellowstone's propensity for regular seismological and geothermal events, and I felt no need to disturb her with what I considered Michael's overly dramatic view about an event that might not happen for another hundred years or longer, if at all. I was skeptical, to say the least.

To break the ice and make everyone comfortable with the prospect of sharing a camping adventure together, I arranged for us all to have drinks and dinner, and discuss our Yellowstone trip over maps after dinner, working out ideas of where to hunt, and what to see.

Michael explained the best route to get there and talked about the trip without bringing up the prospect of an escape route or the dangers he thought we might face, to my relief. We pinky-swore to evenly divide the treasure three ways, should we succeed in finding it, with the infamous autobiography to be mine alone. We set the date well after the end of the planned FEMA drill, and never mentioned the government-sponsored exercise to begin June 7 and involve the three Western states most immediately involved.

We set the dates for our trip and parted company on the best of terms.

Emma and I packed everything we imagined we would possibly need, and she brought along three laminated, waterproof copies of her directions and the solution she had figured out to explain Fenn's 9-clue poem. I admired her cleverness in sussing out the solution she had and crossed my fingers that she was right. We only needed to find the precise spot once we arrived. We allotted six days to search and sightsee, and two days each way for travel, plus a day for everyone to recuperate before returning to our regular routines.

We left early on a Sunday morning, hoping to make good time on our 24-hour trip to West Yellowstone, stopping overnight in Denver. Michael, Emma, and I would take turns driving. The weather held and we found a great place to stay in Denver, next to an outstanding steak place. Emma and I shared a room and dove into our beds as soon as we had washed our faces and brushed our teeth.

The following day took us through Wyoming, where spectacular scenery unfolded before our eyes. We had bought fried chicken for lunch and a slaw without mayo, and ate under a tree by a rushing river.

The Land Cruiser rolled into the town of West Yellowstone late in the evening. We had made reservations – appropriately enough – at the Dude & Roundup – originally The Dude Motel that had been built by Forrest and his brother, Skippy, and which Forrest mentioned in *The Thrill of The Chase*. Michael, whose idea of "slumming" was several stars above the dated two-star motel, was not comforted by the knowledge that he was sleeping in Room 4 - the very same room Ronald Reagan had occupied decades earlier. We repeated the story Fenn recounted in *Too Far To Walk*, but Michael failed to see the prestige in occupying the same quarters as the former two-term President of the United States and Governor of California. I think he wished he had been in charge of the reservations - no offence to the Dude.

We had reserved a spot at Canyon Village Campground because of its amenities, although it was a bit further from the Firehole River site we intended to search than we would have liked.

Michael did nothing that was not first class. He immediately set up a large 8-person, 4-room camping tent with individual sleeping areas, windows, and a covered, screened porch. There were blow-up twin mattresses for each of us, and room to store our supplies and camping kitchen unit, which included a hibachi and a cook stove with two large gas burners. He had a folding table and four chairs for the screened porch area, steel utensils and Melamine dinner ware. Emma and I were amazed.

Each campsite had its own fire pit and picnic table, as well, and the campsite offered flush toilets, sinks, and pay showers, all available at the camper service center at the front of the campground.

We attended a brief course in bear avoidance, bought a large canister of bear spray, and felt ready to sit down and plot out our search the next day.

The following morning, we sat in our screened enclosure enjoying fresh coffee and buttered toast with strawberry jam as we read our laminated sheets. Emma had analyzed Forrest's strange poem and researched a great deal, and she explained her logic.

"You have to ask yourself what is the one place Forrest loves so much he had to mention it in his books" He loved this one spot so much he had to show it to his family, and then was disappointed that his granddaughters were not as enthusiastic about it as he. In fact, Forrest dedicated an entire chapter in *Too Far to Walk* to describing the spot precisely, with the final paragraphs expressing the hope that, in time, his grandchildren would come to love the place, too. Forrest considered it a place where God "had underestimated his ability." So where else would he possibly hide his treasure chest and want his bones buried, as he told the reporter for Newsweek who wrote the article I'd mentioned, than the one place in the world for which he had so much affection? I also worked out this interpretation of his poem:

As I have gone alone in there

He went alone to his secret bathing spot. It is the only place he was truly alone, other than in Laotian jungle before help arrived.

And with my treasures bold

He bathed nude, his "family jewels" exposed. Defined, bold means so confident as to suggest a lack of shame or modesty. He was confident he was unseen there.

I can keep my secret where,

He did keep it. No one knew, until he revealed it in Too Far To Walk.

And hint of riches, new and old.

The riches were the riches of nature – the ancient formations, like the green geyser pool, and the new life in the elk and bison and river otters that surrounded him as he bathed.

Begin it where warm waters halt,

His bathing hole was warmed by the flow from the green geyser pool that ran 50 feet into the water. Moving just a few feet took Forrest into the colder water of the Firehole proper.

And take it in the canyon down,

The spot where he bathed was south of the Firehole Canyon section of the river.

Not far, but too far to walk,

His bathing site was a 20-mile bicycle ride from W. Yellowstone and about a mile's walk from the dirt road (now paved) through weeds and grasses. Definitely too far to walk.

Put in below the home of Brown.

The house of Yellowstone Ranger Gary Brown, built at the turn of the century and on the National Register of Historic Places, is now the Lamar Ranger Station, northeast of and not far from Canyon Village, and definitely north of the Firehole River. So many searchers have given the term "put in" a nautical definition. Actually, it simply means to place in a specific location – his bathing hole.

From there it's no place for the meek,

As Forrest mentions in Too Far To Walk, his bathing spot where the green geyser spills into the Firehole was pleasantly warm, but turned quite cold within only a few feet, changing it from a comfortable temperature, to a cold so intense that it motivated him to climb out immediately and dry in the sun. The cold river is no place for the meek. That is why you both brought wetsuits.

The end is ever drawing nigh;

Life is short. From the moment of our birth we begin the process of existence that only ends in death, which comes ever closer with each passing year.

There'll be no paddle up your creek,

Not only is the Firehole a river, a tributary - not a creek - it is not dangerous at this point, 'up the creek' usually meaning one is in a perilous situation. Although one must be aware of the strength of the current according to the Park literature. From the Midway portion of the river, just a bit north of The Ojo Caliente Bend (from the Spanish, "hot eye" or hot spring – he talks of a geyser pool that seems more of a spring than an actual geyser) which is a weedy stretch, heavy with grasses and with slower, deeper water. The bottom is generally even, however it still has potholes and broken places in the bedrock bottom. Just below the Ojo Caliente Bend is the beginning of the Fountain Flats, where animals graze, so he would have been able to see them as he bathed, exactly as he describes in TFTW.

Just heavy loads and water high.

The heavy load would be his bronze treasure chest, filled with 20 troy pounds of gold - there's that '20' figure he keeps repeating – which works out to 16 pounds, 7.314305 ounces. Plus, with other objects and the weight of the antique bronze chest, I think the whole thing works out to about 42 pounds – quite a heavy load for someone operating alone. Well, a woman, at least. And the water in his swimming hole, he said, was around 4 feet deep. That's considerable, when you consider the potholes and possible shifting o the chest, with the six years of occasional quakes and tremors. And the grass-covered banks that begin in this area are undercut, as well. Now, what's his name – Dal Neitzel? Anyway, he has explored about 8 miles of the river, he says, and has not found it. And all that grass has probably grown around and covered the treasure, so the ability to spend some time under water will be an advantage, as long as it is clear enough to see.

If you've been wise, and found the blaze,

Blaze comes from Old English, and means fire – the Firehole is the 'blaze.'

Look quickly down, your quest to cease.

As soon as you get to the point a few feet from where the warm water ends – and we do not know if he meant to his right, or to his left – look immediately down and the treasure chest should be in that immediate area.

But tarry scant with marvel gaze,

I took this to mean – don't hang around! First of all, Forrest has said that swimming is now verboten –

forbidden – in areas immediately adjacent to thermal activity; then, the road, although it has been paved, is chained off and cars are not admitted. Which does make carrying a 42-pound chest a heavy load!

Just take the chest and go in peace.

No explanation needed.

So why is it that I must go
And leave my trove for all to seek?

Here I think you have to consider that the idea came to him after surviving a battle with cancer.

The answers I already know,

He alone knows his real motivation. We can only guess.

I've done I'm tired, and now I'm weak.

It is apparent he wants to make his mark on the world, and the treasure hunt has done just that, I suppose. At least, there are thousands of people hooked into this search. We are not alone!

So hear me all and listen good,

No explanation needed.

Your effort will be worth the cold,

The river is going to freeze your tushies. Good thing you have the wetsuits!

If you are brave and in the wood

I think here he means, if you're good, and innocent (a babe in the woods?)

I give you title to the gold.

Again, no explanation is needed here!

Emma sat back, self-satisfied, and Michael and I applauded her effort. We planned to start the next day. It had taken us the morning to set everything up and go over Emma's evaluation, and to plot out our search area on a Yellowstone map. Clouds were gathering, with rain forecast for the afternoon, so we went for a walk and returned to the tent just as the first drops fell. The balance of the afternoon was spent on a game of gin rummy, reading, and responding to email.

Reconstituted chili was on the dinner menu, given the weather, and I learned just how advanced camping cuisine had become. It was delicious and satisfying. We discussed our plans for the next morning once more before turning in for the night. The morning would come early.

Chirping birds woke me. The air smelled fresh and clean. What a marvelous way to wake! Michael had been up for a while, and in minutes, he had bacon frying and coffee percolating. Emma was nowhere to be seen. I opened my mouth to ask, and he pre-empted me by saying, "She's up at the front, taking a shower. Want some coffee?"

I nodded and he passed me a steaming cup. We chatted about our expectations for the day until Emma returned, her hair still damp from the shower. "I'm sooooo glad you picked this campground, Stephanie. I heard from other campers that most of the other campgrounds don't have showers!" Our campground was in a thick stand of lodgepole pine. Some trunks were reddened by the feeding of mountain pine beetles. Our particular campsite was conveniently located and, fortunately, not far from the camper services facility.

"Go shower," Michael prompted. "I'll feed Emma and grab some eggs myself, then have your breakfast ready to go in 20 minutes. Is that enough time?"

I nodded and gave Emma a good-morning hug, then gathered soap, shampoo, and toothpaste before heading for the showers. I wasn't sure why I was showering and shampooing if I intended to spend the next few hours under water, but I did anyway, if nothing else but to wake myself up. I hurried back with a growing appetite and was delighted when Michael presented me with a full plate the moment I sat at the table. Michael timed everything perfectly.

We donned wetsuits and rubber shoes and brought tanks and masks to enable Michael and I to stay under water and search while Emma kept an eye on us and managed the

SUV. She would be armed with bear spray. The road ran relatively close to the river. On arrival, we discovered the hard rain the previous evening had kicked up dirt and sand that left the water murky.

Yellowstone is called that because the rhyolite, an igneous rock with a high silica content, was golden-hued. The problem, Michael and I discovered, as we dove four feet beneath the surface and cruised along the bottom to search broken bedrock for the antique chest, was that the piled rocks, half-hidden by the wafting grasses, resembled the carved and adorned top of the bronze chest. I would dig fruitlessly with my trowel, thinking I had spied the edge of the ancient bronze box, only to unearth stone, and Michael would twist square blocks of rhyolite only to recognize the mass as immovable. The murkiness of the water did not help.

As dusk approached and the air cooled, we gave up for the day, vowing to return the next day to search the opposite bank and the center of the river. No telling how the natural forces in the park had shifted the box over six years. And what if it had been found and, as Forrest had said, the finder had refused to share the wealth with the government and so never announced the find to the world? If that were the case, thousands could be spinning their wheels for naught.

Michael surprised us with vacuum-packed steaks that evening. We grilled them over the fire pit and ate with a blend of rehydrated spring peas and pearl onions. The moon rose and the clear sky provided a navy backdrop to billions of stars – a jeweled sky never seen in the city.

The flash woke me from a restful sleep. The light-colored fabric of the tent absorbed no light, but let it all pour through. I'd never seen such brightness except in the worst of thunderstorms. Fearing a downpour, I threw caution to the wind. I grabbed the bear spray, then rushed to use the facilities in our section of the campground, lest a downpour trap me in the tent with a full bladder. I carried my bear spray at the ready and aimed so it would not blow into my face as I walked. As I investigated, I noticed the sky was clear, and that left me puzzled. On my way back to the tent, the sky lit up once again. A mass of white light in the distance filled the horizon and seemed to expand to fill the entire sky. The solid light lingered far longer than a mere lightning strike and turned the nighttime into day, for a total of 1-2-3-4-5-6-7. . . 8 full seconds! Impossible!

Concerned, I lay back on the mattress and watched for several minutes to see if the light would reappear. I eventually fell asleep. In the morning, I booted up my laptop and Googled the Yosemite tapes Michael mentioned in his warning several weeks earlier. And there it was. The videotaped sky blazed with a lingering white light, just like I'd witnessed last night. A chill swept through me. Had he been right to caution me?

But then, the timestamp on the YouTube video I'd just watched was two months ago, and no catastrophe had yet happened.

There were other, more recent videos, however. And so I watched one after the other, seated on my mattress, not yet dressed for the day. Michael finally came looking for me and found me engrossed in a series of videos that echoed the concerns he had expressed at lunch several weeks ago-- concerns I had dismissed.

"Believe me now?" Michael asked.

I nodded. "I saw the sky light up like this twice last night. This has apparently been going on since 2010, though. A lot of these reports have occurred from 2013 through to this year. But it seems to build, then recede. Everyone speaks of that, 'someday.' Well, 'someday' an asteroid or huge meteor is supposed to hit the earth again. And the period from 2003 to 2005 had similar event and sightings – then, nothing. This is fascinating, but it may never happen during our lifetimes, Michael.

"And thousands of diseases can kill us all, as well. I simply can't live in fear, like some people. I know a woman who is so convinced she will be killed by one of the many perils she reads about that she is terrified to leave the house. I can't live that way."

"Well, if it's any consolation, Stephanie, the USGS reports that nothing new is going on – only the usual temblors. I don't feel like diving today. Let's tour the Park. Emma's on board with the idea. How about you?"

"Yes. Absolutely. It would be a pity to spend the week here and only see the bottom of the Firehole River. I thought you didn't trust the USGS."

"I don't, dear Stephanie. However, their reports are analyzed by many other professional sources I keep up with. Besides, we are here, and I haven't seen anything to cause immediate concern. Not even your light flashes. And I do want to see Yellowstone – at least, from the road. We can drive the Loop, and the length of the Firehole, and check out some of the major geysers and pools. Come on. I'll whip you up some scrambled eggs. Emma and I have eaten. Get dressed. I'll have your eggs ready in 5 minutes."

After breakfast in the majestic, wild beauty surrounding us, my mood lifted, and we were all in fine spirits when we set off in the Land Cruiser to see Old Faithful. As we passed through the Lower, Midway, and Norris Geyser Basins, I opened a brochure and read information about the areas out loud for Michael and Emma. These areas had the highest concentration of geothermal features in the park, and were the areas evidencing the greatest recent changes raising concern among park rangers, geologists, Yellowstone tourists, and local residents.

We took the Firehole Canyon loop drive through the Lower Geyser Basin, starting south from Madison Junction, past Firehole Falls and the Fountain Paint Pots - bubbling mud pots that dotted the landscape - and looped off onto Firehole Lake Drive to see Great Fountain Geyser. We continued to Firehole Lake, a hot pool, and the Three Senses Trail, before returning to the Midway Geyser Basin, where we walked to Excelsior Geyser Crater and Grand Prismatic Spring along specially erected boardwalks. In Black Sand Basin, we relished the bright colors of Sunset Lake and the Emerald Pool.

"Wasn't Firehole Lake Drive the road they had to close last year because the asphalt drive was actually melting because of the heat from the ground?" I asked a ranger we met at the Excelsior Geyer. He nodded but did not elaborate. I followed up by asking if he had noted any recent changes we should be aware of. He commented that Norris Geyser Basin had been far more active lately. At Madison Junction, we turned toward the Basin, driving along the northwest rim of the Yellowstone Caldera. Steamboat Geyser was erupting regularly for the first time in years, reaching heights of nearly 380 feet. And it seemed that in the Norris Geyser Basin, every thermal feature was active, including those that - like Steamboat Geyser – had lain dormant for decades.

The mineral oxides and acidic environment of the Porcelain Basin create a quite hostile environment for plants, algae, and bacteria. Spectrums of pink, orange, yellow and red delight the eye, and silica deposits reveal themselves as tiny, sharp spines rather than the thick, beaded deposits common to the alkaline basins of the Park. Steam escapes through the summit of the Roaring Mountain through fumaroles or steam vents rimmed with bright yellow crystalline sulphur deposits. When exposed to moisture, the sulfuric fumes turn into acid that leaches into the ground and is responsible for the stark landscape. The toxic gases have been known to kill even large animals.

North of Norris we passed the Obsidian Cliff, the source of volcanic glass traded across the continent for other essentials by the local Native American tribes. Mammoth Hot Springs presented travertine terraces of calcium carbonate, with geyserite deposits of new rock, which was chemically similar to glass. Tower Junction featured the exquisite Tower Falls, a cascade that tumbled 132 feet into the Yellowstone River. Breathtaking is an understatement.

However, something continued to nag at me, spoiling my enjoyment.

I had read that morning the Shoshone River was boiling, as was a portion of the Yellowstone River. All of Yellowstone seemed more active than it had been for nearly 100 years. Things were obviously heating up. But to what end? It seemed that many of the current fears voiced by observers, rangers and geologists were similar to those voiced in 2013 and again in 2014, and still earlier, from 2001 to 2004. Who knew if these warnings, too, would wane as before, when nothing happened? I tried to still my concerns, then smiled. Michael was always such a worrywart. I was letting his fears infect my mind.

We decided to head back rather than continue east to the other side of Yellowstone. It was mid-afternoon and the sun would set relatively early. Michael didn't want us on the road after dark. Since so many animals were nocturnal, hitting a deer or a bear - or having a tire go flat - could be disastrous.

All I could think of on our way back as I gazed out the window at the astounding scenery was how very fortunate the Fenn brothers had been to spend their summers in this phenomenal place.

And then I wondered what to do about the book-- about Forrest's story.

It needed an ending.

Chapter 44: It Bears Consideration

Morning brought renewed interest in searching the other half of the Firehole in the area of Forrest's bathing pool to see if tremblers in the intervening years after he'd 'secreted' his treasure had perhaps shifted the location of the box.

Yes, it allegedly weighed 42 pounds, and might not be affected by strong currents, but we had to remember that the ground beneath Yellowstone was subject to frequent shaking, changes in elevation and horizontal shifts in terrain that could affect the location of the treasure, with its current site potentially yards away from its original location.

Existing over an active volcano, the surface of Yellowstone rises and falls as the magma builds and shifts beneath the surface rocks, earth, and sands. The Yellowstone Plateau is a work of nature continually in progress, shaping and reshaping itself over the eons in response to unpredictable releases of the planet's energy and the subterranean stresses that bring about tectonic shifts and changes in the caldera. Yellowstone's geysers and hot springs are fueled by the immense heat released by its magma core and, in particular, the huge reservoir that lies beneath the Park.

Following our return to camp the previous evening, I'd been unable to sleep, and so I booted up my laptop and researched Yellowstone for the next two hours, until sleep could be put off no longer. Only once did I notice the intensely bright light spreading across the horizon. It lingered inordinately long – longer than the flashes the night before. Again, there was no indication of lightning.

The U.S. Geological Survey (USGS) created the Yellowstone Volcano Observatory in 2001 and increased the level of sophisticated monitoring of the Park's changes, based on the potential for seriously hazardous changes in the hypothermal, seismic, and volcanic events in the area. The 1970's resurvey of a baseline measurement of the

Yellowstone Caldera taken decades earlier noted an unprecedented uplift that exceeded 28 inches – 72 centimeters – taking place over the interceding 50 years. It was a disturbing change that warranted close monitoring given the potential for near apocalyptic damage a new explosion could cause.

Lava poured from the youngest of the three calderas beneath Yellowstone proper some 70,000 years ago, and no other major eruption has since occurred. But all experts agree it's just a matter of time, since Yellowstone's spectacular and ever-changing geothermal vents, pools and geysers are evidence the volcanic system remains highly active.

I'd read that a southward tilt has been observed along the south shores of Yellowstone Lake, including tilting of the lake basin itself. By the mid- '70s scientists had conclusively established that the center of the Park had indeed risen, just as suspected, with the north end of Yellowstone Lake considerably higher than the south end. Responsibility was attributed to the 640,000-year-old Yellowstone Caldera, which caused resurgent domes to form when magma underlying the surface pushes upward, creating pressures that cause the surface to bow.

The Yellowstone Caldera is an oval, shallow depression that is 53 miles long and 28 miles wide (85 by 45 KM), smack dab in the center of the Park. It was formed during the last major eruption of the Yellowstone Volcano some 640,000 years ago, which caused the ground to collapse into what was then a partially empty magma reservoir, and thus formed the craterlike depression at the Park's center. Subsequent eruptions took the form of more than 20 lava flows, some as thick as 400 feet (120 m), that filled the original Caldera floor and walls. A prominent landmark, Mount Washburn is the one section of the Caldera wall that escaped burial beneath the lava flows.

The University of Utah and the USGS conducted annual surveys from 1983-1998, when new technologies were adopted to provide a more detailed explanation of observable changes. The Caldera floor continued to rise until 1984, paused for a year, and then subsided for the ensuing decade. While portions of the Caldera began to rise again in 1995, a more complex pattern of uplift and subsidence involving the northwest rim of the Caldera centered near the Norris Geyser Basin, has since prevailed.

Over this period, the frequency of earthquakes has varied dramatically, but the raw numbers of quakes have risen steadily over the last three years. We had felt several tremblers since our arrival, but none remarkable enough to cause concern, and they certainly were not what could be termed a "swarm."

The largest swarm, in fact, began in 1985, lasted through 1986, and produced over 3,000 earthquakes in the upper Madison Valley area, moving away from the rim of the Caldera. The swarm was later attributed to a rupture that occurred in a wide layer of impermeable rock above the magma. The rupture allowed heated geothermal fluids to move upward through the rupture, opening other cracks and moving rock, causing a series of small earthquakes that dramatically reduced upward pressure and caused the dome's rise to subside. In 1995 another swarm occurred – this time, accompanied by Caldera uplift.

Current conditions emulated that period of activity, but with increased geothermal activity creating new geysers and bringing dormant ones to life. Heat measurements of the Park increased substantially over recent years, and in 2015, Fountain Flats Drive had actually been closed for repairs when the asphalt melted, with segments crumbling like oatmeal.

Curious, I begged Michael to take us down the drive that morning before we tackled the Firehole River site and spent the rest of the day in the water. He and Emma were amenable, so we set off after a hearty breakfast of oatmeal and fruit, followed by several cups of Michael's excellent coffee while we examined the Yellowstone map and consulted our GPS for directions.

"Fountain Flats Drive is a two-way freight road that runs behind Lower and Midway Geyser Basins," I read out loud. "While this is another interesting side trip off the main road, it does dead end for auto traffic after three miles and then continues as a bicycle and foot trail to rejoin the Grand Loop. The Imperial Geyser and Fairy Falls can be reached from trails along this road."

"Look, it runs alongside the Firehole River, at least for this portion." Emma traced a spot of the map laid out before us.

"I don't think it's as close to the river as it appears on the map," Michael observed. "Looks interesting, though. And it'll give us a chance to do a little hiking. We can sacrifice a few hours, and still have time to search the river bottom this afternoon. What do you think, Stephanie?"

"I'm game. I'd like to see the falls. . . Fairy Falls. Says here the falls are 197 feet high. Hmph. Maybe we'll see a few water fairies. Wonder why they named it Fairy Falls?"

"The road exits west off 191 and traces the Firehole through Midway Geyser Basin and ends after three miles at Goose Lake, which is just a mile off Grand Loop Road. Then the trail follows the old Fountain Flats road from where the drive ends to the Fairy Falls trailhead. It's a hard pack and gravel trail. If we stay on the trail all the way, it'll take us back by Imperial Geyser and Grand Prismatic Spring. So, if we turn around after seeing Fairy Falls. the whole hike should take between 2-3 hours. Then we can picnic on at the Nez Pierce Creek junction with the Firehole and continue up to where we've been looking for the chest near the Ojo Caliente Bend and get some diving in before dusk. Looks like bison and geysers are the trail's two main dangers. And crowds are supposed to be minimal, so it should be a great morning."

After packing a lunch, we drove through the grassy meadows of Fountain Flats, turning west onto the Drive and parking at the lot, where ours was the only vehicle. Two bicyclers passed us, headed to the trail.

We reapplied our sunscreen, slung our backpacks over our shoulders, then took off down the finely-packed gravel path. At the bridge, we walked across the Firehole River, gazing down into its shallow depths, trying to catch sight of the many large trout that ran the river.

The trailhead to Fairy Falls started within a mile. The weather was perfect, and we strode along happily, with water bottles in hand. Occasionally, a pair of bicyclers passed us, waving in greeting.

Bison dotted the meadows, backed by conical pines of dark blue-green, and steaming geothermal features framed the grassy fields where the huge creatures grazed. The shaggy brown ungulates remained at a distance, however, and never raised their heads from their steady munching, so we felt safe and simply enjoyed their presence, occasionally snapping a photo.

When we passed several sites visited the day before from the opposite bank of the Firehole River, we took the opportunity to climb the hill to the left of the Fountain Freight Road. We followed one of the worn footpaths and found that the short scramble to the top was well worth the effort. From our height, we had an exceptional view of the aqua, navy and rose depths of Grand Prismatic Spring, the largest hot spring in the U.S. and third largest in the world. The hill also offered a superior view of the Excelsior Geyser Crater, and the beautiful Opal and Turquoise pools that lay beyond.

We descended the hill and picked up the trail again. On reaching the 1-mile mark, the trail turned to the left. We stopped to read the weathered wood sign that pointed out the distances to various sights, gave the Dos & Don'ts of backcountry hiking and warned us of impending danger: We were entering bear country.

"I thought you said the only trail hazards were geysers and bison," Emma teased Michael. He chuckled. "We aren't carrying food and you ladies wisely eschewed the sweet-smelling lotions and perfumes you usually coat yourselves with, so I doubt they'll find us very appealing."

We passed Goose Lake but decided to check out Fairy Falls first and explore the lake on our way back. Across the landscape, the steam of the many vents and hot pools rose like the smoke from a dozen campfires. Bison moved lazily from one spot to another to partake of the fragrant green late Spring grasses.

This section of the Park, and virtually all of the trail area, had been severely affected by the raging fires of 1988. The landscape was still recovering. Many hillsides were bare, with recently established young pines just beginning to fill out. Older pines that escaped the inferno were occasionally visible on more distant hills, taller and leaner than the young, tender growth that predominated the edges of the meadowland. Before the fire, Yellowstone was covered in aging lodgepole pines that supported far fewer species of animals and plants. In that respect, the fires served a good purpose: The nascent forests were more alive with new growth and animal life than ever.

The 1988 fires opened the dense overhead canopy that inhibited new growth and burned away the underbrush. Grasses new growth took only weeks to sprout anew, with small animals feeding on the plentiful seeds dropped by the many pinecones that popped open from the heat and dropped their contents. With the numerous smaller animals attracted by the plentiful food came their predators, the hawks. Burned tree trunks, weakened by the fire, attracted beetles and other insects that, along with the seeds, provided a nourishing diet for a variety of birds.

As we walked, we appreciated the beauty of woodland and meadow flowers and listened for the sounds of life that filled the adolescent forests the graveled path led us through.

We reached Fairy Falls at the 2.5-mile mark and gasped in delight as the waters of Fairy Creek shot out over the rocky edge of the Madison Plateau, plunging nearly 200 feet to the wide basin below. Recent rains broadened the stream that cascaded down the face of the rocks to form a pool where a few visitors frolicked in the depths. Adult bathers stood chest-high in the cool waters. Youngsters played along the edges. We doffed our shoes and socks and waded in the shallows for a bit, refreshing our feet before the long hike back, which would be made longer by the detour to Goose Lake. The consensus was, "We're here, Let's see it," so we dried our feet on rocks heated by the late morning sun before heading back up the trail.

Goose Lake came into sight. Here, evidence of the 1988 fire has left its mark even more visibly than elsewhere, with fallen trees and scattered trunks covering Goose Lake Meadows and occasional lone lodgepole survivors poking their lean pine trunks skyward, barren of leaves and most branches, silent sentinels watching over the steaming land and placid waters of the lake. A few dark buffalo dotted the landscape. New pine growth lent broad slashes of green to the golden grass-scape, and the hills rose beyond in waves of green. A wide, cloud-free sky drew attention to the snowcapped peaks in the distance. Stillness reigned.

We heard her before we saw her. In fact, had we seen her, we would have backed away immediately, moving slowly in reverse toward the trail, and then beat a hasty retreat to our car.

We had done everything wrong. The hike had gone so smoothly we let our guard down. We separated at the lake, rather than staying together in a tight group. Emma silently picked wildflowers to my left, and I sat on the grass, intently reading the guidebook to learn about the area.

Michael strayed the farthest, about fifty or so feet away. We made no noise, and we all ignored the scavenger birds flying overhead – ravens and hawks circling at differing levels, and a lone vulture riding the higher airstreams to see what the smaller fowl found so attractive-- no doubt a carcass of some kind. The birds were loath to descend, however, while the predators that had brought down the young elk or deer were still feasting upon it.

The wind soughing through the pines and the occasional raucous caw of a raven masked subtle sounds we should have detected--the sounds of carnivores devouring their meal, tearing it limb from limb.

Hidden at some distance behind the bushy foliage of a close-growing stand of young pines, a dangerous scene had been masked by tall meadow grasses.

The attack came when Michael pushed over a dead tree trunk with his foot to see what lay beneath. The unexpected clatter of the loose timber leaning against the log surprised a mother grizzly into a defensive posture. She rose from near invisibility in the high grass to her full height - six feet, at least - and let out a single roar. It was then that we spotted her two cubs feeding on a kill. They raised their heads to see what had angered their mother. The cubs appeared to be about two years of age. They seemed big enough to fend for themselves yet were young enough to still require a mother's protection and instruction. The sow was teaching them to hunt, for themselves. Bringing down their prey had been a family affair.

Michael let out a shout of fear and surprise. I whipped up my head, then rose to my feet, half in shock, frozen. Emma turned toward the noise and also stood frozen, white as a sheet with her hands covering her mouth in horror. Michael's immediate instinct was to back away, then turn and run. But he was no match for the mother bear, who could sprint at nearly 35 miles an hour, and did just that, knocking Michael to the ground and turning quickly to swipe an enormous paw at him as he went down. Her claws tore open his arm. Then the grizzly hovered over him, poking at him with her immense paw. The grizzly sow's large head dove quickly beneath the grass. Was she biting him? Michael's pain was audible, and it seemed he was stifling a scream, perhaps intuiting that it would incite the bear. He'd had the sense to curl into a ball as he went down, protecting his neck by folding his hands behind his head and relying on his backpack to save him from further injury. He lay still, in the fetal position. Gushing blood colored his shirt and reddened his arm.

Had the bear torn an artery? Could he walk? How was I going to going to get Michael back to the car and get him to a hospital in time? And where was the nearest Ranger station? I had my phone, but without nearby cell towers, it might be useless. I couldn't move my hands to fumble for my phone at that point anyway. The sow had lifted her head and was now watching Emma and me. My heart pounded in my chest.

My mind raced as it tried to recollect what to do in this situation. First, I had to worry about the bear. She stood over Michael's still form and was still looking our way.

"Emma, the bear spray. It's in the front pocket of my backpack – get it out! Quick!" I said loudly, evenly, hoping that the low, grim sound of my voice would help the mother grizzly to recognize me as human - not on her list of preferred game. I knew better than to challenge Mama Grizzly by meeting her eyes as she watchfully assessed the remaining threat to her cubs and their kill, but instead kept mine lowered and to the left, with my head angled submissively, all the while beseeching Emma, who I thought was standing behind me, to reach for the canister of pepper spray in the front pocket of my backpack.

But Emma had dropped to the ground the moment the grizzly looked our way, her handful of wildflowers scattering in the wind. I could see her limp body from the corner of my eye. At first, I thought she was playing dead, like the Ranger had instructed us on our first night, but I soon realized she had fainted in terror. I dared not shed my backpack to retrieve the canister myself, nor drop to the ground at this point, and risk a reaction from the huge brown bear in front of me. So I stood frozen, waiting for the grizzly to decide how she was going to handle the situation. It was entirely her call.

I could feel the sow watching me but did not dare to raise my eyes, and tried to refrain from even blinking, alert but docile in my posture. Michael had not moved, and I wondered at the extent of his injuries. The sow had come down hard on him, and he flew several feet from the impact of her paw. I was just thankful he had not landed on his bloodied arm, and hoped his arm was all that her massive blow had injured, and that she hadn't severed an artery. Had she clawed his side and back when she appeared to be poking at him? And had she bitten him when she ducked her head out of sight? Was the blood on her muzzle his, or the slaughtered animal's?

I had no idea how we were going to get out of there without inciting another attack. And Michael desperately needed medical attention.

Suddenly the immense bear turned and lumbered away, pausing for a moment to look behind her before disappearing behind the stand of pine.

"She's gone back to her cubs, Michael. Can you move?" I called out to him in a low voice, hoping I was audible some 20 feet away, where he lay. Panicking, I called out again. This time, I could see him open his eyes. He moved, slowly, cautiously, as if taking physical inventory of his injuries. Michael nodded. But his grimace as he tried to move his bloodied arm was telling.

Why here? I cursed. We were at least a hundred yards from the trail. To escape, we had to cross over meadowland – the terrain strewn with debris from the decades-old fires and occasional rocks tossed by earthquakes that constantly disturbed the surface of Yellowstone. With a grizzly family still feeding beyond the stand of pines, and presumably ready to repeat the aggression, our chances appeared slim. This time, the cubs might join in an attack.

Emma stirred, and I turned my attention to her. "What happened?" she asked, bewildered to find herself lying in the grass.

"Stay down!" I hissed at her. "The bear charged Michael and he's hurt. But I'm afraid for any of us to move, because the mother and her cubs are still over there in the high grass. I think they're still feeding on an elk, or whatever it is. Look at the birds." I pointed skyward.

Emma looked up at the circling ravens and hawks, and the growing number of vultures flying on high. A fresh kill attracted them like a magnet. A few brave ravens appeared to land near the bear, but were immediately lost in the meadow grass, which had grown so high in the spring that the family of bears was nearly invisible. Only the mother was large enough to be seen, and the cubs occasionally moved in a manner that brought their furry ears and the backs of their heads into view.

I realized the grass would hide us, too, if we knelt slowly. I motioned to Emma to retrieve the bear spray and hand it to me from my pack once I had knelt on the ground and was leaning forward. When I reached to take the canister from her, the ground trembled.

The earth's motion was so subtle that I thought I was imagining it. My thoughts were focused on what to do about Michael. Then I felt it again, a vibration that rose from my hand pressed firmly against the ground. I turned to Emma and raised my eyebrows. She had felt it, too, and whispered, "Earthquake – a trembler." Her eyes were wide. I glanced toward Michael, but with my knees and hands on the ground, it was no longer possible to observe him directly, so I asked Emma to watch for any movement of the bears and be ready to call out a warning and was prepared to move slowly toward Michael when I noticed the mama grizzly was no longer paying attention to us, or to their meal. Every animal in sight lifted its head, cocked it slightly, attentively, then trotted away toward – toward what? Animals in the meadow were suddenly on the move, all in the same direction, and the mother bear was watching them, ears alerted to a sound I could not hear.

The earth trembled again, and the mother bear and her cubs rose from the carcass. She appeared torn, not wanting to leave their feast, but apparently troubled by the earth's continued movement and anxiously watching as bison and elk loped out of the meadow – heading where? She reluctantly nudged her cubs and lumbered away in the same direction. The cubs were even more reluctant to leave the food than she was, and the mother promptly returned to lower her head and push the two cubs to their feet before lumbering off ahead of them, looking back to make sure they were following her. The moment they left; the birds descended.

The whole episode concerned me. The tremblers had been so gentle I had hardly worried about them. Was something bigger on its way? Animals were supposed to be sensitive to things like that. Electro-magnetic changes, vibrations, sounds we humans cannot hear, supposedly affected them.

I crept toward Michael, then, reassured by the bear's retreating backsides, I rose to my feet. He lay more relaxed, with eyes closed, and I feared shock was setting in. "Michael, it's okay, they're gone," I called out. "I'm coming to get you. We're coming to get you." Then I recalled that Emma was a nurse.

Turning to Emma, I told her, "Michael needs you. I'll find a location to get him trauma care. Can you see to him? I have no idea what to do." I picked up the guidebook I had dropped in fear and flipped through it desperately. "Go to him – please go to him," I beseeched Emma, who was looking in her backpack for the First Aid kit and bandages. Emma followed my pointing finger, then quietly moved to his side. I followed her.

Blood was still flowing from his wounds, but it did not appear to be gushing, so I was hopeful an artery was not involved. However, there appeared to be damage to his shoulder that I hadn't notice when observing him from a distance. Was it a bite?

"We have to get you out of here," I told him, "get you some medical care. The bears are gone. They're following the other animals, hightailing it out of here, Lord knows where."

Michael opened his eyes and nodded. "I felt it. The shaking. It happens all the time. But if the animals left . . . Ow!

Emma had barely touched him as she inspected his injury. Emma leaned forward and asked, "Can you sit up, Michael, if I help you?" She donned the gloves in the kit then tried to lift away the torn portions of his shirt and reveal the extent of his wounds.

He grimaced in pain but managed to shift his position so she could cut away the shirt and determine the extent of his injuries.

As I watched her take over, my first thought was: Thank goodness she's a nurse! I handed her the various items from the kit as she requested. Emma clucked at the amount of blood Michael was losing. She immediately applied the tourniquet provided in the First Aid kit to staunch the bleeding. She then cleaned and disinfected his wounds before bandaging the areas of torn skin as best as she could. Emma then sat back to check her handiwork. I became worried because she looked worried. The new bandages almost immediately became soaked in blood.

How much blood could a person lose and still live?

"The closest medical facility is the Old Faithful Clinic," I read. "We can call 911 - the emergency number at the Ranger Station - or we can call the clinic directly."

Emma said, "I think it's better if we get hold of a Ranger. They're far more experienced in transporting the injured, and I'm afraid Michael will lose more blood if he exerts himself, or if we try to move him. I have no idea how the two of us could lift him into the SUV. Call 911 - if you can get a signal. Can you?"

The ground trembled again. It was a temblor so slight that even resting on the earth as we were, I barely felt it. The tremors were becoming continuous, as though the earth beneath us was shimmying to a cosmic tune. I reached into my pocket and pulled out my phone. I held my breath as I turned it on. A signal! I punched in the numbers, and in a moment a very competent voice was asking what the problem was and where we were located.

"My friend was attacked by a bear at Goose Lake, not far from the Fountain Flats Freight Road Trail. He's losing a lot of blood," I told the operator. "Please hurry! What? Can he walk? I don't know, we haven't tried to move him.

Another friend – she's a nurse – feels he'll lose more blood if he exerts himself. Yes. Thank you. Please hurry!"

I sighed with relief and addressed the two anxious faces looking at me intently. "The 911 number apparently feeds directly into the ranger station. The dispatcher said someone will be here shortly. They'll have a stretcher and are sending medics. The background was noisy. I could hear people shouting, and lots of voices, commotion - like you hear from a call center - although the fellow I spoke to seemed quite calm. Intense, but calm. I wonder if something is going on."

We were unprepared for the arrival of a helicopter.

As the EIRMC Med-Evac helicopter landed, Emma and I ducked into the grass and covered our heads to keep our hair from whipping our faces. I looked at Michael. His eyes were closed, and he seemed oblivious to the noise and wind of the landing aircraft. No surprise, no interest. No nothing, I was gripped with fear. What could it mean?

"We weren't expecting a helicopter," Emma shouted.

"This your lucky day, ladies," the EMS tech who emerged from the helicopter shouted. "It's been a busy morning, and we were within the perimeter when your call came in – what do we have here?"

I stayed with Michael while Emma explained Michael's condition to the EMS worker. I was grateful for her presence. I was holding Michael's hand tightly and felt the pulse at his carotid. It seemed weak to my untrained touch. Now that I no longer had to think logically, a flood of emotions overtook me, and I began to cry. I kissed his forehead and whispered, "Don't go anywhere, Michael. You can't check out on me. Help is here. You'll be fine."

An EMS worker knelt at his side and took his pulse, checked his eyes, made sure he was breathing steadily, and listened to his heart. He asked if Michael was allergic to anything, and I shook my head, no. He then proceeded to give Michael a tetanus shot, followed by an injection of penicillin. A second tech and placed an oxygen mask over

Michael's nose and mouth. Then they lifted him onto a stretcher.

"I'll have to come with him. He's my husband. Was my husband. He has no other next of kin, and he'll need blood. I'm O-Negative – a universal donor – and Michael's AB." I turned to Emma and asked, "Can you drive Michael's SUV and meet us at the hospital?

The medics looked at each other, then Emma. The unshaven one said, "I'm going to say this fast, and I can't answer questions. There's a Park Ranger coming this way and what I'm telling you is not yet public information, but the ground under and around the Caldera is superheated. They have roads melting all over the Park. New geysers are erupting as we speak. We've been working with scaldings all morning. And we've had small, steady tremblors all morning. They're going to evacuate soon, so if I were you, ma'am, I would hop into that SUV, punch the East Idaho Regional Medical Center into your GPS and hightail it out of here before the roads are overwhelmed."

"But what about our tent? Our things?"

"Things can be replaced. People can't. Your friends will be at EIRMC for a good while. Get the Ranger to take you to your car, and drive out of here, immediately. Forget about your stuff, and don't hesitate."

"Hello, Officer! We meet again!" the second tech shouted to the Park Ranger looming into sight. The approaching Ranger had to be 6'6," so 'looming' was the appropriate term. He carried a shotgun in one hand, and a pocket tape recorder in the other.

"Everything under control, guys? Ladies?" the Ranger asked. "It was a bear attack?"

"Yes," I answered. "Grizzly. The mother and her cubs were feeding – they weren't little cubs. They looked to be – what do you think, Emma? – two years old? They were hidden behind some thick pines, in the high grass. When Michael pushed over a tree trunk with his foot the mother bear freaked. Michael backed away slowly when he first saw her, but then he turned and ran, and that's when she charged him."

Emma added, "I think he was bitten more than once. But he was so bloody . . . ."

"Did you do this? The tourniquet and the bandaging?" one of the EMS workers asked Emma. She nodded.

"Good job," he told her. They carried Michael to the helicopter and a third EMS worker appeared to help load the stretcher onto the Med-Evac.

"It was a long time before we could get to him and apply a tourniquet," I informed the Ranger. He was recording my words, so I made the effort to speak distinctly. "The sow wouldn't leave him alone, though she kept looking back at her cubs, who ignored her and kept feeding."

Emma chimed in, "See – there, where all the birds are – that's where whatever they were eating – where their kill was. We were terrified, and afraid to move to help Michael. We didn't know if moving would make her charge us."

The Ranger quickly walked around the stand of pines, which was about 50 feet away from where we stood and looked down at what we presumed were the remains of the animal they had been feeding on. As he approached, the scavenging birds rose in a dark cloud, only to settle back on the carcass as soon as he turned and walked back to us.

"Elk," he said tersely. "Young, but not a newborn – that would have been just a snack. He was very lucky the bears had eaten well," the Ranger remarked, gesturing toward the waiting helicopter with his head. "There wasn't much left for the birds."

"And he had the sense to play dead, so that's when she went back to her cubs. They ate for a bit longer, then I saw the sow watching some animals that were running in that direction." I pointed. "Quite a few, in fact. She watched them, and then she made the cubs leave what was left of their kill and follow her."

Emma interjected, "There have been so many tremors. Is that why they were running? Is everything okay in the Park? Should we be worried?"

The Ranger spoke immediately to allay our fears. It sounded rehearsed.

"Tremors and small quakes are a way of life in Yellowstone. We don't worry about them much. And the animals are always running somewhere. From predators. To food, or water. Or to protect their young. Interesting that she followed them, though. Maybe the sow saw the opportunity to kill another animal – they do cache their food – bears are opportunistic."

"It was our fault, though, not the bear's. We were stupid. So stupid," I declared. "And the bear was doing what a mother is supposed to do, protecting her cubs." I was surprised I defended the bear's actions. I didn't want the bear killed because of its natural reaction to our errors. We were the ones not paying attention, and we'd surprised it.

The helicopter rotors had never stopped whirring, but now that Michael had been loaded aboard, they picked up speed in order to lift from the ground. One of the EMS team was at the door, beckoning for me to hurry, so I hugged Emma and whispered, "I'll see you in Idaho" I kissed her cheek. Then I asked the Ranger to escort her to the car and gave her Michael's backpack after removing his wallet. I would need his health insurance card and I.D. "His car keys are in the outer pocket. Forget about our other stuff, Emma. All the important stuff is in the SUV. We'll deal with the rest later. I'll need you with me at the hospital. Drive safely."

I ran toward the helicopter and turned to wave to her upon reaching the door, but she and the Ranger were already halfway across the field and on the way to the car.

The helicopter lifted off, and we were on our way, too.

With Michael rebandaged, injected with penicillin, and given IV fluids, the EMS team settled in for the ride.

Once I was seated and belted in, I asked, "Did the bear bite him? How bad is it? Is he conscious?"

Now that crisis was averted, they had time to talk. The two who had rendered immediate care and stretchered Michael to the aircraft were young, but their faces were weathered. One was bearded – he had that scruffy, "Miami Vice" non-shaved look popular with young men. The other was clean-shaven, bordering on handsome. The third member of the EMS team was obviously the supervisor. He wore glasses and was older, quieter and, as I observed during the flight, more judicious in his comments. It was he who answered my queries.

"It looks like he sustained two bites, and a double clawing. The wounds are deep. All bear maulings are serious. He's lost a lot of blood, and that's characteristic of this kind of injury. Many veins and capillaries have been torn. But only a surgeon's thorough examination can tell us how extensive the damage to his nerves and muscles are.

"He said you're his healthcare surrogate; that you can make medical decisions on his behalf."

I was stunned. When we'd had our wills written, while we were still married, we each had signed living wills and had each named the other as medical surrogate, empowered to make any healthcare decisions as were needed, in event of an incapacity. It surprised me that Michael had not replaced my name with Kent's after the divorce.

"The tetanus and penicillin were a precaution against infection. Feeding bears potentially have a lot of dangerous bacteria in their mouths," the EMS supervisor explained.

With the crisis averted for the moment, the medics were more than eager to share their morning's experiences, and everything they knew.

"We've been dealing with a lot of burn victims," one said. "Two new geysers suddenly exploded into existence today, very close to tourist groups walking along open trails - and in two entirely different locations. Six people were scalded by steam. We airlifted a few of them, along with a second Med-Evac helicopter from EIRMC, and we were on our way back for more when we were diverted to Goose Lake to handle this situation."

"He's your husband?" the beardless EMS worker asked. "And you said you can donate blood?" He was the quietest member of the trio. It was the first time I'd heard his voice.

"Yes. No - was. Yes, I can. We're divorced, but still close. It's complicated."

"Isn't everything?" the bearded member said wryly.

"What's this about an evacuation?" I asked.

He replied, "They've got the geologists meeting now to evaluate the situation and

determine the risk level, and last I heard, they were ready to evacuate. I can only remember two other times we've evacuated--the 1988 fires, and a flooding-- but that required the evacuation of only certain sections."

"Same thing with the mudslide." That remark came from the supervisor.

I persisted. "Weren't they planning an evacuation last year – the super volcano thing – after they found that the magma chamber beneath Yellowstone was twice as large as they had calculated?"

"Well, ma'am, I guess you have been doing your homework. Last summer? They had roads melting then, too – closed Fire Hole Drive for a couple of months to resurface it. But they said the evacuation rumors were the result of a false alarm, and they aborted their evacuation plans. But I don't know . . . It's going to happen someday, whenever 'someday' comes around again."

"Thing is, the Park is always changing," the supervisor added. He pushed his glasses up on his nose, and his tone was very professorial. "Yellowstone is on an active volcanic sector – a 'hot spot' on the earth's crust – and there's no doubt it's going to blow again. But it could be another 70,000, or 640,000 or even a million years from now. Or tomorrow. All I know is the geologists say they like these little earthquakes and geothermal features – they say they relieve pressure and prevent a huge buildup that could lead to a still larger event."

"But they *are* contemplating an evacuation? There have been all sorts of tremblors all morning, and this past week –

and light flashes you only see at night that last a long time. Aren't you all worried?" I asked.

The silent one laughed, his handsome face crinkling about his ultra-blue eyes. "We live all live around here. Heck, I grew up around here. West Yellowstone. These guys are imports," he said, uncrossing his arms long enough to point at his companions on the team. "We worry about it every day, in the back of our minds. But if we let worries rob us of sleep, we'd never get a wink of shut-eye. You make your bets; you take your chances. I just can't think of anywhere else I'd rather live." They all nodded assent.

I was thinking of Emma, and of the gear we were leaving behind. I hoped she hadn't gone back for anything. Michael would be pissed. But he had insurance, and he had the money to replace it all. I sensed that he wouldn't be going camping again anytime soon.

I hoped Emma could get out of Yellowstone before panicked Park visitors trying to exit the Park at once clogged the roads. If she left immediately, she should arrive at EIRMC in another hour or so. It was about 110 miles from West Yellowstone.

The helicopter slowed and I detected just the slightest change in the speed of the rotors.

The helicopter descended to the helipad and landed with great care. "We're here. Time to get moving – they're ready for him."

I knew that cell phone use would be limited once inside the facility, so I gave Emma a quick call. She picked up immediately.

"Where are you?" I demanded.

"Stuck in traffic at the head of Grand Loop near the Madison Junction area. Right at the turn."

"Well, hang in there. I have to go, Emma. I'll let them know at the front that I'm expecting you, and where you can find me. Take care."

I followed the EMS team inside, my heart in my throat.

My thoughts were totally focused on Michael. I cared far more about this man than I had thought I would. Next to Dad, Michael was the most important person in my life.

And I had never really cut the cord that tied me to him.

351

Chapter 45: A Time to Weep

It took Emma three hours to get to EIRMC. Michael had already been in surgery for two hours when she arrived. I grasped her hand and hugged her.

"How bad was the drive?" I asked.

Emma spoke of the chaotic exit from Yellowstone, where people had crowded onto the roads ahead of any evacuation announcement and Park Rangers struggled to control traffic.

"The evacuation is going to go on into the night. Park officials finally ordered an official 'temporary evacuation for road repairs' when I was within 10 feet of the West exit. And getting to that spot near the West gate had taken me a full hour to arrive at, after I spoke to you from Madison Junction. I'm exhausted, and starving. Join me in the cafeteria?"

I wasn't hungry, but I wanted the company, so I told the sole occupant of the nursing station where I was going. The nurse promised to call my cell if she had any news, but assured me that the operating room had been reserved for several more hours, and she did not expect that surgery would proceed any faster unless . . .

"Unless what?" I demanded.

"Unless the patient doesn't make it," she replied matter-of-factly.

I couldn't believe my ears, and told Emma what the woman had said, once we were seated in the cafeteria.

"Maybe you should report her to someone in hospital administration," she suggested. "Why? What good would that do?" I asked. "It was insensitive, it was rude, she lacked any warmth or empathy. But I asked, and she told me the truth.

"I blame myself for this, Emma. And it's killing me to know that none of this would have happened if I hadn't insisted on this trip. Michael never wanted me to do this.

He'd warned me about the volcano and the earthquake concerns."

"He warned you? And you talked me into this without telling me?" Emma was horrified, but then shrugged. "I would have come anyway. I would never have let you come out here alone, Stephanie. But you owed it to me to tell me what he had said about the risk – and let me make my own decision, knowing the risks that Michael feared. And now, with this evacuation of the Park, and the continued temblors, it looks like he was right. There appears to have been something to all he said, after all."

"I am so sorry, Emma. You can't know how sorry I am. You're right. I put the two of you in danger because I was so pig-headed. And, although I understood exactly what he warned about, I dismissed the probability of something like that happening, and only realized the possible danger when I personally saw the volcanic flashes of light in the middle of the night."

"What flashes?"

"The other night, a couple bright white flashes lit up the sky. They were so bright they woke me up."

"And you kept this from us? Not a single mention of these flashes to Michael or to me?" Emma's voice raised in pitch.

"I mentioned it to Michael this morning, Emma" I felt terrible. But I was in full confession mode, and there was no stopping me.

"The first night, when the flash woke me, I was an idiot and went to the toilets alone.

They say to never go alone at night. So stupid! I could have come across a bear that night. And I was a fool with this grizzly encounter – I was reading the bear cautions in that Yellowstone guidebook – can you believe that? It said everything we should have been doing. And we didn't do any of it."

"Well, we all heard the Ranger that first night, and yet none of us were paying attention to what we had heard with our own ears. We are all guilty of that. And I love you dearly, Stephanie, but I have to wonder if any of this would have happened if you had only listened to Michael to begin with. What made him volunteer to come out here with us, with all those misgivings?"

"Chivalry. Love. It's the way he has always been with me, and I knew I could make him come out here with us. I have always been able to twist him around my little finger. I'm so ashamed – I owe him so much! And I owe you for all you did for Dad that I never thanked you for properly. So what do I do? I force the two people I love most to put their lives on the line for my stupid ego, and this damned fascination – this need to prove that Forrest Fenn is D.B. Cooper!"

I dissolved in tears and Emma found herself in the uncomfortable position of needing to comfort me.

"I don't deserve your empathy! I am a selfish, pig headed, ignorant fool who can't appreciate others and think about them first, instead of me! I don't deserve your loyalty, Emma, and I certainly don't deserve Michael's love."

Love. What a strange emotion. Did Michael still love me? Did Kent ever love Michael? He had permitted his own need to be with Michael – whatever that need was. It certainly wasn't love – but Kent had permitted that short-lived need to ruin a man who was trying so hard to be a good husband, a father, an upstanding member of the community.

Michael had managed to forget about Kent. Michael had managed to push him and their early, misguided relationship into his past. Michael was trying to be the man he had always wanted to be, and all that he aspired to be. Kent had acted selfishly and was still acting selfishly. However, I had to admit in this matter, I had behaved no better than he.

"I need to call Kent," I announced to Emma. "I hate to do it, but they're business partners. And they are. . . together. He needs to be told about Michael." I rose. "I need to call him."

"Sit down," Emma said sharply. "You don't know a damned thing until you hear from the surgeon. And the last thing we need is for Kent to come rushing out here in some dramatic show of devotion to Michael – which we both know is a lie, even if Michael hasn't figured it out yet – and get you in an emotional tizzy where you'll make even worse decisions. Yes, I am cross with you, Stephanie! Don't complicate things."

Feeling like a chastised child, I heeded Emma's instructions, and sat back in the chair. She finished her meal, then asked, "Are you sure you're not hungry?"

I shook my head, yes – I was sure.

"Well," Emma insisted, "buy a packaged snack of some kind., anyway. You may be starving in a few hours, and the cafeteria may close later, or limit service."

"Yes, Mother," I replied, mockingly, then shrank from Emma's glare. "Sorry, Emma."

"None of this is funny, Stephanie. You get away with a lot because you're pretty, and charming, and you're bright, and funny. But don't interpret all that as a license to be a smart-ass or to walk all over people to get what you want. Actions have consequences! Michael could tell you that. *Will* tell you that - if he makes it."

I had never seen Emma in full fury. I was ashamed of myself.

"Look, I don't hate you," Emma said. "Michael might, though. And you need to realize that before you interact with him again. If he doesn't, then he truly is a saint, because the residual effects of this attack may be fairly severe and last a lifetime."

"Oh, Emma. I don't know how I could live with that."

"I don't see where you get a choice in this, Stephanie. As I just said, every action has its consequences. Our lives are built on the choices we have made.

"What we're experiencing are the consequences of our own – Michael's and my –independent decisions to follow you out here. You are not alone in this, because we followed you willingly. And, frankly, *none* of us followed the Park's guidance regarding bear encounters, so you're off the hook there.

"I have to admit, however, that none of this would have happened without your stubborn determination to pursue your own goals and bend others to your will - even if that meant keeping them in the dark as to the risks they faced! That's how we got into a situation where this could even have happened. And you'd best be alert when you talk to his partner – to Kent. Because of Kent's business relationship your ex, legal action against you in this lawsuit-crazy nation is more than a remote possibility, especially if Michael had revealed at any point that he'd warned you against this trip. Or if Kent otherwise resents you. They may have been equal partners, but Michael was - is - apparently far more important to the company than Kent, as I understand it."

Emma fell silent. Minutes passed, but because there was nothing I could say in my own defense, I dared not say anything at all. The silence between us settled in for a long visit. After two hours, some attention to her email and more than a half dozen magazines, Emma stretched out on the opposite sofa, rested her head on the crook of the arm and fell asleep.

I was left with my thoughts. And they were not pretty.

At long last, the double doors leading into the surgical waiting area swung open and the green-clad surgeon came towards me, after first glancing at Emma's sleeping form. Michael had been in surgery for five and a half hours.

"Are you Mrs. Giordano?" the surgeon asked hopefully.

"I am his next of kin, yes." That seemed a simpler response under the circumstances and required no further explanation. The surgeon's name was stitched on his scrubs: Dr. David Malloy.

"Not the worst mauling I've repaired, fortunately," Dr. Malloy said. "But we had to seriously debride the wound – trim the edges – and clean the deep-tissue injuries before we could stitch him up. Closure took several staples and over 500 stitches. We'll give him a course of antibiotics and intramuscular anti-rabies vaccine injections as prophylaxis.

He has some muscular and nerve damage to his arm, shoulder and back. His hands had defensive injuries, as well. It's a very good thing he used them to cover the back of his neck and scalp, though. Brown bears – grizzlies – usually go for the head and face of a victim. But she spun him around when she swiped his arm and back, and then just bit the highest protrusion – his shoulder. What is he – right-handed? Left-handed?"

"Left-handed."

"Then he's been very lucky, indeed. Only the right side is involved. I'll be following him while he's here.

We'll keep him sedated for the next few days in the ICU as we continue to monitor his progress and reduce the risk of infection."

I nodded. "May I see him?"

"You can see him, but keep it very brief. Try not to disturb him. Mr. Giordano needs total rest for a few days while we give him nutrition and hydration intravenously. When he recovers, he will also need therapy for several months. But he can receive that at home – wherever home is."

"Texas. Temple, Texas."

"Okay, I would advise keeping him here, however, until he is well enough to travel. This is one of the few hospitals with experience with this type of injury. We'll take good care of him."

With that, the surgeon was gone, and within a few minutes, I was led into Recovery.

All it took was a single look at this strong, beautiful, caring man, possibly injured permanently because of me, bandaged and fully immobilized, strapped onto a contraption that kept him from putting any pressure on the affected shoulder, back and arm, and facing long term treatment. I broke down completely. The nurse gently led me back to the waiting room.

As soon as I entered, Emma woke and asked, "Is it over? How is he? What time is it?"

"Michael's fine, he'll be fine. I like the surgeon, Dr. Malloy. Michael will be in Intensive Care and under heavy sedation for several days. It's almost 8:00. Let's get a hotel room and talk about things over dinner. I think we can find someplace that's still open."

The Information Desk had a preprinted sheet for family members that gave several choices of moderately priced extended-stay hotels, and we checked into a Residence Inn in Idaho Falls, just under three miles from the EIRMC, and headed to a local bar and grill. I needed a drink, and Emma concurred.

We selected a sports bar, with televisions everywhere, as was customary for such places, but crowds had gathered around a few sets tuned to news channels showing the events at Yellowstone. The evacuation was still in force and Rangers were combing the park by helicopter to try to locate stray campers in the backcountry who might not be aware of the mandatory evacuation.

Film from the reporting cameras at Yellowstone showed boiling waters in the Shoshone and Yellowstone Rivers and the increased geothermal activity in the area. The Med-Evac airlift of the 6 tourists scalded by the morning's geothermal explosion was reported on extensively, and I recognized the faces of the EMS workers who had come to our rescue. Michael's mauling was duly reported, sans photographs - but was somehow connected with and blamed on unusual animal activity in Yellowstone Park. While Michael's airlift rescue was mentioned, there was no actual footage and was shown with further video of our EMS workers taken from the earlier report. Thankfully, no cameras had been around when they rescued Michael.

Another video clip showed animals running along the trails and roads of Yellowstone. The video clip continued to run as the news story explored the meaning of the odd animal behavior and speculated whether animals could, indeed, predict earthquakes and volcanic events. Shots of animals running through the meadowlands, with steam rising from small geysers and the many meandering streams filled the screen.

"Funny how the news media wove Michael's story into the animal movement at the Park," Emma noted. "Cynical bastards. Anything for a story."

A Ranger was interviewed later in the day and spoke about the evacuation, telling the reporter everything was going smoothly. Emma laughed sharply and uttered a few crude words denying his description of an orderly progression of campers and tourists out of each of the Park's five entrances. Geologists charged with observing the park reported on the geothermal activity and its causes, then went on to describe the underlying magma field, the calderas, and past eruptions, warning the public that, while caution had to be taken due to recent events, the volcanic field was in constant flux, and previous disturbances in the multi-state hotspot had subsided after a few weeks.

"It could be another 650,000 years before the underlying volcano erupts with force, and another 70,000 years before any active lava flows in Yellowstone."

Comforting words, indeed. A waitress appeared to take our order, and the screens around us were switched back to sports as conversation erupted from the patrons. It seemed that everyone had a loud and strong reaction to the news report, until focus shifted to whatever team or game they had chosen to watch.

"I can stay with you for a few days more," Emma informed me, "but the real estate closings are coming up on the new house in Santa Fe, and the Temple home. I have a lot to do to prepare for the move. If Michael's recovery takes as long as you say it might, I can come back in a week or two, for at least a few days."

"Thanks, Emma. I'd appreciate that. We were smart to keep all our electronic gear in the car. I have my laptop so I can finish the book. That will keep me busy and take my mind off things."

"Have you decided on an ending?"

"I think I have, Emma. Thanks to you, I think I have."

Chapter 46: A Time for Every Purpose

Emma and I shopped for clothes and shoes and personal items the next morning, and we each bought carryon bags to transport them.

We settled into a routine that allowed each of us to take care of business while we kept an eye on Michael. I wrote. Emma took care of the details of her condo sale, home purchase, and move to Santa Fe online and by phone. One of us would go to the hospital in the morning at 7 a.m. after an early breakfast; the other would then relieve the morning watch, arriving around noon and staying until visiting hours were over at 7 p.m. We would then go to dinner locally, or cook in the Residence apartment, and compare the day's notes.

Over the next few days, Michael seemed to be progressing well.

I had called Kent to let him know what had happened. He seemed distraught but was not accusatory in any way and asked me to keep him updated.

On the fifth day following the bear attack, Emma took the shuttle to Idaho Falls Regional Airport and flew back to Temple.

That evening, Michael's condition deteriorated.

He began running a fever of 101°. MRSA was suspected and confirmed by tests the next morning. It was not an uncommon development in post-op patients, the ICU attending physician informed me, but this complicated Michael's antibiotic regimen, since MRSA does not respond to most common antibiotics. I was urged to go home and get some rest. He was in good hands.

When I arrived the next morning and asked to see Michael, my request was summarily denied, although I was allowed to look in on him from the other side of the glass. A prominent sign announcing the MRSA infection was placed on the door. I insisted on speaking to his doctor when the ICU physician came on duty.

Shortly, the Intensive Care Unit's attending physician for the day, Dr. Patricia Ahearn, came out to speak with me about Michael. Invasive MRSA had been diagnosed, and intravenous Vancomycin was started immediately. But she assured me not to worry. Michael would be fine.

She explained MRSA as the drug-resistant form of Staphylococcus aureus, a common bacterium found on the skin and in the nose of many individuals, as well as on animals. The MR in the acronym stood for a "methicillin-resistant" staph infection. She assured me it was ordinarily treatable, but Michael's low T-cell count complicated matters further.

"Low T-cell count?" I asked.

"A low T-cell count – a type of white blood cell count – reveals that an individual's immune system is compromised. It can be caused by a number of things such as a viral infection or HIV/AIDS."

This shook me. Michael had complained Kent was cheating on him. Had his partner brought something home to infect him?

"HIV/AIDS?" I could not keep the quaver from my voice as I told the doctor about Michael's relationship with Kent, and Michael's comment about Kent's lack of fidelity.

"I see," was her measured response. "We'll run more tests. Thank you for your honesty, Mrs. Giordano."

"I *was* Mrs. Giordano. Past tense, several years ago. The relationship I just mentioned was what triggered the divorce. We are still friends, though."

"Got it. We'll keep you informed as things progress. Hopefully, we can get the MRSA under control and continue to see improvement in his condition."

"What happens if you can't clear the MRSA?"

"Septicemia is always a risk with predatory animal bites, as I'm sure you've been informed, and in a worst-case scenario, it can lead to sepsis. That is what we're fighting to prevent. You'll be informed immediately if there's any change."

I spent the rest of the day working on the book, using the table in a corner of the waiting room, its plot developing rapidly under my flying fingers. I now knew exactly where I was going – with both the book, and the ultimate conclusion of my investigation of Forrest B. Fenn as D.B. Cooper.

When there was no change in Michael's condition by evening, I packed up my laptop and headed back to my lonely home away from home. I picked at some leftovers in the fridge, drank two glasses of red wine, and watched a report on Yellowstone on the late news.

Yellowstone Rangers complained of a rash of opportunistic thievery, with foolish individuals and groups of petty criminals sneaking into the park to strip rapidly abandoned campgrounds of tents and equipment, personal belongings, and supplies, while the ground continued to rumble and shake beneath them.

Roads continued to melt, with resurfacing costs and the months-long prospective length of closures for repair mounting daily. Rivers continued to boil, and the number of new geysers puncturing the Park's landscape increased, with eruptions occurring more frequently, and with greater force. The monitoring cameras mounted across the Park showed disquieting video images of the glowing ground, of light shooting into the air from the base of geysers, and of events of the kind I had witnessed – lingering flashes of light that weren't lightning, but rather, that lit up the sky with an unholy glow, as if the earth were opening at a distance to show the stars its molten core. Furthermore, Park Rangers flying low over the area had seen a group of dead bison in the Norris Geyser Basin, presumably following exposure to toxic thermal gases emanating from a new geyser in the area.

It was unsettling that all this was occurring within a range of only 180 miles from the hospital. But East Idaho was built on the edge of the Yellowstone Plateau volcanic field composed of four adjacent calderas formed by the

Yellowstone Hotspot, and none of this was new to those who lived and worked in Idaho Falls.

The thought of what could potentially happen terrified me. However, old-timers in the area had spent 60, 70, 80 years or more of fruitful existence perched on the edge of disaster, and had built thriving businesses, raised happy families, and created satisfying lives despite the constant earthquake tremors and ever-changing thermodynamics that periodically increased and subsided, defying media efforts to paint every such disturbance as the beginning of the end, yet hovering as an ever-present threat to their very existence.

I saw fiery images in my dreams--saw the ground boiling, the bear charging, saw Michael being clawed and falling to the ground. I slept fitfully and woke exhausted, but hungry enough to manage a decent breakfast before heading to the hospital. It was there that I would lose my appetite every day, amid hospital smells and the pervasive sense of guilt that haunted me.

Michael's treatment now included the intravenous antibiotic for the MRSA in addition to other antibiotics, the prophylactic rabies vaccines and intravenous fluids and his daily nutrition that dripped from bags that keep Michael hydrated and nourished. and pain-free.

Memories of my conversation with Emma that left me in tears following the bear attack still made me feel even more miserable, if that were possible, but anguished regret only fueled a resolve to work toward the best conclusion.

I dreaded calling Kent, again, but pulled myself together and made the connection. I told him about the possibility of sepsis, and also mentioned the immune deficiency. Michael's health and lifestyle were enough to understand there was only one possible cause for his immune deficiency, and I hated Kent as much as I hated myself for what Michael was suffering. I wanted to scream that it wasn't fair; it wasn't right. But I held my tongue and tried to sound calm.

Kent listened to my report, asked a few questions, then fell silent. He saved me from having to think of anything to add by ending the conversation abruptly. "Thanks for the report, Stephanie. Listen, I've got to run. Let me know if there is any change."

The rest of the day dragged on. I spoke to Emma at some length. Although I could feel her opprobrium, her voice and her words demonstrated nothing but concern for Michael, and for me. "Give me a few more days, Stephanie, and I'll join you again. I know you could use the support. Poor Michael! Such a nice guy. Sometimes life is just not fair."

My thoughts exactly.

Chapter 47: A Time to Be Born, and a Time to Die

I never had the chance to say goodbye. I never had the chance to say I was sorry. I never had the chance to tell Michael that I had never stopped loving him for being the dear person that he was, and always had been.

The MRSA colonized rapidly, and the bacterial infection being held at bay by heavy antibiotics overcame Michael's weakened immune system. A necrotizing soft tissue infection set in, accompanied by the first signs of full-blown sepsis. The doctors fought to keep him hydrated to combat his dropping blood pressure. They gave him medications to elevate his blood pressure and oxygen to improve his breathing.

I continued to spend 12 hours a day at the hospital, writing furiously to keep my mind off what was happening to Michael. The guilt was overwhelming.

And so was the news from Yellowstone. Dead animals. Dead fish. Dead campers found in the backcountry. The ground was glowing. Asphalt was crumbling like oatmeal. Videos of geothermal occurrences in the park were no longer volunteered in an attempt to keep the populace calm, but videos were smuggled out with regularity, appearing on local and national television, creating great concern. Outgoing air traffic exceeded incoming, and alarm was in the air.

And still the physicians battled, but Michael was failing to respond to their best efforts. His blood pressure dropped alarmingly and there were indications of end-organ dysfunction.

I demanded answers, and one morning Dr. Ahearn called me into her office and shut the door. "I know you're wondering why Michael seemed to improve at first, but then began deteriorating," she began, closing the window shades to give us privacy, since her office was in full view of the nursing station. When she came to sit in the chair next to mine, rather than sitting behind her desk, I knew the news was not good.

"Remember when you told me about Michael and his partner?"

I nodded.

"Well, I'm afraid his partner needs to be notified and get tested immediately for HIV. Michael's test came back positive for HIV.

"There are several stages to HIV/AIDS. Following initial exposure, usually within 2 to 4 weeks. Michael might have developed what he thought was influenza symptoms. Sometimes there are no symptoms at all.

"Clinical latency follows, a stage that is also called chronic or asymptomatic HIV, which

can last from 3 to more than 20 years without treatment, although 8 years is the norm. Michael had high levels of CD4 or helper T-cells when he first came in and was evidently not receiving antiretroviral treatment. I doubt he realized he had a problem.

But his CD4 T-cell count fell rapidly when faced with the double-whammy of the bear attack and the MRSA colonization, and we were unsure of the reason until you spoke up. Absent treatment, I feel that Michael would develop AIDS within 10 years from his exposure – and we have no timeline on when that exposure occurred, because he has been sedated or semi-conscious through all this, and unable to be questioned. We are doing all we possibly can, Miss . . . Ward?"

I blinked rapidly to hold back the tears threatening. I nodded.

"And miracles do sometimes occur. But if there are any family members you would like to notify; this would be the time. I am so sorry."

I felt as though she had punched me in the stomach. I began hyperventilating. The doctor leaned forward, her hand on my arm, and instructed me to breathe deeply and steadily. Then she rose and went to the door. "I have rounds. You may stay in here as long as you need to, Miss Ward, to compose yourself."

"Can I see him just one more time?"

"Of course," she said softly, then motioned to a nurse to accompany me into Michael's room.

Michael's paleness and gaunt cheeks hit me like another punch in the gut. *My fault, my fault, my fault.* Fresh tears spilled from my eyes as I lowered myself to his level. I stroked his dark hair, always so perfectly manicured, but now disheveled and listless. I brushed a strand away from his eyes.

"Oh, Michael," I whispered, the onslaught of tears causing me to choke on his name.

There was no reaction, no movement, no sign he knew I was there. Maybe he was already gone.

I spent a few hours with him. I told him how much I enjoyed the life we shared during our marriage and how he was the only man I ever truly loved. How I wished I could have changed things and felt the guilt of how things played out. Maybe things work out for a reason…maybe death was an easier journey than the harsh and difficult road he would have traveled with AIDS. That's what I told myself, anyway.

After pouring out everything in my heart, too late or not, I stood up and leaned over him, brushing a kiss on his forehead. "Goodbye, Michael. I love you. Find peace."

Chapter 48: A Time to Break Down, and a Time to Build Up

It is difficult for the living to understand the legal complexity of death until they have experienced it, and worse yet, the legalities make no concession for grief. There were calls to make and papers to sign and a thousand and one details to take care of, complicated by the distance from the home of the deceased. Nature kindly permits a cloud of unreality to descend that permits the bereaved to function, albeit in a zombie-like state, before collapsing in grief at the end of each day.

My first call was to Emma, to let her know what had happened, and why. She had most of her affairs in order by that time and caught the next plane to Idaho Falls, pausing mid-move to be by my side for those first difficult days. I loved her for it.

The second call was to Michael's lawyer, Dan Morgan. He had been introduced to me as a personal friend of Michael's from their university days, and it was he who had written our wills. Dan would likely have the original copy of Michael's current will since our divorce some years earlier. It would need to be filed with the Probate Court.

After a few minutes of conversation and his sincere condolences, Dan informed me that he had never rewritten Michael's will, except to add one brief amendment that changed my status from spouse to personal friend and executor. Everything else remained the same. Dan confirmed that he and Michael had thoroughly discussed all options, and Michael decided to leave the will unchanged. It was his intention that I still receive everything I had been entitled to as his wife, including his shares in the construction company. Michael owned 65% of the shares. Kent owned the other 35%.

I almost dropped the phone.

After collecting my wits, I immediately hired Dan as my attorney, figuring he knew Michael's affairs intimately – which was invaluable information for me, as executor of the estate. Furthermore, I would need Dan in my corner in the event that Kent contested my control of the company. Dan told me Michael had always had the utmost respect for my business skills, and he knew I would continue to run the business as he had.

As we talked, Dan let slip that Michael had never really trusted Kent, and despite his partner's constant pressure, had never wanted to relinquish ultimate control of the firm to him, even upon his death. In fact, other than some specified personal items – his watches, cufflinks, and personal jewelry, a high-end camera, a pair of virtual reality glasses, his jet ski, and some sports and camping gear, there was no monetary provision whatsoever for Kent.

Whoa! Their relationship was not at all what I had imagined, and if Kent were aware of this, he would be hostile to me, indeed. I wondered if buying him out would be an option and voiced my concern.

Dan promised that on my return to Temple we would meet to strategize. He thought that Michael had told him the corporation's buy-sell agreement was funded. There should be a policy that would provide the necessary funds to buy out Kent's interest, if need be. Dan checked the corporation file, and immediately located the policy. "I'll file the claim, Stephanie. Consider it done. And when we meet, we can go over the details of how a buy-out needs to be handled."

"Bless you, Dan. I am so glad I called you with the terrible news before notifying Kent."

"Well, if he gives you any trouble over any of this, just refer him to me. What are you going to do about the . . . about Michael's body?"

"He wanted to be cremated. I don't believe there was any pre-paid arrangement – unless you know of something – so I'll have him cremated here in Idaho and carry the ashes home myself. I have Michael's car. The SUV."

"It's yours now, Stephanie. I'll have the title transferred."

"I think it's best to have a memorial service in Temple as soon as I can get back. Michael had a lot of friends, and his employees loved him."

The next call was to Kent. It was not going to be pleasant, so I steeled myself.

He was silent as I spoke. I was calm, detailed in my explanation and matter-of-fact when I delivered the information about complications caused by Michael's compromised immune status, and his test results. When I flatly delivered the doctor's recommendation that he be tested for HIV, and enter treatment as soon as possible, he hung up the phone on me.

I attributed his reaction to shock and waited a full ten minutes before calling him back. I was told he was on a phone call and waited a few minutes before he picked up. The first words out of his mouth were a very coldly delivered, "Yes, boss?"

I ignored the pointed sarcasm.

"I will be driving back as soon as I have arranged for Michael's cremation. I'll bring his remains back with me and we can hold a memorial service in Temple. Do you have any suggestions as to where we should hold it?"

"We?" Kent's tone was hostile. He must have called Dan immediately after he hung up and learned the bad news about the company ownership and his limited inheritance. His attitude had transformed from relative apathy to anger in only ten minutes.

"You know I'll fight the buy-out, Miss Ward. And I personally don't care where you have the memorial service. I won't be there."

Again, the receiver slammed down in my ear. Well, I thought, more satisfied than ever that I'd called Dan before Kent and engaged his legal services – situations like this were why Dan got paid the big bucks. I had a feeling he would be earning every penny.

EIRMC had an entire department that assisted families and relatives to deal with what the representative called "the unfortunate event."

Why do people always need to use euphemisms when talking about death?

I was grateful for the assistance in finding a funeral home that could arrange a cremation on short notice and scheduled the service for the day after Emma's scheduled arrival. She and I would receive the ashes together, and then go raise a glass to dear Michael's soul. Then we would drive back together to Santa Fe, where I would spend two or three days with her in her new home before taking Michael back to Texas.

My brief stay in Santa Fe would also allow me to deliver my completed book to Forrest Fenn. The journey would not only be dedicated to Michael, but also to my beloved dad, after which they would both be able to rest in peace, and Emma and I would begin our new lives.

Chapter 49: Let the Chips Fall Where They May

I had spent such a long time ruminating over the book, over the unsolved mystery of D.B. Cooper that Dad and I had dedicated so many years to solving, and over my knowledge of Forrest Fenn, and his amazing story.

I sent him an email with the completed manuscript attached. I knew better than to hold my breath but tried to be as patient as I could. Several days later, he replied:

Done. You are very perceptive. Congratulations. f

True to form, Forrest had handed me a conundrum. This was a man who had always, throughout his long and astounding life, tested the world, tested himself, and most of all, had tested fate. Now, he was testing me.

Would I have the courage to do the right thing?

Emma's arrival was most welcome. There was so much I needed to discuss with a trusted friend, and Emma was just that. She pulled no punches, as I had learned, and her moral compass was unerring. Moreover, she really cared about me, and that was invaluable. I had never felt so alone in the world.

Michael's cremation was quickly arranged and executed. I kissed his cold forehead and let him go, and Emma stood with me to receive his ashes the following day, entombed in the agate box I had purchased for him, in lieu of a traditional urn. Temple was his home, and I would make arrangements for the ashes after his memorial service, planned upon my return.

But other business now occupied my mind.

It was comforting that Emma knew Forrest and Peggy. She knew my moral dilemma and had Dad's intentions in mind as we discussed my choices.

I liked Forrest. He was charming and kind. He had a phenomenal life history and had built his many interests and personal qualities into a true presence in Santa Fe that had to be respected. He had a wonderful family. He had friends and fans worldwide. He had set a challenge for thousands to pursue, enriching some lives, and destroying others through the choices people made in pursuit of Forest Fenn's treasure, of Forrest Fenn's truth. No one knew that better than I.

As we traveled the 830 miles from Idaho Falls to Santa Fe, Emma and I discussed the lives of the three most important men to us-- men whose very existence - and personal choices - had ultimately impacted our own. They were all good men at heart, each with their own faults and foibles. Two were gone, and just one remained.

Once we had stopped overnight at a hotel, I booted up my laptop and found an unsolicited email from Forrest. It was a copy of an email he sent to a movie producer:

I think you will like the story in the link below. It was written by Stephanie Ward (her real name). I think the story is perfect for you and something that I can sign off on.

Stephanie lives just north of Chicago. She claims to have searched for my treasure 100 times and has searched Wyoming, Idaho, and New Mexico.

She thinks I am D.B. Cooper. Really, and that is what this is about. I have been following her with this story since she began writing it. She thought I would hate it. I think it may be the answer for what you and I both want. It is fictionalized, but follows my life almost exactly, even my name. I have no agreement with her. She has found out things about me that I did not know. Please read the first chapter to get a feel for the D.B. Cooper case, which is factual to a fault. Then scroll down to the 5th paragraph in Chapter XXV.

She is hungry. Tell me what you think. ƒ (actual email with the exception of Stephanie's last name changed)

Wow! My mind spun as I reread the entire email. Forrest was trying to make my book into a movie? Wow!

I hastily typed a reply:

Forrest,

Wow! Thank you! It would be so exciting to see my research play out on the big screen! ~Stephanie

Early the next morning, I found another email from Forrest with the movie producer's forwarded message. He was interested. The email included Forrest's reply:

Thanks. I think Stephanie's story has movie written all over it and I am ready to jump and help all I can. f (actual email reply)

I couldn't believe it. My lifelong research was going to possibly be a movie!

Forrest had placed me in an impossible position. He knew that I knew the truth and that Dad had sensed the truth. It was that same truth Forrest wanted to reveal, and yet, needed to keep to himself. So he tried to accomplish both by encouraging me to write my suspicions in book form, and then bought my ultimate silence by promising to publish and promote it. That way, he no doubt calculated, his story would see the light of day, yet be dismissible as fiction.

Forrest had pushed me to join the treasure hunt, promising that the autobiography in his antique bronze chest held the truth I sought.

I was bull-headed – a tendency that has been both a boon and a curse to me. A student of human nature, Forrest read that in me and so pointed me in a direction that both distracted and diverted my efforts away from the book he had hired me to write – or so he thought.

He had found my weakness, and exploited it to his benefit, Emma observed. Forrest was old and getting older. With every passing year the likelihood of criminal prosecution was diminishing in the event that someone actually found his treasure and publicized his "true" life story. Sending me on a wild goose chase to find this treasure would buy him still more time.

My sense of humor has always favored the ironies of life, and I couldn't resist teasing Emma, who sat behind the wheel of Michael's SUV. It was her turn to drive.

"Are you sure, Emma, that 'wild goose chase' is the best terminology to use, in this instance?" I asked drily. She grew flustered, realizing her choice of words was not the best, and actually rather insensitive, under the circumstances. I laughed and said, "We can scratch Yellowstone off the search list. After the shaking, rocking, and rolling the earth is getting in that spot, who knows where Forrest's treasure will wind up? Perhaps buried in one of the fissures that have been opening up."

I didn't want to let Michael go and was seriously debating whether to keep his remains with me rather than sealing them behind a wall in a cemetery that no one would visit. Michael had done so much for me – and yes, to me – since we met on that night of my sister's wedding, what now seemed like eons ago. Everything I had, I owed to him. Not just the material things that had been gifted or inherited, but also the education and encouragement and training and business experience he had given me, along with his belief in my worth as a person, a businesswoman and construction manager, and the unflagging devotion that had led to his death.

When I mentioned this new idea to Emma, as we stopped for lunch, she looked at me for a long time, and then said, "You must do what you need to do."

"Funny," I replied, "that's exactly what Forrest said to me when I threatened to go to the FBI with my story before he offered the book deal: 'You must do what you need to do.'"

"Maybe that was a back-handed way to give you his permission. Maybe this whole thing has been a test?"

"A test?"

"A test of you, of human nature. Of everything – his treasure hunt-- his challenge to you."

"You think he challenged me to turn him in?"

"I don't know. However, I do think this treasure hunt of his is a challenge to people to question their existence, to break out of the mold, to get out of their rut. We are all guilty of not challenging ourselves to reach beyond our comfort zones. Routines become ruts, and before you know it, life is over. Opportunities are gone. If you never try, you will never realize what you're capable of doing.

"I think that's how Forrest has lived his life, always pushing himself to the edge – the edge of glory. He has succeeded where no one would ever have thought he could, by pushing the envelope. And that's why he has been so good at 'hiding in plain sight,' as you call it, Stephanie. Because no one would have ever expected he was capable of pulling off the things that he has-- of doing all that he has done. I also think that's part of his obvious regret about aging. There comes a certain point in life where 'the spirit is strong, but the flesh is weak.' And he feels it intensely – that he is reaching the end of what has been a phenomenal trail. There are still bananas out there, but he is no longer able to reach for them. And it frustrates him immensely."

"I think you're right, Emma. I think he sees all the people who are afraid of life, afraid to be themselves – afraid to take a risk, to try for whatever they want from life – and he wants to push them to change – to grab at those bananas as their train passes by.

"Help me now. Who was it who said this?" she asked, "Thoreau? Wasn't he the one who said, 'The mass of men lead lives of quiet desperation'?"

"Yes. In *Walden.*"

"Maybe – just maybe – Forrest is challenging you to give him one last adventure, Stephanie. One last banana. After all, he's milked the treasure hunt for all the publicity it's going to get – unless someone comes across the damned box, and publicly reveals the find. Which will mean surrendering half of its worth to the government, so even that will operate to keep his secret safe a little longer. Which I don't really think is Forrest's intent."

"You don't?"

"No, Stephanie. I think he is crying out for discovery. What fun is it if people learn that he is D.B. Cooper after he's dead and gone? Forrest has the money to hire clever lawyers to keep prosecution at bay, indefinitely. Think of the notoriety! The interviews! The book and movie deals! The kudos! And the backlash if anyone ever *dared* try to prosecute and jail D. B. Cooper! Besides, if the truth came out, his family and everyone and everything else he cares about would be set for generations to come, and his story would live on forever."

I mulled it over while we paid for our meals and walked toward the car.

As we strolled into the sunlight, Emma added, "You owe him delivery of your completed book manuscript, Stephanie, with the ending that I know you have already written. What you want from me is simply a confirmation of the rightness of what you have already decided."

It was my turn to drive while Emma napped, holding Michael's ashes in her lap. That left me time to think, and I thought deeply about the lessons I had recently learned:

Life is short.

And Nature is merciless.

While often cruel, Nature is absolutely impartial. It does not favor the rich, or the clever, the talented, or even the brave.

Nature teaches us that all actions, all choices, have consequences.

Skippy had found that out. Now it was Forrest's turn to learn that lesson.

At Emma's new place, following our mid-afternoon arrival in Santa Fe, I placed the agate box on the desk beside me in the lovely guest room she had specifically decorated and furnished with me in mind. I downloaded the book from my laptop onto a zip drive, in order to transfer it to Emma's desktop, and then printed out two complete copies of the manuscript. I also printed out a screenshot of another page.

We had an early dinner, and I slept very well that night, for the first time in weeks.

Emma made pancakes for breakfast – my favorite – to fortify me for my visit to Forrest Fenn. I had called from Idaho Falls and told him simply that I was bringing him the completed book., He was awaiting my call when I phoned to let him know I was in Santa Fe and needed to see him.

I had feared the encounter, but our visit was actually very pleasant.

Once I had seated myself in a chair in his study, Forrest went to his desk and picked up the check that sat on its blotter. He then walked over and handed it to me, relieving me of the copy of my book that I had printed out for him as he did so. Forrest sat down at the desk with the manuscript and began reading, flipping through the pages, perusing sections here and there and chuckling at various paragraphs, while pausing at times to read other passages intently.

Meanwhile, I stared down at the $10,000 check in my hands, glancing up at Forrest occasionally, to track his progress.

Forrest suddenly looked up from his reading. "What?" he asked. "That's an advance. There will be much more once it's published. I tell you; we're going to make a lot of money on this, Missy. You'll also receive the profits from the movie when it's made. The sky's the limit."

He quickly read a paragraph or two in each chapter as he worked his way through the manuscript. I would have expected no less from this remarkable man, who'd had no more than a high school education, but who held a world of wisdom between his ears. Finally, he turned to the last chapter, and read every single word. I held my breath.

My heart pounded when Forrest turned to the final page and read the last sentence. Then, as I watched, he just sat there, his hands folded together in his lap, appraising me with an intensity in his gaze that bore right through me. I was frozen in place.

After a few minutes, Forrest rose to his full height and walked over to where I sat, trembling, in my chair. He hovered over me and looked down at me for some time before he put out his hand, grasped mine, and pulled me to my feet, then heartily shook my other hand, in congratulatory fashion.

"I knew I was right about you," he said. "I expected no less." He walked me to the door. "No taxi today?" he asked.

"I drove."

"Well, Missy," he said, "We will definitely be in touch with one another very soon. Good luck."

The following morning, I rose early and dressed with care. The sky was overcast, and threatened rain.

As I drove toward my destination, and upon approaching New Mexico's largest city, I entered an address into the Land Cruiser's GPS:

415 Silver Avenue, Southwest, Albuquerque. The New Mexico Field Office of the Federal Bureau of Investigation.

The parking lot was busy, even at 10:00 in the morning. I parked and gathered my things: a handbag, an umbrella, and a leather satchel containing a copy of the same manuscript I had presented to Forrest the previous day, along with a screenshot of the YouTube page featuring a video clip entitled "D.B. Cooper – Original 1971 Newscast" - CBS announcer Walter Cronkite's original televised lead story from November 25, 1971, reporting on the extraordinary hijacking of Northwest Orient Flight 305 the previous afternoon, and revealing the distinctive image of William Marvin "Skippy" Fenn, passenger number 11, disembarking from that hijacked flight at the airport in Seattle, Washington, where Forrest Fenn's older brother lived, and worked at the time.

Head held high, I walked up to the impressive building before me. At the door, I grasped the cold steel handle, then opened it halfway. I paused, letting the door close again. I gazed up into the blue, blue sky. Just a few wisps of cloud drifted lazily overhead. I looked down at the ground and smiled before getting back into my car and driving away.

Afterword

Stephanie and Mindy are friends who met while searching for Forrest Fenn's treasure. They realized there was a possible connection between Forrest Fenn and D.B. Cooper, and spent countless hours searching and researching possible connections. They believe these connections should not be ignored, and that the possibility that Forrest was D.B. Cooper should be investigated.

Forrest was aware the entire time they were questioning this possibility. He was the first person to read the book and he never once said not to go to the FBI or not to tell this "fictional story." In fact, Forrest claimed he enjoyed the story and thought it would make a good movie. Forrest also gave us permission in an email to use his photos as we wished.

When I asked him originally what he thought about my book, his response was "Your DB book is good. If you could fine a publisher you might make a few bucks. I am not mad about it. f". I was so happy that he approved. I asked him early on if anyone else had questioned him being DB Cooper and at the time he remarked, I was the only one.

On June 6th, 2020, Forrest Fenn announced his notorious treasure chest had been found. Chaos ensued as many questioned the validity of Forrest's Treasure Hunt and the solving of it. Forrest Fenn refused to disclose where the chest had been hidden for over ten years, as well as the name of the finder. Lawsuits were filed. The search community plummeted into confusion, bitterness, and grief. It appeared, and still appears, that we will never receive answers or the closure we feel we deserve.

Since the writing of this book, the finder, supposedly as a result of a lawsuit, has come forward. His name is Jack Steuf, a controversial former writer for *The Onion*, an online satire website. He refuses to say where the treasure was found and denies opening the olive jar containing

Fenn's real autobiography and reading it. We believe it's in this jar that we will be the true solvers of Forrest's secret. We believe there could be an actual DB Cooper bill inside.

Figure 28 Fenn with treasure chest after it was "found." Red arrow points to sealed biography jar.

On September 6th, 2020, Forrest Fenn passed away. Coincidentally, or maybe not, September 6th is also the date Forrest Fenn retired from the Air Force.

As of today, January 21, 2021, Peggy has also passed.

Mindy and Stephanie have spoken of their research on The Cooper Vortex podcast. You can find it at https://thecoopervortex.podbean.com/e/db-cooper-and-the-thrill-of-the-chase-mindy-fausey-and-stephanie-thirtyacre/

The Walter Cronkite video with Skippy exiting the aircraft can be viewed at https://www.youtube.com/watch?v=ksxyp4s6axy

You can find out more information about Forrest's treasure hunt at https://www.chasechat.com/.

We would like to thank Allen K for his connection he's made between the book Hahaha and our belief that the true author was actually Forrest Fenn. A few sentences from the book gave him the initial connection. The term "The Thrill of The Chase" is used.

On page 73 in HaHaHa, it says "unfortunately, impatience was his main shortcoming, and it could be disastrous in our business."

On page 73 of TTOTC, Forrest saw "tenacity was never one of my shortcomings"

HaHaHa is 328 pages long. And Forrest said he flew 328 combat missions.

www.ingramcontent.com/pod-product-compliance
Lightning Source LLC
Chambersburg PA
CBHW060315100726
47907CB00002B/409